THE *NIMROD* MURDERS

Simon Beaufort is a pseudonym for a pair of academics formerly at the Scott Polar Research Institute at the University of Cambridge. One is an award-winning historian, the other a successful crime writer, who publishes under the name Susanna Gregory.

Also by Simon Beaufort

Murder in the Holy City
A Head for Poisoning
The Bishop's Brood
The King's Spies
The Coiners' Quarrel
Deadly Inheritance
The Bloodstained Throne
A Dead Man's Secret

The *Nimrod* Murders

by

Simon Beaufort

THE *NIMROD* MURDERS

First published in 2011 by

The Erskine Press, The White House, Eccles, Norwich,
NR16 2PB
WWW.ERSKINE-PRESS.COM

1SBN 978 1 85297 110 6

Cover photograph and Interior of Nimrod (page vi)
with acknowledgements to HEART OF THE
ANTARCTIC by Ernest Shackleton (William
Heinemann, London 1909)

A CIP catalogue record is available from the British
Library

Typeset by Esme Power
Printed by Ashford Colour Press Limited

For Russell and Gaynor Thompson

Dear Antarctic Friends of Many Years

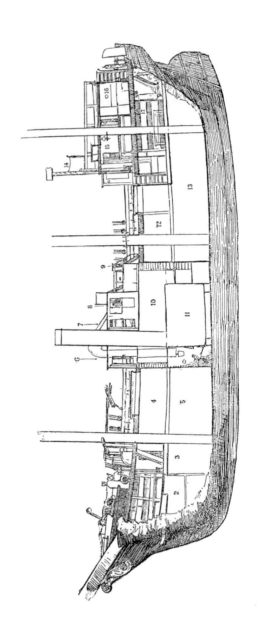

SECTION, SHOWING INTERIOR OF "NIMROD"

1. Forecastle. 2. Stores. 3. Chain locker. 4. Fore hold. 5. Lower hold. 6. Stoke hold. 7. Carpenter's shop. 8. Cook's gallery.
9. Engine room. 10. Engine room. 11. Boiler. 12. After hold. 13. Lower hold. 14. After Bridge. 15. Officer' quarters. 17. Oyster Alley.

Foreword

On 30 July 1907, members of the British Antarctic Expedition, led by Ernest Shackleton, sailed down the Thames on the tiny, refurbished sealer *Nimrod*. Some six months later, in February 1908, the expedition landed in Antarctica. At Cape Royds, a tiny projection into McMurdo Sound dominated by the smoking volcano Mount Erebus, Shackleton and his companions built a hut and set up camp. They then began their long wait for the following spring, when Shackleton would head into the icy unknown in an attempt to become the first man ever to reach the South Pole. In the worldwide fame and glory that followed the return of Shackleton's party to civilisation, little was ever said about a dark incident that almost halted the expedition before it even sailed from London's East India Docks.

Prologue

Cape Royds, Antarctica: March 1908

Philip left today for a place no one on Earth has ever been. Without his broad grin and hearty laugh it seems terribly lonely. Murray, with whom I share a small cubicle, is still puttering around, so it's not the lack of proximity to others that's disturbing. That said, there is a great distance between our party and the rest of humanity, what with us sitting down here at the bottom of the world. I suppose it's just that Philip and I have become such close friends since the terrors of eight months ago.

The day after tomorrow, he's going to be twenty-one years old, the same age as me. But, like me, he could so easily have missed that particular birthday, and all his subsequent ones. And to think he's on the icy slopes of Mount Erebus, not only with the Prof and Mawson – two late additions to the expedition, from whom I hope to learn much about geology – but three others, any of whom we thought at one point might be a killer. Knowing these hard men so much better now, I still think some of our theories weren't unreasonable.

Lord knows what they thought of me prying into their affairs. None of them has been overly friendly since; one is unpleasant in a petty way behind the scenes, and one can be openly nasty – but then, that's been his nature since I met him, and I don't think being the object of scrutiny made him any less nice. I'm sure none of them ever considered how I felt about the whole thing. I can't say that it was a pleasure to be involved in the discovery of dead bodies, to find my face mercilessly shoved deep into a muddy puddle and feel the water begin to enter my lungs, or to have guns blazing at me in a small parlour. Each was a horror of a different kind, which I'd just as soon forget.

Of course, our current situation has just as much risk as those dangers I faced in the less salubrious parts of the London docklands. But even knowing that one of us could disappear down a black hellhole – a crevasse deep enough for one to realise full well what is happening long before he hits the bottom – it somehow isn't as nerve-wracking as prowling around sinister sites late at night in order to reconstruct grisly murders. And even if I were selected to go on the journey to the Pole, I don't think it would seem so difficult a task as that which the Boss assigned me before we ever left England. I've no reason to think I'll be chosen for such a journey, what with competition from the tough, no-nonsense men in our small party, but then I had no expectation to be asked to change from geologist to criminal investigator either, and that happened.

I had assumed that the story of my involvement with those murders would never be fully recorded – I certainly didn't want to write about them. Also, I felt certain that the Boss wouldn't want the story to go on record, as it might overshadow the entire expedition. But I was disabused of that notion late on the night that our ship Nimrod sailed north towards New Zealand, leaving us behind in this God-forsaken place with naught but a tiny hut, a handful of shivering ponies, and some carelessly scattered mounds of supplies, the sum of which seemed all too small to provide for us for a year.

That night, as the lowering sun bathed the peaks in golden rays, and our tiny ship slowly shrank into the distance of a beautiful, deep blue McMurdo Sound broken with slowly floating pieces of pure white ice, the Boss – that is, Ernest Shackleton –plodded through the concrete-hard mixture of ice and scoria up the small rise to where I looked uneasily after our fading connection with home. Only when he was close behind me did I hear his footsteps and I fairly jumped out of my skin. When I turned, I expected to see Frank Wild, the self-appointed nursemaid for Philip and me, the two youngest and – he judged – least experienced of our party. But no, it was the Boss. We stood side by side in silence, admiring the natural setting, so unlike my native Gloucestershire.

'I imagine you've tried not to think much about what happened in London,' Shackleton finally said, while his gaze wandered to where the land behind our base rose slowly, inexorably, up to the smoking summit of Erebus. He was an astute reader of people, but this time he was dead wrong. I hadn't tried to avoid thinking about it – in fact, I think about it almost every day.

'We'll talk more about this later,' he continued, 'but I'm going to want a thorough report on those dreadful events. And I'd like you to write it for me.'

I gazed at him in surprise, but he simply laid his forefinger on his lips to tell me that no more discussion would be had at that moment. Then, taking a deep breath, and with a look on his face that showed his pleasure at being back in the region of everlasting ice after an absence of almost five years, he turned and made his way towards the hut, where sleep beckoned.

For more than a week after that encounter the work was unceasing, as we organised the interior of our small hut, chipped our stores out of the ice that had encased them during a blizzard, and arranged the equipment we will need for the exploration and research to be carried out this next year. Then suddenly, yesterday, Shackleton announced that a party of six would leave today to make the first ascent ever of Erebus, the active volcano that dominates the entire region.

I was sorely disappointed to learn that three of the four specialists in geology – Professor David, Mawson, and Philip – had been selected for the party despite a lack of any mountaineering experience, but that I, who had originally been employed as the expedition's sole geologist, was obliged to remain at base. Nevertheless, I did everything I could to assist the frantic preparations; helping to improvise crampons by poking nails through pieces of leather that were then attached to the soles of the party's reindeer-skin boots. We were at it until well after midnight, and the six were off first thing this morning, the rest of us accompanying them as far as the pond we call Blue Lake before we left them to their challenge.

On my way back to the base, my omission from that party was explained. Shackleton linked his arm with mine and guided me towards Pony Lake, another freshwater pond not far from the hut. It was clear that he intended the constant squawking of the thousand or so Adélie penguins nesting there to prevent us from being overheard.

'I know you wanted to go up Erebus,' Shackleton began, 'and I promise that you'll have a chance later. But I have a task that's far more important. As I said before, I want you to write a report on everything that happened in London.'

My look of dismay did nothing to put him off.

'It must be obvious to you why the Erebus party is structured as it is,' he continued. 'Three of the men were deeply involved in the affair, and I wanted them out of the way when you began writing – they should be gone for at least a week. And the other three are the geologists, so you won't have to worry about doing any of that drudgery while they're gone.'

I could only smile at the typical way Shackleton showed his own lack of interest in geology – in fact, in science in general – while clearly not understanding the passion some of us have for our specialties. But then, the Boss had made no bones about his primary goal from the start, early on proclaiming that the expedition wasn't about science but about reaching the South Pole. Now, he carried on oblivious to my reaction.

'I'd like you to write up that report, and make sure you cover the entire story, Raymond,' he said.

I smiled again: it's 'Raymond' now he's asking me again to do something a little unorthodox, I thought, just like the year before. Not that such familiarity would ever be displayed in front of the other men; this whole issue was one for just the two of us. In fact, despite the roles in the sordid affair played by members of this company, none of them really knew the full story other than Shackleton and me. Not even Philip – my brother confessor, one might call him – and he's the one who, due to the friendship that immediately sprang up between us, has heard more about it than anyone else, during our long watches together aboard ship.

'Step back into that time and place,' Shackleton continued. 'Don't write just about your memories or your experiences, but tell the whole story. Try to capture what we all thought, and feared, and did. Include where we stood, what muttered conversations went on, all the bits and pieces we might forget as the years pass.

Don't write it from your perspective, Raymond. Write it as if you were an independent observer. Then, I think, you'll come closer to the truth of what truly happened. Will you do that?'

It was one of those requests that was in reality more of an order. But it didn't matter. I'd learned long ago that I couldn't deny Shackleton anything. Was it his charm, the admiration in which I held him, or that he'd given me a chance of a lifetime? I don't really know. But whatever he wanted me to do, I'd do.

Shackleton knew that, of course, just like he knew that the two of us and a policeman had, during the previous July, shared experiences and secrets that would never find their way into any official report. What he was asking me to do was to write the only true and full account of those horrific incidents that had joined the three of us in a way that can only happen when men face overwhelming adversity together. He knew, as did I, that very special friendships had been made or extended, friendships that will persist until ended by death.

I nodded my assent, and he headed towards the hut to plan his assault on the South Pole, while the memories rushing into my mind were so strong that they drowned out the squawks of a thousand braying penguins.

Chapter 1

The body was an incongruous sight in more ways than one. First, it was unusual to see someone wearing full evening dress in the shabby, disreputable area comprising the East India Docks, and second, in the experience of Inspector William Taylor, murders in Blackwall or Poplar tended to be the violent expression of alcohol and deprivation. Few were coldly deliberate executions, performed expertly and quickly, with minimal loss of blood despite the brutal nature of the fatal injury.

Next to Taylor, Ernest Shackleton cleared his throat, to remind him that time was passing; the dock came to life early each day, and he had no wish for a delay that might allow the newspapers to get hold of the details of a body found next to his ship. A lurid story in one of the cheap, sensational dailies might be all it took for the funds he was working so hard to raise to dry up. Moreover, there was a great deal to do if his expedition was to sail in three weeks, and while he was appalled by the death of one of his people, he could not allow it to interfere with the vast amount of work still required.

Four living men stood in a silent crescent around the dead one. Three were soon to depart for the distant shores of the Antarctic, and their ship, a refurbished, three-masted barquentine, loomed behind them, its spars and rigging ghostly pale in the pre-dawn mist that rose from the water. The fourth was the policeman, a sturdy man in his early thirties with thick, light-brown hair and a calm, easy manner that had lulled more than one criminal into a false sense of security. He and Shackleton had attended Dulwich College together as boys, before Shackleton had followed the call of the sea and entered the merchant navy. Taylor had continued his studies, reading jurisprudence at King's College, London, before shocking his family by joining the Metropolitan Police.

Taylor liked mornings, although on this particular one, the bells of All Saints Church in Poplar had only just struck five. Mornings were when he did his best thinking, and he appreciated the cleaner, cooler air, and the quiet that allowed him to hear the birds singing in the park near his home. As he always rose early – and he had been awake even earlier than usual that day, because one of his cases was causing him considerable anxiety – he had already washed and shaved when the summons had arrived for him to hurry to the East India Docks with all possible haste.

The gasping messenger had also informed him that his presence had been demanded specifically, and that the 'request' had been made through Chief Superintendent Hamilton himself. Hamilton was well known in the Force for doing favours for members of his Club, but Taylor had been surprised when he had learned that it was Shackleton whom his senior officer was obliging. Then he reconsidered: his old schoolmate was charming, determined and charismatic, and the

11

obsequious Hamilton would be putty in his hands.

'His name is Scudder,' said Shackleton in a whisper, as though he were afraid that loud words might disturb the man who lay on his back in front of them. 'Brice Albert Scudder. He's the expedition's assistant biologist.'

'Was,' corrected Eric Marshall, a tall, powerful fellow with neatly combed hair. '*Was* the assistant biologist. I'd say his days of collecting specimens have definitely ended.'

Taylor found the comment distasteful. He had learned from Shackleton that Marshall was a surgeon – a graduate of the medical school at St Bartholomew's Hospital – and as such was probably more familiar with death than most. But the other two members of the expedition were not, and Shackleton in particular was clearly distressed. Taylor took a moment to study the surgeon, taking in the condescending sneer, the smug demeanour and the sardonic intelligence in the bright blue eyes.

'What are your thoughts about who killed him?' Taylor asked Shackleton, abruptly turning away from Marshall.

Shackleton sighed and rubbed his hand across a chin dark with stubble. He had not taken the time to shave when he had received the awful message, throwing on whatever clothes were to hand and racing immediately to the dockyard.

'I don't know, but none of *my* people will be responsible. Members of an expedition are like a family: they're much closer than normal colleagues. Moreover, to a man, they're keen – desperate – for the ship to be away at the end of the month, and no one will have done anything that might damage that.'

Taylor refrained from pointing out that *someone* had, and that, in his ten years as a detective, experience had taught him that many, if not most, killings occurred within families.

'He's wearing evening dress,' he said, ignoring Marshall's disdainful snort that he should state the obvious. 'Why? Do your people usually come to work dressed for dinner at their clubs, Mick?' He used, without thinking, the nickname by which Shackleton had been known at Dulwich – a reference to the explorer's Anglo-Irish antecedents and soft brogue.

When Marshall snorted a second time, Shackleton glared at him, acutely aware that his surgeon's flippancy might reflect badly on an expedition that needed not only the good graces of the public, if it were to receive the required funding, but of the police, if it were to leave at all.

'Of course not. He was at a formal occasion last night: a reception given by Lady Wallaston – the widow of the former Chinese ambassador – at her house in Eaton Square. He must have come here before turning in.'

'He did, sir,' said Raymond Priestley, the last member of the quartet. It was not unusual for expedition members to arrive at the docks before dawn, in the hope of squeezing a couple of hours of work in before the place became busy. That day, he and Marshall were the early birds, although work had promptly been forgotten when they had discovered the quay swarming with policemen. 'He was worried about his Monagasque trawl.'

Priestley's tone was defensive, and Taylor immediately deduced that the young man had liked the victim, and was shaken by the abrupt brutality of his death. The policeman glanced at him, recalling Shackleton's brief introductions. Despite being just short of his twenty-first birthday, Priestley had been appointed as the expedition's geologist. His fair hair, slight, athletic build and pale complexion made him appear younger still – indeed, Shackleton had mentioned that Priestley was still a student at University College, Bristol. Despite his tender years, the scientist had an aura of quiet dignity that was lacking in Marshall, and Taylor sensed he would prove to be the better man.

'His Monagasque trawl?' Taylor asked, not sure whether such a detail was relevant, or if it was the kind of superfluous information he would later discard. He had dined with Shackleton enough to know that Priestley was not the only one with an affinity for mentioning obscure pieces of equipment in a way that suggested anyone not familiar with them must be from the Moon.

'A device for dredging the sea-bed in the deep ocean – to catch the marine life there. It will…it would have provided Scudder with valuable data,' said Priestley, as Marshall raised his eyes heavenward in mock despair that an explanation was needed. The geologist turned to point. 'You can see it up there on the deck of the ship, below the wooden derrick.'

'*Nimrod*,' said Shackleton softly, gazing at the barque swaying gently at her moorings. 'The ship's name is *Nimrod*.'

The frenzied preparations surrounding Shackleton's venture were so often reported in the newspapers that few Londoners could have been unaware of the name of the vessel that was to transport him and his men to the Great White South. The expedition was the subject of intense national attention, too – indeed, it was rumoured that the King had taken an interest. Taylor felt it a pity that the monarch's curiosity did not extend to his purse, though: the expedition was appallingly under-subscribed, and its leader was obliged to spend his time not only supervising the purchase, delivery and storage of provisions and equipment for an absence expected to exceed eighteen months, but showing an amiable face at fund-raising events too. It was a gruelling business, and only a man with Shackleton's burning energy could have done it.

Taylor looked up at the Monagasque trawl, which squatted on *Nimrod*'s upper deck like some ungainly trapeze, a muddle of nets and pulleys surrounded by crates and boxes. It was not, he thought, the sort of item that would interest thieves – criminals liked goods they could sell, and he did not think there would be much demand for something they could not lift, much less pronounce or explain the purpose of in the shady taverns of Blackwall.

'Why was he worried about it?' he asked. 'It's too large to be attractive to casual thieves, and you've just told me that two crewmen and the first officer…' He twisted his notebook in the gloomy pre-dawn light to read what he had written. '…Mr Davis, had been detailed to guard the ship and the…' He waved his hand to take in the mess of crates, oddly shaped bundles, barrels and boxes that lay in ordered chaos on the quayside.

'Materiel,' supplied Shackleton helpfully. 'Davis came on duty at one o'clock. He and his party relieved the third officer, Cheetham, and two other crewmen who

15

had started at eight last night. You can check with them, but I'm sure it was done properly. I have a good crew, responsible and diligent. I wouldn't have chosen them were they not.'

'Where are they now?' All Taylor could see were his own men – Sergeant Grant and five constables; one placed at either end of the quay to prevent anyone from walking along it until the body was removed, and the others searching for anything that might be construed as evidence. Taylor did not anticipate that they would find much: the murder weapon had been left in place, and the entire pier was so loaded with what he would have called clutter – but which Shackleton insisted were vital components of the expedition – that it would be impossible for a policeman to tell what might or might not be relevant to a murder.

'Cheetham and his men have gone home,' replied Shackleton. 'They're usually keen to get to bed as soon as possible after their watch. Davis, Riches and Berry are on board. It was Davis who found Scudder's... Scudder.'

'Gone home?' asked Taylor. 'They don't live on the ship?'

Marshall's laugh was a derisive bray. 'Of course not! You can see how the quay is awash with equipment, and the ship is the same. There are a couple of bunks in the officers' cabin, and a hammock or two below decks for crewmen with night duty, but there's no room for anyone to sleep here regularly, so everyone goes either home or to rented lodgings. Cheetham and his men are staying in Battersea Rise, near Clapham Junction.'

'And Davis discovered Scudder's body *after* one

o'clock, so Cheetham and his men won't know about it yet,' added Priestley, trying to make amends for the surgeon's curtness by being helpful.

'Is Davis aboard *Nimrod* now?' asked Taylor.

'Going about his duties,' confirmed Shackleton. He shrugged his broad shoulders. 'I've no experience with murders, but it seems to me that carrying on as normal after something like this will help allay the shock, so I ordered him and his men back to work. You don't want them under your feet, anyway – seamen are incurably nosy.'

'Not only seamen,' murmured Taylor, aware that he would not have long to investigate unimpeded before men started to appear for work. The East India Docks were a busy part of the Thames, and would not remain quiet for long, even with his officers barring access. Those determined enough would find other ways in, Taylor knew. He knelt in the sticky, oil- and coal-impregnated muck that formed a thin black carpet across the stone pier, and inspected Scudder's corpse closely, although he doubted the examination would tell him much he did not know already. However, he meant to be thorough.

He had already noticed that Scudder's hands were clean, and that there was no indication that a struggle had taken place. He concluded that the victim had been taken by surprise, and had had no time to defend himself – either because he had been attacked from behind, or because he had not known he had anything to fear from his assailant. Clean hands also meant that Scudder had died where he had fallen – he had not tried to crawl for help, or they would have been as filthy as the knees of Taylor's trousers had just become.

The body was slightly stiff around the face, which Taylor knew suggested he had been dead for some hours, although the warmth of the night and the amount of alcohol the man might have imbibed meant such an estimate was by no means certain. And that was all, except for the unusual weapon that had been used to dispatch him. He jiggled it slightly, assessing the level of violent strength with which it had been driven home.

'Blue eyes,' he said absently, as he pulled back a lid, aware that only Marshall had not turned away during his inspection. Shackleton and Priestley had started a stilted discussion about salted pork, as an excuse not to watch.

'I could have told you that,' said Marshall, a note of censure in his voice. Clearly, he had not liked an amateur performing an examination that was usually the domain of the medical doctor. 'You needn't have looked yourself.'

Taylor did not much care what Marshall thought. He wanted the information instantly, not in several hours after a post-mortem had taken place. He pointed to the spike that had pierced the biologist through the neck, from right to left, in a perfectly straight line. It was some sort of knife, with an ornate hasp and a long, sharp blade.

'I've never seen a weapon like this before, and it's difficult to make it out, embedded as it is. We will have it from the pathologist in due course, but can any of you identify it now? I'd like to include it in my initial report.'

'Certainly,' replied Shackleton. 'That's a Reserve letter opener.'

Taylor frowned. 'I'm not sure I follow. "Reserve"?'

'The emblem on the handle,' explained Shackleton, leaning down to point at it. 'It's the symbol of the Royal Naval Reserve, and letter openers such as these are often used by its officers.'

'I see,' said Taylor. 'Is there anyone aboard *Nimrod* who might own such a thing?'

'Three people, other than me.' Shackleton's reply was hesitant, as though he felt he were betraying a trust. Taylor smiled encouragingly at him, grateful that he was prepared to be practical; the police would have the information sooner or later anyway. 'Captain England, *Nimrod*'s master, was RNR when he served aboard *Morning* on the relief of Scott's expedition.'

'Our expedition's other surgeon – Alistair Mackay – also used to be Royal Navy,' added Marshall, with rather more glee than was appropriate. 'And perhaps more pertinent, so was Jameson Adams, the meteorologist.'

Taylor looked sharply at him. 'Why is Adams more pertinent?'

Marshall gave an unreadable smile, and malice sparkled in his pale eyes. 'Because he looks like the murdering type.'

Shackleton was visibly annoyed with Marshall; his eyes were hard and cold, and his mouth set in a grim line of displeasure. Taylor remembered that look from years before, when classmates had jibed him about his Irish origins, but unlike then, when he had responded with his fists, Shackleton mastered his temper and addressed his companions with quiet courtesy.

'This is no place to discuss such matters,' he said. 'Let's go aboard *Nimrod*.' He reconsidered as he stared unhappily at the inspector. 'Or are you obliged to stay with Scudder until he's removed, Will? I want to do the right thing. Oh, God! I shall have to inform his mother…' He trailed off unhappily.

'It won't take long,' said Marshall carelessly. 'She lives in Norbiton – less than an hour by train – and she won't want you to linger. You'll soon be back to work.'

'I wasn't thinking about the time lost to the expedition,' snapped Shackleton, his eyes blazing now. 'I was thinking about her. What will she do now her only son is killed on the eve of his rise to fame?'

'Oh, he *will* be famous,' said Marshall slyly. 'The gentlemen of the press love a murder.'

'The police will inform Scudder's next of kin,' Taylor said quickly, partly to soothe his agitated friend, but mostly to prevent a tart response – Shackleton's tongue could be barbed and it was no time for an unedifying spat. 'This kind of news is never taken well, but it's often accepted more readily from a man in a uniform.'

He gestured to his sergeant, a short, squat fellow with a low forehead – nicknamed Greasy Grant for reasons Taylor had yet to fathom – to take the body to the mortuary.

Meanwhile, Shackleton led the way towards his ship, indicating with an absent wave of his hand that Taylor was to be careful of the moorings – thick, algae-encrusted lines that moved gently up and down in time with the movement of invisible waves. Taylor watched them, suspecting that if *Nimrod* rocked on the millpond-flat Thames, then she would roll horribly on the open ocean – and some of the seas she would be traversing were among the roughest in the world. He shuddered, grateful he would not be obliged to be on her.

As Shackleton led the way up the gangway, Taylor studied him. He was hatless, and his hair, neatly parted in the middle, was thick and dark. His square face with its wide-set eyes had filled out since they were boys, but otherwise it had changed little, and was capable of sudden, open and infectious laughter, just as it could be stern, hard and sombre.

Taylor certainly did not envy his venture to a region few had ever visited, especially after the lecture he had attended the previous week – the explorer had described icebergs bigger than cathedrals, silent glaciers glittering unimaginably bright as far as the eye could see, and that distant diamond, the South Pole, luring those daring enough to try to reach it. Taylor gave an inward smile: if anyone could do it, it was Shackleton.

The three men familiar with *Nimrod* went up the roughly hewn wooden plank that served as a gangway as though it were a solid marble stairway; Taylor ascended rather more carefully. Once on board, he became aware of unfamiliar sounds and smells, and a sense of pokiness. The companionways and stairwells were impossibly narrow, and a powerful scent of wet rope, seaweed, freshly cut wood and the hot pitch that had caulked the seams pervaded, although these were overlain with something warm, rancid and potent.

'Seal oil,' explained Priestley, seeing Taylor wrinkle his nose. 'It was much worse when she first arrived from Newfoundland, but the holds have been scoured since then, and the decks are scrubbed three times a week. We hope the smell will be gone by the time we put to sea. She was a sealing ship, you see.'

'Lord!' muttered Taylor. The combination of the oily stench, the slight rocking motion and the cramped, airless conditions made him want to gag, and the notion of spending weeks on *Nimrod* as she bucked and rolled her way through the oceans was beyond his imagination.

'You get used to it,' said Priestley with a sympathetic smile. 'You won't notice it at all after a few hours.'

Taylor was sure he would.

Shackleton led the way to a minute room in which every available inch of space held papers, charts, equipment, clothing, tins of food, and even a box containing thermometers. He threaded his way through the chaos to a desk near the window, first tipping a mound of snow goggles from the only other chair for Taylor, and indicating the other two were to sit or stand wherever they found space. Priestley perched on a crate, while Marshall leaned against the closed door. The surgeon took out a pipe while Shackleton shook a cigarette from a packet, and soon the cabin was so full of fug that even the seal oil was masked by the sharp, pungent scent of burning tobacco.

'It's half past five,' said Shackleton, taking a large gold watch from a pocket in his waistcoat and inspecting it briefly. 'And although my people work long hours – either here or at the Expedition Office in Regent Street – it's still too early for most of them to be in. However, you shall speak to each and every one of them, Will.' He hesitated uncertainly. 'I assume that's what you'll be wanting to do?'

'Yes, but it won't be me,' replied Taylor. 'I'm here now because you asked for me, but I'll be handing this to

Inspector Andrews as soon as I've written a preliminary report. We work on a rotating basis, and this will be his case.'

'That's not what Chief Superintendent Hamilton told me,' said Shackleton, with a smile that was an odd combination of rueful and sly. Immediately, Taylor saw that his friend had already been pulling strings, using his considerable charm to get his way. 'He said he can assign his detectives where he pleases, and he can allocate you to this case if that's what I'd like. I would like, Will. I'd rather have someone I know investigating.'

Taylor nodded, suspecting Hamilton had been taken off guard with the demand and had capitulated against his will. In other words, Hamilton would have recanted as soon as he and Shackleton had parted company, and Andrews was probably already en route to the docks as they spoke. Besides, Andrews was clear of his previous investigations, while Taylor was currently overwhelmed. However, it was not the time to discuss the politics of departmental administration, so he held his tongue.

'Right,' said Shackleton, taking Taylor's silence as acquiescence. 'I'll arrange for the men to be ready whenever you want.'

'Very well,' said Taylor, supposing he could make a start. Andrews would appreciate it, as all investigators knew that the most valuable interviews were those conducted soonest after the crime. 'Scudder was obviously killed late last night, because he was wearing evening dress. What time do you all finish work?'

It was Priestley who answered. 'Six to six are the official hours, but there's a lot to do, so we all add at least another couple each day. However, the dockyard gates are closed at dusk – around nine o'clock at this time of year – and once that happens it's difficult to get in or out. Still, some of the dockers may have seen someone lurking.'

'Lurking?' Taylor was not sure what the geologist was saying.

'Robbers,' explained Marshall with exaggerated patience. 'Thieves. The men who killed Scudder. Obviously the culprit is some local criminal.'

'And what about the Reserve paperknife?' asked Taylor, making no attempt to disguise his own sarcasm in response to Marshall's. 'It's not the blade of choice for most dockhands engaging in casual murder-cum-robbery. There's also the fact that nothing was stolen – Scudder's wallet, cuff-links, watch and gold signet ring are still with his body.'

'Then the killers must have been interrupted before they could take them,' said Shackleton, looking alarmed by the implications inherent in Taylor's remarks. 'And the letter opener is something they could have stolen from someone else.'

His expression was unhappy, and Taylor could tell that he was unconvinced by his own explanation. So was Taylor. The lack of a struggle had immediately prompted him to suspect that Scudder had known his assailant. The alternative was that he had been taken by surprise, but if that were the case, and Scudder had died quickly and without a fight, then surely the robbers would have at least snatched his watch and ring before they made their escape?

'So,' he said, resisting the urge to cough – the cabin was too small for the amount of smoke that was being produced by Marshall and Shackleton and he was glad Priestley had not joined in, too. 'While we're waiting for your people to arrive, tell me again what happened. Let's start with this trawl. Why was Scudder worried about it? Is it expensive?'

'Of course it's expensive,' replied Marshall scornfully. 'But it wasn't just the trawl that was worrying him – we have a lot of biological equipment here. As a policeman, you naturally assume he was concerned about theft, but there are other important considerations for men of science. These are essential pieces of equipment, and it is easy to damage—'

Shackleton leaned across his table, hand raised to prevent Marshall from continuing, Taylor was gratified to see the surgeon's mouth close with a snap. Just as Shackleton did not want to offend the police, so Marshall did not want to alienate the man who would decide whether or not to include him on the most important sledge journey in the world – the one to the South Pole. Taylor was no great outdoorsman, but even he could see that claiming one of the last major geographical trophies on Earth for the British Empire would be more prestigious than being left at the base, stuffing penguins for the Natural History Museum, or tending minor cuts and bruises.

'Scudder was conscientious,' Shackleton said. 'It was what made him such a good biologist, according to the references that came with his application. Science of this nature requires a fellow with an eye for detail, a vast amount of patience and a willingness to coax results from temperamental pieces of equipment. Scudder appeared to be equal to the task.'

'Appeared to be?' pounced Taylor. 'You appointed him to your expedition, but you haven't witnessed first-hand the quality of his work?'

A lesser man might have bridled at having his decisions questioned, but Shackleton only gave a lop-sided grin. 'It wouldn't have mattered if I'd heard him address the Royal Society, Will. I'm not a biologist, and I've no way of telling a good one from a bad. However, I've been at pains to appoint men with solid academic reputations. Scudder was such a man – he came highly recommended.'

Taylor's gaze drifted towards Priestley. The geologist was little more than a lad, so surely he did not own a 'solid academic reputation' – he was not old enough. He said nothing, but Shackleton read his thoughts.

'More than four hundred men applied to come south with me. Four hundred! Some wrote, some came in person. However, it's not just competence in their scientific fields that I need, but *mettle*. It takes a special sort of chap to succeed in the Antarctic – resourceful, flexible, careful, single-minded and a good many other things, too. I chose Scudder because he fitted the bill, and also because he was determined to come, and it's that determination – that *drive* – that sorts the men from the boys.'

'Why was he so keen?' asked Taylor, who would not have volunteered to save his life, and failed to understand those who had.

Shackleton smiled again. 'Because men love adventure and the chance to pit themselves against the unknown. You do, when you challenge the felons of a violent, depraved underworld. It's the same with an expedition.'

Taylor did not see that the deliberate courting of extreme danger was anything like apprehending criminals in the course of daily duty, but he raised his hand to prevent Shackleton from continuing. Time was passing and, interesting though it was to be sharing such confidences with his old friend, he needed to concentrate on Scudder.

'So Scudder was worried about his equipment, not because he thought it might be stolen, but because he was afraid it might be damaged,' he surmised. 'Why did he think that? Are these items delicate? Or was he concerned that they were vulnerable to sabotage?'

'We did have a problem with some torn nets a couple of days ago,' replied Shackleton, 'but I think that would be considered unusual. You saw them, Priestley. What did you think?'

Priestley considered. 'They were specially made fine-webbed nets, designed to catch small prey, like krill.'

'Krill?' asked Taylor blankly.

'Antarctic shrimp,' explained Priestley, while Marshall smirked at this latest example of the policeman's ignorance. 'Scudder took the nets out of their boxes, to check them before they were stowed, and some had been damaged. He said someone had cut them deliberately, but I don't think it's possible to say. They might as easily have been harmed on the way down from Hull.'

'And there were his specimen jars,' added Marshall a little slyly. 'A number of them were cracked. He said that was deliberate, too. But the winch set a load of scientific materials down rather heavily once, and I suspect they

27

broke then.'

Taylor nodded, although he was unwilling to dismiss anything until he was sure it was irrelevant. Someone had murdered Scudder, and as nothing had been stolen, it meant the killer had another motive. The fact that Scudder had been experiencing difficulties with his equipment was too pertinent not to warrant further investigation.

'So, Scudder was under the impression that someone was trying to harm his work,' surmised Taylor after a brief hiatus during which strong black coffee was served by a short, moustachioed man in filthy working clothes, whom Shackleton introduced as Roberts, the cook.

Like many men in occupations that encouraged eavesdropping, Roberts lingered after he had poured, obviously keen to hear something interesting. Taylor said not a word while he was present, and even when Roberts had gone, he kept his voice low, determined that nosy crewmen would not hear their discussion.

'He was, but I don't think he had enemies,' replied Priestley. He was pale in the swirling smoke – Shackleton had lit another cigarette, Marshall still puffed on his pipe and Roberts had had some foul-smelling cigar clasped between his teeth, the reek of which still lingered; Taylor supposed the shock of seeing a colleague dead was also beginning to take its toll.

'Perhaps not, but it's what *Scudder* believed that's important now,' he said gently. 'Whether he imagined he had an enemy.'

'I suppose he did,' said Priestley, shooting an apologetic glance at Shackleton, as though he had been manoeuvred into admitting something he would rather have kept to himself. 'Well, not an *enemy* exactly, but someone who was trying to make life awkward for him.'

Shackleton made an impatient noise at the back of his throat. 'I know what you're thinking, Priestley: that you'll bring the expedition into disrepute if you reveal evidence of ill-feeling among its members. But you must tell the police anything – *anything* – that might be pertinent. If we procrastinate, Will might never have his culprit and that could spell the end of us.'

Priestley nodded, albeit unhappily, and turned to Taylor. 'We had hoped to have the biological equipment stowed yesterday, but there was a problem with one of the hatches, so the work had to be delayed until this morning. It meant the Monagasque trawl had to spend the night on deck, while his Nansen-Petterson water bottles were on the quay.'

'Scudder whined about it all evening,' elaborated Marshall. 'He said he should not have gone to a party when his equipment was sitting exposed. He wanted to stay with it.'

'He left early,' added Priestley. He reconsidered. 'Well, I suppose he did. Lady Wallaston had invited a lot of people, and it was difficult to tell who was there and who wasn't – the party spread into several rooms and the garden. I didn't see him leave, but I know he wasn't there later. I was the last to go – with you, sir – and he was certainly gone by then.'

'Priestley and I shared a hansom home,' explained Shackleton. 'Our lodgings are close to each other, and we're doing all we can to save costs, with so many bills mounting up. I tell you, Will, braving the Antarctic is the easy part. It's trying to raise money that sucks the life from you.'

'So, Scudder came here *alone*?' Taylor asked, more interested in the victim than in his friend's financial troubles. 'No one came with him?'

'*I* didn't,' replied Marshall. 'Lady Wallaston had invited all her rich friends to the reception, so it was important that we created a good impression. To have left early would have been rude. I stayed until the raspberry tart incident changed the tenor of the event.'

Shackleton's eyes narrowed, and Priestley's pale face suddenly flushed a deep red.

'Raspberry tart incident?' asked Shackleton, but Taylor waved the question aside, suspecting a ploy on Marshall's part to sidetrack the discussion, and determined not to let it happen. He homed in on the surgeon.

'So what time did Scudder leave?'

Marshall shrugged. 'I have no idea. I was not his keeper.'

'I know he was still there at half past nine,' said Priestley quickly, before Taylor could remark that hindering a police investigation was both unwise and irresponsible. 'I remember because he started on about his trawl again, just as Lady Wallaston's clock started to chime.'

'I hope he didn't slip away too early,' said Shackleton disapprovingly. 'If he did, it would not have endeared us to potential sponsors.'

'He wasn't the only one,' said Marshall spitefully. 'Although you asked everyone in the shore party to stay, a number slipped off when they thought no one was looking.'

'Shore party?' queried Taylor, confused. 'You mean the dockhands?'

'He means the men who will remain *on shore* with me in the Antarctic,' replied Shackleton, cutting into Marshall's snide explanation. 'The scientists, the men who will participate in the sledging journeys and those involved in the logistical side of the operation. We call them the "shore party". The others – the ship's officers and crew – will remain on *Nimrod*.'

'How many scientists do you have?' asked Taylor.

'Six so far,' replied Shackleton with pride. 'All excellent fellows.'

'Five,' corrected Priestley in a low voice. 'You're still counting Scudder, sir.'

'Lord!' muttered Shackleton, rubbing his face hard. 'Five, then. Priestley and Marshall, whom you've met. Our meteorologist is Jameson Adams, the other surgeon is Alistair Mackay and our biologist is James Murray. Five fine men. And I hope I shall have one or two others, too.'

'Your staff isn't complete yet?' asked Taylor, thinking Shackleton was leaving the appointments rather late.

'Obviously not,' drawled Marshall. 'Scudder is hardly in a position to assist Murray *now*, is he? So, there's one – perhaps two – posts left, depending on funding. There are plenty of eager fellows remaining – even with a sailing date only twenty-one days away.'

'But there are three who are on a shortlist,' added Priestley. 'They are named O'Brien, Yaxley and Vallen – we call them the "hopefuls".'

'There was another man I liked a lot,' said Shackleton,

rather wistfully. 'A zoologist called John Gray from some obscure Canadian university. He'd spent two years in Spitsbergen working with sealers, and several more in the Canadian Arctic. His experience would have been invaluable, and he was a strong fellow, willing to turn his hand to anything. But he didn't bother to turn up for a second interview – when I would have offered him the post.'

'Why not?'

'He never said, and I mention it only to show that you're not the only one for whom this expedition holds a distinct lack of appeal. Gray also had cold feet, although I can't imagine why.'

'Maybe he invented his qualifications,' suggested Marshall, ever spiteful. 'And you did tell him that you'd check them. Also, Scudder was against him, remember? He preferred O'Brien for the post. Now that is an opinion I simply cannot understand. O'Brien is a damned fool!'

'He is not,' objected Priestley. 'And you have only taken against him because Scudder approved of him – and you disliked Scudder.'

Marshall rounded on him. 'I *did* dislike Scudder. I deplored the way he ran down Murray all the time, trying to get himself promoted to chief biologist over him. I disapprove of politicking.'

'Nigel Vallen seems promising, though,' said Shackleton lightly, while Taylor listened and drew his own conclusions from Marshall's vitriolic remarks, not least of which was the fact that Scudder was not the only expedition member to 'run down' his colleagues. 'He has just finished a degree in natural history at Oxford, and has been at the docks every day, helping

Scudder. Scudder wasn't an easy man, but Vallen had a way with him.'

'Of course, there's also the fact that Vallen's father lives only a couple of miles away, and is often here watching proceedings,' added Marshall. 'One does tend to be on one's best behaviour when one has a proud parent breathing down one's neck.'

'The Reverend Vallen doesn't breathe down Nigel's neck,' said Priestley firmly. 'He's just interested in the expedition – and after his congregation held a fund-raising fete for us, the Boss said he could visit any time. Besides, the sailors want him here: they say it's good luck to have a man of God watching the preparations.'

'I like him here, too, actually,' said Marshall, and the sudden quiet sincerity in his voice made Taylor glance at him sharply. 'Ours is a dangerous venture, and we need God's blessing.'

Taylor continued to stare. He would not have thought the acid-tongued medic to be a believer, but it was clear that Marshall spoke with genuine conviction.

'Yes,' said Shackleton, a little uncomfortably, although Priestley had nodded heartfelt agreement. 'Although I don't think Scudder would have agreed. Nor O'Brien. Neither of them have…had time for religion.'

Taylor was beginning to be confused with all the new names being bandied about. 'So Vallen, the son of the vicar, and O'Brien, whom Scudder favoured, are the "hopefuls," and Gray was to have been a member, but he decided to give the whole thing a miss?'

'In essence,' nodded Marshall. 'But you missed the third "hopeful" – Peter Yaxley – who, you might want to know, had a quarrel with Scudder only yesterday –

something about the taxonomy of dinoflagellates, would you believe? But Yaxley is better than O'Brien.'

'Why?' asked Taylor.

'Because O'Brien is too old,' replied Marshall promptly. 'He claims he's forty, but if he's a day under fifty, I'll eat my hat. There's no place on a venture like this for the elderly. He may be the best biologist in the Empire, but if he can't climb a ladder without wheezing like my grandfather, then he's no use to us.' He shot Shackleton a glance that indicated there was a good deal left unsaid.

'Murray will rally once he breathes the clean Antarctic air,' snapped Shackleton, verging on anger. 'He's still recovering from the physical strain of his bathymetrical survey of the Scottish lochs.'

Taylor frowned in confusion. 'Murray? I thought we were talking about O'Brien.'

'Marshall is just using an opportunity to make a point he's raised before,' explained Priestley. 'He thinks that at forty-one, Murray is too old for the Antarctic – just like O'Brien.'

Marshall shrugged. 'Medically speaking, Scudder was probably right when he claimed *he* would make a better chief biologist than Murray. I prefer Murray as a man, but sentiment has no place on a venture like ours.'

'No,' said Shackleton coldly. 'However, I appointed Murray, and I stand by my choice. When I want a medical opinion, you'll be the first man I ask. Until then, you will accept my decisions or tender your resignation.'

'So, Scudder favoured appointing O'Brien to the expedition,' said Taylor, after an awkward silence, during which Marshall scowled resentfully, Shackleton glared back and Priestley looked out of the window, obviously wishing he were elsewhere. 'But the rest of you think O'Brien is too old.'

'That's not it,' said Shackleton, reining in his temper with obvious difficulty. 'It's not his age, but something I can't put my finger on. He's always polite and amenable, but I have the sense that he's not the right fit.'

Taylor let the matter drop: he needed hard information, not opinions and impressions. He now had five scientists and three 'hopefuls' to question, and that was more than enough with which to start. He closed his notebook and stood, keen to be out of the cabin. All the time they had been speaking, he had been unpleasantly aware of the ship's swaying, and it was beginning to unsettle his stomach. But Shackleton began talking again, so he reluctantly sat back down.

'Besides the scientists and the hopefuls, there are the four other members of the shore party: Roberts the cook, who just brought us this excellent coffee; Ernest Joyce, in charge of general stores, sledges and the like; Bernard Day, who's going to manage the motor-car—'

'Motor-car?' blurted Taylor, unable to help himself. 'In all that ice? Surely it'll freeze the oil, ice-up the pistons, that sort of thing?'

Shackleton smiled indulgently. 'I see you're no mechanic, Will. Once the engine is running, all those problems will disappear like...like frost in sunshine. Besides, that's why we have Day: to eradicate such inconveniences. Finally, there is Frank Wild, who's in charge of provisions – that's him on the quayside in the blue cap, already about his duties.'

'And there are the members of the *ship's* crew,' added

Marshall, watching Taylor open his notebook and begin to write again. A slight smile crossed his face, as if he knew the inspector was ready to leave and therefore had decided to bombard him with new information out of sheer boorishness. Taylor wondered why. Had the surgeon endured some unpleasant brush with the law that made him hostile to policemen, or was he simply spiteful to everyone? 'Captain England and his five officers, and sixteen crewmen. Would you like their names?'

'Later,' replied Taylor, closing the book with a purposeful and distinctly final snap.

Taylor had had enough of the reek of seal oil, tar and tobacco smoke, all of which were combining with the ship's motion to make him feel rather queasy. He shoved his notebook in his pocket and aimed for the door, intending to be on dry land as quickly as possible. However, when he wrenched it open, he found himself faced with a solid wall of crates, so tall and wide that they covered the entire opening as effectively as if it had been bricked over.

'Damn,' muttered Shackleton. 'It seems stowing has started sooner than I expected today.'

He hollered in a voice calculated to carry over the fiercest of Antarctic storms, then hammered on the nearest box, causing it teeter in a manner that made Taylor hope no one was on the other side. Eventually, Roberts could be heard, breathing heavily, as though he had just run up from below decks. He promised to have the doorway cleared, but nothing happened immediately, so Taylor turned reluctantly back to his chair, pleased to see Priestley opening a porthole. It yielded grudgingly with a metallic shriek, and the geologist shot the policeman a conspiratorial smile as he waved a piece of card in an effort to dissipate some of the fumes.

'Any more questions, inspector?' asked Marshall, relighting his pipe and puffing it in Priestley's direction. 'Or have you finished?'

'Far from finished,' replied Taylor, struggling not to allow the surgeon to irritate him. 'I'd like to know a little more about last night. All six scientists attended Lady Wallaston's function. Who else was there from the ship?'

'Me, of course,' replied Shackleton, 'as well as the four other members of the shore party – Joyce, Day, Roberts and Wild. Two of the ship's officers *weren't* there – Davis and Cheetham had watches – but the other three, including Captain England, were present.'

'But England left early,' added Marshall. 'He was discreet, slipping through the garden so as not to be noticed, but he did leave before most.'

'Would England have come here, to the ship?' asked Taylor.

Shackleton hesitated. 'It's possible. You'll need to ask him.'

'And *I* can ask the others if they saw Scudder leave,' said Marshall.

'No,' said Taylor firmly. 'We'll do that, thank you. You can go about your own duties as soon as Roberts lets us out.'

'I think I did see Scudder go, now I think about it,' said Shackleton suddenly. 'After the loyal toast. He'd been talking to Dr Canning of the Royal Society, and I saw him stand rather abruptly and stride towards the door.

Canning can be a bit long-winded, so perhaps some tedious monologue allowed Scudder's thoughts to stray to his equipment.'

'You saw him exit through the front door?' asked Taylor. 'With his hat and coat on?'

Shackleton grimaced. 'I forget you want us to be literal. No. I saw him leave the room where most of us were gathered around Lady Wallaston and her piano, and I *assumed* he was escaping. Lady Wallaston probably noticed, too.'

'Do you think she was offended?' asked Priestley nervously.

Shackleton smiled, a carefree grin quite unexpected from a man under such enormous pressure. 'No, because I'd anticipated bids for early escape from some of you, so I'd already spun her a tale – said that several of you have sweethearts who are eager to claim your free moments. She would have assumed he was slinking off to a romantic rendezvous, and would have turned an indulgent blind eye.'

'Scudder?' muttered Marshall with a smirk. 'Romantic? She'd be a fool to believe that of him.'

Taylor kept his face carefully neutral, but small pieces of information were beginning to come together in his mind, and he felt he was gaining a reasonable impression of the men on Shackleton's expedition. Scudder had obviously not been the most popular member, and Marshall had disliked him. Marshall himself was outspoken and arrogant, and Taylor imagined he was not liked either. Priestley was serious and decent, eager to do his duty, while Shackleton was just Shackleton, older and considerably wiser than at school, but the same irrepressible chap, entirely committed to the task in hand. Taylor had no doubt that the moment the crates were moved Shackleton would race away to tackle one of his thousand different tasks with the same ebullient cheerfulness with which he approached everything.

'Was Scudder drunk?' Taylor asked. 'Or unsteady on his feet?'

'He was tipsy,' offered Priestley. 'His face gets red when he has too much wine, and it was definitely flushed when I saw him. I'm not saying he was reeling, only that he might have been less inhibited than usual.'

Or less worried about attacks in the dark, thought Taylor. He turned to Shackleton. 'I do not suppose you noticed whether anyone followed him out?'

'I didn't,' said Shackleton. 'But, as Priestley said, the place was busy. It was difficult to tell who was where.'

'Adams,' said Marshall suddenly. '*He* left early – I saw him. So did Mackay, and I've already mentioned England. As for Murray or the others – your guess is as good as mine.'

'Who might be able to tell me?' asked Taylor.

'Not the Wallaston butler,' said Shackleton wryly. 'The whole point about sneaking off early was to do it without being seen, so there would have been no demanding of coats or asking for cabs to be summoned. Priestley?'

'Since we were the last – we were gone by midnight – everyone left before us,' replied the geologist. He regarded his leader soberly. 'And as the inspector said he isn't sure what time Scudder died, I imagine it could be argued that any of us could have made an end of him.'

Chapter 2

A loud knock on the cabin door made Taylor start. Roberts opened it without waiting for a reply, indicating with a silent nod that the crates had been moved. The inspector made an immediate bid for escape, but two seamen blocked his way, caps clasped in their hands. They introduced themselves as Berry and Riches, who had been on duty with First Officer Davis, when Scudder's body had been discovered.

With a sigh, Taylor saw his visit would have to be extended while he spoke to them, and hoped his stomach would not let him down – Marshall was hardly the kind of man to respond sympathetically to seasickness.

'We'll leave you to it, then, Will,' said Shackleton, shooting to his feet and indicating that Marshall and Priestley were to go with him. 'You don't need us any more.'

Riches was the older of the two seamen, grizzled before his time, with hands so callused that Taylor imagined there would be no feeling in them at all. Berry was in his early twenties, but already well on the way to becoming as tough as his shipmate.

'Did you see or speak to anyone other than Davis last

night?' asked Taylor, after they had reported that they had come on duty at one o'clock, and had accompanied Davis on a tour of the ship before beginning their regular patrols along the quay half an hour later. The body had been discovered lying by the tinned sardines at quarter past two – Berry knew this, because he had heard the bells chime at All Saints Church.

'The Boss, sir,' replied Berry. 'He came from home when we sent for him. And then there was the constable what arrived, blowing his whistle to bring his colleagues, and—'

'No, did you see anyone *before* you discovered the body.'

Berry rubbed his head. 'Well, it was quiet like, with everyone gone to the do. These scientists are a rum lot, and it ain't unknown for 'em to stay here all night, poring over their bits and pieces. But not last night.'

'So, you saw none of the scientists – from when you came on duty at one until after you raised the alarm?'

'Well, we saw Mr Adams,' replied Riches reluctantly. '*Nimrod* is moored towards the western end of the South Quay, right? Well, he came up to us, and said he'd been down the *eastern* end. He was worried about a gap he'd found in one of them fences near the railway line, and told us to make sure we paid special attention to it.'

'He told us to keep a weather eye on that whole area,' elaborated Berry. 'Being a former navy man, he thinks he knows better than Mr Davis about how to do things around a ship, but as regards *Nimrod*, it ain't none of his business. Mr Davis is in charge, not Mr Adams. But, like Riches said, he sent us off to the eastern end at about two o'clock.'

41

'So, you saw Adams *before* the murder was discovered,' concluded Taylor, thinking what an art it was to interview witnesses. If the right questions were not asked, the pertinent information might never come to light. 'Did you see anyone else?'

'Well, we'd seen Mr Scudder hisself, on the quay with his equipment, when we came on watch at one o'clock,' said Berry. 'And Dr Mackay was there earlier, and so was Mr Murray, the biologist. Or at least, that's what Ernie Ellis told me – Ernie was on Mr Cheetham's watch. But *I* never saw them.'

'Nor me,' said Riches. 'Mr Scudder and Mr Adams were the only ones I saw until we found the body. Who killed him, sir? The men are saying it was a dockhand, and the dockhands are saying it was us.'

'We can't be sure at this stage,' replied Taylor. 'But we'll do our best to find the culprit.'

He dismissed them and leaned back in the chair, staring through the porthole to a dismal view across the Blackwall Railway Terminus and the skeletal cranes that stood sentinel along the filth-strewn banks of the Thames. He glanced at his pocket watch and wondered why Andrews was taking so long to arrive. The man was not usually tardy. He began to wonder if Shackleton had been right, and Chief Superintendent Hamilton had interfered with his detectives' rota.

He reviewed what he had learned so far. It was not yet known what time Scudder had died, but the biologist had probably left Eaton Square before ten, and was dead by quarter past two, when he was discovered by Davis. The murder weapon was a letter opener of the kind favoured by officers who had served in the Royal

Naval Reserve, and there were four men who might own one: Shackleton, Captain England, Adams and Mackay. All would need to provide alibis.

Taylor considered the facts, and was inclined to think that the killer had wanted one thing: Scudder dead. Scudder may have been slightly drunk, which perhaps accounted for the lack of defensive wounds, but Taylor guessed it more likely that he had known his assailant, and had not considered himself to be in danger. The killer had been able to come close to him, and then drive the blade clean through his neck.

It was a very personal way to kill, necessitating the killer to stand close to his victim when he delivered the fatal blow. Did that mean it was a crime of hate? Taylor's experience told him that a common robber would have been more likely to have stabbed Scudder in the back, not driven a knife through his neck in such a bizarre manner. Marshall had claimed that Adams was the 'murdering kind,' whatever that meant. But, as a policeman, Taylor knew any man could be the 'murdering kind' given the right circumstances. Of course, it was also Adams who had sent Berry and Riches off to the eastern end of the quay, far from where the murder had taken place.

Taylor also knew the victim had not been popular, although Priestley was unwilling to say anything unpleasant and Shackleton had not considered Scudder abrasive enough to cause conflict. However, Marshall had clearly detested him, while someone had disliked him enough to damage his nets and perhaps do something to the loading hatch to prevent the Monagasque trawl from being stowed according to plan. Could the latter have been a ploy to ensure Scudder's later appearance at the dock? Taylor thought it a definite possibility.

Then there were others who had reason to want the victim out of the way: the three 'hopefuls' seemed dependent on his good will in order to be selected for the expedition, but it was clear the victim had not been easy to please. And one of them – Yaxley – had had a public argument with Scudder. Had he been afraid that the row had spoiled his chances, so had taken steps to ensure Scudder was not in a position to do him harm? Meanwhile, O'Brien, whom Scudder had apparently liked, was considered by Shackleton 'not the right fit' for reasons the Boss did not understand himself. Then the awful possibility crossed Taylor's mind that Shackleton might have seen Scudder as an impediment to the smooth running of his venture, and regretted the appointment.

But no. Taylor had been friends with Shackleton for a long time, and even if Scudder had become a problem, no aspect of the scientific programme was worth risking the goal Shackleton had been intent on ever since he had returned from Scott's expedition four years before – the attainment of the Pole. Taylor dismissed Shackleton as a suspect: one of his staff might have made an end to an unpopular colleague, but Mick would have had nothing to do with it.

At about ten o'clock, Greasy Grant arrived with a message from Hamilton, ordering Taylor to continue his enquiries until further notice. There was no explanation. As a result, the rest of the day was taken up with speaking to the night staff employed by the East India Dock Company – a gang of rough, slovenly men employed for security, who were not thrilled to be ordered back to the docks during the day, when they were normally sleeping. They were under the command of a fellow named Ives, a short, bowler-hatted thug with pretensions of respectability, who produced dubious records to 'show' his people had been assiduous in their minding of gates and walls.

Meanwhile, Taylor deployed Grant and several constables to make initial enquiries among the expedition's staff and crew. This was a tactic he had employed before: he would read the statements taken by his officers, then see whether witnesses changed their stories when he later questioned them more closely himself.

When he had finished speaking to the night-watchmen, Taylor turned his attention to two of the 'hopefuls.' He interviewed Yaxley first, using Ives' office to do so, a scruffy lair that reeked of cigarette smoke, located near the dock's main gates. Yaxley perched nervously on a rickety wooden chair far too small for a man of his impressive size.

'I wouldn't have challenged Scudder if I'd known what was going to happen to him,' he said unhappily, shifting so the seat creaked ominously. 'Now I'll have to live with the fact that we argued and I never apologised.'

'The quarrel was your fault, then?' asked Taylor. To anyone who did not know him, his casual tone suggested he was uninterested in the answer, and his attention was on the notebook that lay open in front of him.

'No,' replied Yaxley firmly. 'He said dinoflagellates are more numerous than diatoms, and he was wrong. However, I don't like the thought of my last words to him being angry. I was hoping to be accepted on the expedition as a biologist – like Scudder and Murray – and it was stupid of me to argue with a man who could suggest to Mr Shackleton that I should be left behind.'

'But now you might be appointed in his place?' Taylor's tone was noncommittal.

'Yes.' Yaxley sounded defiant. 'And I hope I am. But I didn't kill him for it.'

Taylor asked a few more questions, then let him go. His next interview was with O'Brien, who was considerably more distressed by Scudder's death than anyone else had been. He sat in the chair and wept openly, tears rolling down his face. His swollen eyes told Taylor that it was not the first time he had given vent to his grief, either.

'He was a wonderful man,' O'Brien gasped, barely understandable as his words came in short, wavery bursts. 'I can't imagine how the expedition will manage without him.'

'You liked him? Admired him?'

'Both. He was a brilliant biologist and an excellent teacher. I've very much enjoyed learning under him these last few weeks, and so did Vallen and Priestley. Just ask them. They worked closely with him. It's only the people who didn't know him well who'll say anything bad.'

'Yaxley worked with him, and he didn't find Scudder likeable or admirable.'

'They didn't get along,' admitted O'Brien. 'It was a pity, because Yaxley has a lot of talent, and Scudder could have helped him with his career. I'm deeply sorry about his death, inspector. Deeply sorry.'

He wept again, and Taylor wondered what it was that had made Shackleton uncomfortable with the man. O'Brien had said nothing to make Taylor share Shackleton's opinion, and he found the man rather sad, someone to be pitied. O'Brien's face was lined, and his hair obviously dyed, so Taylor concurred with Marshall's assessment about his age: nearer fifty than forty. Clearly, he was past his prime physically, and perhaps he had hoped to resuscitate a flagging career by standing on the shoulders of younger men. Taylor did not think O'Brien possessed the strength of character to be a force in the expedition, positive or negative, and imagined that most men would barely notice he was there.

'We're not doing very well, sir,' said Greasy Grant, entering after O'Brien had been dismissed. 'We've now spoken to all the crew and staff on *Nimrod*, and I even went to the Expedition Office on Regent Street to nab a couple that we missed. But no one has confessed.'

'Really?' asked Taylor, wondering whether Grant was being facetious. He had known the moment he had seen the body and the unusual weapon that Scudder's murder would not be easy to solve. 'That's a blow.'

'I looked on all their clothes for blood, but no one had so much as a spot on him.' Grant sounded resentful, as though this piece of initiative had been unjustly thwarted by the clever criminal mind. 'Except Davis, the first officer.'

'He discovered the body,' Taylor pointed out.

'Yes, and he said he touched it, to see whether it was alive.' Grant was dismissive. 'Silly bugger! Of course Scudder was dead, what with a great blade shoved through his neck. What was Davis thinking, prodding a murder victim like a butcher with a slab of meat?'

'Not everyone is as used to violent death as you, or as willing to accept that a man known in life is in fact a corpse,' said Taylor, suspecting he was wasting his breath by trying to explain, but forging on anyway. 'That Davis touched Scudder means nothing other than that he was probably shocked. I can understand.'

'I can't,' countered Grant. He lowered his voice. 'The scientists won't tell you this, but there are some very jealous coves out there who wish it was *them* going off to Antarctica.'

'There's no accounting for taste.'

Grant gazed at his inspector with open astonishment. 'Wouldn't you go, sir, if you had the chance? I would! I'd resign from the Force in a minute.'

Now Taylor was amazed. 'Would you? Why?'

'Because of the fame and the fortune. And the South Pole! I'd love to see the South Pole and make a drawing of it. I'm a fair hand with a sketch, sir. Mr Hamilton told me so.'

Taylor suspected that Grant had a vision of the South Pole as something tall and striped. Ridiculous though he knew that notion to be, he realised his own preconceptions were little better. What was at the South Pole? A mountain? A lake? A frozen plain? Taylor had no idea.

'Did your fair hand draw Scudder before he was taken away?' Taylor winced when the picture was produced with a flourish, vividly portrayed with a good deal of red pencil expended around the neck. Whereas Taylor had been struck by the lack of blood, Grant's picture had allowed poetic licence to intrude on the facts. 'Did you send someone to the mortuary, for the pathologist's report?'

Grant passed him a piece of paper that had been carefully folded, but that was dappled heavily with grimy fingerprints. Taylor was by no means the first person to read it.

As expected, it told him little of use. The cause of death was damage to the windpipe. The blade had missed the major blood vessels, although the pathologist could not determine whether it was a clever stroke executed by someone who knew his business, or by a freak chance.

'Anything else?' he asked.

'Most of the men didn't take to Scudder. He had arguments with almost everyone, except Shackleton and O'Brien, and the seamen thought him a pig.' Grant checked his notebook, and Taylor was amused to see the word 'pig' underscored several times. 'The crew think one of the shore party killed him, so he wouldn't go south with them.'

'And the members of the shore party? What do they think?'

'Well, Dr Marshall thinks Adams did it, because he admitted to coming here after that rich woman's party. Dr Mackay, the other surgeon, says Captain England did it, on the grounds that he's not in his right mind – something to do with spending too much time in the African sun on his last voyage. But the others didn't speculate.'

'What do you think?'

Grant considered carefully. He liked it when the inspector asked for his opinion. 'I think one of the two surgeons is the guilty party.'

'Why? Because of the placement of the blade with such precision?'

Grant shook his head. 'Because I don't like them. In my experience, killers tend not to be nice, so it makes sense to have rotten coves at the top of your list of suspects. It's no good looking at decent men.'

Taylor supposed he had a point, in a hard, feral kind of way. 'Of course we may be barking up the wrong tree, and our killer is isn't a member of the expedition at all, but someone who broke into the docks.'

'Not likely, sir. These premises are very well guarded. It wasn't only the ship's crew what were watching out for their gear, but the guards, who did regular patrols all night – with dogs. The gates are closed at dusk, and no one can get in.'

Taylor thought for a moment, then walked with Grant to inspect the great iron gates that were the only proper entrance to the complex, other than a series of locks on the river. They stood twenty feet high, and were black with the filth that coated most of London – a combination of soot from thousands of chimneys, the stinking black fumes from the belching industries that lined the river, and the oil that was blasted into the air from engines and motors. Taylor ordered them closed.

As he studied them, he recalled the shocking crime levels before the self-contained yards had been built. Now, even without the patrols, the export section of the East India Dock must have seemed all-but impregnable to the average thief. Its western border was flanked by a barbed-wire-topped brick wall that ran the entire length of the unimaginatively named East India Dock Wall

Road, and its northern and eastern boundaries were formed by rows of stout depots, all of which presented unscalable façades to would-be invaders; windows were either absent or so high as to be unreachable without ladders. The southern boundary was a combination of the river, several shipyards, and the fences and walls of the Blackwall Railway Terminus.

Thus, if there were a weak-link, it was the gates. So, regretting the mess it would make of his trousers – and certain his wife Ruby would not be pleased – he put his theory to the test. Watched with mystification by Grant, Ives and the guards, he aimed for the left-hand pillar and began to climb. Some of the bricks had been eaten away by London's poisonous air, and it was possible to use the damage as hand- and footholds, while the bars on the gates provided support in places. It took several minutes for him to reach the top, but he managed it with comparative ease.

'Ye gods!' exclaimed Shackleton, arriving by cab from the Expedition Office. He stood with his hands on his hips and grinned. 'Perhaps we should find a place for you on the expedition. It would be a great bonus to make an assault on Mount Erebus, and you seem to have monkey-like talents that might come in very useful, Will.'

Shackleton was not alone, and as he spoke, the other occupants began to alight. Next out was a short, wiry man whom Taylor recalled had been identified as Frank Wild.

'He's up, but can he get down?' mused Wild, reaching in his pocket and withdrawing a pipe.

'Good gracious!' muttered Marshall, the third man out.

51

He stood next to his leader, shielding his eyes with his hand as he squinted upwards at the unusual sight of a senior policeman atop a gatepost. He looked tired, as though the day had been a hard one, with its early beginning. 'Hardly an edifying spectacle. Is this what we pay our detectives to do?'

The last man to exit the vehicle was Priestley. 'Be careful,' he called uneasily. He alone of the quartet was more concerned than amused. 'It's a long way down.'

Taylor did not need to be told, particularly as it was considerably harder climbing down than up. Acutely aware that he had attracted a sizeable audience, he began his descent, hoping he would not disgrace himself by falling. Eventually, he reached a point where he could jump, thinking, as he landed lightly on his feet, that while he might not be up to Shackleton's standards of fitness, chasing felons across London had kept him reasonably trim. He wiped grimy hands on his freshly laundered handkerchief, realising too late that Ruby would be unhappy about that as well, and turned to Ives.

'If I can do that, you can be sure thieves can, too. You've already told me that your men go on patrols to check various parts of the complex, and that your office is sometimes left unmanned. It wouldn't be difficult for a determined felon to wait in the shadows opposite until he sees it empty, and then make his move.'

'I'll review my security procedures,' said Ives, eyeing him with considerable dislike. He did not like being criticised in front of his men, although Taylor was sure that the demonstration had come as no great surprise. The man was no fool, for all his pompous, upstart manners.

'Good,' said Taylor. He turned back to Shackleton. 'This puts a new perspective on the murder. It means that anyone could have broken in and killed Scudder – not a thief, because if he had taken the trouble to climb the gates, he wouldn't have left without something for his pains – but someone who perhaps doesn't want your expedition to succeed.'

Shackleton shook his head firmly. 'There's no one like that. I've secured funding from a wide variety of sources, and no one has expressed any wish that my expedition shouldn't be a success. Why should they? It's for the glory of the Empire.'

Taylor smiled, aware that even if someone had been critical, Shackleton probably would not have considered it serious. He was too ebullient and optimistic to be dragged down by malcontents, and would have dismissed any complainers from his mind. However, Taylor decided to ask other members of the expedition whether they had experienced any opposition. Still scrubbing his hands, he walked slowly along the quay, which was emptying now that the day was almost over.

'I'm relieved Hamilton agreed to let you look into this nasty affair, Will,' said Shackleton in a low, earnest voice that revealed the depth of his concern.

It was not long past dawn on the following day, and they were again on *Nimrod*, prior to Taylor beginning another round of interviews. Despite working until well past two o'clock the previous night, which had included reading all the statements taken by his constables and inspecting the clothes worn by the entire staff and crew – Grant had grumbled that he had already done it, but the plain truth was that Taylor did not trust him to be sufficiently careful – he had made scant headway with the case. Thus, the day promised to be a busy one, requiring another early start. Moreover, Taylor also wanted to inspect the ship, to gain an idea of Scudder's environment.

'There was talk at the office yesterday about the impact a murder might have on our venture,' Shackleton went on unhappily. 'It kept me awake half the night with worry.'

'I can't see it will be a problem,' said Priestley comfortingly. Shackleton was smoking a cigarette, and Marshall was puffing on his pipe, so the atmosphere was already dense. Priestley was struggling to open the porthole again, but Taylor suspected from Marshall's malignant smirk that the surgeon had done something to jam it. 'People will see us as victims, not villains.'

Shackleton was less sanguine. 'I don't share your faith, I'm afraid. Moreover, after Will's comments yesterday, I spent most of the evening thinking about who'd want us to fail. I discussed it with Emily.'

'Did the lovely Mrs Shackleton come up with anyone?' asked Marshall. There was nothing overtly unpleasant in his tone, but Shackleton regarded him sharply. Taylor could only suppose the surgeon was one of those who put little trust in the opinions of women.

'No one we'd consider as a murderer,' replied Shackleton stiffly. 'Although there are those who would use the situation to make matters awkward for us.'

'Who?' asked Taylor.

Shackleton's face darkened. 'Captain Scott for a start – he thinks he holds prescriptive rights to the Ross Sea region, and doesn't want me anywhere near it. And there's his mentor, Sir Clements Markham, who's all charm and light to my face, but hates the thought of my going south.'

'Clements Markham?' asked Taylor. 'Former president of the Royal Geographical Society? An elderly gentleman with mutton-chop whiskers? I met him while I was investigating a case last year. I found him difficult.'

'By "difficult," do you mean rude, overbearing, condescending and with an unsavoury talent for whispering behind people's backs?' asked Marshall.

Taylor did not reply, unwilling to denigrate a powerful man like Markham to the likes of Marshall, although the surgeon's analysis was certainly accurate. He addressed Shackleton.

'Can his ill-will damage you, Mick?'

'Not really, since the RGS has been miserly with its funding,' replied Shackleton. 'Moreover, much as I'd like to see the vicious old meddler discredited, I don't think he's physically capable of swarming over dockyard gates and stabbing biologists with paper knives.'

'Especially since it's clear Scudder was murdered by some craven dockhand,' added Marshall.

'Yesterday you said Adams was the culprit,' returned Taylor, watching the surgeon carefully. It was not the first inconsistency he had detected in the man: another thing Taylor had done after dark the previous night was to stand amid the crates of provisions, trying to gain a feel for what the murderer had done. As he had kept his silent vigil, he had seen Marshall leave the ship; Adams had been with him. The two men had gone to a nearby tavern, where they had enjoyed a beer together before going their separate ways. Why had Marshall imbibed with a man he professed to dislike?

'We'll help you in any way we can, Will,' said Shackleton when Marshall did not deign to reply. 'We all want Scudder's killer behind bars. All I ask is that you don't reveal details to the press before you have the culprit. Your chief superintendent told me that you've experienced problems with confidentiality on your other case, and suggested I ask you to be careful.'

Taylor said nothing, but his temper began to rise. His department was chronically over-stretched, and Hamilton's reference to his 'other case' made it sound as though it were the only one, when the truth was that he had six or seven investigations in various stages of completion. Most were not murders, but even so there was a daunting amount of work.

Another reason for his ire was the 'other case' itself – Taylor knew perfectly well which of his enquiries Hamilton meant. It was a murder, and he had been hampered by leaks of gratuitously grisly – and invariably inaccurate – details to the press. These had captured the public's imagination and outrage, and during the last month Taylor had been repeatedly castigated in the papers for not catching the perpetrator.

'Bad publicity,' elaborated Marshall patronisingly, lest Taylor's lack of response meant he had not understood the point. 'It may damage our chances with prospective sponsors.'

Taylor ignored him and addressed Shackleton. 'The problem with you asking for me is this: my department has four inspectors, and we're allocated each new case on a rotating basis. There are two other officers who should be given investigations before me, and your request means I'm not yet clear of my others. Andrews is free, however, and—'

Shackleton looked almost sheepish. 'I've already had words with Hamilton, Will. He said your sergeant can finish your other work, and that you dealing with Scudder won't be a problem.'

'Did he?' Taylor was startled, because Hamilton knew perfectly well that Grant was wholly incapable of completing any investigation, but especially the one that was currently causing him so much trouble. 'But he knows I'm overwhelmed with a complicated case that requires attention – *my* attention. I can't delegate it to Grant, Mick. I really can't.'

'He told me that particular enquiry was at a standstill,' stated Shackleton bluntly. 'He said you haven't found a new lead in ages.'

Taylor was even more astonished, amazed that his chief should be so indiscreet as to discuss police files with a member of the public, albeit a famous one. Shackleton was his friend, but he resented the notion of Hamilton revealing such information regardless. Hamilton was also wrong. 'One of my informers gave me a lead only last night,' he said stiffly.

Coincidentally, when Taylor had covertly followed Marshall and Adams to the tavern, he had met a man he had not seen for months. His name was Joe Bacon, and he had secured work as a gardener at Southwark Park, which explained why he had not been in any of his usual haunts. Bacon had quickly immersed himself in his new local underworld, and had heard whispers about the curious, month-old murder that had stumped Taylor.

Marshall's face broke out in its sardonic smile. 'Let's not beat around the bush here, Taylor. The case you mention so obtusely is what the newspapers have been calling the Headless Bishop, one of the nastiest crimes to have taken place in London for years. The press has been following it for many, many weeks.'

'A *month*,' corrected Priestley admonishingly. 'Only one month. You make it sound much longer—'

'How do you two know about it?' interrupted Shackleton, startled. 'Hamilton rattled on about it to me at length yesterday, but I'd never heard of it before that.'

'Because we read the papers in their entirety,' replied Marshall, 'not just the parts that refer to the expedition. Taylor is quite famous, in an unfortunate way. The Headless Bishop was the talk of London in June, and even now, weeks later' – here he shot an unpleasant glance in Priestley's direction – 'it still gains headlines. I wondered yesterday why his name was familiar to me, and then it clicked: he's the investigating officer – the one who is hopelessly flummoxed.'

'A sorry claim to fame,' sighed Taylor ruefully, supposing there was no point in denying it – or in defending himself against the unfair diatribes of the press. It was unpleasant being the scapegoat of the dailies, but there was a grain of truth in the allegations: he had no idea who had committed the murder next to a sordid little jetty called Fountain Dock, in an area not far from where he now sat, and he feared that his chances of uncovering the killer were remote.

'I don't have time for newspapers at the moment,' said Shackleton, as if he imagined Taylor might think less of him because he did not relish such salacious tales.

'You've time to read the parts that concern us,' said Marshall. He pointed to a copy of *The Standard*, in which Shackleton had pencilled a ring around a small, humorous piece relating to the recent donation of a prodigious amount of chocolate. 'But *I'm* especially well acquainted with the Headless Bishop because my cousin, a medical student at Bart's Hospital, is working with the police surgeon who examined the body. Peter told me about it when we met for a drink a couple of weeks ago.'

'Anything the surgeon said to him would have been confidential,' said Taylor, disliking the notion of police business bandied about in taverns. 'I hope your cousin is discreet.'

Marshall gave what could only be described as a sneer. 'What's there to be discreet about? All the police know is that a body was found next to the Thames *sans* head, feet and hands. The newspapers – particularly *The Star* and the *Daily Mail* – are having a grand time, claiming that London is prowled by a maniac, and that the Metropolitan Police are bumbling incompetents.'

Shackleton regarded his surgeon uneasily. 'I don't think Will's other work is any of our affair, Marshall. I'm sure he's doing his best.'

But Taylor had been called a lot worse by the press, and Marshall's comments failed to sting him. The so-called Headless Bishop had been a difficult case from the beginning – bodies found on the banks of the Thames without identification invariably were – and the leak of ghoulish details to the press and the subsequent reaction by the public had done nothing to help. However, while he was not so naïve as to imagine that he could solve every crime he investigated, the criticism had taken its toll on his confidence even so.

His mind returned to the Headless Bishop, as it often did, even when he was working on other matters. Joe Bacon had suggested that he speak to a fellow known as Long Ron, who lived close to where the body had been discovered. Long Ron had boasted to his drinking mates that he had seen someone carrying a heavy bag at the time of the murder, which, he had concluded, contained the Bishop's missing parts.

Such men tended not to volunteer information to the police, but they sometimes did not mind sharing it over a free beer or two. Taylor intended to find Long Ron, although he was painfully aware that he was pinning a good deal of hope on what might prove to be no more than a drunkard's fevered imagination. It would not be the first time a promising lead dissolved into nothing, but he was anxious to leave no stone unturned regardless.

'We're considerably closer to unravelling the mystery now than when we first found the body,' he said shortly. 'Of course, there are details we don't reveal to the press or to gossiping medical students, so no one outside the Force can know the real status of the enquiry.'

Marshall regarded him coolly. 'Well, I wish you luck,' he said insincerely. 'However, when one policeman meets a total lack of success, surely he should pass the case to another, who will look at it with fresh eyes?'

Personally, Taylor was surprised it had not happened already, and had even suggested it to Hamilton. However, Hamilton had demurred, claiming it was better to stick with the man who knew the details, which Taylor had interpreted as meaning that his superior did not want another inspector lambasted in the press. It was better to let Taylor be the sole sacrificial goat to feed the press's undying appetite for a victim.

'It won't prevent you from helping us, though?' asked Shackleton when there was no reply. 'Hamilton said you're capable of juggling several cases at once – that your department is too short-handed to do otherwise.'

'Yes, it is,' agreed Taylor unhappily. 'I suppose I can squeeze it in. My wife won't mind if she doesn't see me for the next month.'

Shackleton regarded him uncertainly, then laughed. 'I imagine Ruby will be displeased, but you can blame it on me. However, since it appears you'll be strapped for time – and probably for men, too – I've a suggestion. You can use young Priestley as your assistant.'

'What?' asked Priestley, sitting bolt upright. 'I've no experience with this kind of thing!'

'I should hope not,' said Shackleton. 'It would be a curious qualification for a geologist.' He turned back to Taylor. 'When you arrest the guilty party, and it's only a matter of time before you do, you can tell the press what you like. As Priestley says, we'll be seen as victims, to be pitied and – with luck – showered with compensatory money. But, until then, there's always something slightly insalubrious about an unsolved murder. Do you take my point?'

Taylor nodded. 'I can see a violent death may have an adverse effect on your plans.'

'Quite,' agreed Shackleton. 'You'll have total and unrestricted access to *Nimrod* and her people – officers, crew and shore party. And Priestley will remain with you, to answer any questions you might have, or to provide you with information.'

Taylor considered. He was used to working alone, or occasionally with Greasy Grant, and had never had an assistant before. However, it occurred to him that there would be many questions of a basic nature that would need answering before he came to grips with the unusual circumstances of the case. It might be useful to have someone like Priestley when they arose. Besides, the geologist did not seem to be someone who would be a nuisance. It was irregular, but so was being invited to investigate a murder by an old school friend. With a smile, he nodded acceptance of the offer.

Cape Royds: March 1908

As much as the Boss wants me to write about
the events surrounding Scudder's murder,
there are things happening here that are
much more important. At the moment, the
ponies have to be our first concern. We
sailed from New Zealand with ten, but two
were put down during the voyage and then
Zulu died a week ago, after eating some
corrosive material that was leaking from
the batteries. And yesterday, Sandy died.
With both surgeons on Mount Erebus, it fell
to Joyce and Day to perform an autopsy.
When they cut open the poor beast's
stomach, they found fourteen pounds of
volcanic sand. Now Billy is sick with the
same symptoms, and all I can think is
that we haven't given them enough salt,
so they've been eating the sand because
it was covered with seawater in a recent
blizzard. If we lose many more ponies,
Shackleton's chances of reaching the South
Pole will become chimerical.

I was helping to stable the remaining
ponies away from the sand when the Boss
told me to get back to my writing. I said

I thought the ponies should come first, but he stated – firmly – that there were other men who could handle that, whereas no one else could write about last summer's events. So here I am, pencil in hand again. I'm not pleased with his decision, but then I wasn't pleased when he offered me as skivvy to Will Taylor either.

I still don't understand why he picked me to help the police. Certainly I'd shown I could work hard, but that didn't mean that I possessed the skills to assist in a murder inquiry. In fact, the Boss didn't really know that much about me. Our meeting had essentially been a fluke.

I'd just finished my second year at University College, Bristol, where I'd been captain of hockey and a member of the cricket XI. Unfortunately, I hadn't been quite so hot in the studying part of the university experience.

One morning I was in the library, fed up, because I wanted to be outside, when my brother Bert approached me with a startling proposal. Shackleton had been interviewing a man named Piercy from the Bristol Museum for the position of expedition geologist. Piercy had just refused the job, when Bert, a lecturer in botany, happened into the interview room, which was on an upper floor of the library. 'What about your brother,' he was asked.

'He's a geologist isn't he?'

So Bert came down to where I was sitting and said, 'How would you like to go to the Antarctic, Ray?'

'I'd go anywhere to get out of this place,' I'd said miserably.

It seems so simple in retrospect. Two days later I received a letter from Shackleton asking me to go up to London to see him, which I did immediately. I remember very little about the interview except that Adams was there, and that Shackleton asked me if I would recognise gold if I saw it and if I could play a musical instrument. I replied in the affirmative for the one but not the other, then left without being sure whether I had been taken or not. Yet I was so elated with the whole business anyway that, on getting back to Tewksbury, I leaped over a tennis net and seriously injured my left knee when I landed awkwardly.

I was ordered to stay in bed for two weeks, but halfway through I received a wire from Shackleton: 'Why are you not in London collecting your equipment and helping with the expedition?' To my amazement, I'd made the grade. I sent for the doctor, had him cut my leg out of the cast, and hobbled up to London, determined that no one would find out about my knee.

I was the official geologist for a fully-fledged Antarctic expedition. What could be better? I did everything I possibly could, every moment of the day, to create a serious geological component to the expedition, while at the same time lending a hand with anything else I could help with. And then the Boss pulled me away from my duties to assist a policeman! I wasn't happy. Probably even less than I am now, having to ignore the poor, suffering ponies, just to write about those events.

Chapter 3

While Taylor had no objections about accepting Priestley's help, the geologist had other ideas. He waited until the inspector had gone on deck, and then asked for a private word with Shackleton. The Boss said he had an important appointment with a sponsor, and was keen to be away, but Priestley was uncharacteristically firm.

'I can't do this,' he said, standing by the closed door to make it difficult for Shackleton to slip past him. 'I'm a geologist, not a detective, and I have a lot of work to do. It wasn't that long ago that you were demanding to know why I wasn't getting everything in order, and now I'm here...'

'I know, and I appreciate your plight,' said Shackleton impatiently. 'But this is important – the entire venture might flounder if things turn out badly, and I need a man I trust on the inside. I'd do it myself, but I can't delegate these fund-raising meetings to anyone else. I need you to do this, Raymond, for the good of the expedition.'

'You know I'll do anything to help. But surely, there's someone better qualified?'

'I'm not asking you to solve the case, just keep an eye on it, and report to me if it looks as though it might go wrong for us – not that there's much I can do if it does, but forewarned is forearmed.'

'Taylor is your friend. He'll keep you abreast of matters.'

'Yes, he is, and I asked for him because I trust his judgement, his impartiality and his abilities. He knows nothing about the Antarctic, which may afford you the occasional degree of amusement, but I also want to help him as much as we possibly can. It wasn't easy convincing Hamilton to oblige.'

'How do you know Hamilton?'

'I met him at the RGS. He *is* interested in the Antarctic. It appears he had a distant relative on some Arctic expedition in the last century, so he's always had a fascination with high latitudes and gave us a donation of ten pounds. Little did he imagine that his good wishes would translate into me asking for a favour. He admitted it would put Taylor under an intolerable amount of strain, but Will's the kind of man who rises to a challenge.'

'Perhaps he is, sir, but you don't know that I am,' said Priestley unhappily.

Shackleton laughed. 'Of course you are: that's why I hired you. Besides, you're quite advanced with your preparations already.'

'So because I'm efficient, I'm to be penalised with monitoring this investigation?'

Shackleton smiled. 'I'm afraid so, but it's not just that. I *trust* you, Raymond, in a way that I don't some of the others. I'm paying you a compliment: there aren't many men I'd grant free rein to deal with something so desperately important. I *need* you to do this.'

It was difficult to say no to a man whom he not only

liked and respected, but who was also his leader, so Priestley nodded reluctant agreement. Shackleton clapped him on the shoulders. The comradely gesture of affection turned Priestley to one side, and Shackleton had his hand on the door latch in an instant, opening it and sliding past in one easy, sinuous movement. With the knowledge that he had been expertly manoeuvred – and not only physically – Priestley shook his head as the Boss clattered along the corridor, shouting greetings and orders as he went.

With a wistful sigh for the plans he had made for that morning, he went in search of the inspector, hoping he wouldn't prove too much of a boor. His previous dealings with the police had been confined to the local constable at fetes in Tewkesbury, where his father was headmaster of the grammar school. Although Priestley was sure the Metropolitan Police's officers were worthy fellows, they were not the company he would willingly have chosen.

'You'll be wanting a bit of information about *Nimrod* and the expedition, I expect,' he said when he found the inspector staring thoughtfully down to where Scudder's body had been found. Priestley tried a willing grin, but there was little warmth or enthusiasm in it.

'If you please.' Taylor did not return the smile, so Priestley sensed he knew perfectly well that his newly appointed assistant would rather be doing something else.

He indicated that the inspector should stand next to him at the taffrail – a quiet spot at the back of the ship where they would not be disturbed and would not interfere with the loading. Roberts arrived with mugs of powerful coffee, which Priestley accepted graciously, although the brew went over the side as soon as the man had retreated. Priestley's Wesleyan Methodist upbringing had conditioned him to abstain from strong drink and tobacco, and in his mind, the powerful drugs in coffee were just as heinous as alcohol. He watched Taylor sip his and followed suit with a grimace.

'The plan is for *Nimrod* to sail on the first of August, heading to New Zealand,' Priestley began. 'However, only Murray and the other biologist – whoever that might be – will be aboard, so that they can carry out dredging operations en route. *Nimrod* is slow, you see, and will be jammed to the gills with equipment, so the rest of us will travel on faster passenger ships, and meet her in Lyttelton – that's a port in New Zealand.'

'Yes,' said Taylor dryly. 'I have heard of it.'

'Of course.' Priestley flushed, and hurried on. 'We will all sail to the Antarctic from New Zealand at the beginning of next year, with a shore party of eleven or twelve. Scudder's position needs to be filled, so *two* of the hopefuls might get jobs, since there was a post open anyway. Although there's also a rumour that the Boss wants to appoint an artist instead of a scientist.'

'An artist?' Taylor had a sudden vision of a man in a beret at an easel, wielding a palette while a blizzard raged around him.

'To record our successes with paintings and photographs,' elaborated Priestley. He saw the inspector look bemused, but pressed on. 'Once we reach the Antarctic, we'll establish a base, and *Nimrod* will go north for the winter, to conduct oceanographic work near Australia and New Zealand.'

70

'You mean she's going to sail away and leave you?' asked Taylor incredulously. 'What if she can't reach you the next year? Shackleton told me that no one knows what the ice will do from one season to the next. Or worse, what happens if you can't land where he planned, and *Nimrod* sinks on the way home without telling anyone your new location? You could be lost forever.'

'True,' said Priestley matter-of-factly. 'But the Boss knows what he is doing, and there are a limited number of places where we can land, so it shouldn't be too difficult to find us.'

'I see,' said Taylor unconvinced, and thinking more than ever that Shackleton's volunteers must have a death wish.

Priestley shrugged. 'No one said it was going to be easy; it's just one of the risks associated with this kind of venture. You take risks in your line of work, Inspector. The Boss tells me you were shot by an armed robber last year. It's the same with us.'

'It's not the same at all,' argued Taylor. 'I'd sooner face a desperate villain than a hungry polar bear.'

'Then you *should* come with us,' said Priestley drolly, supposing this sort of remark was what Shackleton had had in mind as amusing, 'because you'll be as far away from polar bears as it's possible to be. They don't live in the Antarctic, only the Arctic.'

'Really?' Taylor handed his empty cup to Roberts, who had come to collect them. 'Well, you learn something new every day. However, I still don't envy you.'

'Good,' said Priestley. 'Then you won't try to persuade the Boss to take you in my place. You may not want to travel south, but there are hundreds who do.'

'So, it's possible that one of these hundreds killed Scudder?'

Priestley thought for a moment and then nodded. 'I can take you to the Expedition Office, and you can look through the applications the Boss received.'

'Later. Before that, I need to understand how Scudder spent his last few days. So first, a tour of the ship.'

Space was at a premium on *Nimrod*, because most supplies were ready to be stowed, but had not yet been allocated their final positions, so every deck, hold and cabin was a chaotic jumble. Taylor was amazed that the crew saw order in the frenzied anarchy, and that each man went about his business with a calm efficiency.

Captain Rupert England, a finicky man with a powerful voice and hair that looked as if it was being worn off by his habit of constantly rubbing his crown through his cap, curtly informed Taylor that he was far too busy to give him a tour. He then did just that, lovingly explaining the purpose of every space, stairwell, hold, sail and mast. He was assisted by his tall, thin, ginger-haired first officer, John King Davis. Also present were two of the shore party: Jameson Adams, a former naval officer who was officially the meteorologist and who spent much of his time at the Expedition Office, and a brusque Scottish surgeon named Alistair Mackay. Priestley tagged along behind.

Taylor immediately liked Davis' enthusiasm, and warmed considerably more to Adams than to his protagonist Marshall, although he was taken aback by the fact that Adams' speech was peppered with colourful obscenities, his language being a good deal saltier than that of the sailors. Mackay was more of an enigma, and Taylor struggled with his heavy Scots accent.

It was a large party to be crushed together in such cramped confines, and Taylor had the impression that Mackay was enjoying his growing discomfort. It was not only the overriding stench of rancid seal oil – something England tartly informed Taylor he was imagining – that was disagreeable, but the low ceilings, narrow companionways and teetering piles of crates that looked like accidents waiting to happen. Then there was the ship's incessant rocking motion, an unpleasant sway that again made Taylor wonder whether he might be sick.

He was sure there were many in London who would have given their last shilling to be shown around *Nimrod*, but his focus remained on putting Scudder's killer behind bars. So it was not just a desire to help an old friend that made him chafe at England's ponderous explanations, or his eagerness to escape before he disgraced himself with *mal de mer* – an arrest would regain his credibility.

'You know *I* was the one who found Scudder,' said Davis in a low voice, when the others were temporarily out of hearing. His thin face was sombre. 'I told your man yesterday that I relieved Cheetham at one in the morning, with Berry and Riches.'

'Yes,' replied Taylor. 'We have your statement. Is there something you forgot to mention?'

'Not really.' Davis looked awkward and embarrassed. 'But I felt I didn't express myself very well – shock, probably. I've seen corpses before, but never one murdered, and I couldn't get the image out of my head. But I'm better today, and I want to make sure I told you exactly what happened.'

'We can go through it again, if you like.' Taylor smiled reassuringly, concealing his immediate suspicion: sometimes when witnesses asked to do such a thing, it meant they had said something they wished they had not, and were eager to rectify the matter.

Davis nodded. 'I'd like to, to make sure I didn't omit anything important.'

Taylor glanced behind him. Mackay, Adams and England were involved in an intense discussion about some minute aspect of the engine, and Priestley was trapped on the other side of their small circle. No one would hear what Davis had to say. He gestured that the first officer was to begin. Davis cleared his throat and took a breath, as though he was about to give evidence to a hostile judge.

'The captain and the Boss have arranged for watches – an officer and two seamen – to be kept all night for as long as *Nimrod* is at the East India Docks. We know the place is locked at night, but you can't be too careful. Cheetham has the first watch, and I have the second.'

'Except that the hours you keep are different from those of normal naval watches, because of the times the docks are open and closed,' said Taylor, recalling Grant's summary. 'The first night-watch is usually eight to midnight, but *Nimrod* keeps eight until one; the regular middle-watch is midnight to four, but *Nimrod* keeps one until six.'

Davis nodded. 'Precisely. It's just temporary, you understand – we'll be back to normal once we're at sea. So I was on duty from one until six. Cheetham prefers to stay on board during his watch, but I like to wander around a bit, stretch my legs.' He gave a sheepish shrug. 'I tend to doze off otherwise, because it's so still and quiet. I checked the ship with the two seamen, to make sure all was in order, and then we went on patrol.'

'On patrol?'

'Well, any theft isn't going to come from *on* the ship, but from *off* it – from thieves breaking into the docks. So, on my watch, we patrol the pier, where it's easier to see intruders.'

Taylor considered. 'I disagree: there's far too much clutter – materiel – on the quay for that sort of strategy to be efficient for three men. A thief could easily hide among the boxes and approach the ship without being seen while you explore elsewhere.'

'That's what Cheetham thinks,' said Davis unhappily. 'And obviously he's right, given what happened. He and his men remain *on* the ship – he posts one seaman aft and one forward, while he remains amidships, looking over the rail. But Berry, Riches and I include parts of the South, East, and West quays on our patrols. It's quite a large area.'

'It's a *very* large area.'

'But we've been doing it without problems for weeks,' protested Davis, agitated. 'My rationale was that thieves would be deterred by men on the move all night. The docks also employ their own guards, who wander about with dogs – nasty brutes kept on leads – but my remit was to prevent theft, not murder. I never thought there would be a murder.'

'People seldom do. Who do *you* think killed Scudder?'

'A robber, I suppose,' replied Davis unhappily. 'I imagine the villain thought twice about tackling fit guards armed with cudgels, but a fellow reeling along in evening dress would be a different proposition altogether.'

'Scudder was reeling?'

'I *assume* he was reeling. Scudder liked a tipple, and there would have been a lot to drink at that reception. Berry and Riches saw him over by his equipment when our watch started, but none of us spoke to him. Of course, I can see what happened: along he comes, all spruced up and not in any state to defend himself, and so he's stabbed for his wallet.'

'His wallet was in his pocket, along with a valuable fob watch, and he was wearing a gold ring and cufflinks. If the motive for his death was robbery, then the thief wasn't successful.'

'Perhaps he heard Berry, Riches or me coming,' suggested Davis. 'I told you the timing: Cheetham noticed nothing amiss when I relieved him at one o'clock. I spent half an hour checking the holds – we're worried about pilfering, but fire would be even more devastating, because it could wipe out the expedition permanently – and then we went on the quay. And it was forty-five minutes after that when I found Scudder, dead next to the tinned sardines.'

'Here's what we call the gun cupboard,' said England, drawing attention to a locker with a padlock as he continued his tour once again, Priestley, Adams, Mackay and Davis in tow. 'We carry three rifles, a shotgun and ammunition. Of course, I also have a revolver in my cabin.'

'Why do you need firearms?' asked Taylor, not liking the 'of course.'

'For the tribes of Antarctic cannibals,' said Mackay, making a trigger motion with thumb and forefinger. He laughed at his own joke. 'For seals, laddie. They'll feed men and dogs, and provide us with a source of fresh meat that may ward off scurvy.'

'And the revolver?'

'In case of mutiny,' said England darkly. 'You never know what might happen when the cold settles on a man's head.'

'Or the heat,' added Mackay with a wink. 'Such as that in *West Africa*.'

Taylor watched the captain undergo some sort of inner battle. Anger was clear on his face, and he seemed on the verge of making a curt retort, but in the end he merely waved a dismissive hand, indicating that his first officer was to lead the way forward, as though he simply could not be bothered with Mackay's obtuse jests. Taylor regarded Priestley questioningly. It was this sort of interaction that he wanted the geologist to explain.

'The captain was unwell when he returned from Senegal recently,' obliged Priestley in a low voice. 'He said it was the result of the sun on his head, although Dr Mackay says he has never heard of such a condition – at least, not with the symptoms the captain claims to have suffered. As a consequence, England dislikes being out on deck during the day, and tends to leave the ship only after the sun has set.'

'Like a wee vampire,' said Mackay, overhearing the last comment and smirking. 'Tell me, inspector, have you come across any sudden deaths where exsanguination is the cause?'

'The captain has a thing about women on board, too,'

said Priestley, ignoring the Scot's irritating jocularity. 'He refuses to let them on.'

'Why?'

'They're supposed to bring bad luck, like sailing on a Friday,' explained Priestley. 'Sailors are a superstitious lot, but the captain seems more extreme than most.'

'Here's the chain locker,' said Davis, his voice loud in the confines of a dank and smelly room. Taylor only half listened to the ensuing monologue about the room's relevance, most of his attention focused on England, who was mopping his face with a handkerchief. The captain seemed nervous, making Taylor wonder whether it was the natural strain of a man with a great deal of responsibility, or whether it was the presence of the police that unsettled him. Meanwhile, Adams was busily poking his penknife into the hold's timbers.

'Look at this,' he said, showing Taylor that the tip of the knife barely penetrated the wood. 'The old girl may have a decade or more on her than we do – forty-one on her last birthday – but she's a bloody good ship.'

'Solid,' agreed England with pride. 'If she was bad, that knife would be through her timbers like they were butter, but she has a sturdy heart. She'll get us safely down south, God bless her.'

'And perhaps even back again,' added Mackay with a laugh.

'What do you mean by *perhaps*?' England snarled. 'Stupid fellow!'

Mackay's good humour disappeared abruptly at the captain's remark, and when a crewman asked a question about sleeping bags, the surgeon barked a reply that made the man back away in alarm. Taylor made a mental note that the Scot had a quick temper and was sensitive about being jibed, although he doled out a good deal of ribbing himself. Mackay was mercurial: he could be amusing and witty, but he could also be moody and temperamental, and might just as easily destroy a good atmosphere as create one.

'Here is Nigel Vallen – and his father with him,' said Davis, as a short trip along a narrow companionway brought them inconveniently head-on with a party coming from the opposite direction. Since the others were laden down with boxes, the captain's party retraced their steps, and they met in a tiny vestibule with a stairway that led to the upper deck and a massive pipe that Taylor assumed had something to do with the boiler.

'I've just heard what happened to Brice Scudder,' said a young bespectacled man, breathless from manhandling an awkwardly shaped parcel. He had fine, floppy hair, and looked as though he would be more comfortable in a library than on a ship. 'His poor mother!'

There was a short silence, during which everyone stood with heads bowed, as if to do otherwise might be construed as a mark of disrespect. Taylor watched with interest, knowing the abrupt adoption of proper mourning procedures stemmed not from any sense of loss, but because Nigel Vallen's father was a priest, instantly recognisable by his round hat, white collar and black suit. There were also the clerical teeth – long, slightly splayed incisors that were well suited to baring themselves genially at old ladies during afternoon tea.

'I shall visit Mrs Scudder tomorrow,' announced the vicar, after a suitable interlude had passed. 'I have no wish to intrude on her grief, but I wouldn't like her to think we're insensitive to her distress.'

'I'm sure she'll appreciate that,' said England, adopting the stiff, formal tone that many people reserved for clergymen. 'It would be a great kindness.'

'I'll come, too, if you like,' said Adams. 'Losing a son must be damned awful, and we should let her know we're bloody sorry.'

'Inspector Taylor is leading the investigation,' said England, indicating the policeman with a nod. 'We're showing him the ship, so he can see where Scudder worked.'

'I suppose it may allow you to gain a picture of the unfortunate victim's last hours,' mused the vicar. 'I read an article on crime detection in *Reynolds's Newspaper* last month. Most educational. One must have sharp wits to foil such wicked criminals.' He proffered his hand to Taylor. 'Charles Vallen, sir.'

'The Reverend Vallen is the incumbent of St James's Church, Rotherhithe,' added England. 'You probably know it, inspector. It's on Jamaica Road. I've attended Communion there on occasion, and have been treated to some very edifying sermons.'

Mackay gave a snort of suppressed laughter, while even Priestley looked dubious. Taylor could see why: England did not appear to be a man who would listen to sermons, edifying or otherwise, and the inspector could only suppose it was another example of a sailor's superstition – currying favour with the Almighty and his ministers lest favours needed to be asked while at sea.

'Thank you,' said Vallen, a little warily.

Taylor shook the vicar's hand. 'Actually, our paths

have crossed before, although we have never met. You often provide tea for my constables when they're on duty near your home, and they speak very warmly of you.'

'Then your men will have met my son, who read natural sciences at Oxford,' said Vallen, indicating the youth with unfeigned pride. 'He earned a first, and hopes to be part of this expedition when it sails. It's good to travel when one is young, and opportunities like this don't come along often.'

'I need to pass muster first,' said Nigel uncomfortably shifting his parcel, which slipped from his hands. Davis lunged and stopped it from hitting the ground, but the look on his face indicated that it was not the first time he had come to the rescue. 'There are others who want to be a part of Mr Shackleton's expedition, too. One of them – O'Brien – has a great deal of experience, being twice as old as me, while Yaxley once spent a summer in Greenland!'

'That's a big island in the Arctic,' whispered Priestley in Taylor's ear, not sure whether the inspector's ignorance extended to the north, too. 'With polar bears.'

'O'Brien will never be selected over you, Nigel, laddie,' said Mackay with considerable conviction. 'The Boss doesn't like him.'

'Scudder did, though,' mused Adams. 'God knows why, but he did.'

'Because he doesn't argue,' explained Mackay. 'Unlike Yaxley. That was the appeal for Scudder: he didn't like to be challenged, as you found out, eh, Nigel? Tell the inspector about your fracas.'

'We had a brief disagreement a week ago,' Nigel explained, as he flushed red, clearly chagrined. 'But it wasn't violent – we didn't have a *fracas*.'

Taylor suspected it was true: the clumsy graduate did not seem like the kind of man to get into a passion about anything. He had seen the type before: gentle, unassuming and tentative, who tended to be buffeted and abused by those with stronger, more forceful characters. He had one or two just like Nigel in his division, young men who were unlikely to last long in the harsh world of policing.

'It was about evolution,' Nigel went on. 'And the modern linking of geology and biology that has been used to prove Darwin's theories about natural selection. I pointed out that Darwin wasn't so arrogant as to state that God played no role in the Creation – if you read *On the Origin of Species*, you'll see what I mean. But Scudder claimed that religion has no place in twentieth-century scientific thought. Naturally, I disagreed, and we had a bit of a barney.'

'I should hope so,' said the elder Vallen with a fond smile. 'I have always taught you to stand up for your principles, and no vicar's son should hear that sort of thing without issuing a challenge.'

'Scudder was being bloody provocative,' said Adams, angry on the youngster's behalf. 'He saw a man who takes religion seriously, and homed in on him like a damned vulture. I'm no great God-botherer myself, but I won't see others mocked for their beliefs.' He rested a thick arm around the young man's shoulders. 'To hell with Scudder and to hell with anyone else who gets in your way. Don't you be intimidated by them. Sod 'em, is what I say. Sod 'em all!'

Nigel blushed scarlet at the colourful expression of

support, while England cleared his throat in a noisy, meaningful way, catching Adams' eye and flicking his head towards the astonished vicar, to suggest he moderate his language.

'I've dreamed of going to the polar regions since I was a boy,' said Nigel with a wan smile, while Adams frowned his bemusement at England's gestures; clearly he saw nothing wrong with his choice of words. 'I don't think I've ever wanted anything more. I hope Mr Shackleton will appoint me – I've been aboard *Nimrod* ever since she arrived, making myself useful, and I'll do anything he asks. Even the cooking.'

'We have that old bugger Roberts for the kitchen, thank God,' said Adams, although his friendly expression took the sting from his words. 'You're all fingers and thumbs, and I dread to think what you'd be like among boiling liquids and hot fat.'

'I'd learn,' said Nigel with quiet determination.

Vallen patted his son's arm. 'It's all in God's hands, Nigel, and there's no use fretting about it. We must put our faith in Him, and accept what He deigns to give and take away.'

'Amen,' said Mackay putting his hands together and casting a stagy glance above his head. 'But look on the bright side, Nigel. Now Scudder is dead, there are two positions free, not one. Your chances of coming south have doubled.'

Nigel gazed at Mackay, and his jaw fell open. 'Oh,' he stammered. He turned to Taylor. 'Sir! I didn't think of that when I told you how much I wanted to go south. I do, but I don't delight in Scudder's death…'

'I'm sure the inspector doesn't think anything of the kind,' said Priestley, glaring at Mackay. 'No decent Christian man celebrates the untimely demise of another.'

'Scudder?' asked Mackay in disbelief. 'Where are you coming from, laddie? He was neither Christian nor decent. Remember what he said to our three hopefuls?'

'Did your mother never teach you not to speak ill of the dead, Mackay?' asked Davis sharply. 'It shows an appalling lack of charity.'

Mackay was unmoved, and turned to the inspector. 'Scudder taunted them. He said the Boss would never raise funds for the final post, so he was making use of their labour with no intention of rewarding one of them with an appointment. It was all rubbish, of course – Shackleton would never do something so underhand – but Scudder was the kind of man to say that sort of thing.'

While the discussion had been going on, Reverend Vallen had been regarding Taylor thoughtfully. 'You said we haven't met, but you look familiar. Are you sure our paths have never crossed?'

'Yes,' said Taylor shortly. He knew the turn the conversation was about to take, and was keen to avert it. But before he could ask the captain to resume the tour, the vicar released an exclamation.

'Hah! I have it! I've seen sketches of you in the paper. You're the officer in charge of the Headless Bishop case. Poor Scudder's demise must have robbed me of my wits, because I should have known immediately. I've followed your progress very carefully in the newspapers, although it's sometimes difficult to distil fact from fiction.'

'Not really,' said Taylor flatly. 'If you assume it's all fiction, you can't go far wrong.'

'*I've* been following that case, too,' said Mackay keenly, while Taylor gave an inward groan. He had lost count of the times that members of the public had regaled him with theories and solutions based on 'evidence' gleaned from the newspapers. 'And I can tell you that slicing head, hands and feet from a corpse isn't easy. I keep expecting the police to announce that the villain is a surgeon.'

'Is that so?' Taylor turned to England before Mackay could elaborate. 'Where next, captain?'

But Mackay overrode him. 'Perhaps he's even someone I know. There were any number of fellows at my medical school in Edinburgh who were up to the task, and who now live in London. Would you like the names of a few likely candidates?'

'I don't think that would be very productive,' said Vallen firmly. He turned to Taylor. 'Forgive me. I shouldn't have initiated this discussion. I should have guessed where it would lead.' The glance he threw in Mackay's direction would have silenced a more sensitive man, but did nothing to quell the Scot.

'And now we have the same investigator to help *us*,' Mackay crowed. 'I hope you have more success with Scudder than you have had with the Headless Bishop, laddie. I read in The *Daily Telegraph* only yesterday that the matter will be raised in the House.'

'Why?' asked Adams. 'What will that achieve? The House has more pressing matters to consider than some pathetic bloody murder!'

'It might win more funding for the police,' replied

Mackay. 'Which is why Taylor's superintendent...what's his name? Hamilton...doesn't mind his officer's failure being paraded in the press. What's the sacrifice of one of his detectives, when it means additional money?'

Taylor was careful to keep his expression neutral, although the truth was that Mackay had voiced something that had recently started to tease at the back of his own mind. Hamilton was usually supportive of his officers, but this time he had not stepped forward to shield his beleaguered inspector. Was that why Hamilton had acceded to Shackleton's request – that the additional workload would mean no progress on the Headless Bishop, and thus set his sacrificial lamb firmly in place for when the House debated the murder?

'I have every confidence that the police will prevail,' said Priestley, trying to end the discussion. 'Now, we should—'

'The Headless Bishop was murdered just a few streets from our vicarage,' interrupted Nigel ghoulishly. 'I heard a lot of commotion outside my window – people running and shouting – all very early, before we were up. Then I heard that a body had been washed up at Fountain Dock, which is a dirty, disused little wharf in the middle of the part of the Thames known as London Pool—'

'These are sailors, Nigel,' said his father gently. 'They don't need the geography of the river explained to them.'

Nigel grinned an apology, and went on. 'My father was obliged to spend the next week visiting elderly parishioners, assuring them that the same thing wouldn't happen to them.'

'They were all terrified,' said Vallen. 'Well, it is understandable. No one likes the notion of a dismembered body on their doorstep.'

'Why is the body referred to as the Headless *Bishop*?' asked Davis. 'The headless bit even a simple sailor can grasp. But why Bishop? The victim wasn't a cleric, was he?'

There was silence, and everyone seemed to be awaiting the answer. Taylor considered making a curt reply that would end the discussion, but alienating potential witnesses would serve no useful purpose.

'Because one reporter claimed that a bishop's mitre had been scratched into the corpse's chest,' he explained reluctantly.

'And had it?' asked Mackay, fascinated.

Taylor shrugged. 'Where are we going next? To see the Monagasque trawl?'

On Taylor's orders, the area on the upper deck containing the Monagasque trawl and the part of the quay where Scudder had been murdered had been designated off-limits. Unfortunately, this meant several crates had been left open to the elements, and as he and his guides descended the gangway to the pier, it became obvious that not everyone had complied with his instructions.

'Bloody pigeons!' cried Adams in dismay, shooing out three that had set up house in one crate. 'Stupid God-damned birds!'

'Please, Adams!' said Priestley tiredly. 'Must you swear so?'

'Jesus Christ!' cursed Adams, ignoring him as he reached into one of the boxes. 'Look at this!'

'I'm glad the Reverend Vallen isn't here to hear your uncouth tongue,' snapped the geologist. 'Or perhaps he can. We are standing very close to the ship, and sounds carry.'

'Yes, they do,' agreed England sternly. 'And that sort of language is only heard on the lower decks, never in the mouths of well-bred men.'

'I said *look*, damn it!' Adams exclaimed. He held in his hand half a dozen scalpels from the dissection kits. All the blades had been snapped off. 'More sabotage to Scudder's equipment!'

There was a shocked silence, before Mackay broke it. 'Nonsense!' the Scot said briskly. 'They were almost certainly broken in transit. Scudder found them and whined bitterly about them the night he was killed. Finally I had to walk away because he wouldn't stop griping about them.'

'When was this?' Taylor asked. 'Before he went to Lady Wallaston's house?'

'After – midnight perhaps,' replied Mackay, most of his attention still on Adams, who was rummaging through the boxes to see if more damage had been done. 'Or later. I've no idea. I don't wear a watch.'

'Were you at Lady Wallaston's?' Taylor asked. He was aware that a debate had broken out between the two sailors and Priestley, with the geologist and England arguing that bad language was inexcusable under any conditions, and Davis maintaining that it was occasionally unavoidable.

'I slipped away after the toasts to the King,' said Mackay, his Scots brogue seeming stronger suddenly. 'I wasn't in the mood for English foolery.'

'Did you see Scudder leave?'

'Not that I recall. But as I just said, I saw him here

at about midnight. When I arrived, the dockyard gates were locked, and I yelled myself hoarse trying to get in. I was a bit squiffy, and since you can never find a cab around here so late, I decided to sleep on board. I used the officers' cabin. Ask Davis. He saw me, because I woke him up when I came in. He was game about it though – said he had to be getting up soon anyway to start his one o'clock watch.'

'Why did you come here at all? I was under the impression that the shore party all stayed in lodgings or with friends and family.'

'I had forgotten the key to my rooms – again,' explained Mackay. 'And the last time that happened, my landlady was curt with me. All in all, it seemed better to stay here. However, before you start thinking that *I* killed Scudder, Cheetham saw me come aboard, and Davis was with me until he relieved Cheetham.'

'Then what about *before* you came aboard?' pressed Taylor. He was not sure the alibis counted for much, given that he did not have a precise time of death for Scudder.

'Before that I was at the party, laddie.'

'What about *between* the time you left the reception and the time Cheetham saw you come aboard?' asked Taylor patiently, wondering whether Mackay was being deliberately obstructive. He had not forgotten that there were four men who might own a Royal Naval Reserve letter opener – and that Mackay was one of them.

'I was travelling from Lady Wallaston's house – on foot and alone. When I arrived, I saw Scudder standing next to these crates, and he called me over because of the scalpels. I recommended he get a good night's sleep rather than worry about it. That was the last I saw of him.'

'Did you do anything else before or after this encounter?' asked Taylor, wondering why the Scot had not mentioned it to the constable who had taken his statement the day before. He consulted his notebook. 'I understand the toasts were around nine forty-five, and you were among several people – including Scudder – who left when they were over. I imagine they took roughly ten minutes, which takes the time to nine fifty-five or a little after. Yet you say you arrived here around or after midnight.'

'I stopped for a wee dram at the Queen's Head.'

'The Queen's Head?' asked Taylor warily. 'On the High Street? Don't you think that was rash for a man in evening dress?' The words 'are you insane?' formed, but did not find a voice.

Mackay's expression was defiant. 'The dockhands know me. Besides, I was a policeman in Baden-Powell's force in South Africa. I know how to look after myself.'

Taylor regarded him askance, thinking the Scot was fortunate not to have been found himself in a brawl. The Queen's Head was notorious for the frequency and violence of its fights. 'And you left there at what time?'

'When the bell rang for closing. Then I walked here, and hollered to be let in. I saw Scudder, went to bed and the next thing I knew was being woken up by Davis with tales of murder.'

'You didn't mention meeting Scudder in the report you gave to my constable. Why?'

Mackay shrugged. 'I didn't think it was important. He was alive at the time, and why would the police be interested in me telling him to go home?'

'Because you may have been the last person to see him alive.'

'I doubt it,' said Mackay dismissively, although his eyes were uneasy. 'I imagine Adams saw him after I did, because he was hanging around the ship, too. I saw him myself when I got up to go to the head. Why don't you ask *him* what he was doing, instead of picking on a poor beleaguered Scot?'

Mackay would answer no more questions, so Taylor beckoned Adams away from the crate, and asked him for his story. The Scot declined to leave, and leaned against Scudder's boxes, listening to the interview with open interest.

'As I told your Sergeant Grant,' Adams began, 'I left the party when everything was in an uproar because of the raspberry tart incident – that happened at ten o'clock – and I put my nose in here before I went to my lodgings.'

'What time did your nose arrive?'

'Jesus, I don't know. Late, because I had to knock, like Mackay. However, not having a Scottish foghorn of a voice, I couldn't make the guards hear, so I climbed over the gates. I understand you demonstrated how easily it can be done yesterday.'

'Why did you come here at all?'

'To check on things. I'll be the expedition's second-in-command, and it's my duty to make sure all is well. I don't drink to excess, but most of my colleagues were pissed to the gills, including Scudder and Mackay, and I wanted to make certain none of them did anything stupid. We have a lot of valuable equipment, and it could all be lost if some bloody fool falls asleep with a lighted cigarette in his hand. I've seen how fast a fire can destroy a ship.'

'Did you see Scudder?'

'No, but I wasn't looking for him.' Adams waved an expansive arm. 'You can see how much materiel is here, inspector. We could have wandered around for ages without crossing each other's paths. Especially in the dark'

'What did you do, exactly?'

'I inspected the supplies out here. Then I met Berry and Riches, while they were on that damned-fool route Davis makes them follow – it's predictable, and all a thief needs to do is slip past when the time is right. I've pointed this out, but he's a merchant seaman and he told me that those of us from the real Service know nothing other than swords and brasswork, and ordered me to mind my own business.'

Mackay released a short bark of laughter. 'And he may well be right, laddie. I was a Royal Navy surgeon before I joined this expedition, and what I could tell you about military inflexibility would make your hair curl.'

'I ordered them away from the western end of the South Quay,' Adams continued, 'because the really vulnerable part is the more isolated east. Then I wandered around a little longer before going home.'

But Taylor saw an inconsistency in the tale. 'Riches and Berry were on Davis' watch, and didn't come on duty until one. If you left the party at ten o'clock – perhaps five minutes or so after Scudder – you would have arrived here on *Cheetham's* watch.'

Adams blinked. 'Then I must have left later, because it was Berry and Riches whom I saw. Ask them. They'll tell you I ordered them to concentrate on the eastern end of the pier.'

'I am not questioning whom you met,' said Taylor. 'I'm questioning your timing. Even if you walked slowly from Eaton Square, it would not have taken you three hours. Besides, Mackay here says he saw you when he went to the lavatory.'

'I did,' nodded the surgeon. 'I can't give you a time, because I don't have a watch, but it was long after midnight.'

Adams rubbed his chin, then spoke in a low, resentful voice. 'All right, I did come later – probably after two o'clock. I have a friend, and I went to see *her* first. However, I shan't reveal her name, so don't expect her to confirm my tale. I may marry her, and she can't be expected to take me if I send the bloody police after her, can she?'

'A woman!' crowed Mackay in delight. 'Who'd have thought it!'

'You may have no choice,' warned Taylor, ignoring the Scot. 'She'll be even less inclined to accept you if you're inside Pentonville, on suspicion of murder.'

Adams gazed at him in horror. 'But Scudder was probably dead long before I arrived. Look, there's Cheetham. Ask *him* whether I was here on his watch: he'll tell you I wasn't.'

'I will,' said Taylor. 'But whether he saw you or not doesn't *prove* that you weren't here. Your tale is unconvincing, and that makes you a prime suspect for killing Scudder.' He turned to Mackay, who had started to grin. 'And that goes for you, too.'

Chapter 4

Third Officer Cheetham was a smiling, round-faced man a decade or more older than most of his shipmates. Taylor interviewed him on *Nimrod*'s upper deck, where he was informed that Cheetham had seen nothing unusual during his watch. Cheetham also confided that he had started two hours earlier than scheduled, about six o'clock, because he was concerned about theft. He confirmed what Davis had said: that he preferred to remain on board, rather than prowling the quay.

'There's no right or wrong, though,' he said, glancing at Davis, who was rearranging some of the crates near the gangway, using Mackay, Adams and Priestley to help. Adams and Mackay obliged only reluctantly, both resentful and alarmed to learn they comprised the inspector's chief suspects. 'It's just personal preference.'

'What is your rationale?' asked Taylor.

'I think it's the best vantage point. I station Ellis at the aft gangway and Kemp on the forward gangway, while I remain here, midships. If you go and stand in each of those places, you'll see they allow us to cover pretty much the whole area. The best place is midships, though, which is why I always take it myself.'

'Because you don't trust the others?' asked Taylor, writing in his notebook.

'Because an officer should always opt for the most arduous duty,' replied Cheetham.

'What did you see two nights ago?'

'Nothing that will help you, inspector. Various members of the expedition came and went, but all my attention was on the materiel. We're on a tight budget, and can't afford theft.'

'Have you lost anything so far?'

'No,' responded Cheetham proudly. 'Although I've certainly seen shadows lurking, waiting for their chance. But it was quiet that night, and I didn't see anyone who shouldn't have been here.'

'Who *did* you see?'

The third officer rubbed his chin. 'Not the Boss and Priestley. They both left the docks just after six – cutting it fine to dash to their lodgings and don their finery. They'd been fiddling with that equipment of Scudder's, trying to get it stowed. They didn't succeed, and Scudder was vexed to think of it sitting out all night.'

'He didn't trust you to guard it?'

Cheetham grimaced. 'It wasn't that – he thought I wouldn't be able to resist the temptation to play with it, indulging my natural sailor's curiosity to see how things work. To take it apart and reassemble it in a way I thought was better, or so he said.'

'And would you?'

'Of course not! I have a ship and materiel to monitor, and cannot waste time meddling with the scientific equipment. Scudder was just venting his spleen, because he was annoyed that the broken hatch meant his crates were still out, when they should have been safely stowed.'

'So, Shackleton and Priestley left the ship at six. When did they return?'

'As far as I know, after Davis found the body. He sent Riches to fetch the Boss. Priestley had arrived early, hoping to get some work done.'

Davis, hearing his name, came to join the conversation. Mackay followed.

'Who else did you see?' Taylor asked, turning a page in his notebook.

Cheetham considered. 'The captain. He wanted to make sure all was in order before he retired for the night. He was the first to come – probably about eleven o'clock. I didn't see Adams, though.'

'I did,' said Davis. 'He was walking around the supplies, checking they were all shipshape and Bristol fashion, just like I was. That was about one forty-five.'

'See?' asked Adams in relief. 'I *wasn't* here earlier, just like I told you.'

'You weren't *seen* earlier,' corrected Taylor. 'It's not the same thing. Who else, Cheetham?'

'Mackay. He said he was going to sleep in the officers' cabin, because he'd forgotten his key.'

'He woke me up when he came in,' interjected Davis. 'I've never seen a man so lubricated. I had to get up and put him to bed, because he couldn't do it himself. That was roughly twelve-fifteen.' He paused. 'But he was gone a short while later, when I got up to start my watch.'

'Just to the head,' said Mackay quickly. 'I don't remember going, but I always do after a few beers. I certainly wouldn't have left the ship. And I wasn't *lubricated*. I could still walk!' He glared at Davis.

'Was Mackay asleep when you turned in?' asked Taylor of Cheetham.

The third officer shook his head. 'I can't say. I went straight to my lodgings, leaving the dock at roughly ten past one. I didn't go below decks again that night.'

'I was asleep, though,' said Mackay firmly. 'You can take my word for it.'

Taylor nodded, writing steadily. 'Anyone else, Cheetham?'

'Marshall was here for a while. He came at about eleven-thirty with Murray, who was also worried about the equipment – he's the chief biologist, after all. I saw Scudder shortly after, but they didn't arrive together.'

'Of course they didn't,' said Mackay acidly. 'Scudder couldn't abide Murray. I saw a formal letter he drafted to the Boss, stating that his credentials were better than Murray's. It's all nonsense of course. Scudder thought he could use Murray's age against him.'

Cheetham snorted his disgust. 'Murray's only a couple of years older than me, and I don't consider *myself* past usefulness.'

'In reality,' the Scot went on, prudently saying no more about age, 'Murray is better than Scudder in all respects – a better man, a better scientist and a better type to have on an expedition. He isn't in the best of health, but physical fitness isn't everything.'

'Do you think Murray objected to Scudder's claims?' asked Taylor, supposing here was another motive for murder, and another suspect, too.

Mackay shrugged, and it was Cheetham who answered. 'I certainly would have done.'

'So you never saw Murray with Scudder the night of the murder?' asked Taylor of the third officer.

Cheetham shook his head. 'I didn't say that – I said they didn't *arrive* together. I saw them standing by the trawl together, shortly before Mackay arrived so drunk that he had to be assisted up the gangway.'

'I was not drunk,' objected the surgeon irritably. 'I wouldn't have been able to advise Scudder to go home if I'd been three sheets to the wind, would I?'

'Did anyone else talk to Scudder?' Taylor asked, ignoring him.

Cheetham was thoughtful. 'Marshall did, and the captain called out a greeting to him, too.'

Taylor consulted his notebook. 'So, Mackay, Captain England, Murray and Marshall had some sort of interaction with Scudder that night. And Adams was in the vicinity, but failed to see him. Anyone else?'

'Yes, Wild came by, as he does every night,' replied Cheetham. 'Then there were the hopefuls. Yaxley came alone, and young Vallen and O'Brien were together.'

Taylor sighed, scanning the notes he had made the previous day, seeing that Cheetham's tale was wholly consistent with his earlier statement. Basically, the entire scientific staff and more had been present at one point or other, and the watches had been managed in such a way that anyone could have slipped on or off the dock. Only two men could be exonerated: Shackleton and Priestley, whose alibis after Lady Wallaston's party had already been confirmed by Sergeant Grant.

'Is there anything else that might help us?' he asked.

'One thing,' replied Cheetham. 'As I said, I stand where you are now when I keep watch. I move a few feet in either direction, but my view remains essentially the same.'

Taylor stared down at the quay. Greasy Grant was kneeling next to the tarpaulin that lay across the spot where Scudder's body had been, poking at the ground with a penknife for some reason known only to himself. Taylor realised that a corpse would have been visible, even in the gloom of an unlit dock. Grant saw he was being watched, and headed for the gangway, looking more squat than ever by the addition of a new bowler hat that was entirely the wrong style for a man of his proportions.

'You would have seen the murder or the body from here,' surmised Taylor, addressing the third officer. 'And your watch finished at one.'

'Yes, which means that Scudder was killed between then and a quarter past two, when Davis found him.'

'Twenty past one, sir,' said Grant, overhearing. 'I forgot to mention it yesterday, but Scudder's watch was broken, and it stopped at twenty minutes past one. That must have been when he died.'

Taylor groaned inwardly at the sergeant's oversight. 'Assuming his watch kept accurate time,' was all he said in front of the others.

Taylor stayed by the rail, deep in thought, while his witnesses and suspects took the opportunity afforded by his pondering to slip away and be about their own duties. Silently, Taylor cursed Hamilton for lumbering him with a case that was likely to be just as complex and difficult as the Headless Bishop, and that might well transpire to be unsolvable. He already had a list of suspects as long as his arm – not to mention the fact that literally hundreds of applicants might have dispatched Scudder in the hope that they would be accepted on the expedition instead.

Moreover, he had not taken to either of the surgeons, and thought the feisty Mackay or the acerbic Marshall might well commit murder to suit themselves. He *did* like the foul-mouthed Adams, but the man's story contained too many inconsistencies, and his alibi was a woman he declined to name.

And could he trust the testimony of his other witnesses? Instinctively, he felt Cheetham and Davis would not lie, but it would have been easy for a cunning killer to fool them – neither officer's system of guarding the supplies was perfect, and anyone familiar with them and their routines would know it.

In fact, the only reliable detail Taylor had was the time of the victim's death – twenty past one. Fortunately, the discovery had been made by the pathologist, not by the unreliable Grant, and he had used his initiative to examine the watch carefully. The report about it, which Grant eventually produced from one of his grimy pockets, was unequivocal: the watch would have kept good time, and it had certainly been broken when Scudder fell as he was murdered. Taylor opened his notebook and saw the jumble of times and names his witnesses had given him. As soon as he had a quiet moment, he would have to reassess them all in the light of that fateful moment: twenty minutes past one o'clock.

Eventually, aware that time was passing, Taylor went in search of Adams, feeling the meteorologist's testimony was by far the weakest, and thus needed clarification. The man not only had declined to name his female alibi, but he had confessed to wandering among the crates near where the murder had occurred, and confirmed that he had ordered the two seamen to the other end of the dock. Adams was on the quayside, kneeling next to a weather balloon.

'I need to know exactly what time you arrived here the night Scudder died,' Taylor began. 'This is important.'

Adams frowned uneasily. 'I left Hel...I left my lady friend's house at half-past twelve, because I heard the church bells chiming. It takes about thirty minutes to get here, walking briskly.'

'So you arrived at one?' asked Taylor. When Adams nodded cautiously, he added, 'So why did you tell me earlier that you arrived at two?'

Adams regarded him with dislike. 'If I did, then it was a slip of the tongue. It was *one* o'clock.'

'Very well. Then what?

'I climbed over the gates – as I told you – and inspected the crates, to make sure all was well. You heard what Cheetham said: he's seen shadows lurking – greedy bastards after our equipment. You see the box with the green top? It contains a Robinson anemometer and those are expensive. I can't afford to lose it to a thief who wouldn't know its purpose if it was stuffed up his bloody arse.'

'Don't you people ever rest?' asked Taylor. 'You spend all day here or at the Expedition Office, and you pass your nights crawling about on dark quays, pawing over your belongings. Do you all operate constantly without sleep?'

'When you're in a state of high excitement, and the days are long and warm, you don't need much sleep,'

101

replied Adams. He relaxed enough to manage a rueful smile. 'We're on tenterhooks, inspector, with three weeks to go, and I find sleep evades me. I lie awake, thinking about theodolites and hypsometers. Will we have enough thermometers? What happens if we get south and I find Nigel Vallen has broken them all? What shall we do if the mercury freezes? You know the sort of thing.'

Taylor could hazard a guess. He had spent restless nights himself of late, fretting about the Headless Bishop, and about the intricate political dance that Hamilton seemed to be performing. He pulled his thoughts away from his own troubles, and stared towards the place where Scudder had died.

Was Adams telling the truth now? *Had* it been a slip of the tongue when the meteorologist had claimed a two o'clock arrival when he meant one? Taylor found himself uncertain. Then should he arrest the man? Unfortunately, a dubious alibi and confused timing were insufficient for such a course of action – Taylor needed more. He added his thanks for Adams' cooperation and sauntered away, aware of the meteorologist's immediate relief. Did it signify a guilty conscience, or was it just the entirely understandable reaction of an innocent man who had never been questioned by the police before? Taylor wondered how he could find out.

The inspector continued his prowling, gradually gaining a sense of order in what had first seemed to be an unruly state of chaos in the materiel. Eventually, his wanderings took him back aboard *Nimrod*, where he discovered several expedition members in the throws of an argument. Because both surgeons were present, the atmosphere had grown explosive, Marshall goading the others to anger with snide remarks, and the prickly Mackay quick to take offence. Adams and Captain England were also irate, and although Priestley was trying to calm troubled waters, he was meeting with scant success.

'You're worse than bloody Scudder,' Adams was snarling. 'He was always whining about my language. Well, it's none of your damned business, England.'

'It is when you're on my ship,' retorted England coldly. 'I won't countenance obscenities on a Christian vessel, just as I won't countenance women on it. They bring a ship bad luck.'

'Did Scudder complain about your language?' asked Taylor of Adams, breaking into the debate. Everyone jumped to see him standing there, and Taylor was intrigued to note that Priestley was the only one who did not immediately assume a guilty expression. As a policeman, he was used to those sorts of reactions, even for the innocent, but he could not help but wonder whether they might be significant here, among his prime suspects.

'Once or twice,' Adams admitted eventually. 'He was a prissy fellow. He didn't even like his fingers being dirty, and was constantly wiping them on his handkerchief.'

Taylor recalled the body's pristine hands.

'He did,' agreed Davis. 'And a ship in the process of being loaded with provisions is no place to stay clean. He was always trying to dust himself off, and I told him more than once that white suits were not appropriate for our kind of work.'

'He didn't *work*,' said England bitterly. 'He pestered my crew into doing it for him.'

'Complaining about Adams' ripe language wasn't all he moaned about,' added Mackay. 'He was always griping about something – the captain's refusal to give him a sailor for his exclusive employ, the smell of Marshall's Autumn Gold tobacco, Wild's singing, the fact that Murray was his senior…the list is endless.'

'You didn't like him, then,' said Taylor mildly.

'No, I didn't,' replied Mackay firmly. 'And neither did anyone else, although they will lie and tell you they did. Except wee Priestley here, of course, who likes everyone.'

'I most certainly do not,' said Priestley, fixing Mackay with an intent look.

The Scot merely laughed.

Taylor was thoughtful as his suspects dispersed. It was clear that there was a good deal of ill feeling aboard *Nimrod*, and he said as much to Priestley.

'We're all under a lot of pressure. You can see how much there is to do, and the Expedition Office has work piled almost to the ceiling, too. You're not seeing us at our best.'

'Most murders are committed when the killer isn't at his best,' Taylor pointed out. 'That's the point – circumstances combine to push someone over a boundary he wouldn't normally cross.'

'I suppose so,' admitted Priestley. He started suddenly. 'Heavens! That's *my* chest they're stowing, and if they put it there, I shan't be able to get at it until we arrive in the south – and it contains all my notebooks!'

He hurried away and Taylor noted that his manner was so pleasantly affable that the seamen immediately tipped their caps and agreed to do as he asked. He was sure Mackay and Marshall would not have been so amiable, and was equally sure their belongings would not have been treated with the same care, either.

When Priestley was satisfied that his chest was safe, he led the way back to the open deck, where they bumped into Shackleton. The expedition leader opened his mouth to speak, but before he could say a word, a short, wiry fellow with a carefully clipped beard hurried up. It was Frank Wild, the man in charge of provisions.

'The tobacco has just arrived from Bristol, Boss. We should stow it as soon as we can.' Wild nodded towards the quay, where a number of dockhands had converged to help with the loading. Unlike scientific equipment, tobacco would certainly be something that could be spirited away, and sold to customers who asked few questions.

'Good thinking, Frank,' agreed Shackleton. 'See it brought aboard immediately. Stow it in the galley for now – but tell Roberts first.'

Wild immediately hastened to oblige, collecting Davis en route to help him. Taylor became aware of someone standing very close behind him, and turned to see the captain, who had fixed his lanky first officer with a beady glare.

'I didn't want Davis, you know,' he confided hotly in Taylor's ear. 'I had in mind someone with qualifications that can only be described as transcendent. But he let me down, so I was obliged to recruit Davis instead. And *he* is too tall.'

Taylor raised his eyebrows. 'Why should that be a problem?'

'Because this is a small ship,' snapped England. 'Didn't you notice the way he's obliged to walk below decks – more like a crab than a man! Officers shouldn't scurry along bent double – they should stand upright and walk easily, like me. Would you like to see my cabin, by the way? You should – it is the centre of operations.'

Without waiting for an answer, he scuttled along the cluttered deck, moving quickly with his head pulled down like a frightened turtle. Taylor wondered how the captain could dare remark on Davis' gait when his own was so peculiar. Once below decks again, England took a deep, shuddery breath.

'The sun,' he whispered, wiping his sweating face. 'I don't like it on my head. Still, I'll be better once we're at sea. There's nothing like the ocean for getting rid of cobwebs brought on by the sun.'

England led Taylor into a tiny cabin that smelled of linseed oil. The scent reminded the inspector of cricket, and he wondered whether he would be far enough advanced with Scudder's murder to play for the Metropolitan Police Second Eleven against the Ecclesiastical Commission on Sunday. He was a respectable all-rounder, and his cunningly delivered off-spinners had seen the end of more than one incautious batsman.

The captain's cabin comprised a small cupboard-like space full of odd angles. There was a photograph of the King on one wall, and a roughly drawn sketch of *Nimrod* and her various holds on another, covered with notes made in pencil. Several shelves were piled high with books and papers, all well-thumbed, and a narrow bench was so loaded with boxes that its presence was only revealed by the corner of a cushion protruding from one end. Sea chests stood in an unsteady pile behind the door, and the table, inconveniently large so as to accommodate the Admiralty's generously sized nautical charts, was awash with lists of supplies, requisitions and correspondence.

'Eventually, I'll share this with Shackleton and his second-in-command,' said England, gesturing for Taylor to take the only empty chair, while he perched on the edge of a chest.

'Who is the second-in-command?' asked Taylor, then answered before England could reply. 'Adams, of course. He told me so himself.'

'He tells everyone that,' said England. 'But Marshall claims the position was promised to *him*. Shackleton says he'll decide once the ship is underway, and we have time to draw breath. I stay out of such matters, of course. The hierarchy of the shore party is nothing to do with me.'

'Is the choice limited to those two?' asked Taylor, recalling that this post was not the only contentious one: Scudder had set his sights on Murray's, too. It occurred to Taylor that Shackleton was wrong to leave his men in uncertainty, and that he should make his decision sooner, but supposed the expedition leader had his reasons.

'Yes,' said England. 'No one else is interested.'

'How important is the post?' asked Taylor. 'Shackleton is in charge, and you are master of the ship. What's left?'

'It could be extremely important,' replied England. 'It

will determine who leads one of the sledging parties, who will be in charge at base while the Boss is gone, or even who accompanies him to the Pole. One of them is going to be in for a big disappointment.'

Taylor nodded, thinking to himself that in his experience, disappointed men tended to make excellent candidates for murder suspects.'

With Priestley at his side, Taylor spent the rest of the day assessing the whereabouts of the crew and staff at the time of the murder, dispatching constables to confirm their alibis, and then collating the resulting information. This necessarily included a number of dockhands and casual labourers – anyone who had had contact with Scudder – and was tedious and time-consuming. Thus, it was past seven when he announced that they had done enough, and gave Priestley leave to go.

They disembarked from *Nimrod* together, Taylor unsettled to find the quay unsteady under his feet now he had grown used to the sway of the ship. While he issued a batch of instructions to Grant and two constables for the evening, Priestley reflected on his own day.

Although he had not enjoyed prying into his colleagues' affairs, there had been a certain satisfaction in collecting and organising information. He had also discovered that although Taylor had asked some astonishingly basic questions about the ship and her mission, he had learned quickly, and Priestley had detected a sharp mind. The geologist still resented the squandering of his time, but as Taylor was willing to include him in his interviews and even share some of his speculations, the day had been considerably more interesting than he had expected.

'This is painstaking work,' he said as they walked toward the gates. 'Like science. You have to be careful with that, too, because carelessness might give false readings and lead you to erroneous conclusions.'

'Unfortunately, that doesn't stop most people,' said Taylor wryly, thinking about some of the wild theories with which he had been regaled regarding the Headless Bishop.

Priestley grinned. 'Some academics can certainly be precipitous on occasion, but that won't happen on our expedition. Maybe we won't discover anything stunning, but we shall push the boundaries of knowledge back a little, and that's the basis of good science. Fabulous discoveries are all very well, but it's the groundwork that allows them to be made.'

Tiredly, Taylor thought about some groundwork of his own that would need to be carried out that night: namely, interviewing the man who had claimed to have seen the killer of the Headless Bishop. He would far rather have gone home, especially as his wife was tired of him leaving for work before six each morning and not returning until late – a situation that was not going to improve now he had another investigation. But tips of the kind offered by Joe Bacon needed to be followed up quickly, or the witness might melt away. Taylor would just have to make it up to Ruby another time.

'Would you like to stop at a chop-house for some dinner?' asked Priestley. 'Neither of us has had much to eat today.'

It was a tempting offer, especially as Ruby's skills in the kitchen were mediocre, to put it kindly, but Taylor knew where his duty lay. 'I wish I could, but I must visit an alehouse near London Pool.'

'London Pool?' asked Priestley startled. 'That's no place for a decent man.'

'True. Unfortunately, witnesses tend not to take such things into account when choosing their watering holes.'

Priestley realised he had said something foolish; of course the inspector was obliged to go where his witnesses lived.

'Would you like me to come?' He had no desire to visit London Pool, but getting to know the policeman in different circumstances would not be a bad thing if they were to work together. 'I never touch alcohol, but barley water and some company would be pleasant.'

'Not tonight,' Taylor said, smiling at the notion of the naïve geologist in the kind of tavern Long Ron was likely to frequent. 'Another time perhaps.'

'Very well,' said Priestley. He grinned suddenly. 'The Antarctic has no rough taverns, and no one has ever been murdered there, either. Just imagine – a whole continent, free of the sin of Cain!'

They parted company, Taylor to walk to London Pool, and Priestley to catch a cab to his lodgings. The inspector thought about Priestley's last comment as he went, and he hoped he would solve Scudder's death before the expedition left, because he did not like the notion that his failure might be responsible for a killer travelling south, especially if he then struck again – the first ever murder on an entire continent.

The following morning saw Taylor and Priestley waiting at the East India Dock gates at five to six, along with several others. One was a smiling, soft-spoken man with spectacles and a thick moustache, whom Priestley introduced as Murray, the chief biologist and the man whose post Scudder had coveted. Grant had interviewed him, and Taylor recalled from his sergeant's notes that Murray had left the party at ten, visited *Nimrod* until roughly midnight, then gone to enjoy a cup of cocoa at his club before retiring for the night.

Murray asked in a pleasant, affable way how the investigation was going, and Taylor was aware of total silence as everyone waited for an answer. When he gave his stock reply – that he was pursuing several lines of enquiry – they looked disappointed, and he was left with the sense that they felt he was letting them down.

'Never mind,' said Priestley kindly. 'Today, you're almost certain to discover something that will take you forward.'

Taylor hoped the confidence was not misplaced. He had been to his station before coming to the docks, where a memorandum from Chief Superintendent Hamilton had curtly informed him that he was to solve the Scudder case with all possible speed. He was also to continue investigating the Headless Bishop with all due diligence, using Grant if he found himself unequal to managing two murder enquiries plus his less-important cases.

Taylor had read the order in disbelief, outraged that the chief superintendent should feel the need to tell him to work hard. Then – exasperated that Andrews should be lounging idly while he himself struggled against an unreasonable burden – he had hurled the scrunched-up paper into the wastepaper bin so violently that the thing had fallen over with a metallic clatter.

111

He dragged his thoughts away from departmental politics, and studied the men who were waiting to begin work. Some of Shackleton's people were yawning and rubbing sleep from their eyes, but all were in good humour and were obviously keen to be about their duties. They formed a distinct contrast to the dockhands, for whom work was work, something that put bread on the table and beer in their stomachs. As the gates opened, Shackleton arrived.

'Priestley told me last night that you intend to re-interview my men today,' he said without preamble. 'I asked Wild to tidy up the officers' cabin, so you'll have somewhere private to work.'

'Won't that interfere with your provisioning?'

Shackleton smiled ruefully. 'Yes. But I said I'd offer you every convenience, and I intend to fulfil that promise – especially as this case has come at such a bad time for you. The Headless Bishop.'

'I'll manage,' replied Taylor, unwilling to admit that he might be unequal to the task when the burdens on his old classmate were probably heavier still.

'Emily told me last night that I abused our friendship by asking for your help,' Shackleton went on. 'And if that's the case, I'm sorry. But you understand, don't you, Will? If the expedition is to leave in less than three weeks, we *must* have Scudder's murderer caught. Giving you an office is a small price to pay. Have you made any headway?'

'We're pursuing several...' began Taylor. Then he relented: this was Shackleton. 'No, not yet, but we haven't finished the interviews, and nor have I established who owned the murder weapon.'

He had ordered it photographed the previous day, and copies sent to men who were considered experts in naval affairs. But these were details the harried expedition leader did not need to know.

'You think the culprit is one of us?' asked Shackleton uneasily. 'I was hoping it was a random attack – that Scudder was in the wrong place at the wrong time.'

'Perhaps he was,' said Taylor. 'I know it sounds as though I'm speaking in clichés, but we really will leave no stone unturned.'

They arrived at the ship to discover that Wild had sacrificed much of his night's sleep to convert the little cabin from a storeroom into a functional office. Taylor stepped inside and looked around.

'How was your visit to London Pool last night?' asked Priestley cheerfully, while Wild's eyebrows shot up at the mention of such a disreputable place.

Taylor shrugged, unwilling to admit that several hours sipping sour ale in extremely unpleasant surroundings had yielded no result: Long Ron had not appeared.

'I think we should begin with Murray this morning,' he said, declining to talk about it.

Priestley sped off to fetch him, leaving Taylor with Wild, who chatted amiably as they waited for him to return. His favoured subject was the loading of the ship, and the antipathy that existed between seasoned sailors, who knew about such matters, and scientists, who did not but who nevertheless had strong ideas about how their equipment should be stowed. He laughed as he described how Murray had wanted a delicate piece of equipment left free-standing in the aft hold. Taylor regarded him blankly.

'It would topple over before we left the Thames,' explained Wild, his grin fading when he saw Taylor had no more understanding of nautical matters than the biologist. 'And by the time we reach New Zealand, there wouldn't be a piece left bigger than my fingernail.'

'Lord!' muttered Taylor. The rocking of the ship was making him queasy again, a feeling that intensified when Wild began to describe the monstrous seas *Nimrod* would face on her way south.

Of course, he suspected the unappetising clots of half-raw pastry and stringy meat that comprised Ruby's so-called Cornish pasties might be to blame, too. He had eaten three of them that morning in an effort to make up for forgetting their trip to the theatre the night before, which had gone clean from his mind until he had returned home from London Pool and seen the tickets placed meaningfully on the kitchen table.

'This excursion sounds remarkably unappealing, yet you have men lining up to go.'

'Fame and glory, Mr Taylor, fame and glory.' Wild straightened from where he was stacking finnesko – reindeer-skin boots – behind a bulkhead. 'When the expedition leaves from Lyttelton, this cabin will be home to five officers.'

'Five?' asked Taylor, wondering whether he was being made sport of. 'That's not possible. We're cramped in here with just you and me.'

'They'll work watches, which means they won't all be bunking down at the same time.'

'And the shore party?' asked Taylor. 'They won't keep watches, so where will they sleep? I know they will sail on another ship to New Zealand, but what about the journey to the Antarctic?'

'Wherever we can stow them,' replied Wild. He grinned a little wickedly. 'They complain about the lodgings they have been allocated here in London, but those are palaces compared to what they will have to endure in the south.'

'Why do they need to be in London at all?' asked Taylor. 'From what you've said, the loading of a ship should be managed by experienced seamen – like you.'

Wild nodded. 'It should, and between you and me, the scientists are a nuisance with their demands. They don't understand the difference between their equipment and important supplies.'

'Their equipment isn't important?'

Wild shrugged. 'It has its place, but let's be honest, the main goal of the expedition is to bag the Pole. But even if not, their instruments aren't as vital as coal – both for running the ship and for keeping us alive through the winter. Then there's food – we need to take enough to last a dozen men for two years. And there's the hut, which—'

'Hut?'

Wild made no attempt to hide his surprise at the question. 'We can hardly sleep in tents during an Antarctic winter, Mr Taylor. We need proper shelter.'

'I suppose you do.' Taylor had not given the matter much thought. Wild continued.

'The Boss has designed a hut that will house everyone, and that has space for science, cooking, sleeping and so on. So, these things comprise the main part of the cargo, but much of the equipment the scientists will need for their research is fragile, so they want to stow it

115

themselves. That's where the friction comes in.'

'What kind of friction?'

Wild pursed his lips. 'Well, Marshall and Mackay fuss over the medical supplies, Adams is touchy over his meteorological equipment, and Scudder was a nuisance about everything. But enough of that – here is Murray come to talk to you, and Priestley with him.'

Taylor gestured for the genial biologist to sit on one of the crates, while he took the stool behind the table, so he could make notes. They exchanged pleasantries for a few moments, during which Taylor saw that Murray was breathless. As *Nimrod* was not a large ship, he thought the man must be very unfit.

'I feel quite guilty about it, actually,' said Murray, when Priestley offered to fetch him some water. 'My health, I mean. I'm not what you'd call in prime condition, although I'm a bit worse than usual, because I'm recovering from a nasty bout of 'flu. I'm trusting this wheeziness will ease soon, although I cannot but help worry that it may become problematic after we sail.'

'Why go, then?' asked Taylor bluntly.

'Because I'd give ten years of my life to study the tardigrades and rotifers of the southern oceans and Antarctic lakes. Have you ever seen a tardigrade, inspector?'

'Not that I'm aware,' replied Taylor cautiously, hoping it was not some kind of flea and Murray carried samples of them in his pockets. He began to feel itchy, but resisted the temptation to scratch.

'Then I'll whisk up a microscope and give you the thrill of your life,' offered Murray generously. 'Tardigrada! The

116

prince among taxa! I cannot imagine anything more wonderful than to fish them living from the icy waters of the south, and study them in their native environments. Glorious, glorious little beasts! I have framed drawings of them all over my house.'

'I see,' said Taylor. He met many odd people in his line of work. 'Did Scudder share this particular passion? He was to have been your assistant, I understand.'

Murray's face fell. 'Actually, he didn't. He was more interested in salps, which are fascinating, of course, but he was rather dismissive of rotifers and tardigrades, which I found hurtful. I suspect we would have argued about it, had he lived.'

'Are you saying you didn't argue?'

'I didn't; he did – or he tried. However, you can't have an argument when only one person participates, so he found himself thwarted. He even went to Shackleton, and told him that he should be head biologist – that I should be *his* assistant.'

'Yes?' probed Taylor, seeing the indignation in the biologist's face. Here was a very good motive for dispatching Scudder.

Murray sighed. 'It would have been inappropriate, inspector. He was a careful and painstaking researcher, but he was still unknown in his field. Perhaps he would have become famous in time, although I doubt it. He was too unwilling to work with others.'

'He was jealous of you, then?'

Murray was embarrassed. 'If so, then he didn't tell me.'

'Was he, Priestley?' asked Taylor.

'Yes,' replied Priestley immediately. 'Murray was

117

recommended to the Boss not only by Sir John Murray – not a relation, by the way – but by William Speirs Bruce, too.'

'I see,' said Taylor, supposing he was meant to be impressed.

'Many consider them the world's two most renowned polar scientists,' elaborated Priestley, seeing his point had been missed. 'Their endorsement speaks for itself. Scudder had good references, too, but nothing like Murray's.'

Murray reddened and stared at his shoes.

'So you weren't friends?' asked Taylor to the biologist. 'And you didn't admire each other.'

'We may have come to like each other, in time, although I suspect he would have driven me to distraction with his litany of complaints. But no, we weren't friends.'

'Is there anything you can tell me that might be relevant to his death?'

Murray thought, and the sounds of the dock drifted in through the open porthole: the hammering of nails as crates were sealed, the yells of men busy about their duties, and the squeak and groan of winches.

'No,' he said eventually. 'But I have a consignment of formaldehyde waiting on the quay, and I don't want it sitting in the sun. Do you have any more questions, or may I be excused?'

Chapter 5

While Taylor waited for Priestley to fetch the next person to be interviewed, he gazed out the porthole, watching a gull wheel over the grimy roofs of the depots. Closer to the ship, members of the expedition were threading through the supplies. Some were opening crates to check their contents, while others were making notes or discussing items with the sailors.

He saw Adams direct Nigel Vallen to a box, which the lad picked up only for the bottom to drop out, scattering its contents across the ground. Marshall stormed up to him, and some of his vicious diatribe drifted up to Taylor's porthole. Nigel bowed his head and seemed on the verge of tears, while the others watched uncomfortably. Eventually, Adams intervened, so Marshall exploded at the meteorologist instead. Adams merely replied with several pithy obscenities before going back to his own work, leaving Marshall stunned into blessed silence.

As Priestley was taking some time to return, Taylor began to review his notes from the previous interviews. Suddenly, the door flew open and Marshall strode in. Priestley was at his heels, and evidently had tried to stop him, because his youthful features were apologetic and exasperated in equal measure.

'Am I disturbing you, inspector?' asked Marshall carelessly. 'I forgot you were here. Have you seen a theodolite, by any chance?'

'No,' replied Taylor, watching him rummage through the neat piles Wild had arranged, creating a good deal of disorder in the process. He would not have known a theodolite if it had marched up and announced itself, but he was not about to admit it to the abrasive surgeon.

'I gave it to Nigel to mind, but it wouldn't surprise me to learn that he broke it, and is too embarrassed to confess. It's a pity he's so clumsy, because otherwise he'd be a walk-in for the expedition. Yaxley is too hot-headed, and there's something about O'Brien that I don't like at all. Shackleton feels the same. Of course, none of them are as good as Gray. It's a shame he got cold feet and did a runner. Have you seen the paper this morning?'

Before Taylor could reply, Marshall had dropped *The Star* on the table.

'You're mentioned,' the surgeon said slyly. 'I've finished with it, so feel free to peruse it at your leisure. There! I thought you said you hadn't seen my theodolite.'

He leaned across the table and grabbed a complicated-looking instrument from near Taylor's hand. He inspected it closely, as if he imagined its proximity to a policeman might have damaged it.

'So, Nigel didn't break it after all,' said Priestley coldly. 'It was in the officers' cabin, quite safe and unharmed, just where he told you it would be. I imagine an apology is in order.'

'Nonsense,' said Marshall, walking out. 'If a man can't take a bit of ribbing, he has no business on an expedition.

We can't be wondering whether we're hurting delicate feelings every time we ask a question. Enjoy the paper, inspector.'

'Throw it away,' advised Priestley. 'He only brought it to taunt you.'

Taylor sighed. 'I suppose there's another piece about the Headless Bishop? I thought the fact that nothing has happened would mean there was nothing to report.'

Priestley perched on the edge of a crate. 'The press is a mystery to me. On the few occasions when the papers report on matters I know about, they're nearly always wrong or misleading. It makes me wonder about the truth of the things that I *don't* know about.'

'Especially *The Star* and the *Daily Mail*,' agreed Taylor. 'If the facts don't fit their stories, they simply ignore them. And the astonishing thing is that people accept them as truth. Ruby showed me an article last month that claimed house sparrows are turning carnivorous and attacking children. The next day, someone came into my station with three boxes of dead birds and asked if there was a reward.'

Priestley raised his hands, to express his mystification. 'And why does the press lay hold of some cases like a pack of dogs, but ignore others? Here we are, about to sail for the last great, unknown area of the world, but are they interested? No – they give precedence to Lady Davenport changing her dressmaker.'

Taylor picked up the paper and leafed through it. He did not have to look hard for an editorial entitled 'Are the Police Doing Right by the People of London?' by a reporter named Bernard Faris, who was well known for his scathing attacks on the Force. He read it quickly, picking out the adjectives and phrases that told him all he needed to know about the tenor of the piece: incompetent, half-hearted, ineffectual, negligent, should be dismissed, superior officers deeply dismayed. He closed it and tossed it on the table, where Priestley immediately took it between his thumb and forefinger, as he might lay hold of something repulsive.

'I wouldn't be seen dead purchasing a disreputable organ like this,' he declared. 'And nor would any other decent, right-minded person. Anyone who believes this squalid nonsense doesn't deserve to be treated as a gentleman.' Taylor was astonished when he hurled it out of the window, sending its sheets fluttering down into the oil-covered slick of the harbour. 'There. That's the best thing to do with *that* rubbish.'

Taylor was beginning to like Priestley.

While Taylor interviewed Joyce, a taciturn man with a devotion to the expedition that verged on the fanatical, Priestley worked on a chart that would tell them at a glance who had been where on the night of Scudder's murder. It contained the name of everyone on the expedition, with a column for each hour of the night, listing where they had claimed to be. There was also a column labelled 'alibi,' to hold a tick if the claim had been verified by constables.

It was not long before they were interrupted by Grant, who was carrying something wrapped in brown paper. It was the letter opener that had killed Scudder, extracted by the pathologist and now returned to the police. Taylor studied it properly for the first time. Joyce took the opportunity to escape, and Priestley followed, leaving the two policemen alone.

The letter opener was ornate, and had been crafted to emulate the shape of an officer's dress sword. It had a plated-silver blade of about six inches, and the hilt was engraved with a 'foul' anchor and the lettering 'RNR.' What made it unique, however, was that the blade had been honed to a wicked sharpness, and its tip was like a needle, still speckled with its victim's blood. Taylor regarded it thoughtfully. Its modifications went far beyond what would be needed to open letters, so someone had clearly intended it for another purpose.

'Have you discovered who owned it yet, sir?' asked Grant, watching his inspector in a way that made Taylor feel slightly uncomfortable. It was how the sergeant treated the villains he interviewed, hoping to make them nervous with unwavering scrutiny. 'You said there were four men who might have one – Shackleton, England, Adams and Mackay.'

'I'll show it to them this morning, and see whether anyone recognises it.'

'They won't,' predicted Grant. 'Why would anyone confess to owning a murder weapon?'

'Owning it isn't the same as killing with it,' Taylor pointed out, wishing Grant was capable of a little more imagination. 'It may have been stolen. However, if our four potential owners don't recognise it, we may have to cast our net wider, and see whether any of their colleagues do. It's quite distinctive.'

Grant took it from him. 'Captain England says you can buy these from any naval supply store. Perhaps you're right, and we're barking up the wrong tree – maybe some enterprising sailor bought it in anticipation of a promotion. I've done much the same thing myself, by buying inspector's epaulettes for my uniform.'

Taylor was startled. It had never occurred to him that Grant might yearn for advancement, although he doubted he would get it. Grant might be ambitious, but the cold reality was that he did not possess the intelligence to be an inspector, and was destined to remain a sergeant for the rest of his career. He was not sure what to say.

'If we solve this case, it'll help me a lot,' said Grant, when no response was forthcoming. 'And if we get the Headless Bishop tied up, too – well, it'll be even better.'

'We'll do our best.' Taylor turned his attention back to the letter opener. 'No one can do more.'

'We can,' said Grant, making Taylor regard him sharply. 'We can do a lot better.'

'I'm not sure what you mean.'

'I mean that in this life, God helps them who help themselves, and that's what I intend to do.'

Taylor continued to regard him warily, uncertain what he was saying. 'Help yourself to what, exactly?'

'To what's rightfully mine,' said Grant. 'To promotion.'

'Oh,' said Taylor, wondering whether he was being warned that the sergeant was after his job. Somehow, he suspected that even Hamilton, with his low and moveable standards, would baulk at that. 'Well, you won't get it by wasting time. We need to do some serious thinking. Look at this knife and tell me what you see.'

Grant complied eagerly. 'I see something that was used to kill a scientist. Something so sharp that it sliced through his neck like butter and severed his windpipe. That's what killed him, not blood loss.'

'Fair enough. But what I see is something fairly

old. You can see the hilt is worn through use, and the blade is slightly concave, suggesting it was habitually sharpened, not honed for the express purpose of a single murder.'

'An heirloom?' asked Grant. 'That would be good, because we can get others to identify it.'

'Possibly. I'd also say that its owner has used it regularly over a period of years. He'll miss it – whether he was the one who used it to kill Scudder, or whether it was stolen from him.'

'But he won't admit that to us,' said Grant. 'He'll have to be forced. Personally, I find a spell in prison does wonders for concentrating the mind – of the innocent and guilty alike.'

'Right,' said Taylor, aware that not everyone responded to force. It was another reason why Grant would not make a good inspector: he did not think through his actions and strategies.

'I'll fetch the captain,' offered Grant eagerly. 'We'll have a go at him first.'

'Let me ask the questions,' said Taylor hastily, suspecting nothing would be achieved if Grant charged at England like a ravening wolf. 'You stand behind me and keep the sun off him.'

At that moment, however, Priestley returned with his completed chart, followed by Roberts with a tray of tea. Taylor studied Priestley's work, while Grant asked the other two about the value of the materiel on the quay. The sergeant was open-mouthed at its worth, and promptly declared that men would murder for a good deal less. Priestley and Roberts were transparently relieved to think that Scudder might have been murdered by a

125

common thief, and Taylor was aware that they wanted *him* to say something to suggest he concurred. But instead, he hailed England as he passed the cabin door. Reluctantly, the captain entered.

'I'll wait outside,' said Priestley, seeing the letter opener on the table and guessing what the interview was to be about. Roberts had already disappeared.

'No, stay,' countered Taylor. He had no desire for England to claim he had been insulted or browbeaten, and the captain struck him as the kind of man who might do just that. Priestley would be a better witness to the conversation than Grant, whose looming presence was doing nothing to put the captain at his ease.

'Pour me some tea, Priestley,' ordered England peremptorily. 'And put your questions, Inspector. I am a busy man, with no time to waste.'

'What did you think of Scudder?' asked Taylor, watching England down the beverage black and with more sugar than could be dissolved in the limited amount of liquid.

'Not much,' replied England, indicating to Priestley that he wanted a refill. Although there was a substantial amount of sugary slush remaining in the bottom of his cup, he sweetened it again. 'I don't usually speak ill of the dead, but I feel I should be honest. I'm relieved Scudder won't be coming with us: his presence would not have made for a happy ship.'

'Sir!' blurted Priestley, dismayed.

England shrugged unapologetically. 'I thought Scudder was a pompous fool, always demanding things and ordering my men around. He will not be missed, and we have many others who are eager to take his place.'

126

'Who do you think killed him?' asked Taylor. 'One of the hopefuls?'

'I doubt it. They're too intelligent – they know they'd be your first suspects.'

'Well, whoever did it used this,' said Taylor, indicating the paper knife. He pushed it across the table. 'Have you seen it before?'

England barely glanced at it. 'I've got one rather like it, but as I told your sergeant yesterday, they can be brought from any naval outfitters.'

'Where is yours now?'

England stared at him. 'I hope you don't think I am the culprit. And I certainly hope you don't think me stupid enough to have done it with my own knife, if I were.'

Taylor stared back. 'Are you saying you would use someone else's letter opener, then, if you were of a mind to kill?'

England's stare turned hostile. 'Don't put words in my mouth, Taylor. That knife isn't mine, and I didn't kill Scudder. And now, if you'll excuse me, I'm busy.'

Grant moved quickly to block the door. 'You can't go until you've shown us your paper knife, matey,' he snarled. 'This is a murder enquiry, and you can't just walk out when the questions become uncomfortable.'

England turned to Taylor, rage blazing in his eyes. 'My knife is somewhere at home, but I can't possibly waste time searching for it. And don't say you will look yourselves, because I don't trust you – you might just plant this one. Besides, there are confidential papers and delicate nautical equipment to consider. Now, tell this oaf to move before I have him ejected from *my* ship.'

Taylor nodded to Grant, who edged to one side with

barely concealed fury. When the captain had gone, Grant's angry eyes fastened on Taylor, who smiled.

'Well done, sergeant,' he said, taking the wind from the man's sails. 'You made him tell us exactly what we needed to know: he doesn't have his paper knife, and he's worried about it. It made him aggressive and then he invented reasons why we shouldn't be permitted to look for ourselves. So, he remains on our list of suspects.'

'He certainly does,' growled Grant. 'Shall we put these questions to Shackleton, Mackay, and Adams now?'

'I'll see if they're here,' offered Priestley unhappily.

Mackay and Adams were both at the Expedition Office, although Shackleton was on one of his flying visits to the ship, dashing through it like a whirlwind between meetings. He stopped long enough to inspect the knife.

'Is that it?' he asked uncomfortably. 'The thing that did away with poor Scudder?'

'Do you recognise it?' asked Grant baldly.

Shackleton picked it up and turned it over in his hands. 'No. Lord, it's so sharp you could shave with it! I've never had much time for letter openers, personally – life's too short to be messing around with slitting, when tearing and ripping do the job much more quickly.'

'Emily never gave you one?' asked Taylor. 'Or some friend from the Service? This is important, Mick. It's imperative we know how many of these things might have been aboard.'

Shackleton nodded. 'I know. But *I've* never owned a letter opener – from the Reserve or anywhere else – so the killer can't have got it from me. You can ask Emily if you like, but it's simply not the sort of thing I ever wanted.'

Taylor believed him, although Grant wrote down the address at which Emily might be found, obviously intending to take the Boss at his word. Shackleton did not object, clearly ready to do anything to assist the investigation, even subjecting his wife to Greasy Grant.

'Have you seen anyone else with one?' asked Taylor, as Grant wrote, licking his pencil and moving his lips as he scrawled the words.

Shackleton hesitated. 'England uses a letter opener, although I can't tell you whether it's fancy like this, or something fashioned from wood. I just recall him slitting envelopes.'

'And Adams? Mackay?' asked Taylor, as England moved up another notch on his list of suspects.

'Not that I recall. Besides, they are careful with their belongings, so I doubt that the killer could have stolen it from one of them.'

'You seem very certain the killer is someone else,' said Grant. 'Not Mackay, Adams or England.'

'Of course I am,' said Shackleton impatiently. 'None of them would have killed Scudder, not when it might spell the end of the expedition.' He turned to Taylor, a frown of concern creasing his face. 'Do you suspect one of those three in particular?'

'We're keeping an open mind,' replied Taylor vaguely. 'As I said to you earlier, we must leave no stone unturned.'

'I hope to God you're wrong,' muttered Shackleton, rubbing his hand across his face. 'But I must leave you to your work. Speak to Emily, sergeant, so you can eliminate the possibility that Scudder was murdered with a knife of mine. I don't want you wasting your time barking up the wrong tree when time is of the essence.'

Despite his determination not to let it worry him, *The Star's* editorial had upset Taylor. It was not easy being the most reviled policeman in London, seen as the epitome of all that was wrong with the Force. He dreaded to think what would happen if he failed to solve Scudder's murder, so with a growing sense of urgency, he decided to go to Regent Street and speak to Mackay and Adams at once, rather than wait for them to appear at the dock.

He and Priestley hailed a cab on the East India Dock Road, but it was lunchtime, and the traffic was heavy, especially around The Strand, where carriages and motor vehicles were jammed together in a solid mass.

'*This* is the sort of issue that should be raised in the House, not the Headless Bishop,' said Priestley irritably, as black smoke from a motor-car belched through the open window. 'London grinding to a standstill three times every day. And the smell! I cannot abide the reek of rotting horse dung and engine fumes.'

'You will be free of it in the Antarctic,' Taylor said absently, his thoughts more on the investigation than Priestley's rant. 'You will be in a place with no engines and no horses.'

Priestley grinned. 'Actually, there will be both. We're taking fifteen ponies to help pull the sledges, and we've been given a motor-car.'

'I'd forgotten about the motor-car. I still don't think it'll work, though. The Force had a couple, but they kept breaking down, and when the driver went for help, he invariably returned to find it stripped of everything a thief could carry. Now we only use them for ferrying bodies to the mortuary, on the grounds that folk tend not to steal from hearses.'

Priestley cleared his throat. 'Forgive me for mentioning it, but I understood that the Headless Bishop's corpse was stolen.'

Taylor sighed, sorry that even a discussion about motor-cars should revert to the case that so haunted him. 'Yes, he was stolen – before the pathologist had had a chance to examine him properly. However, he wasn't taken from the vehicle, but from the mortuary itself.'

'Do you know why?'

'No. The press – well, Bernard Faris of *The Star* to be precise – claimed it was the killer reclaiming his victim, which had the city in an uproar for a day or two. But there was no evidence to suggest it was true. However, we should be discussing Scudder, not my other cases. Will you explain your chart to me? Since we're stuck, we might as well pass the time usefully.'

Priestley obliged, spreading the piece of paper on his knees, and beginning to go through his findings. Taylor had surprised himself by discussing the stolen body, but there was something about Priestley that invited confidences. He was young, and had not yet acquired the natural confidence of maturity, but he still exuded the sense that he could be trusted.

'So,' concluded Priestley, after a concise explanation of his work, 'you don't have as many suspects among the expedition as you initially thought. Let's take the ship's officers – first. There are five of them, but two were

131

outside London at the time of the murder, which leaves England, Davis, and Cheetham. Davis and Cheetham were asleep half the night and on watch the other half, but either – along with the seamen assigned to their watches – would have noticed the other sneaking off to kill Scudder, so they can be dismissed as suspects.'

'Not necessarily,' said Taylor. 'Scudder died at twenty past one, but Riches and Berry were on patrol then, and Davis was on his own.'

'Not so,' said Priestley, consulting his chart. 'Davis was still below decks with his men at half past one. *Ergo*, he was only alone *after* Scudder was dead. All three men are in the clear.'

And Cheetham?' asked Taylor.

'He left *Nimrod* immediately after his watch, and he took his two men with him. All three were let out of the docks at ten past one – we have Ives' testimony to corroborate that. Cheetham and his men are in the clear, too.'

'Good,' said Taylor, impressed by the geologist's careful analysis. Although he had already deduced as much himself, it was satisfying to hear it from another source. 'So that only leaves England.'

'Now there, matters become a little blurred,' admitted Priestley reluctantly. 'He left Lady Wallaston's shortly before ten o'clock, and arrived at the dock an hour later to check his ship. Masters do that, Taylor – a vessel is their responsibility at all times, and they're always concerned about them. England says – and Cheetham confirms – that he left *Nimrod* at half past twelve, but he has no alibi until he reached his home shortly before two. And then there's the paper knife.' He glanced at the

132

wrapped package in Taylor's hand.

'Where are his lodgings?' asked Taylor. Priestley pointed to the address written neatly on another piece of paper – he had been thorough. 'That's less than two miles away. It shouldn't have taken him an hour and a half to get there.'

'He claims he walked,' said Priestley. 'Grant asked why he didn't hail a cab, and he said he needed the exercise, because he can't be outside about much during the day. Because of the sun.'

Taylor nodded, but said nothing: the captain would remain a suspect.

'Next, we turn to the crew, of which there are sixteen,' Priestley went on. 'All are being worked very hard – from six in the morning until six at night, although they tend to stay even later. It's gruelling physical labour, and they are all exhausted by the end of the day.'

Taylor nodded a second time. He had seen for himself how feverishly the sailors laboured, their only respite being when the scientists pestered them with demands, necessitating time taken for explanations.

Priestley continued again. 'The night Scudder died, twelve of them were either with their families or friends, or – for those rooming at the Albion Hotel – with other members of the crew. Your sergeant has confirmed their alibis. Moreover, we have already dismissed the four who were with Davis and Cheetham. Thus *all* the crew are in the clear.'

'What was to stop one of the men at the Albion from rising during the night, killing Scudder, and coming back while his crewmates were asleep?' asked Taylor.

'I checked that,' said Priestley. 'I went there myself.'

'You did?' Taylor was increasingly impressed; Grant would never have done such a thing.

'Basically, it's a hostel used exclusively by seamen, and because they can be unruly, it's run differently to other guesthouses. It has a strict locked-doors policy: all residents must be in their rooms by midnight, and they aren't allowed out until five the following morning. There are bars on the windows and a ferocious one-legged veteran from the Boer War guarding the door. No one can escape without being challenged.'

'What about the shore party? You and Shackleton are exonerated, because you have alibis.' Taylor glanced at Priestley's sheet. 'So have Roberts, Wild, Joyce and Day.'

'Which leaves Marshall, Adams, Mackay and Murray,' said Priestley, 'all of whom left the reception before the Boss and me, and came to the ship at some point during the night. Murray says he went to his club for cocoa afterwards, and arrived there at about half past twelve, but no one there can confirm it. At least, no one has yet.'

'Meanwhile, Mackay went to a rough pub, then came drunk to the ship,' Taylor said, taking up the tale. 'Cheetham says he talked to Scudder about his broken scalpels at midnight, and fifteen minutes later, he staggered into the officers' cabin, where he woke Davis.'

'And where he stayed the rest of the night,' said Priestley.

'Not so,' said Taylor. 'Davis reported him missing when he woke shortly before one o'clock for his watch. Mackay claims it was just a visit to the lavatory, but he was gone long enough to spot Adams prowling on the quay.'

'I suppose so,' said Priestley unhappily, amending his chart accordingly.

'Marshall was vague about *his* timing, too,' said Taylor. 'All I know about him is that Cheetham saw him at the ship at eleven-thirty. He claims he doesn't recall what time he left to go home. He doesn't seem to care that he hinders our progress by being unhelpful.'

'That's because he thinks he's above suspicion,' explained Priestley grimly. 'He'll be in for a shock if he's not more forthcoming.'

'And finally, there's Adams,' said Taylor. 'Who has changed his story several times, leaving me uncertain of the truth. I think he probably did leave the party at ten, after which he may or may not have visited this nameless lady. Davis saw him at quarter to two. Mackay saw him, too, but can't say when.'

'He didn't see Scudder, though,' said Priestley defensively.

'Yes, but I'm not sure whether to believe him. Then there's the letter opener.' Taylor tapped the package in his hand. 'Adams is one of those who might have owned one. So is Mackay.'

'True,' acknowledged Priestley. 'But neither is stupid, and it seems foolish in the extreme to have left it in the body, if it could be used to identify them.'

'People rarely think rationally when they commit crimes. You'd be surprised at the number of people I've caught because of something like an easily identifiable weapon. Another thing is that Mackay, Adams, Marshall, England and even Murray admit to disliking Scudder. They found him arrogant and argumentative, while he made brazen moves to have Murray's position for himself.'

'And lastly, we have the three hopefuls,' continued Priestley, leaning forward to consult his timetable. 'Nigel Vallen left the party at about eleven o'clock with O'Brien. They had planned on going sooner, but Nigel felt he needed to stay so that no one blamed him for the raspberry tart incident. He stopped briefly at the ship, then took a cab home to his father, who says he arrived home at eleven-forty. He went to bed, and his father confirms that he did not leave the house until the following morning, so he's out of our reckoning. That leaves O'Brien and Yaxley.'

'Yaxley had quarrelled with Scudder, and I see a blank on your page for his whereabouts.'

'He claims he was out walking, and O'Brien can confirm this to a point. They strolled around together, discussing how they might raise money to ensure that both of them were selected for the expedition, but they parted at half past twelve. O'Brien has an alibi in the form of his landlady, who was angry that he made noise when he came in, but Yaxley has no idea what time he arrived home.

'So,' concluded Taylor, 'there's our rogues' gallery: Marshall, England, Murray, Adams, Mackay and Yaxley. And then there are the dockhands, at least ten of whom have been unable to prove their whereabouts. Of course, people have told me from the start that Scudder's death was a bungled robbery.'

'I know you don't believe that, though,' said Priestley. 'You think Scudder was too fastidious to mix with dockhands, and that he was killed by someone he knew. And much as it grieves me to say it, I think you're right.'

Chapter 6

Number Nine Regent Street was an excellent office for the expedition. It was centrally located, and a large banner above its windows proclaimed to passing London that here was the headquarters of what Shackleton had grandly named the British Antarctic Expedition. Visitors were urged inside where, for a nominal fee, they could visit a small exhibition of polar equipment, with an expedition member often available to explain details. Bowls and bottles were discreetly placed in the hope that people might find the venture worthy of a further donation.

'Do they?' asked Taylor of Priestley as they walked inside. It was busier than he had expected, with a score of visitors inspecting the displays and talking to those who had been detailed to liaise with the public that day.

'More than you might think,' replied Priestley. 'A troop of boy scouts came, and were so taken with us that they went away and raised twenty-five pounds with a jumble sale. Then one old lady handed me what she said was a trifle, but turned out to be a ten-pound note. Of course, most of the time we're counting shillings and pennies. Still, the purpose isn't *just* to get money, but to raise awareness. The expedition is for the glory of the Empire, after all.'

While Priestley went to fetch Mackay and Adams, Taylor took the opportunity to explore the headquarters. Only one room had been given over to the exhibition; the others were offices where Shackleton, Adams and the expedition manager, Alfred Reid, could host suppliers or sponsors, interview prospective members, order and receive equipment, and carry out the thousand and one tasks that needed doing before the expedition left. They also served as a repository for delicate or valuable items, until they were ready to go aboard *Nimrod*.

The entire building was alive, and the hubbub indicated that a lot of work was being done in the dwindling time left before the departure. As Taylor wandered around, several expedition members nodded greetings, and he could read the question in their eyes: have you caught the killer?

Among them were Wild, Joyce and Nigel Vallen, the latter identifiable by the sudden sound of something being dropped. Taylor watched him retrieve it, inspect it carefully, and then place it gently on a table. He noticed that everyone seemed so used to Vallen's clumsiness that the sound of items bouncing off the floor had attracted little attention. Nigel grinned sheepishly when he saw Taylor watching him, and turned to a pile of papers, some of which promptly skipped through his fingers to flutter in all directions.

'Poor lad,' said Wild indulgently. 'Some folk are dainty, like fairies, and others lack the gentle touch. Still, he's a willing chap, and there won't be much he can break once we get south. We'll just have to remember to keep him away from the scientific equipment and chemicals.'

'Did Scudder have a gentle touch?' asked Taylor.

Wild nodded. 'Oh yes. Your own mother couldn't have been more tender. That alone would have made him valuable.'

'Of course, he wouldn't have been as good as that other fellow we all liked,' added Joyce, taking what looked like a large pocket watch from a box and inspecting it with great care. 'The one who didn't reply to Shackleton's letter inviting him to a second interview. What was his name, Frank?'

'John Gray,' replied Wild. 'No, Nigel! Stay away from the marine chronometers, there's a good lad. The Admiralty have only lent them to us, and they'll be wanting them back after the expedition, preferably whole and working.'

Joyce reached out a hand that just prevented the hopeful from blundering into the boxes he was examining, and sent him on his way with a firm but well-intentioned push. He and Wild exchanged a wary but indulgent smile.

Unwilling to interrupt their work, Taylor entered the more sedate atmosphere of the exhibition room, which displayed samples of cumbersome polar clothing and rations of food. He was alarmed to note that the ship's biscuit looked disconcertingly similar to one of Ruby's ginger nuts. He joined three elderly ladies staring at a pair of woollen gloves, and fully concurred with their opinion that they would be wholly inadequate to keep out the cold in such a bitter, nasty place.

'Those are mine,' said Priestley, coming to join him.

Taylor was shocked. 'They wouldn't keep *me* warm

during a *London* winter! Surely, they're going to provide you with something better than that? They are so...*thin*.'

'They're standard wool ones, no thinner than normal. But remember: they're only under-gloves. Outside them, we'll be wearing wolfskin mittens, which the Boss has ordered from Norway.'

'So you'll be fully attired in fur?'

'No, the Boss has decided to use furs only for gloves, footwear, and sleeping bags.'

'Well, at least you'll be warm when you're asleep, then.'

'That's the plan, and the bags might be cosier than you imagine. Most are singles, but some are for three men, which should provide a lot of additional warmth.'

'Then I'll keep my fingers crossed that your sleeping companions don't have my wife's icy feet. You wouldn't want the likes of *them* on you in the middle of the night.'

'That's what husbands are for,' said one of the old women haughtily. 'They're certainly not much use for anything else, the idle buggers!'

Priestley pursed his lips as she and her companions moved away to inspect a pair of skis. 'She must be Adams' mother. He said she might visit today, and that she wouldn't refrain from speaking her mind. But here he is now, and Mackay with him.'

'Make this quick, will you, laddie?' said Mackay without preamble. 'Some of the medical supplies have just been delivered, and I need to do an inventory at once. I don't want to get south and find we haven't been given the correct medicines.'

'Of course.' Taylor removed the letter opener from its wrappings and laid it on a nearby table.

'What's that?' asked Adams, bemused.

'A letter opener,' said Mackay impatiently. 'Although I can't imagine why the inspector should consider it of interest to us. We won't need one where we're going.'

'It's the weapon that was used to kill Scudder,' said Taylor, watching them intently, and aware of Priestley doing the same. 'Have either of you seen it before?'

'Jesus, God Almighty!' cursed Adams, bending down to peer at it. 'Is it really?'

'No blasphemy, Jameson,' came a shrill voice from across the room. 'What have I told you before about taking the Lord's name in vain? You're just like your father with your bloody bad language.'

'Sorry,' called Adams. He smiled apologetically at Taylor. 'It doesn't look familiar to me.'

'Well?' asked Taylor, when Mackay made no effort to reply. 'Is it yours, then?'

'No,' said the Scot shortly. 'And I don't have time for this nonsense. I didn't kill Scudder, and I resent you implying that I did. Why ask *me* about that knife? Why not Wild or Joyce?'

'Because they haven't held commissions in the Royal Navy,' said Taylor, unperturbed by the man's hostility. 'You have, so would be in a position to own an implement like this one.'

'First, this knife is RNR, not Royal Navy. I was in the *real* Service,' snapped Mackay angrily. 'Second, it's common knowledge that one can buy these from any naval outfitter. *You* could have one, for all I know. However, I assure you that *I* do not.'

'Captain England said the same thing about acquiring them,' Priestley agreed. 'So have you seen anyone else with one? This is important, Mackay. Please think carefully.'

Mackay relented at Priestley's appeal, and leaned down to pick it up. Almost immediately, he dropped it with a cry. 'Jesus Christ, that's sharp! I've just cut myself.'

'Jameson!'

'That wasn't me, mother.'

'I'm bleeding!' shouted Mackay, fumbling in his pocket for a handkerchief. 'What are you thinking of, handing such a dangerous thing to unsuspecting people? I might have sliced a tendon or sustained a serious injury that would have prevented me from travelling south! I wasn't expecting a letter opener to be sharp – they're not supposed to be honed like that.'

'Exactly,' said Taylor mildly. 'As a murder weapon, it's unique, perhaps designed specially for the purpose.'

'But not by me, laddie,' fumed Mackay, wrapping the cloth around his finger. 'And now, if you'll excuse me, I have important work to do.'

He shouldered his way through a gaggle of people who had stopped inspecting a sledge to watch the altercation, leaving Priestley embarrassed and Taylor wondering whether the vehement denial could be a case of 'he doth protest too much.' Was Mackay's temper a response to the pressure of an approaching sailing date, or was there a more sinister reason – especially as the cut had been little more than a nick? He turned his attention to Adams, who blew out his lips in a sigh.

'I can't deny that I was in the RNR for a number of years, inspector. I was offered a permanent commission in the Royal Navy last year, but turned it down to join this expedition. But unfortunately, I can't help you either.

I don't own one of these things – I'm not a letter opener sort of man. I prefer to use my teeth in the rare event of anyone writing to me.'

'Nonsense, Jameson,' said the old woman. 'Don't you tell falsehoods to that man! I gave you a pretty brass letter opener for Christmas, and you bloody well told me you wouldn't be without it.'

Adams looked indescribably guilty. He gave a smile that lacked humour, muttered something about having one or two such items lying around at home, and shot away when Nigel dropped something that sent purple liquid splattering across the floor. He busied himself by rushing for mops and water, and made it clear that he had no intention of returning to Taylor.

'I'm not a man for tales, but I don't like to see the police misled,' said Wild, watching the chaos with an unhappy face. 'Mackay is wrong, and so is the captain: I've been to naval outfitters, and you *can't* buy such letter openers.'

Taylor frowned. 'Are you sure?'

'I'm positive, Inspector. A friend of my father's was desperate to have one of these things, but he never received the official approval he needed to buy one. I'm afraid our captain and surgeon have both got the wrong end of the stick.'

'Yes,' said Taylor blandly. 'I expect that's what happened.'

Taylor and Priestley showed the letter opener to the rest of the staff at the Expedition Office, but no one admitted to seeing it before. Priestley started to hand it to Nigel, but Wild intervened hastily, claiming that it would be like giving a stick of dynamite to a baby. Thus, Nigel was enjoined to inspect the weapon from a distance. Jokingly, Wild steered him to the far end of the room, claiming it was the only place Nigel would be safe from it, so Taylor doubted he could see more than the wrappings. Wild's antics made the others smile, and the tension that had filled the room after Mackay's explosion began to dissipate. The laughter stopped abruptly when Shackleton arrived.

'You must think we don't care, Will,' he said, glaring admonishingly at his people. 'Sniggering and cackling over a blade that was driven through the neck of a colleague.'

'Not at all. It's just a way of dealing with a shock.'

'I might agree, if it had been anyone other than Scudder,' said Shackleton unhappily. 'But I've a feeling he won't be much mourned. Speaking of mourning, have you visited his mother yet?'

'Sergeant Grant took her the news, and I'm going to see her tomorrow. Do you want to come?'

'Not tomorrow.' Shackleton consulted a piece of paper heavily scribbled with notes and dates. 'I'll go on Saturday, and ask Emily to come with me. This kind of thing may go better with a woman's gentle touch. It's a pity you can't take Ruby.'

'I don't think *she'd* provide a gentle touch,' said Taylor, surprised his friend should think she might.

Shackleton considered. 'No, perhaps not. But Emily will.' He glanced at his watch. 'Ye gods! I must get back to the ship. The Earl of Iveagh is due to visit at four. Care for a lift?'

Taylor and Priestley accepted, but none of them spoke

144

during the journey. Taylor was preoccupied with Adams' lie about owning a letter opener – which he would have believed if the man had not been contradicted by his mother. Worse, Adams had sent Berry and Riches to patrol the far end of the quay on a flimsy pretext. And what of the woman he claimed as his alibi? Was she real, or an invention? Singly, the facts were nothing, but taken together they set Taylor's senses jangling.

Meanwhile, Priestley had also found Adams' stories wanting and was distressed by it. And Shackleton was a man bowed down with care: had the pressure under which he had placed his men caused one to crack? Would *Nimrod* sail loaded with debts he would spend the rest of his life trying to pay off? And how was he to tell one or two of the hopefuls that their labours in helping the expedition had been in vain?

He was also uneasy about Taylor. He had asked Hamilton to allocate him to the enquiry because he knew him to be solid, careful and discreet. But he had been appalled to read that the Headless Bishop's murder remained unsolved because Taylor was incompetent. He did not like to think ill of his friends, but he was beginning to wonder if he should have asked for someone else.

They arrived at the East India Docks, where Shackleton hurried away to greet the Earl – the scion of the great family of Irish brewers famous for Guinness – who was ten minutes early. Taylor and Priestley, meanwhile, went to re-interview a score of dockhands.

As he went, Shackleton wished one would leap to his feet and confess, but he saw the dark, weather-stained, surly faces, and knew these were not men to be moved by remorse. No, if the murder had been committed by a dockhand, the only way Taylor would ever have him in a cell would be with hard evidence and cunning detection. The Boss only hoped he was capable of it.

It was almost nine o'clock and dusk when Taylor and Priestley finished with the dockhands. One man had confessed to burgling three houses in nearby Bloomsbury Street, but they had nothing else to show for their labours. All those interviewed had met Scudder, about half had worked with him, and several had admitted that they disliked him because he treated them shabbily. But that was all. Taylor was disheartened as he passed the statements to a constable to take to the station for typing.

'Ruby won't be pleased with you,' remarked Priestley, as left the East India Docks office. He breathed in deeply, although the air reeked of hot dust and stagnant water. 'You're late again.'

'She's staying with her mother tonight,' replied Taylor, trying to ease a kink from his neck. He felt grimy, full of the stink of the cheap cigarettes favoured by the dockhands. 'It's her birthday.'

Priestley stared at him. 'You missed your wife's birthday?'

'Her mother's birthday. I should have been at a cake-hack…cake-*cutting* ceremony at six, which I forgot, so I'll be in trouble tomorrow. Still, I have tonight free.'

'To do what? Visit rough taverns in London Pool again?'

Taylor nodded. It was the last thing he felt like doing, but unless he found Long Ron soon, the man might disappear forever, as was the way with such people.

'Then I'll come with you,' determined Priestley suddenly. 'I'm sure I've seen worse, and besides, maybe I'll bring you better luck than last time.'

Taylor smiled. 'Thank you, but no. You're tired, too, and—'

'Nonsense! I'm as fresh as a daisy. Besides, if your witness fails to show up, then at least you'll have me to talk to.'

Taylor started to argue, but then capitulated. He liked Priestley, and his company would certainly make a tavern-trawl less objectionable. They left the docks just as the great wrought-iron gates were closing for the night. Ives was there, and Taylor had the impression that his patrols would be assiduous for a while – at least until the police had gone.

It had been a hot day, clear and blue, and the setting sun silhouetted the dockside cranes. Twilight was descending, although it was still too early for lamps to be lit. Priestley jumped in alarm when a man suddenly scuttled out of some nearby bushes and approached them, touching his hand to a greasy bowler hat.

'Evening, gents,' he said in a hoarse growl. 'Finished for the day? I expect you're in need of a glass of cool beer. I know a place that sells the best in London—'

'What do you want, Faris?' asked Taylor wearily.

Priestley made a moue of disgust. 'Not Bernard Faris of *The Star*?'

'The very same,' said Faris proudly. 'And what I want is a chat, inspector. I've been told by my contacts in the docks that someone was murdered here – a gent of the scientific persuasion.'

Taylor raised his eyebrows. 'And?'

'And I was wondering whether you could give me a quote – a quote, say, about the fact that he was stabbed in the neck, but that it wasn't robbery, because nothing was stolen.'

'What makes you say that?'

'Well, it must be an important murder, or they wouldn't still have an inspector on site – even though it's only the man who lets the Headless Bishop's killer walk free among decent folk.'

'Now just a minute,' started Priestley indignantly. 'I don't—'

Taylor stopped him from saying more. 'This is Faris' way – if wheedling doesn't produce information, he tries insults, in the hope that his victim will object and let something slip in anger. But he knows it won't work with me.'

Faris scowled. 'The East India was swarming with coppers a couple of days ago, although most have gone now. Your station cutting costs again, is it? Giving inadequate service to the people of London to save a few pound?'

'Good night, Faris,' said Taylor, walking away.

Priestley was obliged to trot to catch up with him, leaving the reporter behind. 'What a grubby little fellow! Now I've seen him, I can imagine him sitting in some dirty alehouse, jotting his nasty thoughts on the backs of envelopes. Do you think he'll write about Scudder?'

Taylor nodded. It was only ever a matter of time before the press smelled the case, and he supposed he had been fortunate not to have been cornered by Faris sooner.

'But he doesn't know much, or he wouldn't have tried

his luck with me. We've crossed swords previously, and he knows I won't talk to him. He's obviously desperate.'

'I hope he doesn't find out about our list of suspects,' said Priestley worriedly. 'That was exactly what the Boss was hoping to avoid. Crikey! I left that sheet in Ives' office, with all those names and alibis on it. Supposing he gets hold of it?'

'It's in my pocket,' said Taylor, still walking briskly. 'I've learned never to leave things like that lying around, not even in my station.'

Priestley rubbed his chin, then caught Taylor's arm, forcing the inspector to stop and look at him.

'Faris knows that Scudder was stabbed, but that nothing was stolen. That's not general knowledge – his contact at the docks couldn't have known it. The information had to come from somewhere else.'

'Yes,' said Taylor shortly. 'I had worked that out.'

'None of *us* would have gone to the press with that sort of information, so it stands to reason that one of your officers tipped him off.'

'We can't know that for certain,' said Taylor, although his voice carried no conviction.

Priestley gazed at him intently. 'But you're not surprised. You've experienced problems like this before – that's why you took my notes when we left Ives' office.' He paused for a moment. 'This is what happened with the Headless Bishop, isn't it? There's a rotten apple among your colleagues, and he's making your job more difficult than it should be. I suppose that's why you agreed to let me help you – I'm not police, and therefore I'm untainted.'

Taylor returned the stare. 'You're too astute for your

own good.'

Priestley frowned unhappily. 'This isn't good news! The Headless Bishop has become a dreadful scandal, and I hope the same thing doesn't happen with Scudder.'

'So do I,' said Taylor softly.

The two walked along Limehouse's main road, and then trudged through grimy, warehouse-lined streets, ultimately reaching the seedy alehouses – the Speckled Hen and the Lord Nelson – that Joe Bacon had claimed were the favourite haunts of Long Ron.

The journey gave them ample time to discuss Scudder's murder, Faris' appearance having intensified the pressure on both to solve it. Taylor felt he was reaching the end of his tether: his wife was resentful because he was rarely at home, and he trusted no one at his station, not even his chief superintendent. Meanwhile, Priestley had less than three weeks to carry out his first direct order from the Boss, *and* to ensure the geological part of the expedition was in order.

Taylor soon found himself confiding to Priestley in a way he had not spoken to anyone in months; the young man was an attentive and sympathetic listener, and had a clarity of thought the policeman found helpful.

'Logic tells me Adams is our man,' he said. 'For four reasons: his only alibi is this mysterious woman whose name he refuses to divulge; he forged the opportunity by sending Riches and Berry to the far end of the quay; he had a motive, because he disliked Scudder; and the murder weapon was a letter opener, and he lied about owning one. I imagine he's having strong words with his mother tonight.'

'His lady *might* exist,' hedged Priestley. 'You tell me he said "Hel" before he stopped himself, suggesting her name is Helen or Helena. He wouldn't have made that slip if she were a figment of his imagination.'

'True.'

'And think about the timing. Adams told Riches and Berry to go to the east end of the quay *after* Scudder had been killed. Scudder died at twenty past one, and Adams gave the men their orders at quarter to two or so. That's twenty-five minutes later.'

Taylor sighed. 'My suspicions are all based on circumstantial evidence in any case – I can't arrest Adams, because a good lawyer will have him out in a trice. Your Boss would be unimpressed that I couldn't prove my case, while mine might use it as an excuse to demand my resignation.'

'I don't like the sound of your chief superintendent.'

Taylor shrugged. 'He has a tiny budget, yet is expected to stem a rising wave of crime. With scant resources, it's his duty to provide plenty of well-trained detectives, an army of constables, surgeons for post-mortems, the storage of murder victims in a mortuary – which costs more than you might think – a staff of clerks to file and prepare paperwork, the upkeep of the station, various chemical tests…the list is endless, but the funding isn't.'

'Would he throw you to the dogs in order to acquire more?'

Taylor nodded. 'He could use my failure in the Headless Bishop case – and perhaps Scudder's murder – to prove under-funding is responsible.'

'And you're content to let him do that?'

'Of course not, but I don't see how I can stop it –

unless I manage to solve both cases in the next few days, before the matter is raised in the House.'

'Then we'd better get on with it,' suggested Priestley. 'Here we are at the Lord Nelson. Let's see whether Long Ron can help you out of your predicament.'

The Lord Nelson was not the kind of place two respectable men would normally have chosen to spend an evening. It was squalid, with paint peeling from the walls, dirty brown ceilings and sawdust on the floor. Sawdust was usually used so it could be swept out with the other filth on a daily basis, but this was ancient stuff, and it vied for space with cigarette butts, spilled food, slimy secretions that Priestley thought were gobs of phlegm, and mud from boots.

The clientele was equally sleazy. Most wore greasy caps pulled over their eyes, giving the impression they did not wish to be identified, and the sharp scent of urine and body odour vied for dominance with the stench of cheap tobacco. Several dogs sniffed around the milling legs, noses to the floor as they occasionally swallowed something they deemed edible. Priestley muttered that they made him feel sick.

'Don't watch, then. And pull up your coat collar. Your clean shirt is drawing attention.'

'Well, you look like a policeman,' Priestley hissed back. 'And this is the kind of place where policemen aren't welcome.'

'I'm used to not being welcome. But if it bothers you, you should wait outside.'

'I'm not leaving you in here alone. Besides, I'm not entirely useless in a fracas.'

'For God's sake don't start a fight in here!' whispered Taylor, appalled. 'That would see the end of both of us for certain, and then we'd have the likes of Grant investigating *our* murders. Smile. Pretend to be a bit witless. Don't let anyone but the barman know that you aren't drinking alcohol. And *please* don't try to pay for the drinks with that half-sovereign! Use coppers.'

They found a seat near the door, and once the tavern's occupants had stopped staring at them, Taylor leaned across to the next table, slipped a coin across the surface and asked if Long Ron was in that night. The coin disappeared without a word, and Taylor went back to his beer.

'Is that it?' whispered Priestley, startled. 'They've taken your money, but haven't told you where Long Ron is sitting, or even if he's here.'

'Wait.'

They did, and eventually a man of extraordinary height unwound himself from a chair near the empty hearth and made his way towards them. Long Ron settled himself at their table, and Taylor pushed a glass of beer towards him. Long Ron drank some, sat silently for a while, then finished the glass. Taylor made no move to ask questions, and Priestley looked from one to the other in confusion, not understanding the rules or the ritual that was being played out in front of him.

'Right, Mr Policeman,' said Long Ron, once a second glass of beer had been bought and consumed. 'What can I do for you?'

'I'm told you know something about the Headless Bishop,' said Taylor. 'You saw someone running away from the river at about the time he was killed. Someone carrying a bag.'

'That's right.' Ron sounded pleased with himself. 'I seen a gent leaving Fountain Dock the night before the news came out about what happened. I never knew at the time, obviously, or I might have took a bit more notice of him.'

'What can you remember?'

'Not much. It was one o'clock in the morning, because I heard the bells going in St James's Church. I was coming home from work – from work. D'you know what I mean?'

'No,' replied Priestley.

'He does,' said Ron, nodding at Taylor. 'So shut up.'

'He means he was sober, so we've no reason to doubt him,' explained Taylor briefly. 'What else, Ron?'

'Fountain Dock, like all them wharves off Bermondsey Wall, ain't got no public entrance, but there's a bit of the fence what's broken. Nippers use it for fishing on Sundays. Anyway, I was coming home, and I saw this chap slide out through the hole in the fence. Obviously at that time of night he was up to no good, so I ducked into a doorway to wait till he'd gone. He was carrying a bag.'

'What kind of bag?'

'It's awful hot in here, and me throat's cruel dry.'

Priestley gathered the empties and headed to the bar. When he returned, he was surprised to find Ron had waited before continuing his tale, and saw he had underestimated the power of free beer.

'A big bag,' Ron went on, after a substantial gulp. 'And heavy. He was struggling with it, gasping under its weight, like. Now I look back, I realise it contained the head, feet and hands of the Headless Bishop.'

'Head, feet and hands wouldn't have been that heavy,' said Priestley, earning a resentful glare from Ron. 'Well, they wouldn't! It's not like this villain was carrying a whole corpse.'

'Well, the man *I* saw was struggling,' said Ron shortly. 'And I heard him mutter to himself.'

'What did he say?' asked Taylor.

'He was whispering about forgiveness and the like. I reckon he was sorry for what he done, and was praying to his god. But it didn't stop him from making off with them hands, feet and head, did it?'

'Did you see his face?'

'No, thank the good Lord, because I'd have seen the face of Satan. All I saw was a cove in a dark coat carrying a bag.'

'Did you follow him, or see where he went?'

'He came right past me hiding place, and continued up Salisbury Street before turning right along Jamaica Road. I was going to follow him, see where he went, but, to tell the truth, I never liked his muttering. It was...well, it was creepy.'

'In what way?' asked Priestley.

'Like he was deranged. I didn't want to get involved with a lunatic, so I stayed hiding till he'd turned onto Jamaica Road. But then I got to wondering about what he might have been doing, and whether he might have left something of interest to a fellow like me.'

'You mean something you could steal?' asked Priestley before Taylor's heel digging into the top of his foot told him to keep quiet.

'I mean something I could take to the police and claim

a reward for finding, like any honest citizen,' replied Ron stiffly. 'I went to the loose fence and squeezed through. And then I seen someone lying on the ground, by the water.'

'A dead someone?' asked Priestley, drawn into the tale, despite himself.

'A body,' nodded Ron. 'Naked and headless, lying on the moonlit mud as it waited for the tide to come and take it.'

'I see,' said Taylor. 'And then what did you do?'

'I buggered off home, and I ain't never seen the killer since, thank God.'

'No, that's *not* what happened, Ron,' said Taylor softly. 'He wasn't naked, he was covered with a blanket – I saw the impressions of it in the mud. And he was moved, too. He wasn't where the killer left him.'

Ron's expression was furtive. 'Someone else must have took the blanket.'

'Listen, Ron. I don't care about the blanket. All I want is the truth. Supposing next time it's your sister or a friend – one of the people drinking with you tonight? You can help me stop him.'

Ron underwent a visible inner battle, which Priestley watched in fascination. He had never seen so many clearly etched emotions in a human face: guilt, fear, shame, avarice.

'All right,' said Ron eventually. 'I seen the body on the mud, and I knew the tide would have it if I left it where it was, and I didn't like the notion of that queer cove getting away with murder, like. So, I took hold of it and I pulled it clear. Then, as I was setting it down, the blanket came loose. It felt like a nice one, so I thought I might as well have it. My woman washed it good, and sold it in the market for a shilling the next day.'

'Did you look at the body?'

Ron shuddered. 'I ain't no lover of corpses, not since our Annie copped it in the night, and I woke up next to her. I glanced back after I'd whipped off...after I gently removed the blanket what it wouldn't be needing no more. It was mostly in shadows by then, so I couldn't have seen it good, even if I'd wanted to, but I seen the carving of the mitre on its chest, like what they mentioned in the papers, and I saw he was short.'

'What did the man you saw leaving look like?'

'Medium height and average build – not fat, not thin.'

'Was he wearing a hat?'

Ron frowned. 'Yes, now I think of it. Not a cap, but a proper hat. Hard. One of them bowlers what city gents has. He must have nicked it, or had it off the Salvation Army.'

'And what about his coat? It was warm that night, but you say he was wearing a coat.'

'He was,' said Ron, nodding vigorously. 'And it was loose, like it didn't belong to him.'

'Did you see anyone else that night who might have run into this man?'

Long Ron shook his head. 'It was late, so most of the pubs were closed, and it's always a bit deserted around there, on account of there not being many houses – just factories and the like. That's why I decided against following him. What would I have done if he'd come at me? I could have hollered, but no one would have come to help.'

'Thank you, Ron,' said Taylor, with apparent sincerity. 'You've been very helpful.'

Cape Royds: March, 1908

Mount Erebus has been conquered. After seven days, the party returned late last night, five having made it to the top. Only Philip didn't reach the summit; his feet were badly frostbitten, so he was left in his sleeping bag at a camp, while the others finished the ascent to the active crater. This morning he's been hobbling about in his pyjamas and overcoat, his feet a horrid sight, all black, red and green, and bloated beyond measure. I pray that he doesn't lose them.

Everyone was greatly pleased with the achievement and full of plans for the future, particularly the Prof and Mawson, who want to begin work on their geological samples immediately. But not me: the Boss won't permit me to work with them until I've finished writing about Scudder's murder.

It's hard to believe that it happened only eight months ago. Looking back, I was so inexperienced, so unsophisticated, so credulous – my naïveté is amazing to me now. I suppose it was a reflection of my upbringing as a non-smoking, non-swearing, teetotal Wesleyan Methodist. I'd been raised in a non-conformist atmosphere: chapel twice on Sundays and the Wesley Guild in the middle of the week. London was the farthest I'd ever been from Tewkesbury, a town of less than six thousand souls. Then I was selected for a role on a stage that the whole world was watching, not to mention a separate stage where much of the production went on behind the scenes, so to speak. And all of this before my twenty-first birthday.

It had been one thing to associate with Wild, Joyce and Roberts, men who lived hard, played hard and never liked to hear someone say 'no' to the offer of a drink. Even I, after a night of many rounds of whiskey and beer – or, in my case, ginger ale – had helped get Roberts (Bobs as we call him) aboard ship by slinging him in a coal-basket and hauling him up; then we rolled him into a bunk where he remained motionless for most of the next day. There was no coffee from him that next morning.

But it was another to be involved in two murder enquiries, where everything was deadly serious and dangerous, and where high jinks never entered. The places I was being taken by Will Taylor, the things I was being shown, were of a different order of magnitude. Even the drinking, gambling and selling of women's bodies that was going on in the Lord Nelson wasn't the worst of it. Corpses were part of the investigation, too, and there seemed every chance that one of my colleagues had sent Scudder to meet our Maker. For someone whose worst sin to date had been dozing off in Chapel, this was all too appalling, despite my attempts to put a brave face on the matter. Little did I know that it was soon going to become even worse.

Chapter 7

Outside the Lord Nelson, the air was mercifully free of smoke. Priestley took a deep breath, then hurried after Taylor, who was moving away at a rapid lick.

'What's the hurry,' he gasped, breaking into a trot to keep up.

'We can't linger here. The word will soon get around that the police were questioning Long Ron. Hopefully, the word will include that we're investigating a murderer no one much likes, but someone still might take umbrage at our presence here.'

'So you have your first witness,' said Priestley, glancing around nervously. 'Someone who saw a man carrying parts of your Headless Bishop from the scene.'

'I have a witness,' agreed Taylor, still walking fast. 'And I know two things I didn't before. First, the killer left the body for the tide to take – I saw the drag marks in the mud and assumed he'd had second thoughts, but that was Long Ron's doing. And second, the killer left the corpse decently covered – when I saw it, it was exposed.'

'I don't see why either is important.'

'They reveal a state of mind. A body stripped and

dumped in a place where it might be eaten by rats is a lot different to a body wrapped in a blanket and set carefully at the water's edge.'

'They both sound nasty to me,' said Priestley with a shudder.

'I'm not saying one is better than the other, only that they're not the same. That the killer was muttering is interesting, too, and suggests, as Ron said, that he was uncomfortable with his actions.'

'You don't think he'll do it again, then?'

Taylor shrugged. 'I'm told a second murder is easier than the first. However, a man leaving a blanket-swathed body on a riverbank is a far cry from the decapitating monster portrayed in the press. It makes me wonder whether the culprit even knows that we've found his victim! He's probably thanking his lucky stars that *he* didn't meet the Headless Bishop's killer while he dumped his own corpse.'

'He may become curious enough to check,' suggested Priestley hopefully. 'He may revisit the site, to make sure the evidence of his own crime has gone.'

'I had a constable there for three weeks, but he only ever caught boys carrying out dares. The sensational newspapers have everyone else too frightened to go near the place – probably including the killer. But Ron's statement has allowed me to answer several questions that have been niggling since the case began, although it has raised others – such as what was in the bag.'

'We know what was in the bag,' said Priestley. 'Bits of your Bishop.'

Taylor smiled grimly. 'No, it wasn't. And your assumption underlines the danger of believing everything written in the papers. You see, the Headless Bishop wasn't *headless*, nor was he handless and footless. He was perfectly intact, although his corpse was stolen before the pathologist could examine it properly. Unfortunately, its disappearance meant we couldn't refute the stories about is missing parts.'

Priestley gaped at him. 'The Headless Bishop is just the Bishop?'

Taylor nodded. 'Just a normal corpse in all respects, except for the puncture wound in the chest that probably killed him. I remarked to some of my colleagues that there were no identifying features on the body – meaning no clothes, jewellery or papers – and this was eventually interpreted as meaning no head, hands or feet. It was like Chinese Whispers, where words become warped with repetition.'

'There was a report of a broken knee – of torture.'

'Yes, but that was untrue, too.'

'This is incredible,' breathed Priestley. 'The real horror about the Headless Bishop story is that parts of the body were missing. Now you say they weren't.'

Taylor nodded again. 'The press whipped up a frenzy about what was just a simple stabbing.

'But Ron said he saw...' Priestley trailed off. 'But he didn't, did he? He was afraid to look at the body, and it was dark.'

'Yes, and he just told us that he pulled it – wrapped in the blanket – from the moonlit shore to the shadows of the upper bank. It was only when he got it there that he took off the covers – at which point, he couldn't have seen the body, even if he'd wanted to. He saw enough to think it was short, and assumed that was because it was lacking a head. However, Long Ron has earned his nickname for a reason: most people will appear short to someone his height.'

'So Ron went to Faris and told him all this rubbish,' surmised Priestley. 'But he left out that the body was decently covered by a blanket, and his testimony encouraged Faris to believe the lie about the mutilation. But none of it is true, so why didn't you refute Faris' claims?'

'I was ready to do just that, but Hamilton ordered me to wait for the furore to subside of its own accord. Of course, it hasn't, and now it's too late. We can't prove our point anyway, because the body is gone.'

They had reached London Bridge, which was better lit, so Taylor slowed down. It was a considerable relief to discuss the case, and although he had only known Priestley for a few days, he already trusted him more than colleagues with whom he had worked for a decade.

'What a mess,' said Priestley, appalled. 'No wonder you haven't been able to solve it. What *do* you know that's accurate?'

'The victim was in his early or middle thirties. Dark hair, worn slightly long. I didn't look at his eyes when I was at Fountain Dock – I assumed the pathologist would do that.'

'You looked at Scudder's eyes,' said Priestley, recalling his revulsion and Marshall's sharp reprimand. 'Now I understand why.'

'Rough hands, as though he was used to manual work,' Taylor continued, 'and strong, well-muscled arms and legs. There was a bruise on his hip that was several days old: it looked as though he had walked into a table.'

'You searched Fountain Dock, I assume?'

'Of course, but all we found was a cap, which I can't be sure was associated with the body – it might have been washed there by the river, or thrown away or lost by someone completely unrelated.'

'How close was it to the corpse?'

'Not very. There were all sorts of other items we discounted, too – mostly because of the amount of mud covering them, which was indicative of their length of stay. However, while the killer's plan to have his victim claimed by the Thames might have been thwarted, he was careful to leave no other clues. We couldn't find anything, despite searching for a good six hours.'

'What sort of cap was it?'

'A cotton one, like those worn by sportsmen. It was trampled into the mud, perhaps by the killer, perhaps by the victim, but more likely by the first constables to arrive. However, as I said, we can't be sure to whom it belonged.'

'Would Long Ron have stolen this hat, had he seen it?'

'Possibly. However, I had a constable make inquiries at the Lord Nelson yesterday, and the amount Ron has spent there recently is about what he would have had from Faris, plus the shilling for the blanket. I don't think he took anything else.'

'So, which part of his tale *do* you believe?'

'A man emerging from Fountain Dock wearing a hat and a baggy coat, even though the night was warm, rings true, because the killer had probably disguised himself. Then Ron almost certainly did follow the man until the muttering unnerved him, but being naturally greedy, he risked returning to the dock to see whether he could find anything to his advantage.'

'And got the fright of his life by discovering a corpse.'

Taylor nodded. 'I also believe he moved it, because murder and theft are two very different kettles of fish, and he was loath for the body to be washed away by the tide as the killer clearly intended. Ron is a thief; he doesn't condone homicide.'

'And which bits *don't* you believe?'

'If the killer was carrying a bag, it didn't contain body parts, since our corpse wasn't missing any. Ron didn't see the carving of a bishop's mitre on the chest, either, because there wasn't one. He included it in what he told us because I imagine he believes it lends a certain ghoulish credence to his tale.'

'Did Faris invent that particular detail, then?'

'No. I did.'

Priestley gaped at him. 'You? How? Why?'

'When the story first appeared in the press, I suspected one of my colleagues had been to Faris, and was angry enough to want to catch him out. I invented the tale of the carved mitre to trap him. I told Grant.'

'Then Grant is the leak?'

'Unfortunately, Hamilton overheard me, and included it in a briefing to the entire station the following day.' Taylor laughed bitterly. 'So, the Headless Bishop was neither decapitated nor marked with a mitre, and his hideous nickname is almost entirely my fault. Since then, the case has degenerated into a gruesome nightmare. My only hope is to solve the murder and expose the truth, but since Long Ron is the closest I've come to a witness, my chances of success are virtually non-existent.'

The next day was cloudy, and the air still, humid and sultry. The leaves on the trees hung limp and flat, and Priestley sweated inside his cotton suit as he waited outside Waterloo Station for Taylor. The atmosphere was not improved by the belching engines that hissed and wheezed at their platforms, sending palls of soot-filled steam towards the lofty Victorian ceilings. Normally, he would have been delighted to leave the city for the cleaner air of the suburbs, but the prospect of visiting Scudder's mother robbed the jaunt of any potential enjoyment.

At ten to nine, two minutes before the train was due to leave, Taylor arrived at a run, indicating with a flap of his hand that Priestley was to lead the way to the platform because he was too breathless to speak.

'I was beginning to think I might have to go alone,' said Priestley accusingly as he went. 'You said you'd be here half an hour ago. Did you oversleep?'

Still grumbling, he dashed to where the London and South Western Railway's eight fifty-two to Twickenham – where they would change for Norbiton – was ready to depart. He shot through the last open door, engaged in a brief tussle with the guard to keep it ajar until Taylor staggered in, then sat on a seat that had seen better days. He had purchased First Class tickets, and the carriage was Second, but they had it to themselves and he saw no point in changing. Taylor looked as though he might refuse anyway, still breathing hard after what had apparently been a furious dash.

'Gas explosion early this morning,' he gasped, opening the window as far as it would go, and then flopping back on the seat. 'The laundry at the Poplar Workhouse. Two dead.'

'Another case?' asked Priestley, wondering what would happen to Scudder now.

Taylor nodded, eyes closed as he recovered. The traffic had been at a standstill, and he would have missed the train if he had waited in his cab. Running had been the only option, but a race of more than a mile at full pelt had left him spent.

'Taps left on,' he added, trying to control his breathing. 'Deliberately. Makes it murder.'

'And you're the investigating officer?' asked Priestley. He had thought extensively about Taylor's predicament after they had parted company the previous night, and had concluded that the inspector had a dangerous enemy within the Force. The more he mulled over the leaks to the press, the misinformation and the amount of work being piled on him, the more he felt there was something rotten happening in Taylor's station.

Taylor nodded again. 'But we've made an arrest – or Grant has. Billy Hopkins from Limehouse way. Done it before. Didn't mean to kill anyone, though. Says it was an accident.'

'Two unlawful killings solved before breakfast? That should impress Hamilton.'

Taylor managed to laugh. 'Not at all. Most of our cases are like this. A body covered in stab wounds, and someone standing over it with a bloody knife saying, "I didn't mean to kill him, officer." But even though Hopkins has confessed, there are still witness statements to collect, evidence to catalogue, circumstances to investigate.'

'Why put you on the case? You said Andrews was next in line.'

'He has gone away, which leaves three of us, and this is the third incident since Scudder. Hot weather is usually associated with a rise in violent crime, so we're always busier in summer. Still, at least it's not another Headless Bishop. Hopkins has tampered with gas taps before – he likes the smell and noise of a fire. He's never hurt anyone, but it was only ever a matter of time before he did, so it was no surprise when we saw him at the scene and learned that he's been living in the workhouse the last few weeks.'

Priestley nodded, then stared out the window. If Taylor was already being forced to work on other cases, would Scudder's murder ever be solved? Or would Adams be arrested because the evidence they had accumulated so far, albeit circumstantial, pointed in his direction? The policeman seemed to read his mind.

'I'm becoming increasingly convinced that Adams killed Scudder, but I won't make an accusation until I'm sure. I still have some professional pride left, and it's always far more satisfactory to arrest the real killer than to hang an innocent man.'

Priestley glanced at him sharply. 'Good. But you owe me a breakfast. You promised me bacon and eggs at the Hotel York before we caught the train.'

Taylor groped in his pocket and produced several round, brown discs wrapped in a linen napkin. 'Have one of these instead. Ruby made them before she went to her mother's house.'

Priestley gnawed on one. 'She doesn't work for a ship's chandler, does she?' he asked when his teeth made virtually no impact. 'This is like hardtack.'

'She says it's her finest shortbread,' replied Taylor, who had not taken one himself. 'She makes them for the Women's Institute every Tuesday and I get the ones that are left, which tends to be most of them.' He consulted his notebook. 'Grant tells me that Canbury Station is better than Norbiton for Mrs Scudder's house.'

They alighted at a pleasant country-style station that was painted brown and white, and that boasted pots of brightly coloured flowers hanging in baskets from the eaves. The station-master gave them directions to Ham Road, saying it would be quicker to walk than to wait for a cab, and returned to his newspaper. Birds sang, and despite the inevitable gas works, the place had an almost rural feel about it. The air smelled of cut grass, and the Thames meandered sluggishly through a pretty water-meadow.

Scudder's mother lived in a sturdy Victorian villa that afforded pleasant views across the river. Its paintwork was pristine, and a gardener tipped his hat to the visitors as he moved through the roses with his pruning shears. The scent was heady, and the flowers stood in regimented blocks of red, yellow and white.

Taylor knocked at the door, which was answered by a woman in her sixties, who looked eerily like the body he had seen lying on the East India Docks – the same small face and slightly petulant features. Her wispy fair hair clung to her round head, and she had pale blue eyes. Taylor introduced himself and Priestley.

'It's good of you to come, Mr Priestley,' said Mrs Scudder, ushering them into a parlour, a large room with bay windows. Taylor was studiously ignored, and he wondered uneasily what Grant had said when he broke the news no parent should have to hear. 'The police have been, of course, and Mr Shackleton sent a beautiful telegram. He means to visit me tomorrow, with his wife.'

'I really am very sorry,' said Priestley. He sat in the chair she indicated, and accepted a slice of Dundee cake. Cups and saucers stood ready, too: Mrs Muriel Scudder was well prepared for the anticipated onslaught of sympathetic friends, relatives and neighbours. 'Is there anything I can do?'

'You are a sweet young man,' she said bravely. 'My Brice mentioned you when he talked about the expedition. He liked you very much.'

'Who else did he talk about, ma'am?' asked Taylor, whose slice of cake was considerably smaller than Priestley's. Clearly, Mrs Scudder preferred expedition members to policemen.

She regarded him with barely concealed dislike. 'Why?'

Taylor was used to hostility, although not usually from respectable middle-class women. He had asked Grant to ascertain whether Scudder had ever fallen foul of the law – it was something he did routinely with every murder victim – and the sergeant had reported that there was nothing amiss in Scudder's background. However, Taylor sincerely hoped that the information had not been obtained by asking the bereaved woman whether her son had ever been in prison.

'Because it's important that we gain an accurate picture of what he thought about the people he worked with,' he explained gently.

She glowered at him. 'I've already been through all this with that odious sergeant. Can't you ask him, and spare my feelings? I *won't* be bullied by you.'

'Please, Mrs Scudder,' said Priestley, with a smile that would have melted the heart of the most forbidding of gorgons. 'Brice's death was a terrible shock to us all, and everyone wants to catch the vile wretch who did it. That's why *I* came here today – to stress the importance Mr Shackleton places on the official enquiry.'

'I thought you were here to make sure *he* behaves himself,' said Mrs Scudder, scowling at Taylor. 'Mr Shackleton said in his telegraph that he'd do all he could to protect me from anyone who might distress me. Like policemen.'

'Like reporters,' corrected Priestley, aware of Taylor's startled look. 'He said he'd try to protect you from newspapermen who might demand stories. He didn't say anything about the police – and I know, because I delivered the telegraph to the Post Office myself.'

'Did you now,' she said coldly.

'This is excellent cake, Mrs Scudder,' Priestley said, to win back her good graces. It wasn't entirely sycophantic: her Dundee was a world apart from Ruby's so-called shortbread, and a good deal less unkind on the teeth.

She softened. 'Brice always liked my baking.'

Priestley finished the slice and placed his empty plate on the table, pleased when it was immediately refilled. He hated missing breakfast. 'Brice was an excellent biologist. You must have been very proud when he was invited to join the expedition.'

Mrs Scudder smiled for the first time. 'I was. He

172

deserved something good, after what happ…' She trailed off and glared at Taylor, as though he was responsible for her almost revealing something she intended to conceal.

'What happened?' he asked, instantly alert. 'He had some bad luck?'

'You could say that,' she said, pursing her lips.

'Will you tell us about it?'

'No,' she replied flatly. She folded her arms and gazed at him defiantly.

Taylor sighed. 'Shall I ask your neighbours, then? Or your friends who—'

'No!' she cried. No respectable woman wanted police asking acquaintances whether they had heard anything sordid about her family. 'Leave them alone. Leave *me* alone!'

Priestley went to sit next to her, taking one of her hands in his. 'If there's one thing I've learned recently, Mrs Scudder, it's that the police always get their answers in the end. It may not be something you want to reveal, but it's better to volunteer it than to have it dragged out piece by piece.'

'You don't understand,' she said in a low voice. 'It's the shame of it all.'

'I can guarantee discretion,' said Priestley. He saw Taylor start to object, and hurried on before the inspector could point out that if the information was pertinent, it might be a promise that could not be kept. 'Not everything the police learn ends up in the newspapers or a courtroom.'

Taylor was not so sure, especially with someone supplying Faris with information. He tried again to speak, but Priestley overrode him a second time.

'Please, Mrs Scudder,' he said gently. 'It's to help us catch the monster who hurt Brice.'

Mrs Scudder dabbed away her tears with a handkerchief, and assessed the two men with eyes that were suddenly calculating. Taylor wondered if Priestley could see that she was a good deal tougher than she had first appeared. She was silent for a few moments, and then made her decision, her face full of unconcealed resentment.

'Very well,' she said stiffly. 'I suppose I can trust you not to make this information public.' She took a deep breath. 'Brice was accused of *loitering*.' The last word was spoken in such a low whisper that it was all but inaudible.

'Loitering where?' asked Taylor.

'Outside Cannon Street Railway Terminus. I say *accused*, because nothing was proved, and the police were obliged to let him go. Of course, they were nasty about it, furious to be deprived of a conviction.' Another scowl came Taylor's way. 'He was only waiting for a hansom.'

At that moment, there was knock on the front door. Taylor stood politely as she went to answer it, and when she had gone, Priestley rounded angrily on him.

'You should be ashamed of yourself! There was no need to threaten a poor old lady with enquiries to her neighbours.'

'We needed to know what she was hiding,' said Taylor, unmoved. 'And that "poor old lady" was trying to conceal important information.'

'You can't blame her for trying to protect her son.

Besides, you should have known about this loitering business already. Don't you check on that sort of thing?'

'Yes, I should have known,' admitted Taylor, thinking he would have words with Grant. Still, at least the information explained Mrs Scudder's hostility. The arrest had soured her attitude towards the police in any guise.

'And you could have been more sympathetic,' Priestley went on, unappeased.

'I have every sympathy for her, but my first duty is to catch her son's killer. I can't do that by tiptoeing around every witness who declines to be open.'

'I could have persuaded her to confide in us without recourse to threats,' objected Priestley.

'No, you couldn't. She would have fobbed you off with a tale that would have wasted our time. And you should be wary of promising things not in your power. It may prove impossible to keep Scudder's trouble quiet.'

Priestley threw up his hands in exasperation. 'So he tried to hire a lady of the night. I don't see how forcing his mother to tell you that helps. You upset her – and alienated her – for nothing.'

'Not nothing – her confession tells us a great deal. You obviously don't understand the significance of Cannon Street Railway Terminus, but she does. That particular station isn't known for its "ladies of the night," but for male prostitutes.'

Priestley looked at him blankly.

'The area is frequented by homosexuals in search of paid favours,' elaborated Taylor. 'The place where hansoms are hailed is at the opposite end of the station, and you'd have to be drunk or stupid to confuse the two. So if Scudder was arrested there, then the chances are that he was where he shouldn't have been.'

Priestley's face reddened with embarrassment. 'Scudder was a homosexual?'

'I've no idea. However, he was caught in an area known for homosexual activities. I would need to read the file to know what sort of evidence was gathered against him – not much, if the case was dropped.'

'Did you ask Grant to find out if Scudder had a criminal record?' asked Priestley, changing the subject suddenly. Taylor nodded. 'Then there are two possibilities: he's either inefficient or he's depriving you of information.'

'Probably the former. He doesn't want me to fail, because my lack of success will reflect on him.'

Priestley sighed. 'So now you know this nasty little fact about Scudder, how does it help?'

'It may explain his relationships with other members of the expedition, and may even have induced one of them to kill him – not all men like the notion of living in a tiny hut with someone of unorthodox sexual preferences. Some men won't care, but others may mind very much.'

'We'll talk about it later,' said Priestley, as voices sounded in the corridor. 'Here come Adams and the Reverend Vallen.'

It was an uncomfortable gathering in Mrs Scudder's parlour. Adams had not expected Taylor to be there, and seemed to realise that his changing stories about the night of the murder had been treated with scepticism. He spilled his tea, dropped his cake and forgot that he was in the presence of a lady and a vicar, as curses and blasphemies dripped from his lips like leaves from a tree in autumn. He became so flustered, that even Vallen and Mrs Scudder regarded him warily.

Meanwhile, Mrs Scudder was furious with Taylor for forcing her to reveal the Cannon Street incident, and even the presence of a man of the cloth did not prevent her from glaring and making tart remarks. Reverend Vallen tried desperately to keep the peace, while Priestley lapsed into silence, thinking about the implications of Scudder's secret life.

'My son Nigel spoke very highly of Brice,' said Vallen, baring his incisors in an ecclesiastical smile and clasping his hands in front of him as he perched on the edge of a horsehair sofa.

'Brice liked Nigel, too, although he did say he was all fingers and thumbs,' said Mrs Scudder with a wan smile. 'He talked a lot about the expedition and his research, and he was always going on about the things he wanted to discover in Antarctica.'

'Such as what?' asked Taylor, when she gazed out the window, waiting for someone to encourage her to elaborate.

She might have been keen to expand, but not to a policeman. She rounded on him. 'How could he know that, when he hadn't discovered them yet? What a stupid question!'

Taylor stifled a sigh. 'I'm not entirely unacquainted with scientific method, ma'am. Biologists don't race off to an unknown continent, stand in the snow and wait for discoveries to jump out at them. They have hypotheses they want to test, and they set about collecting data to do it.'

'True,' nodded Priestley with a bright smile. 'Brice hoped to discover evidence that dinosaurs once walked where penguins now stand – that the continent was once covered in trees rather than ice, and that the weather then changed, so a different kind of beast evolved.'

'He was interested in evolution,' agreed Mrs Scudder proudly. 'Darwin was his greatest hero, and he enjoyed many debates on the subject with Nigel, Mr O'Brien and Mr Murray. Mr Murray is the expedition's chief biologist, although Brice told me that once they set sail, Mr Shackleton intended to promote *him* to the post.'

'Evolution is an intriguing notion,' mused Vallen before Taylor could pursue that confidence. 'Although there's a tendency to take it literally, and ignore God's role in the matter.'

'I believe the two can be reconciled,' said Priestley. 'It's just a question of balance.'

'Yes,' said Vallen, accepting another piece of cake. 'A question of balance. How nicely put.'

'Was Brice looking forward to going south, ma'am?' interjected Adams. He blushed at the inanity of the question. 'Jesus Christ Almighty! What a bloody stupid thing to say! Of course he was looking forward to it. We all were. All are. Well, he was…before…' He trailed off and ate more cake in an attempt to conceal his mortification.

Taylor watched him. Did this coarse-tongued man really expect the police to believe that he was courting a woman so respectable that her name could not be revealed? It did not seem likely that such a paragon would entertain a fellow like Adams.

'Brice couldn't wait,' said Mrs Scudder. 'He was desperate to be away from London and its unpleasant characters.' She threw another black look at Taylor.

'It is nice to be outside London at this time of year,'

interjected Vallen pleasantly, gesturing to the sun shining through the window. 'The weather is unseasonably hot for July, I find.'

'Too bloody right,' agreed Adams, relieved to be on neutral ground. 'I sweated like a pig over the loading last night, even though it was cooler than at noon. I shall be glad to feel the brisk southern winds on my face.'

'Brice liked the cold,' said his mother. 'And he told me that many members of the expedition felt the same. That's why they joined up. That charming Mr O'Brien – he came to tea once with that opinionated Yaxley – said he usually spends his summers in Scotland, and was finding London beastly hot. Dr Mackay is from Scotland.' A shadow crossed her face. 'Brice mentioned him on several occasions. He is a vile man.'

'Is he?' asked Taylor, when no one else made any response.

Mrs Scudder's expression was spiteful. 'He plays cruel jokes on the hopefuls. He got them to do unpleasant things with the promise that he'd put in a word for them with Mr Shackleton. But he never intended to do anything of the kind.'

'I don't think—' began Adams uncomfortably.

'And Brice detested Marshall, whom he said was worse. I met Marshall at a lecture Mr Shackleton gave. He told me that most of the expedition members were lily-livered disbelievers, and that he doubted God would smile on *Nimrod* when it was full of men who thought they were independent of Him. Those were Marshall's exact words.'

She gazed challengingly at Vallen, and although Vallen had undoubtedly heard far worse, he nonetheless

179

obligingly composed his face into an expression of pious dismay, and shook his head. The reaction seemed to satisfy her, and she continued.

'Brice also said that Captain England was insane, and that Murray is so stricken with ill health that his presence on the expedition is dangerous. *Brice* should have been chief biologist.'

Priestley cleared his throat to defend his colleagues, but he was no match for Mrs Scudder now she was in full flow. She overrode him. 'Murray came to tea once, and I saw for myself that Brice was right. He clearly has something wrong with him, because he was puffing and panting even after the walk from the road to my front door.'

'He has had 'flu, objected Priestley. 'And—'

'Then there was the meteorologist, Jameson Adams,' Mrs Scudder went on. Everyone gaped at her: she had evidently not paid attention when the introductions were made and was oblivious to the fact that the object of her diatribe was sitting on her chaise longue. 'He was nasty when Brice borrowed some silly animal meter and it was broken. He made Brice pay for a new one.'

'She means "anemometer",' whispered Priestley to Taylor. 'A device for measuring wind speed.

'Oh, dear,' said Vallen unhappily. 'I do hope Nigel wasn't to blame. He tends to be accident-prone where fragile equipment is concerned, although it's only his nerves. He'll be perfectly steady-handed once he's on his way south. If he's successful, of course.'

'I think he will be,' said Priestley, making the vicar beam with delight before realising that such a reaction was wholly inappropriate in the presence of a woman whose son had just been cruelly deprived of his own opportunity. The vicar struggled to assume a more sombre expression.

'It wasn't Nigel who broke it,' said Mrs Scudder, rampaging on in a way that suggested no one would be able to stem the tirade. 'It was Adams himself, because his animal meter was old. In other words, he tricked Brice into buying him a new one.'

'No, by God,' said Adams vehemently. 'That's *not* true. Brice did break my anemometer, because I saw him. Then he tried to conceal the fact by shoving it under a table, ready to blame some other poor sod, I imagine. He was angry when I caught him, and I gave him a few home-truths he didn't like hearing.'

'When was this?' asked Taylor.

'Christ!' muttered Adams, anger turning to alarm when he realised he may have just admitted to a motive for murder. He stood abruptly. 'I've said enough. Goodbye Mrs Scudder. Despite what I just said, I'm sorry Brice is dead. Good morning to you.'

As Adams aimed for the door, Vallen leapt to his feet and said it was time for him to be on his way, too. Since it was hardly polite for Priestley and Taylor to escape at the same time, they were obliged to linger a while longer, Taylor cursing himself for being slower witted than Vallen, and Priestley squirming with embarrassment as Mrs Scudder continued with her character assassinations. It soon became clear that the comments were no longer Brice's assessments, but her own vitriol. Taylor saw it as a reaction to grief, and let the flow of spite wash over him, but Priestley was shocked.

'Crickey!' he said eventually, breaking into a claim that one of the seamen had a shameful pox. 'Is that the time? We must be on our way, or the Boss will wonder what's happened.'

It was difficult to extricate themselves, but they managed eventually, Priestley promising he would visit her again before the expedition sailed, and Taylor promising he would not, both of which pleased her. She pressed the remains of the Dundee cake into Priestley's hand, claiming that he would need to build himself up for Antarctica.

'This should be safe for you to eat,' said Priestley, passing a piece to Taylor as they returned to the railway station. 'If she'd given it to you, I'd have advised you to toss it in the river.'

'Why?'

'Because she'd have soaked it in poison or added splinters of glass. She obviously detests the police, and she's a vengeful woman. When we first arrived, I thought she was a gentle old lady, but she proved herself to be something of a tartar with her vicious tongue. Now I see where Scudder learned his manners.'

'Scudder was like her?'

'In some ways, although not as brazenly slanderous. I'm glad to escape, and only wish we'd seized the opportunity earlier.'

Suddenly, Taylor stopped walking and turned around. The street was a wide one, and trees had been planted on the pavement, which not only afforded the road some welcome shade, but also provided the rural feel of an affluent London suburb. To their right lay the Thames, with a meadow full of long grass that rolled down to its wood-fringed banks. Shaking his head, he started to move forward again.

'What is it?' asked Priestley.

Taylor spun around again, and this time there was no mistaking that someone was behind them. Oddly, for so hot a day, the person was wearing a coat and a cap that concealed his face. Taylor was after him in a trice, and Priestley was not far behind.

Realising he had been spotted, the figure turned to flee towards the river, coat tails whipping behind him. He vaulted awkwardly over a fence and staggered across the uneven grass, glancing behind him as he went. He ran clumsily, as though unused to it, and it was not long before Taylor and Priestley began to gain on him. He ran harder, but so did they. He reached a path that wound through the trees lining the river, normally a pleasant route for Sunday strollers.

'He's going to jump in the river!' cried Priestley in alarm. 'To swim for it!'

The man, seeing that he would not outrun his pursuers, hesitated before making an ungainly dive that raised spray in all directions. His coat flew upwards and wrapped itself around his head, where the sodden material encumbered him so he could not see or use his arms. It was one of the most dismal attempts at escape that Taylor had ever witnessed. He leaned out, seized one of the kicking feet, and together he and Priestley drew him out of the water to stand dripping and gasping on the river bank.

'Well, Mr O'Brien,' said Taylor amiably. 'Fancy meeting you here.'

Chapter 8

Connor O'Brien had a miserable journey back to London. Not only was he soaking wet, he was questioned relentlessly. His waterlogged shoes had shrunk and pinched him, his trousers clung moistly around his aching legs, and there was water in one ear that he could not dislodge, no matter how much he shook his head and blew his nose.

'So,' said Taylor, leaning back in his seat and folding his arms. 'Why did you run?'

'You startled me. I was happily walking down the street, and all of a sudden I saw you two bearing down on me like Zulus at Rorke's Drift. What was I supposed to do?'

'Don't lie,' said Taylor mildly. 'You ran because you didn't want to be caught, and the dive in the river was an act of pure desperation.'

'I don't know what you're talking about,' insisted O'Brien stiffly. 'I ran because I was afraid. If someone starting chasing you out of the blue, you'd be frightened, too.'

'Actually,' said Priestley, 'we just turned and looked, and you took off like a hare. We chased you *because* you started running.'

O'Brien looked from one to the other and licked his lips. 'I came to pay my respects to Brice's mother,' he said. 'But first Adams came tearing out of her house as though the hounds of Hell were on his tail, then Reverend Vallen dashed after him. I waited a while, and then you two emerged and started driving me towards the river. My only thought was that if Adams and the vicar had seen fit to run, then maybe I should, too.'

'You ran because Adams and Vallen did?' asked Taylor, in a voice that said he did not believe a word.

O'Brien nodded vehemently. 'You're clearly looking for someone – anyone – to accuse of Brice's murder. Marshall says you're so desperate for an arrest that you'll pick on anyone, just to save yourself from being castigated by the press.'

'Is that so?' asked Taylor flatly. 'What else has he been saying?'

'That you think the killer is someone Brice knew, whereas it's obvious that he was murdered by a passing thief. Unfortunately, that sort of random crime is hard to solve with no witnesses, just like the Headless Bishop, so you're looking to frame an expedition member instead.'

'Do *you* think Scudder's death is a case of a robbery gone wrong?' asked Priestley, while Taylor did not bother to grace the claims with a reply.

O'Brien nodded. 'No one who knew Brice would want to harm him. He was kind and gentle.'

'I've heard of not speaking ill of the dead,' said Taylor. 'But you've taken it to a new level. Everyone else found Scudder boorish and difficult. Even Priestley, who seldom has anything bad to say about anyone, acknowledges that Scudder had his faults.'

'I told you before, he had one face for the outside world, and another for the people who took the trouble to know him,' argued O'Brien. 'Underneath, he was good, decent and thoughtful.'

Taylor sensed they would have no more out of him, and watched the depressing approach into London out of the window until, with an ear-splitting hiss, the train shuddered to a halt. A guard opened their door, then looked with disapproval when he saw the mess O'Brien's damp clothes had made of the seats.

'This is first class,' he objected indignantly. 'You should have gone third if you wanted to bring a wet dog with you. Where is it? Did you buy it a ticket?'

The guard was so persistent in demanding payment for the non-existent dog that Taylor was obliged to accompany him to his supervisor. The moment the inspector had gone, O'Brien tried to make a bid for freedom, but Priestley grabbed his arm.

'You live in Walter Street, I believe,' said Priestley. 'That's near Captain England's lodgings.'

O'Brien nodded. 'We walk home together sometimes.'

'Do you? I thought he avoided daytime exercise, because of the sun.'

'Like all of us, he comes to work before the sun is up and leaves only when it's getting dark. Marshall used to accompany us, but he complained – nastily – that England's pace is too stately, and he goes on his own these days.'

'How was he nasty?'

'He made sport of the captain. For some obscure reason, England reckons he strides along at a

186

tremendous lick, and that it's difficult for others to keep up. Perhaps his sister – who keeps house for him – told him so. Anyway, Marshall claimed he couldn't accompany us because England was far too brisk on his pins. England didn't know he was being mocked, but the crew did.'

'But you don't mind this snail's pace?'

'Not in the evenings, and the captain is good company. He has some odd superstitions, like scratching backstays to make wishes come true, and whistling to call up a wind. However, I take the time to get to know people I think I'll like, although it seems to have landed me in trouble with your policeman friend. He has me in his sights for killing Brice.'

'Is he wrong?'

O'Brien gave what was almost a sob. 'Of course he is! What motive would I have?'

'Scudder's death means a second empty place on the expedition. And you are a hopeful.'

O'Brien gulped. 'But I would rather win my place by merit than murder. What sort of man do you think I am?'

Priestley changed the subject abruptly. 'Did you know that someone had been damaging Scudder's equipment, and that there was trouble with his Monagasque trawl?'

'It couldn't be stowed because of a problem with a hatch,' recalled O'Brien. 'So what?'

'I don't suppose you know anything about it, do you?' asked Taylor, speaking behind O'Brien and making him jump in alarm. He had not noticed the policeman's soft-footed approach.

'No!' cried O'Brien, although his expression bespoke abject guilt. His eyes were wide, and his face drained of

187

what little colour he had left. 'That had nothing to do with me. Perhaps whoever tampered with the hatch *did* want Brice to return later that night to check his equipment. But it wasn't me.'

'Interesting,' mused Taylor. 'You say the hatch was "tampered with," but everyone else says it was broken. If you're right and someone did engage in sabotage, then you're confirming that Scudder was murdered by someone he knew.'

O'Brien's shoulders sagged and he seemed near tears. 'This is all too horrible! Can I go home now, or do you want to arrest me?'

'Go home,' said Taylor.

O'Brien escaped with relief, while Priestley stared after him. 'Was that wise? Even I could see he knows something about the hatch, and he certainly has a motive for murder: with Scudder gone, he might be appointed assistant biologist.'

Taylor shook his head. 'O'Brien has an alibi, if you recall. He was with Nigel Vallen, and then his landlady. We can uncover all the villainous motives in the world, but they mean nothing when our suspect can prove he was elsewhere at the time of the murder.'

Because Priestley knew Adams was scheduled to work on *Nimrod* that day – and he did not relish meeting the meteorologist after the incident in Norbiton – he went to the Expedition Office. Taylor accompanied him, and they batted ideas back and forth, although it soon became obvious that most of their opinions were based on suspicion, not facts.

'I've known killers to hide behind their geniality,'

188

remarked Taylor. 'And there have been some I've liked very much. Murray's gentle manners don't preclude him from sticking a knife into Scudder. It must have been extremely galling to have Scudder telling people that he was unfit to be chief biologist, and that Scudder should be appointed in his place.'

'I accept that. However, if you use that line of argument, then it means you can't accuse Mackay or Marshall: they certainly don't hide behind *their* geniality.'

'True. But, while I've known *some* murderers to be pleasant, I've known far more who were aggressive and arrogant, which puts Mackay and Marshall firmly on the list again.'

'I still don't believe one of my colleagues killed Scudder,' said Priestley unhappily. 'Such an act would jeopardise the entire expedition.'

'You assume it was thought through, whereas it was probably on the spur of the moment, like most murders.' Taylor hesitated. 'Although the weapon suggests a degree of premeditation – how many people happen to have a pre-sharpened letter opener to hand when the urge comes upon them to kill? But the broken hatch is on my mind: *was* it damaged to ensure Scudder visited the docks after the party?'

Priestley had no reply. He sighed. 'So, to summarise, our chief suspects are still Marshall, Adams, Murray, Mackay, Yaxley, Captain England and a few dockhands? We have eliminated none of them, and Mrs Scudder's testimony tells us that her son had reasons to dislike them all?

Taylor nodded.

'Will you come see Shackleton with me?' asked

Priestley tiredly. 'I don't think I can bear to tell him that you're gunning for his captain, his second-in-command, his surgeons, his biologist and a hopeful.'

Shackleton declined to discuss the case at the Expedition Office, and in an act of spontaneous extravagance typical of him, suggested lunch in the elegant dining room of the illustrious Cecil Hotel on The Strand, a popular venue for bankers, barristers and those involved in high finance. They walked the short distance, then strolled up the opulent staircase to the first floor, where a waiter hurried to greet them. The expedition had made Shackleton sufficiently famous that he and his companions were immediately fussed over and escorted to a table in the window that afforded a commanding view of the bustle in the street below.

The Cecil's dining room was light and airy, dominated by a massive central chandelier that glittered in the noonday sunlight. The wallpaper sported a design that looked Japanese, and the wooden floorboards had been polished almost white. The room was full of men in dark suits and starched collars, and the atmosphere was genteel, informal and relaxing.

'Salmon,' said Shackleton, ordering for everyone in his expansive way. 'And boiled potatoes with peas. Good honest fare, for good honest men.'

'But most of the men in here are lawyers,' remarked Taylor, looking around him.

'True,' agreed Shackleton. 'So they'll probably order the pheasant gitana.' He became serious. 'Have you made any headway? I've been worried to death about the whole business, and Emily is getting tired of me talking about it. Ruby's probably the same with you.'

'We have a lot of circumstantial evidence, but no real clues,' replied Taylor. He seldom discussed his work with Ruby, even when their paths did cross. 'It may be that we never do.'

'So far, all we know for certain is that Scudder left the party just before ten o'clock, and then went to the ship.' Priestley began to summarise what few facts they had accumulated. 'No one saw any odd characters there, and there's no evidence that the murder was committed by a thief.'

'Damn!' muttered Shackleton. 'I was hoping you'd find he was killed by a greedy dockhand. Do you have *any* suspects?'

Priestley looked down at his food and declined to answer.

'We do,' said Taylor steadily. 'Including six members of your expedition. However, the two who stand out most at this stage of the investigation, at least my mind, are Adams and England.'

Shackleton gaped at him. 'Surely, you must be mistaken! Adams is a capital fellow, and while England comes over as a little odd, he's my captain, and it won't be easy to find another sailor with his experience and skills. He's not a killer, either.'

'We shall see,' said Taylor noncommittally.

Shackleton stared at him. 'I hope I haven't put you under too much pressure, Will. You look exhausted, and I know you have other pressing cases. Perhaps I should ask Hamilton to assign us another officer.'

'No, don't do that,' blurted Priestley. He flushed when Shackleton and Taylor regarded him in astonishment, and hastened to explain. 'I think we're coming close to a solution, and all it wants is a few more days and a bit of luck. It would take another inspector a long time to become acquainted with the facts, time that could be spent far more profitably in pursuit of the killer.'

'Then I shan't keep you from it,' said Shackleton. He started to raise his hand for the bill, but a waiter was already moving towards him with an envelope in his hand. Taylor realised they had been served remarkably quickly, far faster than other customers, and recalled how Shackleton had charmed servants into giving him privileged treatment at school, too.

While Shackleton thanked the manager – not only for a free meal, but for a donation, too – Priestley and Taylor waited outside. It was a stifling afternoon, and dark clouds suggested a thunderstorm in the offing.

'We had an awkward encounter with O'Brien,' said Priestley, as Shackleton joined them on the street. The expedition leader held several banknotes in his hand, money thrust at him by other patrons who had been inspired by the fuss made by the manager and his staff.

'O'Brien?' asked Shackleton, raising an arm to wave down a cab. Immediately, one started to make its way across the street towards them.

Priestley nodded. 'We caught him hovering around Mrs Scudder's house, and he made a run for it when we spotted him. He fell in the river eventually and we brought him back to town.'

'He ran away from the police?' asked Shackleton. He was thoughtful, pausing with his foot on the cab's lowest step. 'Poor O'Brien. He's having a hard time.'

'What do you mean?' asked Taylor.

Shackleton withdrew his foot, and Taylor was astonished when the driver made no objection to the delay. On the contrary, the fellow was only too happy to wait, indicating with gestures to passing colleagues that *he* had a passenger whose picture was often in the newspapers.

'I was discussing the hopefuls with Murray and Scudder a couple of days before Scudder's death,' Shackleton went on. 'Murray wanted either Nigel Vallen or Yaxley, in that order, but Scudder wanted O'Brien.'

'They were friends,' said Priestley. 'O'Brien really liked Scudder.'

Shackleton shook his head slowly. 'I suppose that accounts for it. But while O'Brien is a pleasant enough fellow, he's very average intellectually. Anyway, to cut a long story short, I told them O'Brien definitely wouldn't be going.'

'Have you told O'Brien that?' asked Taylor.

'I haven't had the chance. These things can't be bellowed along the length of the quay, and I've been waiting for the right moment. I asked Scudder and Murray to say nothing until I'd spoken to him, but he's been odd these last few days, and I cannot help but wonder whether Scudder disregarded my request and told him anyway.'

'Or Murray did,' suggested Taylor.

'Definitely *not* Murray,' said Shackleton. 'He was distressed to think his opinion had carried enough weight to destroy a man's ambitions, and fretted about how the news could be broken. He was indescribably relieved when I told him that unpleasant duty fell to me.'

'I don't think O'Brien knows,' said Priestley. 'If he did,

he would have said something – if not to me, then to Nigel or Yaxley.'

'Poor O'Brien.' Shackleton began to climb into the cab at last. 'Losing a friend and being dropped from the expedition. He's definitely not having a good week.'

'No,' agreed Taylor. 'But its better than Scudder's.'

Priestley went with Shackleton to the Expedition Office, while Taylor headed to the still-smouldering rubble that once comprised the Poplar Workhouse's laundry. The workhouse was a rambling, scruffy building sandwiched unattractively between a terrace of untidy hovels and the grimy façade of the London and Blackwall Railway's goods depot. The Thames slid in an evil-smelling curl behind it. It was depressing in all respects – from its gloomy location to its institutional architecture.

Taylor found the workhouse devoid of police, and business seemed back to normal everywhere except the demolished washrooms. Some inmates had been detailed to salvage what they could from the ruins, and they poked about with iron bars in a desultory manner, retrieving a brick here and a tile there. They stopped working when they saw Taylor, and had to be urged to start again by a man in a uniform. He was a fat, slovenly fellow, with oily hair and stains on his clothes that suggested a cavalier attitude to personal hygiene. His grin of welcome showed several missing teeth, and his hands were dirty, scabbed and scarred.

'Lazy buggers,' he said to Taylor, as the inspector looked at what was left of the building. He indicated the workers with his thumb, and settled more comfortably in the chair he had carried outside for himself. 'It's almost time for tea, so they ain't much interested in labouring.'

'Well, it *is* hot,' said Taylor, thinking he wouldn't be overly keen on pawing through partly baked bricks in such heat either.

'Not as hot as it was at three o'clock this morning,' said the guard with a meaningful smirk. Taylor remembered him from earlier that day; his name was Leonard Vine. 'You should have seen the place go up! It was like one of them firework displays. Hopkins did a lovely job.'

'Where are the police officers I left here? Inside?'

'Gone home. They took statements, and were done by noon. Sergeant Grant said he didn't need too much detail, on account of the fact that he already had Hopkins locked up, and no one would ever read what we said anyway.'

'He said that?' Taylor was disgusted.

Vince nodded. 'He said it was an open-and-shut case once Hopkins confessed. Shame about them two women what copped it, though. Still, they weren't supposed to be in the laundry in the first place.'

'Why not?'

'It's against regulations. All inmates are supposed to be in their dormitory beds by ten o'clock. But these old buildings are stuffy in summer, and we're pretty full at the moment, so them two women got into the habit of sleeping in the laundry, because it was cooler.'

'Did Hopkins know they were there?'

'It wasn't no secret.'

One of the inmates overheard. 'The laundry was more convenient for their business, if you catch my meaning.'

'Shut your face, Joe,' snarled Vine, outraged that an inmate should dare to butt into his conversation. He turned back to Taylor. 'He's right, though. Them women never said no to a few pennies from a needy man.'

'Including you?'

Vine feigned shock. 'Gracious me, no! My wife wouldn't approve of that at all.'

Inside the workhouse, Taylor spoke to some of Hopkins' friends, who began to clamour his innocence. Hopkins had been asleep in the men's wing when the explosion had occurred, they said, and as it was hot and several of them were awake, he couldn't have gone out, because they would have seen him. Taylor had been told the same story at four o'clock that morning, when the flames had still been dancing across the bodies of Meg and Franny White.

However, Grant had been tugging on his sleeve to say he had already apprehended the culprit, so Taylor had left him to interview these witnesses, while he himself had gone to calm the workhouse superintendent and ensure the place was safe from further explosions before allowing the inmates and nearby residents to return. Now, as he gave the witnesses his full attention, he realised he had made a mistake.

He listened and asked questions until he had enough information to rectify it, then returned to Vine, and asked if the man would accompany him to Poplar Police Station to give another statement. Vine was suspicious at first, but obliged when Taylor told him that his word would carry more weight than that of inmates.

Taylor found Greasy Grant in the station, too, gloating over a frightened Hopkins, whose hands were encased in heavy manacles. Grant was pleased with himself, indicating the small pile of statements with a satisfied grin, and informing his inspector that all that was needed was a signature, and the entire file could be sent for processing: case closed. Taylor stared at the hapless arsonist.

'Who told you to confess to the explosion, Hopkins?' he asked softly.

Hopkins blanched, and his terrified eyes became wilder than ever. 'I never...I didn't...'

'I know you didn't do it,' Taylor continued, aware of Grant's gaping shock. 'A dozen people say you were asleep at the time. So, who told you to confess?'

'A gent,' replied Hopkins unhappily, looking everywhere but at the policemen. 'He promised me fifty pound if I did, and said he'd get me out of prison in a day or two.'

'Next time don't be so trusting,' advised Taylor. 'You'll never see that fifty pounds, and you might have been hanged for murder into the bargain. As it is, you'll have a spell in gaol for wasting police time.'

'But I was only doing what I was told!' objected Hopkins. 'You can't lock me up!'

'The bastard!' exclaimed Grant, as they left Hopkins howling that he had done nothing wrong. 'I thought we had this solved – that it would go down as a good result in my file.'

'Then you shouldn't be so trusting, either,' admonished Taylor. 'A convicted arsonist at the scene of a fire is indeed cause for further investigation, but you should know by now that things are seldom as they seem.

'Bloody hell!' muttered Grant angrily. 'Now what?'

'Now we interview the real culprit, who obligingly came with me to the station. His name is Leonard Vine, and

I suspect he set the explosion because of some falling out with the White sisters over the division of spoils from their prostitution.'

Grant's small eyes widened under his heavy brow. 'How do you know?'

'His eyebrows are singed, although he claims he was nowhere near the explosion or the fire; he was seen by several inmates outside the laundry just before the blast, although he was supposed to be off duty; his hands are covered in that black sheen you get from touching lead pipes, although he has taken no part in the physical labour of dismantling the damaged building; and two inmates heard him boast about fooling the police in a public house at lunchtime. Doubtless we'll uncover more evidence in time, but we have enough to arrest him now.'

'Thank God,' muttered Grant fervently. 'This could have been a catastrophe.'

'Especially for Hopkins. What I'd really like, though, is to speak to the "gent" who bribed him into making a false confession.'

'I wonder why anyone would do such a thing.'

'I imagine either because he wanted a quick – albeit inaccurate – solution to the crime, or because he wanted to make us look stupid. Regardless, we outmanoeuvred him. So, arrest Vine, then come with me to the workhouse and help me take witness statements – proper ones, this time, with *all* the details, not just the ones you think will incriminate the suspect you have in custody.'

'Yes sir,' said Grant sullenly.

It was after ten o'clock by the time Taylor and Grant

had finished recording the rambling accounts of the inmates, and had conducted a formal interview with Vine. The guard denied the charge at first, suddenly "remembering" that he had actually seen Hopkins set the flame, but he crumbled once his wife – afraid she might be accused of complicity and hang at his side – turned over the equipment he had used.

At the same time, desperate to co-operate, she related a sordid tale of his wages supplemented by the female inmates' nocturnal exertions in the laundry, and a good deal of aggravation regarding how the proceeds should be divided up. Weary, but relieved that he had managed to salvage the situation in time, Taylor left Grant to deliver the statements to the station, while he walked to the docks. As he approached them, he saw a figure near the clock tower, lurking suspiciously.

'Priestley,' he called softly, watching the geologist leap ain alarm at the sound of his voice. 'What are you doing, hovering here like a timid whore?'

'Like a what?' asked Priestley, shocked.

Taylor rubbed his eyes tiredly. 'I'm sorry. It's what comes of listening to people talk about prostitution half the day. You forget there's such a thing as decent society.'

'Well, I advise you not to forget when Ruby is around,' recommended Priestley tartly.

Taylor was amused by the prim reaction, but managed to keep a straight face. 'I thought you'd have gone home by now,' he said.

'I'm waiting for Captain England. I thought I'd follow him home, to see if he was telling us the truth about the time it takes,' explained Priestley. 'We know he may have owned the murder weapon. He didn't like Scudder. And there's a lot of unaccounted time between when he left *Nimrod* on the night of the murder, and when he arrived home – getting on for two hours.'

'You think England is our man?'

Priestley shrugged. 'I don't know, but if I follow him, I shall know whether he can stride the two miles briskly, thus giving him plenty of time to murder Scudder, or whether he dawdles, in which case he was probably telling us the truth.'

'O'Brien said he walked slowly,' mused Taylor.

Priestley nodded. 'I asked Marshall about it this afternoon, too, and he confirmed that England ambles along so haltingly that he can't bear to accompany him. He makes excuses if England offers to go with him. So, I think England is innocent, but if I watch him myself, I can be sure.'

'There he is,' said Taylor, pointing to where a figure in a distinctive blue cap was being ushered outside the gates. 'Do you want company?'

'No, you look spent. Go home to Ruby.'

'She's decided to stay with her mother until I can guarantee to spend more than five minutes a day with her. An empty house and one of her suet puddings – cold and hard as a rock – is even less appealing than stalking a suspect through London. So let's go.'

'Very well. Besides, if England walks as slowly as we've been told, I shall need company to keep me awake. And if there are two of us, it will look less suspicious if he spots us.'

Taylor laughed. 'You don't think he'll see anything odd in Shackleton's agent and a policeman shadowing him at this hour? That West African sun must have done him more damage than we imagined! But come on – we'll lose him if we dally.'

But there was no possibility of losing England. He used the middle of the street, avoiding unlit pavements, and always came to a complete standstill at junctions, to ensure there was no oncoming traffic. The difficulty was in moving slowly enough not to catch up with him.

While England strolled with leisurely grace down the East India Docks Road, Taylor found himself telling Priestley about the Poplar Workhouse case. He confided that he now felt unable to delegate any task to Grant, no matter how simple, because the potential for disaster was too great.

'But you can't do *everything* yourself,' Priestley pointed out. 'You have to delegate, or you'll end up getting nowhere.'

'The devil and the deep blue sea,' murmured Taylor. 'But I shouldn't be burdening you with my problems. You have enough to think about with your own affairs.'

'I'll manage. Besides, friends are supposed to burden each other.'

Taylor smiled in the gloom, both surprised and flattered to learn he was considered a friend. He held back while England took his time negotiating the complex junction where the West India Dock Road joined East India Dock Road, Burdett Road and Pigott Street, waiting until it was absolutely clear of cabs and other vehicles before ambling across as though he had all the time in the world. He continued up Commercial Road, stopping once to light his pipe, and then again to inspect the window of a tobacconist's shop. He did not seem to like bridges, studying them uneasily for some time before scooting across or under them with uncharacteristic bursts of speed, and he was always careful near uneven surfaces.

Shortly before midnight, an hour and forty minutes after he had left the docks, England stopped at a house on Jubilee Street and rummaged in his pocket for a key. Taylor and Priestley had grown careless as it had become increasingly clear that the captain had been telling the truth about the length of his journeys home, and Priestley had embarked on a detailed description of the fossils that had been collected in the Antarctic by a Swedish expedition five years before. He was inspiringly eloquent, and by the time Taylor realised they were standing in full view, they had been spotted by the watchful eyes that had been waiting behind the net curtains in England's lodgings.

'Rupert, dear,' cried England's sister, bustling out of the house. 'You're always in such a world of your own when you're walking. Didn't you see poor Raymond Priestley hurrying after you, desperately trying to catch you up? Look at the poor boy! He's dead on his feet with weariness.'

'Ye gods!' exclaimed England, peering behind him. 'I didn't notice, because I've been pondering the question of azimuth mirrors. The Admiralty has lent us a pair, but I'm wondering whether I should ask Shackleton to purchase more. We had several on our voyage to rescue Scott, and it's better to have too many than too few.'

'Good evening, sir,' said Priestley, stepping forward

and preparing to brazen his way out of the situation. 'Will and I have just been to…to an evening of Gospel readings at the Wesleyan Chapel on Commercial Road, and when we saw you passing, we thought we'd wish you good night.'

'Will, is it?' asked England disapprovingly, while Taylor thought that if the captain believed such an obvious lie, then he was even more gullible than Hopkins. 'Well, I suppose even policemen are entitled to hear the Word of God. Would you like to come inside and catch your breath, have a spot to drink? Marshall complains that I walk too briskly for him, so I've probably tuckered you out if you've been trying to catch me. So come in, if you're coming. Break out the rations, Gertrude.'

'Thank you, sir,' said Priestley.

'I should go home,' replied Taylor at the same time. He was bone-weary after a day that had started before three-thirty that morning, and he wanted to sleep.

'Goodnight, then,' said England, pulling Priestley inside and beginning to close the door on Taylor.

'No, you must have a little refreshment, too, Mr…er,' said Gertrude, pushing her brother aside to take Taylor's arm and draw him across the threshold. 'It's been hot today and you must be thirsty.'

Unable to escape, Taylor allowed himself to be hauled into a parlour she had made homely and welcoming. She insisted that he and Priestley remove their coats to cool down, pointing out that most people became overheated if they tried to keep up with her fleet-footed sibling. Then she fetched a bottle of rum, and poured measures that would have been deemed generous by even the most gluttonous standards.

'Actually,' said Priestley, 'I never touch alcohol. But a glass of barley water—'

'Nonsense,' interrupted England, setting it in front of him. 'Everyone likes rum.'

'No, really,' protested Priestley, trying to pass it back, 'I don't drink strong liquor.'

'Rum isn't strong liquor,' stated England. 'It's rum. Come on. Down the hatch.'

He swallowed the contents of his own glass in several long, careful gulps, while Priestley regarded him in dismay. Gertrude followed her brother's example, so that for a few moments, the only sounds in the room were those of rhythmic swallowing.

'You'll have to dump this in her potted plant,' hissed Priestley urgently in Taylor's ear. 'I can't reach, and they'll think me an ingrate if I leave the lot.'

Taylor leaned back in his chair, and deftly tipped his own drink into one of Gertrude's flourishing aspidistras. In a neat sleight of hand, Priestley swapped glasses, concealing the fact that his was empty by cupping his hands around it. Unfortunately, the discarded liquid sat on top of the soil in a solid, unmoveable puddle – it was too hard and dry to allow it to drain, and Taylor would certainly not be able to repeat the exercise without making a mess on the carpet. But he did not want to imbibe vast quantities of neat rum either, knowing it would exacerbate his exhaustion.

'Drink up, inspector,' England ordered. 'Even the boy has outstripped you while you sip away like a nun. We'll be here all night at this rate, and I want to go to bed.'

'Manners, Rupert!' chided his sister. 'Perhaps the inspector prefers milk. I have some in the pantry. It's

204

been there a couple of days, and the weather's been hot, but I should be able to strain out some of the larger lumps…'

'Put some whiskey in it,' advised England, as she stood to fetch it. 'Take away the taste.'

'Thank you, no,' said Taylor hastily, drinking more of the rum than he wanted in an effort to stop her. It was powerful stuff, and it was not easy to prevent himself from gagging. His next words were spoken rather hoarsely. 'But it's very late, and we mustn't trespass on your hospitality.'

'Finish the rum,' England ordered, while Gertrude sat again. He glared at Taylor until the inspector took another swallow that made his throat burn. Taylor tried to read the label on the bottle, not surprised that there wasn't one: England's rum was some home-brewed potion that was probably illegal and certainly more powerful than anything available from legitimate sources. He tried not to cough, but could not help himself.

'It *is* good, isn't it?' said Gertrude, interpreting the hacking as a sign of approval. She refilled Priestley's glass before he could stop her, then did the same for everyone else's.

'Incidentally, I'm a suspect for murder, Gertie,' said England, after downing another substantial draught that made Taylor wonder whether he had any stomach lining left. 'The inspector here thinks I killed Scudder.'

'Does he?' asked Gertrude placidly. 'That must be tiresome.'

'And I have more than enough to worry about, without being obliged to answer silly questions about where I keep my letter openers,' England went on, irked.

He buried his nose in his tumbler and took another enormous mouthful, washing it around his teeth before swallowing with a sigh of relish.

'You know where your letter openers are, dear,' said Gertrude. 'You have the old wooden one from Dakar in your sea chest, and the others are here. I told you I'd keep them until your cabin is ship-shape. You'll only lose them if you take them aboard in all that chaos.'

'I don't suppose my Royal Naval Reserve one is to hand, is it?' asked England hopefully.

Gertrude stood and opened a drawer in a bureau. 'It's here. Why? Did the wooden one break?'

'Hah!' exclaimed England, leaping to his feet and snatching the implement from her. 'Here it is! So, it wasn't my letter opener that killed the biologist, just as I told you.'

'We know, sir,' said Taylor wearily. The rum was taking its toll, and he knew that if he closed his eyes he would fall asleep. 'You've been off our list of suspects for some time now.'

'Have I?' asked England, suspicious but relieved. 'Good. I didn't care for Scudder, but I certainly didn't kill him. And neither did any of my officers or crew.'

'No,' agreed Taylor, aware that his voice was slurring. There was nothing he could do to stop it. 'They're innocent, too.'

'Whom *do* you suspect, then?' asked Gertrude conversationally. 'A thief who wanted Mr Scudder's watch? Mr Adams told me it was particularly valuable.'

'Adams,' mused Taylor. 'He certainly has good reason to hope we believe a thief was responsible.'

Chapter 9

With no Ruby snoring next to him, half a pint of neat rum and the cumulative effect of more interrupted nights sleep than he could remember, Taylor did not wake until seven o'clock the following morning. He stared at his watch in disbelief before leaping out of bed, trying to recall the last time he had slept so late. He cut himself by shaving in haste, pulled a button off a new collar and when he finally shot downstairs at a run, was startled to detect the rich aroma of coffee.

'Ruby?' he called in surprise.

'You said Ruby was staying with her mother,' said Priestley, pouring the coffee into two cups. 'Would she be back this early?'

Taylor rubbed his eyes. 'No. I forgot you were here.' He glanced at the table, neatly laid and piled prodigiously with buttered toast. 'You made yourself at home, I see.'

'You told me to,' said Priestley, unabashed. 'Last night, you said whoever was awake first should brew the coffee.'

'So I did.' Taylor was so used to being up before guests that it was unthinkable one should have made his own breakfast. 'Did you sleep all right?'

'I can sleep well anywhere,' replied Priestley airily. 'Which is just as well, given that in the Antarctic there will be a dozen of us crammed inside a hut that's hardly bigger than your sitting room. Were you about to rush out?'

'I'm late,' said Taylor, gulping the coffee. He remembered the previous evening now: he and Priestley eventually escaping the Englands' alcoholic hospitality, and his offer of the spare room when he realised it was well after one o'clock. 'I'm normally at my desk at least an hour before this.'

'Then no wonder you were dead on your feet last night. I thought it was England's rum, which is why I didn't dare leave you to find your own way home.'

'I've been doing it quite successfully for some years now.'

Priestley grinned. 'But I'm not sure you would have managed last night. I know you didn't want to talk to England, but it was worth it. We've eliminated one suspect totally, and that's certainly a good thing.'

'Indeed,' said Taylor. The geologist's enthusiasm was infectious, and Taylor had to admit it was a relief to feel that the case had moved forward, even if only by a little. 'The first thing I need to do is check the paperwork for the Poplar Workhouse. Then I think it's time for another word with Adams.'

'Is there anything you can do for the Headless Bishop?' asked Priestley, reaching for more toast. He thought for a moment. 'How long was he in the mortuary before he was stolen?'

Taylor struggled to contain his impatience at the questions: the thought of hours already lost was bothering him. 'He arrived there at about midday on a Sunday, but had gone by nine o'clock the following morning, when the post-mortem was scheduled. Why?'

'Because someone must have been there to *accept* the body – a technician, perhaps – and he might remember something about it that you missed. These people are trained to look for specific things, after all.'

'Actually, Robert Bradwell – he's the Force's most experienced pathologist and also a friend of mine – was at the mortuary when the body arrived, and he signed for it. He did inspect it briefly, but he planned to perform a detailed examination the next day, and as he was busy with another case, I didn't press him. At the time, of course, it was just a simple stabbing.'

'But if Bradwell was in the mortuary, then how was the body stolen?' asked Priestley, gesturing that Taylor should sit and eat some toast.

'He doesn't *live* there, Raymond. He went home on Sunday evening, and discovered it gone the following day. Someone stole it during the night.'

Priestley frowned unhappily. 'I thought I might be able to come up with something to help you, but you've reached a proper dead end, haven't you?'

Taylor winced at the blunt appraisal. 'But at least the press can't stick with it much longer. Even tales like the Headless Bishop must have an ending somewhere.'

'But, unfortunately, not today. I assume Ruby reads *The Star*, because it was in the letter box.'

Taylor became aware of the paper lying on the table. 'I'm usually at work by the time the papers are delivered, so I'm not sure what she orders.'

He knew, however, that she had not been a subscriber

for long, and supposed she had taken the rag because she wanted to read for herself the reports about her husband's handling of the case that had London in such a turmoil. He did not blame her: he declined to discuss it with her, so the newspapers were the only way for her to find out what was being said about him.

'There's a piece on page three. I don't point it out to upset you, but so you know what to expect if you meet Marshall today.'

Fighting his distaste, Taylor opened it to an article entitled 'Bungling Inspector Makes Wrongful Arrest.' It told how Hopkins had been dragged from the Poplar Workhouse protesting his innocence, while the real killer had imbibed tea with Taylor in the wreckage of the laundry. The two women who had lost their lives were industrious, honest seamstresses, and there was no mention of brothels or arguments about the division of spoils. The account was by Bernard Faris, who had contrived to make Taylor appear callous as well as inept. It concluded by mentioning the Headless Bishop, rolling in his grave – wherever that happened to be – while a dangerous executioner stalked the streets around London Pool looking for his next victim.

Taylor gazed at the florid words. 'I wonder if this would have been reported had I left Grant to conclude the case on his own – if I hadn't discovered our mistake and rectified it.'

Priestley's expression was sombre. 'Probably not – it wouldn't have made such a good story. So, who told Faris all this rubbish? Grant?'

'Grant is portrayed as negatively as I am, and the sketch makes him look like an ape.'

'Hamilton, then – he was alarmed when he heard a miscarriage of justice had almost occurred, and reported it to Faris as further evidence of your incompetence, to strengthen his case for getting money to hire better detectives.'

Taylor stood up and tossed the paper in the fireplace. 'I can't waste time on this. Share a cab with me as far as the City, and I'll meet you at *Nimrod* at eleven.'

The Star was not a newspaper normally purchased by policemen, because it was consistently hostile to them. Most preferred the *Daily Mail*, while their senior officers favoured *The Times* or *The Daily Telegraph* – any man with a desire to move up the chain of command needed concise analyses of the quagmires created by his political masters.

However, that day virtually everyone had a copy of *The Star*, although most were hastily shoved out of sight when Taylor entered the station. Some men would not meet his eyes, while others returned his smile uneasily. He was acutely aware that he had become a pariah, and his colleagues were loath to be associated with him, lest they be tarred with the same brush.

He and Grant went over the paperwork for the Poplar Workhouse case, then talked to Vine, hearing again his frightened claim that he had been driven to wickedness by poverty and deprivation. He confided that he would escape the noose by telling the judge that he had been rendered temporarily insane by the summer heat. Taylor wished him luck, Grant sneered his disdain and they left him inventing increasingly wilder plans. When he emerged from the station, Taylor felt soiled and depressed.

Once at the docks, he walked along the South Quay slowly, not looking forward to what he was about to do. He could predict exactly how Adams was going to react to a further interview – with anger, hurt, indignation and shock – and the galling thing was that the confrontation would almost certainly do no good. Adams was unlikely to confess to the crime, especially as he probably knew hard evidence was lacking, and the whole encounter would be unpleasant. However, it would be a dereliction of duty not to speak to him, and it was an ordeal that could not be avoided or postponed.

Nimrod was busy, as usual. Men moved through the materiel, and winches and cranes creaked as they transferred it to holds and decks. When Berry asked whether Taylor had caught the 'thief what done for Mr Scudder,' there was an expectant hush, and the entire quay seemed to be waiting for the reply. Taylor could only say that the investigation was moving ahead, and that he hoped to have a solution soon. Several of the men started to discuss the comment, trying to penetrate its meaning, but Davis called them to order, and the chatter died away.

Meanwhile, Reverend Vallen was handing two large Bibles to Marshall, who took them with careful reverence, and started to climb the gangway.

'I'll stow them safely,' the surgeon called over his shoulder. 'Thank you for bringing them.'

Vallen smiled at Taylor as he approached. 'At a busy time like this, essential items like Bibles are often overlooked, and I wouldn't like to think of these men gone for years without spiritual comfort.'

'We have plenty of Scotch, vicar,' called Mackay, making several of the crew laugh.

'I was thinking of something a little more useful,' retorted Vallen, equally good humoured. 'Even you won't want to swallow Scotch when you wake restless and unsettled at four in the morning.'

'Don't be so sure, vicar, don't be so sure,' quipped Mackay, to the cheers of the crew.

Vallen chuckled, then turned back to Taylor. 'Marshall will make sure the Bibles are available for those who need them.'

'Will he?' asked Taylor. He recalled that the surgeon had made remarks that suggested he was devout, but owning a personal faith and ministering to others were two very different things. Taylor did not believe Marshall was a compassionate or understanding man.

'He has a deep, unshakable faith. He planned to join the Church when he was up at Cambridge, but went into medicine instead.' Vallen lowered his voice. 'Mackay doesn't have his strength. He jests and laughs and pleases the crew, but Marshall is the stronger of the two, because of his religious convictions.'

'And Adams?' asked Taylor. 'Does he possess this piety?'

'We haven't discussed it,' said Vallen. 'But I imagine he's like most of my flock: he doesn't think much about God until there's a need, and then he'll grip religion hard with both hands. Perhaps you should try a prayer or two, inspector. You must be deeply wounded by what has been written about you in the newspapers, and a few words with Him may restore your inner strength. My door is always open, should you feel the need to unburden yourself.'

'Thank you,' said Taylor awkwardly. With the recent exception of Priestley, no one else had been particularly sympathetic to his situation, and he was uncertain how to respond.

'Sergeant Grant told me you were shot by a robber last year,' Vallen went on. 'I counsel the victims of violence in hospitals, and I know the shock of an attack can last many months after the physical wounds have healed. So if you find your skills have become blunted these last months, don't despair. They'll return in time, I promise.'

'Right,' said Taylor, wondering whether anyone else thought his lack of success with the Headless Bishop was due to the incident that had occurred the previous November. Seeing Priestley waiting at the gangway, he excused himself with relief.

Priestley was unhappy when he heard what Taylor wanted to do, but went off in search of Adams, returning a few moments later to say the meteorologist was in the officers' cabin. Wordlessly, he led the way there, fidgeting restlessly while they waited for their chief suspect to finish signing papers for a supplier.

'You wanted to see me?' he asked, perching on the edge of a crate. 'Is it about yesterday, and that damned anemometer that Scudder broke? I can explain that.'

'Please do,' said Taylor. He saw Priestley wince at his cool tone.

'I was bloody angry, I admit, but once he bought me a new one, I relented. I was irritable with him for a day or two, but that's all. Yesterday, his damned mother got me unsettled with her ruddy insinuations, and that's why I reacted as I did.'

214

'I see,' said Taylor. 'However, while you may have forgiven Scudder for his transgression with the anemometer, you disliked him for other reasons. You said as much when we talked earlier.'

Adams nodded. 'Yes, I did, and I've never pretended otherwise. He was the most god-awful reptile, if you want the truth. He was a good biologist, though – knew his salps.'

'Salps are free-swimming chordates,' elucidated Priestley, although the policeman was none the wiser for the aside.

'You have no alibi for the time of Scudder's murder,' said Taylor, watching Adams intently. 'You say you met a woman, but you refuse to give us her name. You were seen very close to where the body was found, and you even ordered Berry and Riches to the far end of the quay.'

'My God!' breathed Adams in horror. 'You think *I* did it! I've explained all these things to you, but you don't believe me!'

'And then there's the Reserve letter opener,' Taylor went on relentlessly. 'There are only four members of the expedition who could have owned one. Shackleton and England are exonerated; you and one other remain. And you lied about yours.'

'My bloody mother,' said Adams bitterly. 'She's old, inspector, and gets confused. I *do* have a box of the damned things – she will insist on giving them to me for Christmas – but I never use them, and as far as I know, they're packed up in a chest in her attic.'

'The one I showed you yesterday,' said Taylor. 'Is it yours?'

215

'No! I've just told you where mine is. The one you showed me is completely unfamiliar, and I'd never hone one so bloody sharp, anyway. It would be dangerous with my mother poking around my things.'

'Are you prepared to tell us about the woman you were with? She might be able to exonerate you once and for all.'

'No!' Adams' face was white with anger, and he took a threatening step towards Taylor, fists clenched. 'She has nothing to do with it, and I won't let you pester her with questions.'

'Not even ones that will allow us to eliminate you from the investigation so we can concentrate on the real killer?'

Adams glared at him with dislike. 'No, not even those. And if I find out you have gone after her, I'll…'

'Yes?' asked Taylor mildly.

Adams controlled himself with difficulty. 'Never mind. You'll just have to find some other way forward with your bloody investigation.'

Taylor nodded. 'We will. I sent the knife to the Royal Naval College in Greenwich yesterday. It won't be long before we have their report.'

'Good,' said Adams harshly. 'Because they'll be able to identify its owner, and then you'll *have* to believe that it's not me. And when you do, I'll be demanding an official apology. So, if there's nothing further, I've a lot of work to do, and don't have time to talk bloody nonsense.'

He turned and stalked to the door. When he hauled it open to leave, someone stood up quickly in the corridor outside, and Adams swore when he almost tripped over him. It was Marshall, who was gathering some papers he appeared to have dropped. The surgeon grinned when Adams stormed towards the deck.

'I *knew* it was him,' he crowed. 'I told you, right from the start.'

'You were listening?' asked Priestley, shocked.

'What if I was? This is a small ship, and sounds carry, so you can bet your trousers that I wasn't the only one. I knew he did it!'

'How?' asked Taylor coolly. 'Did you see him stab Scudder?'

'I didn't need to,' said Marshall, still gloating. 'I just made an assessment of the evidence and drew my own conclusions. There are too many coincidences for Adams to be innocent – the lack of an alibi, his odd dealings with Berry and Riches, his refusal to show you his letter opener. It all adds up. I can't imagine why you haven't arrested him. Surely the facts speak for themselves?'

'Not in court,' replied Taylor shortly.

'Well, I'm sure you'll soon have all you need to convince the judges,' Marshall gushed. 'The Boss will be delighted.'

'I'm not so sure,' said Priestley. 'Adams was to have been his second-in-command.'

'Nonsense,' said Marshall briskly. 'Officially, the matter has yet to be decided, but I am the better candidate anyway. Well done, inspector. You must allow me to buy you a drink. You probably need one after what I read in *The Star* today.'

After Marshall had gone, Taylor became aware that many of the crew were regarding him coldly. Adams was

217

popular, and they resented what the police were doing. Taylor sighed, and hoped the anger would not focus on Priestley, too. In an effort to ensure it did not, he informed Marshall – who obviously had a talent for spreading tales – that Priestley had objected strenuously to the police's conclusions and had argued on Adams' behalf.

Shackleton came to see him, as he was preparing to leave the ship. Taylor had done all he could aboard; now it was a case of waiting for the Royal Naval College to tell him about the letter opener, and of sifting through statements and reports to look for inconsistencies he might have missed. The Boss' expression was grim as he sat on the crate recently vacated by Adams.

'So,' he said in a tired, hoarse voice. 'You think Adams killed Scudder. I wish you'd kept it quiet until you were sure. You may be wrong, and it would have been better to be discreet.'

'You should take that up with Marshall.'

Shackleton grimaced. 'The whole business is a damned shame, and I'm heartily sorry. Are you sure about this, Will? Could there be a mistake?'

'There's always room for error. Certainly Adams may never be formally charged, due to insufficient evidence. But I'm sorry too, Mick. I wish you hadn't asked me to investigate.'

'So do I,' said Shackleton, grimacing again. 'It wasn't the sort of thing a man should demand of a friend. I'd have been better with Grant, because then I could've railed against him and accused him of gross stupidity. But regardless, may I assume that you'll continue your enquiries, so you can be absolutely certain, before you take this to a more official level?'

Taylor nodded.

Shackleton cleared his throat. 'May I make a request, then? Can we keep this business on the ship until you've either enough evidence to charge Adams or to leave him alone? It would be a pity to let the press drag him through the mud...'

'I won't tell my colleagues. So if you read in *The Star* that Adams killed Scudder, it won't have come from the police.'

Taylor spent the rest of the day in his station, sifting through reports and the statements taken from members of the expedition. He made a list of inconsistencies and contradictions that would need to be ironed out, although most were minor and were of a type common in cases where many people had been interviewed by different officers. He finished at five o'clock, when the words began to blur on the page, and left thinking he would surprise Ruby by going home early – she had promised to return that day.

But when he arrived, the house was empty, and there was a curt note on the mantelpiece saying she would be staying with her mother until his current glut of cases had diminished. In an ominous postscript, she added that there was a meat pie in the scullery. Taylor regarded the specimen without enthusiasm, knowing that once he had managed to saw through Ruby's pastry – no mean task, even with a sharp knife – there would be a mass of uncooked mutton and perhaps some raw carrots within. He left it where it was, and aimed for the front door.

He wandered aimlessly, thinking about Vine, Adams and the Headless Bishop, wondering how he could redeem himself. The arrest of Adams would not help. The expedition was popular, and the notion of London's worst detective nabbing a man whom Shackleton had selected to go south was likely to render him even more loathsome in the eyes of the public. He would do what had to be done, of course, but he would not relish the task or its consequences.

A short while later, he knocked on a door, wondering whether he had remembered the address correctly. He was not even sure of his welcome, but he was strangely lonely and craved company. He supposed he could have caught a train to see Ruby, but he did not want to spend the evening listening to a lecture by his mother-in-law on his failings as a husband.

'I'm in danger of wallowing in self-pity,' he said, when Priestley answered. The young man's hair was wet and there was a towel around his neck. Priestley stood aside so he could enter.

'I assume from your morose mood that you haven't discovered anything new?' Taylor shook his head. 'I still think you're wrong, although Adams is a fool to refuse to tell you the name of this woman he's supposed to have been with.'

'To be honest, I'm not sure it would help anyway. He's told so many lies about when he left her, when he arrived at *Nimrod* and what he was doing here that I no longer have any idea what to believe regarding him.'

They talked for a while, then Priestley announced he was hungry, and Taylor realised he had eaten nothing all day but breakfast toast. They strolled towards Leicester Square, and its profusion of chop houses and oyster bars. After dining on lamb cutlets, boiled potatoes and some sort of pale-yellow mash, all smothered in a glutinous, lumpy gravy, they walked along the Embankment. Then Priestley stopped abruptly.

'I've just remembered that Murray is giving a lecture tonight – at Somerset House on The Strand. That's only five minutes from here, and I'm sure he'd be delighted to see friendly faces in the audience.'

'After what happened with Adams, he might not consider mine friendly,' warned Taylor, but he followed his youthful companion anyway.

They arrived to find that Priestley was not the only one who had come to support his colleague: Marshall and Mackay were there, and so were the hopefuls. Yaxley sat between Nigel Vallen and his father, who had dispensed with his clerical collar and was dressed in a suit of navy blue. O'Brien, perched on the other side of the vicar, started guiltily when he saw Taylor, who had the impression that the man would have bolted had he not been in an inside seat.

Taylor had expected to be bored, regaled with intricate descriptions of microscopic creatures bearing unmemorable Latin names, but Murray was a skilled and entertaining speaker. His quiet, unassuming modesty quickly won the audience's support, and he used lantern-slides to illustrate his points. Bowls were set out for donations to the expedition afterwards, and the audience responded with generosity.

'Fascinating,' said Reverend Vallen as they stood at the back of the hall, waiting their turn to congratulate Murray. 'I never knew there were so many wonderful creatures living in a continent covered in ice. It's quite extraordinary. God has certainly created marvels.'

'Evolution,' said Yaxley, one of a small group that included Vallen, the two surgeons and the hopefuls, with Priestley and Taylor on the periphery. 'They've *evolved* that way to make use of an ecological niche that was hitherto unexploited. They weren't created with those features.'

'I disagree,' said the vicar. 'There's far too great a tendency to see the world in terms of cold science these days, and we forget that the hand of the Creator is at work.'

'Amen to that,' said Marshall piously. 'His hand can be seen in all things, even science.'

He and Vallen began a religious discussion, which was interrupted by Murray, a cup of tea in one hand and several bankers' orders in the other. The conversation immediately reverted back to the lecture.

'I love these occasions,' said Murray, glowing with happiness. 'It's an honour to tell people about the wonders of Antarctica, and I derive great pleasure from it. And they're good for raising funds, too.'

'Not for all of us,' said Marshall snidely, glancing at Priestley. 'You didn't have the pleasure – if that's the correct word – of attending Priestley's talk at a local school. He drew a large crowd but shot through his fifty lantern-slides in under fifteen minutes, and then just stood there, squirming.'

Mackay joined in the fun. 'The whole presentation was so fast that one wee bairn got up and asked him to do it again, because they had forty-five minutes in hand and nothing else to do,' he hooted. 'It was hugely embarrassing. And we only made two-and-six.'

'I'm sure Priestley did an admirable job,' said Murray

kindly. 'But as long as you're here, Marshall, will you take this money to Shackleton?' He shoved the night's takings at the surgeon. 'Now poor Adams is under something of a cloud, you're the expedition's second-in-command.'

'I have always been his second-in-command,' said Marshall sharply. He grinned, suddenly and unexpectedly, when he saw how much Murray had collected. 'The Boss will be delighted, because the funds aren't rolling in as they should – probably because of this murder and the fact that it took such an unconscionably long time to solve. Oh, good evening, Inspector. I didn't see you there.'

'I'm surprised he dared show his face after what happened earlier with Adams,' drawled Mackay. 'But he bought a ticket, and his money is as capable of buying cans of corned beef as anyone else's, although I doubt Adams would eat any of it.'

'Our poor fund-raising can't have anything to do with the investigation, because it hasn't been made public,' said Priestley coldly, treating both men to an angry glare. Taylor was intrigued: over the last few days Priestley had started to assert himself, and the two least likeable members of the expedition were now bearing the brunt of his developing confidence. 'You are speaking drivel.'

Marshall's eyes blazed, but he held his temper. 'Then how do you explain the fact that donations have slowed to a trickle? Of course the inspector's dubious skills in thief-taking – or should I say meteorologist-taking? – are responsible. And because of it, Shackleton told me this evening that he's going to eliminate the last position, to cut costs.'

'You mean the hopefuls' post?' cried Reverend Vallen, dismayed. 'Surely not!'

'Yes,' said Marshall, either oblivious to or careless of the fact that such news would be a bitter blow to the three men clustered around him. Taylor saw their horrified faces, and was sorry the news had been broken in so callous a manner. It was cruel and unnecessary, and showed Marshall to lack the leadership qualities that Shackleton possessed in abundance.

The vicar turned to his son, Yaxley and O'Brien. 'My dear boys! I'm so sorry…'

'Actually, all is not lost,' said Murray, frowning at Marshall with disapproval. 'There's still Scudder's place to fill, so we're back to where we were before: one place and three applicants.'

'Think yourselves lucky, then,' said Marshall with a shrug. 'Are you walking home, Mackay? I'll need some protection if I'm to have charge of all this money, and you're a fair hand in a brawl.'

Mackay nodded in a way that said he took the remark as a compliment. Yaxley went with them, while Murray was snagged by a large lady swathed in a copious quantity of crinoline, asking questions about the 'poor penguin babies' and how they managed in the cold. Should she and her friends crochet little coats to see them through the worst of the weather, as they had knitted socks for the troops in the Boer War?

'No, ma'am,' replied Murray with cool aplomb. 'They're quite capable of knitting for themselves.'

Once outside, O'Brien tried to slink away, but was obliged to stop when Nigel called out in his good-natured manner that he and his father had promised to drop him off en route to their home. Trapped, O'Brien hovered uneasily, obviously wishing they would hurry up and leave. He kept glancing towards Taylor, so it took no imagination to see where the source of his discomfort lay.

'I heard you identified your culprit, Inspector,' said the vicar sadly. 'But although I'm relieved that the waiting is at an end, it's difficult to rejoice in your success.'

'I agree,' said Nigel unhappily. 'Poor Adams. He was the last person I'd have suspected. Well, perhaps Mr Murray is the *last* person, but Adams isn't far off.'

'Everyone feels sorry for Adams – except Marshall – but what about Brice?' demanded O'Brien, his voice unsteady. '*He's* the one who was murdered, but he's not missed, it seems.'

'That's untrue,' said the vicar gently. 'Nigel grieves for Brice, as do I.'

'Yes, *you* do.' O'Brien shot a dark, resentful glower to where Mackay, Yaxley and Marshall were walking down the road. 'But *they* don't, and neither do the crew. Even Murray, who's generally a gentle soul, doesn't show Brice's memory the proper respect. I know Brice wanted his position, but that's no reason to celebrate his death.'

'Murray isn't celebrating!' exclaimed Nigel, aghast by the claim. 'And you're mistaken: we are all appalled by what's happened, but you feel his loss too keenly. I know you were friends, but I don't think you should withdraw from the expedition over it. He wouldn't have wanted that.'

'You've withdrawn your application?' asked Priestley, startled.

'Actually, I withdrew before Brice died,' said O'Brien.

'Or I intended to. I just haven't got around to telling the Boss yet.'

Taylor regarded him intently in the unsteady light of the street's gas lamp. 'Is your withdrawal anything to do with the fact that Shackleton decided you weren't to be included anyway? He, Murray and Scudder discussed it, and Shackleton said he intended to tell you the bad news.'

O'Brien winced. 'He never found the time for such an insignificant duty – he still hasn't,' he said bitterly. 'So Brice told me.'

'I'm sorry,' said Reverend Vallen gently. 'And these last few days I've been rattling on about how two of you hopefuls will have the experience of a lifetime.'

'One,' said Nigel. 'It's back to one place again now. One place and *two* hopefuls.'

'You're in a strong position, Nigel,' said O'Brien with a wan smile. 'The Boss likes you, and Yaxley's too argumentative. However, don't rest on your laurels just yet, because Yaxley has some talent with charcoal and paints. In other words, he could also serve as the expedition artist, which gives him a distinct advantage.'

'Why did the Boss take against you?' asked Nigel, obviously sorry for O'Brien. 'Was it because you and Scudder were…close?'

There was a momentary silence, and Priestley's jaw dropped as he finally understood the nature of O'Brien's relationship with Scudder.

'He didn't know about it,' said O'Brien in a small voice. 'No one did. I confided in you, and I know you kept our secret – until now. But no one else was aware.'

'Close?' asked Priestley, to be sure. 'You mean you

and Scudder…?'

'We were of the same mind,' said O'Brien softly. 'Why do you think I volunteered for this miserable expedition in the first place? Because I didn't want to be parted from him. I *loved* Brice, and intended to spend as much time with him as possible.'

'Such…friendships are illegal,' said Priestley, glancing uneasily towards Taylor.

'I don't *care*,' cried O'Brien, his voice wavering with emotion. 'I don't care what people think *or* about narrow and unjust laws. Taylor can throw me in prison if he likes. I don't care about anything any more.'

'You don't seem surprised, Will,' said Priestley in an undertone. 'Did you guess? It answers why O'Brien was so devastated by Scudder's death; why Scudder was determined to have O'Brien appointed; and why O'Brien was loitering at Scudder's house – he was grieving and wanted to be near his lover's home. It also explains the Boss' uneasy feeling about O'Brien – he must have sensed a deeper partnership than would be appropriate. You knew, didn't you?'

Taylor nodded. 'My suspicions were confirmed when I read the Cannon Street arrest report. O'Brien was taken into custody with Scudder that night.'

'You didn't tell me,' said Priestley reproachfully.

'There was no need – it was irrelevant to the murder. Technically, I should prosecute O'Brien, but I don't see what good would come out of it.'

'Your liberalism is a credit to you,' said Priestley. 'But you're wrong to assume that the relationship is irrelevant to Scudder's murder. It resolves some of the details.' He turned to O'Brien. 'You say you don't care, but you may have helped to bring about Scudder's death in an indirect way, and you know it. It's guilt as well as grief that haunts you at the moment.'

O'Brien stared at him, then lowered his head. 'The Monagasque trawl,' he said in a low voice.

Priestley nodded. 'It was you who tampered with the hatch so that the trawl couldn't be stowed. Now I understand why: you couldn't go on the expedition, so you decided that Scudder shouldn't, either. You hoped to exasperate him into resigning, which is why you continued to offer your services as a volunteer, even after it was clear you would never be appointed.'

'It's dangerous,' whispered O'Brien, as he paced. 'I didn't want him to go without me to watch over him.'

'If you damaged the hatch, then you must also have cut Scudder's nets, broken his specimen bottles and snapped his scalpels,' surmised Taylor. 'He thought someone had sabotaged his equipment, and he was right.'

'I didn't do it for malice,' said O'Brien miserably. 'I did it to protect him.' He regarded Taylor with tragic eyes. 'But his murder was my fault. If I hadn't tampered with the hatch, the trawl would have been stowed, and he wouldn't have returned to the docks that night – to meet his killer.'

Chapter 10

There was little Taylor or Priestley could say to soothe O'Brien's troubled conscience, but Reverend Vallen showed dutiful compassion. He insisted that the unhappy man stay with him and Nigel at the vicarage that night, and led him away by the hand, as though he were a child. O'Brien responded to his sympathy, and Taylor had the feeling that Vallen's understanding would save him from a night of dreadful torment.

'It's fortunate that Vallen is an open-minded man,' said Taylor. 'Not all priests would react with kindness to a bereaved homosexual.'

'Not all policemen, either,' pointed out Priestley. 'However, Vallen isn't as open-minded as you think – at least, not as regards evolution and the Creation.'

'Those are religious issues,' said Taylor. 'Vicars are supposed to be inflexible on them. He can hardly go around saying that God played no part in the Creation, can he?'

'It's more complex than that,' said Priestley. '*I* believe God created our universe – of course He did. But the issue isn't *whether* He did, but *how*. Vallen is a fundamentalist in that respect, which is unusual these days.'

'Perhaps you just haven't discussed it with many clergymen,' said Taylor, not very interested. 'But while O'Brien might have company tonight, I won't, so I think I'll use the opportunity to visit the Lord Nelson and have another word with Long Ron. It's late enough that he may be drunk, and he might let slip some detail he forgot to mention last time.'

It was an act of desperation, but it was better than doing nothing. Uninvited, Priestley fell into step at his side, but Taylor did not have the heart to order him home. They walked in silence, both reflecting on Scudder's life and the repercussions his death had had on those left behind.

As they drew near London Pool, Taylor changed direction suddenly, walking to where a crumbling brick wall separated the Thames from a row of ramshackle wharves and warehouses. Broken glass had been cemented into its top in some places, while in others it was virtually derelict. Taylor aimed for a place where the bricks had tumbled into a heap, and had been replaced by a crude fence of rough wood. A brighter patch showed where a gap had recently been plugged, but next to it was a yawning hole, where someone had made another entrance in the rotting panels.

'What are you doing,' asked Priestley in alarm, when Taylor started to climb through it. 'Long Ron isn't going to be in there.'

'Fountain Dock,' explained Taylor. 'Where the Headless Bishop was found. The moon and weather conditions are about the same tonight as when he was dumped, and I want a few moments to stand and think.

230

Wait here.'

Priestley watched him disappear, then followed, muttering irritably under his breath when splinters tore his jacket. Once through the fence, he paused to survey his surroundings in the moonlight. He was on a narrow strip of wasteland that extended to the river, hemmed in on either side by the thick, featureless walls of warehouses. They were windowless, black-stained and loomed in a way that was claustrophobic. Underfoot, the earth had been baked hard by the summer sun, and straggly weeds grew to knee height, giving the place an air of desolation. It ran flat for a few yards, then sloped sharply towards the water.

The Thames itself was dark and sinister, streaked with moonlight. It stank of sewage and decay. The tide was out, so Fountain Dock boasted a small, grimy beach, littered with mud-coated rocks, discarded rubbish and something large, jagged, and broken that looked like part of a boat. Taylor was silhouetted there, standing with his hands in his pockets as he stared at the water.

Priestley wondered where the body had been when the police had found it. He studied the terrain, and guessed that it had been discovered slightly forward and to his right, where the shadows were deepest – if the Bishop had been left on the beach where Taylor stood, Long Ron would have dragged it upwards by the shortest possible route. He was about to ask, but the words died in his throat. He strained his eyes in the gloom. Had something moved?

Suddenly, a figure darted out of the shadows and launched itself at Taylor. Priestley had a fleeting glimpse of a cudgel raised, ready to smash downwards. His warning yell came just in time, and the inspector ducked away from what would have been a debilitating, if not fatal, blow. Taylor crashed to the ground, and Priestley raced down the slope and drove back the attacker with a smashing punch to the jaw. While the fellow staggered away, Priestley adopted a fighting stance, fists clenched and knees loose.

'Police!' cried the man furiously, wielding the cudgel. With a shock Priestley recognised the weapon as a truncheon, thick and sturdy, and with a pale gold gleam where the Force crest was emblazoned. 'If you know what's good for you, you'll put your hands in the air and stand still.'

'Grant?' called Taylor, peering into the gloom. 'Is that you?'

The truncheon was lowered. 'Sir? What are you doing here? And who's he? Whoever he is, he punched me, and I'll have him for it.'

Taylor clambered to his feet. 'More to the point, what are *you* doing here? And what precipitated that wild attack? If Priestley hadn't yelled a warning, you might have killed me.'

'The Headless Bishop, sir,' explained Grant sullenly. 'You aren't going to solve it – you're more interested in Scudder and the Poplar Workhouse. The Bishop's been forgotten.'

'Of course he hasn't been forgotten,' objected Taylor, stung. 'Why do you think I'm here now?'

Grant sounded exasperated. 'But you never confide in me, so how am I supposed to know that? It *looked* like you'd given up, so I thought I'd have a go at cracking it myself. I'd been here for about ten minutes when I saw you – a shadowy figure wandering around a murder scene – and I thought you might be the killer. You can't blame me for striking out, sir. Not under the circumstances.'

'Then you can't blame Priestley for punching you, either,' retorted Taylor. 'What did you hope to learn by coming here?'

Grant shrugged, slipping the truncheon inside a specially made pocket in his trousers. Taylor watched disapprovingly, not liking plain-clothed officers carrying weapons that were part of a uniform. It suggested a propensity to violence that he had long suspected in Grant.

'I'm not sure,' admitted Grant reluctantly, 'but I've watched you revisit the scenes of murders, to think about what might have happened, so I decided to try it myself. *I* didn't see the body, remember? *You* sent me off to take witness statements – and what a waste of time that was! – and so I thought I'd come here to see if I could imagine what it was like that night.'

Taylor gazed at him in surprise. He had not realised his sergeant harboured such resentment at being assigned to house-to-house enquiries, rather than being a part of the group that had remained with the body. At the time, Taylor had considered interviewing potential witnesses far more important than sifting through the garbage washed up on the Dock, although Grant clearly did not agree.

Grant turned his scowl on Priestley, in a way that said he was jealous of the fact that the geologist had accompanied Taylor, while Grant was excluded from his inspector's confidences.

'You haven't explained what *he's* doing here yet,' he said eventually. 'Sir.'

'We came to do the same as you,' replied Taylor evenly, ignoring the smouldering resentment. 'To try to see whether there might be something I missed. Did you learn anything?'

'No.' Grant sounded disgusted. 'I suppose I shall visit a few local taverns now, to ask questions, but I'm not hopeful. I've done it before without success. I heard a rumour that there was a tall man who witnessed the dumping of the body, but no one will tell me his name.'

'I know his name,' said Taylor, walking towards the road. Fountain Dock, with its air of hopelessness and abandonment, was beginning to depress him. 'Come and talk to him with me. Who knows? Perhaps the sight of a truncheon will achieve what free beer has not.'

Because it was a Saturday night, the Lord Nelson was heaving, and its patrons had spilled out onto the streets, yelling and shouting in ale-fuelled voices. The evening shift of a local foundry had just finished, and the workmen had been advised about a number of redundancies; this was being discussed in indignant bellows. The mood was ugly, and it was beginning to spread to other customers. Someone remarked that the foundry owners would employ the police to keep the dismissed workmen away, and the prediction resulted in a growl of universal disapprobation.

'I don't think this is the night to speak to Long Ron,' said Taylor, holding back.

'*I'm* not scared,' said Grant, hauling out his truncheon. 'I'll get him for you.'

'Fear has nothing to do with it,' replied Taylor, putting out a hand to stop him. 'There will be a brawl if you go in there now, and while you might be capable of looking after yourself, and even of arresting Long Ron, others will be less fortunate.'

'Others?' sneered Grant. He flicked a disdainful nod in Priestley's direction. 'You mean him?'

Taylor looked pointedly at the sergeant's bruised chin. 'No. I was thinking about the women and youngsters in the crowd, not to mention men who are too drunk to protect themselves. Put that thing away, Grant. With luck, these folk will disperse peacefully and go home. To incite them would be irresponsible.'

'If you say so,' said Grant shortly. It was clear he did not agree.

'There's Long Ron,' said Priestley, pointing suddenly to where the tall labourer was reeling unsteadily away from the tavern. 'He must be going home.'

'Good,' said Grant, moving forward. 'We can talk to him after all.'

'I don't trust Grant,' whispered Priestley, when the sergeant was out of earshot. 'He solves problems with violence, rather than his wits.'

Grant immediately proved Priestley's point by bringing Long Ron crashing to the ground with a well-aimed swipe of his night-stick, and then hauling him a short distance down an alley while the man howled in pain and confusion. It all happened too quickly for Taylor to stop him.

'Steady, Grant,' he ordered sharply, catching him up. 'Let me—'

'Who killed the Headless Bishop?' snarled Grant,

leaning close to Long Ron so that the prostrate man cringed away in terror. 'I want a name or you can kiss goodbye to your kneecaps.'

'I don't know!' screeched Ron, terrified. He gestured to Taylor. 'Like I told him the other night, I ain't never seen the cove before. And I ain't seen him since. I swear!'

'I don't believe you,' hissed Grant, raising his truncheon.

'Sergeant!' snapped Taylor, seizing the upraised weapon and wresting it away from him.

Grant rounded on him with such fury, that Taylor gripped the cosh in anticipation of using it to defend himself, certain the sergeant was going to attack him. Grant eyed it for a moment, then growled, 'You said we should see whether a truncheon worked where free beer—'

'I said the *sight* of a truncheon; I didn't intend you use it.' Taylor crouched next to the cowering Ron, using his own body to shield him from Grant. 'You weren't entirely honest with us the other night: you told one or two lies. We both know what they are, so we don't need to go over it all again, but I want to know one thing. Did the man carry a bag, as you claimed, or was he empty-handed?'

Ron swallowed hard. 'He had a bag,' he whispered, eyes flicking nervously towards Grant. 'Maybe it wasn't as big as I said…Well, maybe it wasn't a bag, either. Maybe it was an armful of clothes.'

'An armful of clothes?' echoed Grant in disbelief. 'What would a killer want with an armful of clothes?'

Taylor ignored him, his attention focussed on Ron. 'Did you see what kind of clothes?'

'All of them.' Ron eased farther behind Taylor as Grant clenched his fists. 'He had a coat over one arm, and I saw braces attached to trousers and the white gleam of a shirt. And shoes with socks stuffed in them. But no hat – it must have been in his pocket.'

'You seem very certain,' said Taylor. 'Yet you've never mentioned it before. Why?'

Ron licked his lips uneasily. 'Because a bag with a severed head, hands and feet was more interesting to Mr Faris,' he mumbled sheepishly. He became defensive. 'He wouldn't have given me a penny if I'd said the killer was toting a bundle of garments! And a man needs to look out for hisself in this world, tweak the truth a little, to get by.'

'You're absolutely sure about this now? It's important.'

Ron nodded. 'I ain't lying now. I'm telling the truth.'

'No hat?' asked Priestley. He glanced at Taylor when Ron nodded again. 'Then the one you found might well help you identify the victim.'

'It won't,' said Grant sulkily. 'I was given that cap to investigate, and the lead went nowhere. No one recognised it, and no one reported one missing that matched. Like this piece of dung says, the victim's hat was probably in the killer's pocket.' His face took on a malicious cant. 'Along with the Bishop's head, hands and feet.'

'That's right,' said Ron, eager to please. 'The killer's coat was loose, like I told you, so perhaps the body parts was in his pockets. But all I saw was clothes, sir. Can I go now?'

Taylor helped him to stand, which he did slowly and with obvious pain. Grant growled his disapproval as

Taylor handed Ron some coins, then turned on his heel and stalked to the end of the alley, to see whether the crowd had dispersed and it was safe for them to leave.

When he had gone, Ron turned to Taylor. 'You want to watch him. He's been around here before, asking questions and making threats. One of my pals told him a lie, just to get him to piss off, but the next day it was in the papers as fact. I'm telling you this because you done right by me.'

'What lie?' asked Taylor.

'My pal told him that the Headless Bishop had one of his knees smashed before he died, which he made up on the spot. The next day it was in *The Star*. I told Mr Faris it was a lie, but he said what was printed was printed, and that was the end of it.'

'But *you* lied to Faris, too,' said Priestley, bemused by Ron's contorted moral code.

'That was different,' said Ron. '*I* saw the body, and so I got a right to say what I like, but my pal never did. And that sergeant didn't have the right to sell my pal's lies to Mr Faris, neither.'

Greasy Grant slouched away on business of his own once Long Ron had limped into the darkness. Taylor started to walk towards London Bridge and home, but Priestley had other ideas.

'Where's this cap, Will? At your station?'

Taylor stared at him. 'You want to see it now? It must be nearing midnight.'

'So what? I don't trust Grant to have performed an adequate job of tracing it – and Ron just said the killer wasn't carrying a hat, so I suspect it did belong to the

Bishop. The killer was wearing his own hat to conceal his face, so it wasn't his. However, as this might be the only item of the victim's in your possession, you *have* to follow up on it. And now that Grant has heard Ron's testimony, who's to say that the cap might not just disappear?'

'Ron may have been mistaken – a cap would be easy to miss in the dark. You may not think much of Grant, but he's tenacious when it suits him, and if the cap held a clue, I think he'd have run it down.'

Priestley was becoming exasperated. 'But he hasn't. Why? Because he's hoping you'll fail, so he can step into your shoes. Remember what Ron said: Grant's the one who's been leaking information to *The Star*. The business with the smashed knee proves it.'

Taylor made no reply. He was both hurt and shocked by the betrayal, although he supposed he should not be surprised: Grant had never shown him much loyalty, which was why Taylor had always treated him with a cautious reserve.

'So where's this cap?' Priestley asked eventually. 'I have a liking for headgear myself, so maybe I can recognise where it was bought.'

'It's at the mortuary.'

Priestley gazed at him. 'Why? Surely it can't be normal to leave evidence in there? Especially after the Bishop was stolen from the place?'

'It's locked in one of the offices,' Taylor shrugged. 'After the leaks to the press, I was wary of my station, so I left it with my friend Robert Bradwell.'

'Very well,' said Priestley gamely. 'We'll go to the mortuary. Lead on.'

They hired a hansom, and arrived at a section of the city that was probably depressing by day, but that was positively Hadean by night. The mortuary comprised a squat, brick building that was black from decades of soot, and those of its windows that were free of wooden boards were cracked or broken. A tall wall topped with barbed wire surrounded a dismal little courtyard where dead visitors were admitted, while living ones used a heavy door that someone had painted red. Taylor aimed for the yard, where the twin gates stood open and a lamp flickered unsteadily.

'We're in luck. They must have opened to accept a customer.'

'You fetch the cap; I'll wait here.' Priestley didn't like the look of the dirty enclosure, or the sinister aura of the door at its far end.

'Come on. It won't take a minute. Besides, you'll look like a pervert if you lurk out here. Someone might send for the police.'

But Priestley shook his head. 'Scudder is in there,' he said in something of a gulp.

'Stored in a separate room,' said Taylor. 'You won't see him, I promise. Come on.'

With considerable reluctance, Priestley followed him across the cracked flagstones, and through the door. He found himself in a dark corridor in which their footsteps echoed eerily. Immediately, they were assailed by a sickly cloying stench that he imagined was the uglier side of death, grotesquely overlain by the chemical reek of a concentrated cleaning agent. He thought the combination of the two was far worse than either would have been alone.

Taylor opened another door at the end of the corridor, and ushered him into a brightly lit chamber that had been painted white. It was an unfortunate choice of colours, because it showed stains that would have been less obvious had the decorator opted for green or blue. Priestley glanced around quickly, relieved to note that Taylor had been telling him the truth, and that none of the still forms lying on trolleys were his erstwhile colleague.

'Robert!' said Taylor, smiling at the room's sole living occupant. 'I didn't expect to find you here so late.'

The man straightened from where he had been studying the body of a young woman. Priestley looked away; there was a livid bruise around her neck and her tongue was lolling swollen in her mouth. Robert Bradwell was in his late fifties or early sixties, with grey hair and a matching moustache. His brown eyes were kindly and intelligent, and the wrinkles around them suggested he laughed a lot. He laughed now, obviously pleased to see Taylor.

'I didn't expect you, either, Will. It must be almost one o'clock.'

He offered his hand to Priestley when Taylor introduced them, and Priestley would have taken it, had Taylor not stopped him. The geologist shuddered when he saw what he might have touched, although Bradwell guffawed uproariously at what he thought was a fine joke, and continued to cackle while he stood at a sink and rinsed his fingers.

'You shouldn't be here alone,' chided Taylor, as they followed Bradwell into an office as small, cramped and cluttered as anywhere aboard *Nimrod*. 'Not with the gates unlocked.'

'Did I forget to close them again? Blast! I promised you I'd be more careful after last time.' Bradwell pinched the bridge of his nose. 'And blast again! You told me not to say anything about it, and I blurt it out in front of our visitor without a second thought. I must be getting senile, Will, prattling on like an old woman.'

'It's all right. We can trust him.'

Priestley regarded Taylor intently: here was something else the inspector had not told him before. 'The Headless Bishop was stolen because the mortuary gates were left open?'

'I think he would have been taken regardless,' said Taylor. 'The gates being unlocked just made the theft easier.'

'Will agreed to keep my carelessness quiet,' confided Bradwell ruefully. 'If the newspapers had got hold of *that* little detail, I'd have had every criminal in London flocking here to see what he could steal.'

'Steal?' asked Priestley weakly. 'You mean body parts?'

Bradwell chuckled. 'No, I mean personal effects. Most of my customers arrive in clothes, and some come complete with purses, jewellery, watches and other valuables. If word had got out that I'm in the habit of occasionally neglecting security…well, it doesn't bear thinking about.'

'You also promised not to work here alone,' said Taylor. 'It may not be safe.'

'I'm not alone: I have three medical students with me. They're in trouble for some prank or other, and have been ordered to work here for a month of their summer vacation, as penance. You see how the noble skills of pathology are regarded in medical schools these days?'

'Where are they?' asked Taylor.

'Smoking in the chapel.' Bradwell shrugged when Priestley's jaw dropped in shock. 'It's disrespectful, I know, but better there than here, where the gas pipes leak. I'd rather be accused of sacrilege than end up in pieces on one of my own slabs. You're looking pale, lad. Would you like a tot of brandy?'

'He doesn't drink alcohol.'

'Good for him. If you saw some of the livers I have in here, you'd never touch a drop again either, Will. But to what do I owe this visit? Am I to expect another client tonight?'

'Raymond is going to solve the Headless Bishop case by looking at that cap.'

'Thank God,' said Bradwell, going to a desk and unlocking a drawer. He removed a package rolled in brown paper and handed it over. 'It's about time. I don't know how you can stand it, Will, reading those lies written about you almost every day.'

Priestley unrolled the paper with considerable trepidation, fearful of what he might find. He had not imagined himself to be squeamish, but he had not reckoned on the chamber of horrors that comprised Bradwell's domain. The shelves of pickled specimens, some containing entire limbs and organs, had not escaped his attention, and neither had the bucket of red slops that stood near a drain. Taylor was doubtless inured to such sights, but they were new to Priestley, and he did not like them. However, his concerns about the cap were unfounded. It had been cleaned. Relieved, he turned it over in his hands.

It was cotton, and comprised an uneven selection of red, silver and black stripes, broken at the front by a coat of arms. He looked for a label, and was disappointed to see that where there should have been a piece of cloth giving the name of its maker, there was only a row of ragged holes: it had come away from its moorings. The holes were frayed, and he supposed it had been lost naturally. However, he was sure about one thing.

'This is a college cap,' he said, breaking into Bradwell's graphic description of the strangled woman in the other room. 'Worn by men who row or play cricket for their college or university.'

Taylor nodded. 'We'd already surmised that. What we haven't worked out is which one.'

Priestley experienced a wave of indignation on Taylor's behalf: it was obvious that the cap was part of a uniform, and Grant should have persisted until he had identified it. It was not from a well-known institution, such as an Oxbridge college, but that was no excuse.

'It shouldn't be difficult,' he said. 'The coat of arms is distinctive: three red birds in flight beneath three peaks, an open book with silver crowns above them, and what I think is a fleur-de-lis. And it says *In Domino Confido*, which is Latin.'

'Meaning, "I trust in the Lord,"' said Taylor. 'But He hasn't shown us the way on this one.'

Bradwell patted his arm comfortingly, then turned to Priestley. 'I took the thing to Bart's, where I teach, and showed it to a few colleagues, but no one recognised it. And Grant spent days touring gentlemen's outfitters. If it *is* a college cap, then it's not a very well-known one.'

'Nevertheless, can we conclude that the Headless

Bishop was a student?' asked Priestley, aware of a hammering in his chest. It was exciting to be unravelling a clue in a case that had so perplexed the police.

Bradwell shook his head. 'He was the wrong age – late twenties or early thirties. Yet the hat itself is only four or five years old and we can't conclude that he continued to wear an old school cap for sentimental reasons. It must be a college cap, although not one any of us recognise.'

'I'll ask my father about it,' said Priestley, rolling it in the paper and slipping it in his pocket. 'He's a headmaster, and his students enrol in colleges all over the country. Many keep in touch with him.'

He determined to make a start the next morning, and to succeed where Grant had failed. If nothing else, it would underline to Taylor that Grant should not be trusted. Or worse, that he was deliberately obstructive.

Bradwell had turned to Taylor, concerned. 'Are you sure about this, Will? That's police evidence, and there'll be hell to pay if someone finds out you're entrusting it to a civilian.'

'I'm sure.' Taylor shrugged. 'The alternative is to leave it in your drawer. If Raymond thinks he can —' He broke off at a sudden commotion from outside.

'More visitors,' said Bradwell, with a predatory smile. 'I am in demand tonight.'

As it turned out, the rumpus was not another body arriving, but the three medical students. They had caught Grant loitering outside, and had sneaked up on him and pinned his arms to his sides before he could grab his truncheon. He was yelling furiously as they dragged him in.

'Let him go,' ordered Bradwell, eyeing the sergeant in disdain. 'He's a policeman, although you might not believe it to look at him.'

Priestley saw he was not the only one who had taken against Grant.

'He was trying to climb in through one of the windows, sir,' explained the leader of the trio, a burly, thick-set fellow whose face seemed vaguely familiar.

'I was doing a security check,' snarled Grant.

'Did you hear that, Marshall?' asked Bradwell facetiously. 'Sergeant Grant was ensuring we were safe. Where would we be without such dedication?'

'Marshall?' echoed Priestley. He studied the student closely. 'Are you related to Eric Marshall, the surgeon? He mentioned a cousin who was a medical student.'

'That's me,' the lad said proudly. 'Peter Marshall. My cousin's going to the Antarctic as Shackleton's second-in-command.'

Taylor beckoned to Grant and led him down the corridor, away from others. For the first time in their brief acquaintance, Priestley saw he was genuinely angry, and understood why: Grant had doubled back after slinking away, and had followed his inspector as he might one of his suspects. Uneasily, Priestley wondered whether Grant had overheard what he planned to do with the cap. If so, he might cause trouble, since the implication was that his own efforts had been lacking.

While the policemen were talking, Bradwell showed Priestley and the three students the strangled woman. He explained in grisly detail the physical signs that were indicative of throttling, which deeply fascinated the others, but had Priestley sidling away to stand near the door. It was all too horrible, and unlike the medics, he saw not a collection of physiological symptoms, but a young woman whose life had been cruelly snuffed out. He tuned it out, and tried to hear what Taylor was saying to Grant, but caught nothing but the occasional murmur. The inspector was not a man who yelled when his temper was up.

When they eventually rejoined the others, Grant was grey-faced and shaking, although Priestley could not decide whether from rage or shock. Taylor was impassive. He nodded a farewell to Bradwell and aimed for the door, but before he could reach it, there was another chaos of voices and more visitors arrived. There were several constables and a man in an expensive suit.

'Chief Superintendent Hamilton,' said the pathologist with a distinct lack of warmth. 'I assume you're here about the Mayfair murder?'

Hamilton was a heavyset, balding man with eyes that Priestley thought were sly. He had soft white hands, a sizable paunch and there was something about him that made the geologist feel as though he should be on his guard. Priestley rarely took against people on first sight, but all his instincts clamoured at him to be wary of Taylor's chief superintendent.

'I thought I'd better put in an appearance,' Hamilton said smoothly. 'She's the daughter of an eminent banker, and I don't want it said that I lie in bed while wealthy Londoners are strangled. What are you doing here, Taylor? I certainly don't want *you* working on this.'

'He's here for the Headless Bishop,' said Bradwell, sharply defensive. 'You remember him? The case that

247

blew out of all proportion, because the police elected not to deny certain rumours?'

'Don't be impertinent,' snapped Hamilton angrily. 'It's not our fault it dissolved into a shambles – the police certainly didn't tell Faris about the missing head.' He shot Bradwell an unpleasant glance, making it clear whom he blamed. Then his gaze swivelled to Priestley. 'Who are you?'

'A witness in the Scudder case,' said Taylor with an expressionless gaze that Priestley thought made him look rather dangerous.

'Here to identify marks associated with frostbite on a body,' fabricated Bradwell blithely.

'At this time of night?' Hamilton was not so far promoted that he had lost all his policeman's instincts, and was still able to detect a lie when he heard one.

'Of course,' replied Bradwell coldly. 'The dead decompose, so Mr Priestley's expert opinion was a matter of urgency. If all witnesses were so accommodating, your officers would have a far easier time of it.'

'Have you made an arrest yet on the Scudder case, Taylor?' asked Hamilton, whipping around suddenly to address his inspector.

'No,' replied Taylor, so shortly it was insolent.

Surprisingly, Hamilton softened. 'I appreciate your dedication in working such gruelling hours. I know the last few weeks haven't been easy on you. So what have you learned? And how does it relate to frostbite?'

'Unfortunately, it transpired to be a false lead,' interjected Bradwell, thus saving Priestley from the need to invent an explanation.

'Pity,' said Hamilton with genuine regret. 'Then what

248

about the Headless Bishop? Bradwell said you came here looking into some aspect of that, too.'

'He came to study the photograph I took of the body before it was stolen,' said Bradwell. Priestley had never heard so many falsehoods uttered in such a short space of time.

'I remember that photograph,' mused Hamilton. 'You took it because you happened to have a spare plate left from an earlier case, and we were grateful we had something to go on after the Bishop disappeared. May I see it? Then I can state, with complete honesty, that I've been looking at the Headless Bishop tonight, too.'

Bradwell opened a cabinet, and passed a large picture to Hamilton, who held it at arm's length in the manner of the long-sighted. Priestley noticed Grant straining to see it, too, and recalled the sergeant saying he had never seen the Bishop's body; he had probably not seen the photograph, either. With uncharacteristic spite, Priestley moved slightly, to block Grant's line of sight, then braced himself to look at the black-and-white image.

He was relieved to find it not too dreadful: a picture of a torso with arms. Head, legs and hands were not in the frame, and Priestley wondered whether the photograph had been shown to Faris to 'prove' the Bishop was missing certain parts, although anyone with sense should have seen that the extremities had simply been outside the photographer's field of vision.

The wound was not much to look at, and comprised a single pear-shaped slit on the left side of the chest. Priestley knew nothing about weapons, but it seemed that it could have been made with something as small as a dinner knife. To one side and just above the injury was a faint mark etched into the skin. Priestley frowned. It looked like a cross, and it occurred to him that the victim might have been wearing a piece of jewellery that had pressed into him and left an indentation.

'I need to make a sketch. Fetch a pencil from the office, sergeant,' said Taylor in a quiet voice that nonetheless held sufficient authority to send Grant scuttling to do as he was told.

'Why did you want to see this?' asked Hamilton, handing it to him. 'It doesn't tell us anything we don't already know.'

'I think he may have been a silversmith,' replied Taylor. 'Do you see these marks on his forearm? Such burns are common in that particular trade.'

Hamilton peered at the picture. 'They look like muddy streaks to me.'

Taylor shrugged as Grant returned. 'Perhaps, but the possibility warrants further investigation.'

He made his sketch – a deft one that Priestley thought surprisingly accurate – watched Bradwell replace the photograph in the cabinet, and took his leave.

There was a cluster of newspapermen standing outside the mortuary when Taylor and Priestley exited, Grant at their heels, and they surged forward hopefully. Taylor's grimly forbidding expression led all but one to fall back.

'A posh murder in Mayfair,' said Faris with relish. 'Come on, inspector. I'm only making an honest living here. Don't give me a hard time. Or maybe you've something to say about the Headless Bishop instead?'

Taylor pushed past him without a word. Scowling, Faris returned to his colleagues. When Taylor reached the end of the road, he stopped walking suddenly and turned to Grant, who immediately began to regard him warily, clearly still smarting from whatever had been said to him in Bradwell's hallway.

'Looking at that photograph reminded me of something,' Taylor said. 'The stains across the Bishop's chest, which we assumed were made by mud, looked like the dirt-marks I saw on the itinerants at the Poplar Workhouse the other day. Perhaps the Headless Bishop was a vagrant. First thing tomorrow, I want you to look at all the reports listing missing tramps.'

'But there will be hundreds of them,' objected Grant, horrified. 'And their friends report them missing, but they never bother to let us know when they come back again. It'll take hours.'

'Days more like,' agreed Taylor with a certain malice. 'But look on the bright side – it's a perfect opportunity for you to amend our files accordingly. I'm sure Hamilton will be delighted, and such initiative could be your ticket to greater things.'

Grant glowered, not so stupid as to believe it. He left, slouching along the road and kicking viciously at a stone. A sharp crack indicated that it had hit a window, at which point he started to walk a good deal faster.

'Do you think it'll work?' asked Priestley, when he had gone. 'That *The Star* will report that the Headless Bishop is either a tramp or a silversmith, so you'll know for certain who is the snake in your station? Of course, I thought we'd already concluded that it was Grant. Long Ron told us as much.'

'But Grant has been damaged by these reports, too, and I need to be certain.' Taylor sighed tiredly. 'Although

I find myself so sick of the whole business that I'm not sure I care. Still, I ought to make an effort for Bradwell's sake. He lied to help me.'

'And you lied for him. It was *his* fault the Bishop went missing, because he was lax with his security. You covered his mistake, and bore the brunt of his carelessness.'

'Not really. He made it easier for the thieves, but if there is a scheme to discredit me in order to improve the station's funding, and the perpetrators are willing to go as far as stealing a body, then a couple of gates – locked or not – aren't going to deter them.'

Priestley suspected he was just being loyal, but Taylor's face was grey with exhaustion, and he saw it was not the time to argue. He changed the subject. 'Did you know there was an imprint of a cross on the Bishop's body?'

'Of course, although you're the only person to have commented on it, apart from Bradwell. It was the cross that made me concoct the tale about the mitre. I assume the victim was wearing one when he died. Some men do. Dr Marshall, for example.'

'Does he?' asked Priestley. 'I hadn't noticed.'

'Under his shirt.' Taylor was silent for a moment. 'Thank you for your help tonight – especially at Fountain Dock. Grant would have dashed out my brains if you hadn't stopped him.'

'Hitting him was a pleasure,' said Priestley. 'Is there anyone else you'd like me to punch?'

Taylor laughed, and some of the bleakness in his expression lifted. 'I'm going to the East India Docks now. It might help to prowl around those crates, to see what it's like in the middle of the night. No, you go home, Raymond. You've done enough for one day.'

'I'm not tired,' said Priestley, falling into step at his side. 'And I'll have to be aboard *Nimrod* in a few hours anyway. I may as well come with you, then find a quiet corner for a nap.'

They hailed a cab that happened to be rattling past, saying little as the dark streets slipped by. It started to rain, a light drizzle that made the air more humid than ever. With no traffic, they reached the docks in record time.

'Shall we climb over the gates?' asked Priestley gamely.

'Not tonight,' said Taylor. 'Here comes Ives, proving he's doing his job. He's lucky he still has it, because the East India Dock Company can't be pleased to learn that murders take place on their premises with him in charge.'

'Inspector,' said Ives with relief. 'I was about to send for you. There's a young woman here, and she says she won't go until she's seen you. Her name is Mrs Underhill. Mrs Helen Underhill.'

The woman was emerging from the office before Ives could complete his explanation. She was in her mid-to-late-twenties, and was clad from head to toe in black, suggesting a recent bereavement. Her hair, neatly gathered at the nape of her slender neck, was a rich auburn, the same hue as her striking eyes. She nodded her thanks to Ives, and indicated with an authoritative wave of her hand that he should leave.

'I hoped you would come, inspector,' she said in a deep voice that was strangely melodious. 'My prayers have been answered. I couldn't go to your police station, and this was the only other place I thought you might be. Thank God you are conscientious, and work long hours.'

Taylor regarded her blankly. 'I don't understand—'

'I can't afford to be seen,' she said quickly. 'Not at the station and not here. That's why I had to visit at night.'

'Do you have information about the murder of Brice Scudder?'

'I do,' she replied. 'And my information is that Jameson Adams is completely innocent. The reason I know this is because Jameson was with me when Scudder was killed.'

Cape Royds: April, 1908

Revenge, it's been said, is a dish best served cold. Well, as our short autumn at Cape Royds heads towards the long darkness of winter, there must no place in the world where it's colder than here, so Adams must be enjoying his platter of vengeance immensely. Unfortunately, I appear to be the main course.

I've always considered myself friendly, considerate, easy to get along with. And I've tried to overlook foibles that would normally annoy men when they're placed in close contact with others for an extended period. I've worked hard to help build an esprit-de-corps with everyone who's stranded in this tiny hut at the edge of world. But since that night last July, when Will Taylor and I talked to Helen Underhill, Adams hasn't wanted any of it. He's always publicly civil, he hasn't openly insulted me, he'll work alongside me when he must, but there's a rift between us of the deepest magnitude, one that seems unlikely to be bridged in this lifetime.

It's surprising, because Adams is

normally a thoughtful, generous man, one of the most popular members of the expedition. But he clearly believes that I stepped beyond the pale, and has cut me off from any chance of redemption. I first began to realise it when Shackleton sent eight of us to New Zealand together to meet Nimrod. We steamed from Liverpool in the emigrant ship Runic, and the Boss paid the princely sum of nineteen pounds for eight men to share one cabin.

We spent six weeks together, and friendships and loyalty were created that will help us go successfully through all manner of hell this winter and in sledging next spring. Wild and Joyce virtually replaced my parents in introducing me to whole new aspects of life. Day proved to be as much cynic and philosopher as motor mechanic. And Roberts – Bobs — transpired to be fabulous entertainment, perhaps most so unintentionally, when he became so drunk that a possum we'd adopted in Australia gnawed off one wing of his moustache without him waking up.

But Adams, while he could be the life and soul of the party, was more a menace than a delight for me. It was just little things – an unpleasant stare, blowing pipe smoke in my direction, the constant swearing that seemed to increase when I was present – matters so insignificant that had I complained, I'd have looked churlish.

His dislike of me has continued since we've been at Cape Royds, and it was just last week that we finally had a bit of a barney. He is responsible for the routine at our winter quarters, and told me to exercise the ponies. I'd no interest in that at all. Although I'd wanted to help when several sickened and died, I don't really know one end of a horse from the other: both are lethal so far as I'm concerned. No, I wanted to be with the Prof, doing geological fieldwork. In the middle of the ensuing argument, Adams said hotly: 'You needn't bloody well think, Priestley, that you were taken on this show because you were a great scientist.'

I didn't. In fact, I'd always had a sneaking desire to know why I was chosen, because I'd discovered that at least a dozen Honours graduates had been after the job. I was about to find out.

'I was present when Shacks interviewed you at number nine,' Adams went on, blowing smoke at me. 'He was damned worried at the time because he'd got hold of a lot of real hard nuts.' He had – Adams was one of them. 'When you left the room, he turned to me and said, "Well! I can manage that fellow!" That's the only reason why you got your sodding chance, lad, so don't give me any of your lip, and get out there to exercise the bloody ponies.'

I did, of course, despite the Boss' reproachful glance that I was abandoning the project he had set me. Oddly, I resented the time away from it, since writing down what happened has allowed me to understand things I previously hadn't. But I obeyed Adams, and I have continued to do so, abandoning geology – and my writing for Shackleton – to play the veterinary surgeon to a herd of kicking, nipping, bucking nags that heartily wish they were elsewhere. I've nursed them through colic; I've escaped braining by a handsbreadth twice when I was valeting Grisi, the most cantankerous of them; and I've mucked them out. And it all seems to have given Adams great satisfaction. But now Armytage, who like the Prof and Mawson was hired on in Australia, has agreed to take over the day-to-day care of the ponies, so I've high hopes of making a real contribution to geology. The only thing now standing between science and me is my report for Shackleton about the investigation that caused my problems with Adams in the first place.

Chapter 11

Helen Underhill refused to return to Ives' office and declined to board *Nimrod*, insisting that she would remain at the docks only as long as it took to tell her story. So they stood by the gates, with the cab waiting to take her home the moment she had finished answering Taylor's questions.

'Adams claims he was with you on the night of Scudder's murder,' he said. 'That he came to you after Lady Wallaston's party, and that you remained together until half past twelve. Then he came here. Unfortunately, Scudder was killed at twenty past one, which is a time Adams cannot give an account of himself.'

'He was with me then, too,' she said softly. 'On *Nimrod.*'

'You were on the ship?' asked Priestley, startled. 'But you can't have been! The gates are locked at that time of night, and I don't see you climbing over them.' He laughed nervously.

'Of course I can climb over them,' she replied scornfully. 'Or do you imagine women to be physically incapable of simple acts of balance and agility? How do you think I got in tonight?'

'I imagine you asked Ives to admit you...' began Priestley uneasily.

'He wouldn't have done that,' she said, truthfully enough. 'So I climbed in and *then* I presented myself at his office. We made a pact: he would let me stay until I'd spoken to you, and I wouldn't tell his superiors that I'd eluded his patrols.'

'In a skirt?' asked Priestley, regarding her cumbersome garments in disbelief.

'Not when Scudder was murdered: then I borrowed a pair of Jameson's trousers. But these are the clothes I wore this evening, and if you care to inspect them, you'll see several dark stains from those dirty railings half-way up.'

Priestley watched a smile flicker across Taylor's face. The inspector was taken with this spirited woman, who cared nothing for convention.

'So, you and Adams scaled the gates,' Priestley said. 'He already told us that's how he got in. But then what?'

'Then we hid among the materiel while we waited for the watch to change. We left my house at twelve-thirty, and we were here a few minutes before one. Scudder was there, hovering around the crates containing his instruments. I'd show you, but they've been moved.'

'Did he see you?'

'Of course not – I was careful to stay concealed. At one o'clock, Davis and his two men replaced Cheetham and his pair, but they all went forward for two minutes for a bit of a chat. Jameson knew this was going to happen, so we slipped aboard at that point. As Davis prefers to patrol the quay, we had the ship to ourselves – except for Mackay, who was asleep in the officers' cabin, too drunk to know anything about us. Jameson showed me every inch of *Nimrod*.'

'If Scudder was among the materiel, why didn't *he* see you go up the gangway?' asked Taylor.

'He was too busy with his own affairs – he was a self-absorbed man. I saw him – alive – when I went aboard. Then, sometime between quarter to two and two o'clock, when we were ready to leave, Jameson ordered Berry and Riches to explore the far end of the quay, so I could slip away unseen.'

'I see!' exclaimed Priestley. 'I've always been puzzled by that particular order. Now I understand, and it makes perfect sense.'

She ignored the interruption and continued. 'Scudder must have been dead by then, but it was dark and we were intent on escaping, so we didn't notice anything that might help you. Then Jameson took me home, and as it was a warm night, we sat together in my garden until he left for work at six. We were together the whole time from when he left Lady Wallaston's party at ten o'clock until dawn. He didn't kill anyone.'

Taylor stared at her. 'I believe you,' he said eventually. 'However, what I don't understand is the reason for all the secrecy.'

'Because I'm a widow, and still officially in mourning. My husband was a good man, but many years my senior, so don't be too severe when you judge a young woman who falls in love for the first time, and who breaks social convention to be sure the man of her choice knows of her affections before he embarks on a long and dangerous journey.'

'You want Adams to know you'll be waiting for him

when he comes back?' surmised Priestley.

She nodded. 'My official mourning ends in October, but he'll be gone by then, and I couldn't lose him for the want of a few weeks. However, my family are strict about such things, so our courtship has been restricted to clandestine meetings at night.'

'It sounds romantic,' said Priestley, a little wistfully.

She smiled for the first time, and both men saw she was extremely beautiful. 'Yes, it is.'

'But even so,' said Taylor, 'I still don't see why you couldn't come openly to *Nimrod*. With a member of your family, for example. Visitors arrive all the time, and you could have applied for a guided tour.'

'Actually, Will, she couldn't,' said Priestley. 'The captain is odd about women on his ship – he claims it's bad luck. So it's extremely difficult to inveigle an invitation if you're not the Boss' wife or a major sponsor. Adams couldn't have shown her around any other way.'

'And Jameson is very sensitive to the captain's idiosyncrasies,' she elaborated. 'He's a kind, dear, considerate man, and didn't want to distress England by having him come face to face with the nautical equivalent of the devil on his vessel. And yet I so desperately wanted to see where Jameson will work, sleep and eat. He thought long and hard about how he could accommodate me *and* the captain, and invented this plan. Of course, now I wish he hadn't, because it has brought him so much trouble.'

'Can you prove any of this?' asked Taylor. 'I've already said I believe you, but corroborating evidence would put it beyond question.'

'My old governess accompanied us as far as the

gates,' said Helen. 'She can confirm the times I've given you, and she'll also tell you that there was no blood on our clothes. I can describe the inside of the ship, to prove I've been on her, and I even made some sketches – which I brought with me tonight. I drew them so I'd be able to imagine Jameson on his way south.'

Priestley scanned them. 'These are very good, and Adams couldn't have done them – I've seen his attempts at drawing.'

'And there's this,' she said, holding out something small and silver. It was a letter opener, similar to the one that had killed Scudder, although this one looked as though it had never been used. 'When he told me you believed him to be guilty because he couldn't find his paper-knife, I went to his mother's house, and she and I conducted a search for it.'

'Did you tell her what you were doing?' asked Taylor.

'Tell a mother that her son is under suspicion of murder?' Her eyes twinkled with mischief. 'If I had, then this blade would likely have ended up in you, inspector. I told her he needed it for the expedition, and she helped me hunt through the chests in her attic until we found it. You can ask her to confirm this if you like, although I recommend you make no accusations.'

'Does she know about your relationship with her son?'

'She does, and she approves. Helen regarded him intently in the lamplight. 'I'll take any oath you like, inspector, and you can ask about my standing in society – as long as you do it discreetly. You'll find me a credible witness.'

'Yes,' said Taylor, leading her towards the waiting cab. 'I'm sure you are.'

'You'll make it known that Jameson is innocent?' she asked, her eyes intense in the gloom.

He nodded. 'As soon as I see him.'

The sailors on night duty always had strong coffee ready to help them through the quiet hours, and Davis was more than willing to share it with Taylor as he prepared to compose a carefully worded report that dismissed Adams as a suspect in the investigation. The first officer was delighted to learn the news, and Taylor again saw the popularity of the meteorologist.

While the inspector wrote, Priestley disappeared, and Taylor assumed he had gone for a nap. Taylor knew he should rest himself, but his thoughts were racing, and he knew he would not sleep. He remained in the officers' cabin when he had finished the report, drinking more of the powerful coffee than was wise on an empty stomach, and reviewing his dwindling list of suspects. Eventually, Priestley returned. The geologist's expression was grim, and Taylor saw that whatever he had been doing, napping had not been involved.

'We're running out of suspects,' Taylor said tiredly. 'According to your chart, we're left with Mackay, Yaxley, Marshall and Murray.'

'After the fiasco with Adams, we should make sure we have more than unfounded speculations before accusing anyone else.'

'Then let's consider what we have. Yaxley had a recent argument with Scudder, but the two surgeons loathed the man, too. However, Murray has an even more powerful motive: Scudder made efforts to have himself promoted at his expense.'

'No,' said Priestley firmly. '*Not* Murray. And I can prove it.'

'How?'

'With a medical report. It's confidential, and I'll lose my job if anyone finds out what I've done. But the alternative is to tell Shackleton that you suspect Murray of murder, and then ask his permission to see our records. And I'd just as soon avoid that.'

'You've been in Shackleton's files?' asked Taylor uneasily. 'You shouldn't have done. You could have told me what you suspected, and let us acquire the proper permissions.'

'Listen to me,' said Priestley fiercely. 'This entire affair has been nasty in the extreme, and potentially damaging to the expedition. I didn't enjoy what I did, but if it prevents you from issuing another accusation to a man I know is innocent, then it's worthwhile. Murray will be spared what Adams has gone through, and you'll be spared the indignity of being wrong – again.'

'All right,' said Taylor, taken aback by his vehemence. 'Tell me what you have.'

Priestley took a deep breath, mastering his temper. He had not been exaggerating when he said he had found the episode distasteful, and he was angry, not just with himself for ploughing through Shackleton's files, but at the whole unsavoury business.

'Even with a sharp knife, it takes power to ram a blade clean through a man's neck, and I don't believe Murray – in his present frail health – could do it. So I looked at his medical file, which contains reports that say he's currently afflicted with a certain feebleness, especially at night when he's tired. In short, killing Scudder would have been a physical impossibility for him. The weakness is reported by three independent physicians.'

Taylor was puzzled. 'Then why does Shackleton want Murray to go to the Antarctic?'

Priestley pursed his lips. 'He obviously believes the parts that say Murray is on the mend and will be healthier by the time we leave. We can only hope so. But now, if you don't mind, I want to dismiss Murray from our discussions.'

'Done,' said Taylor. He smiled. 'Besides, we may have a witness who saw Murray arrive at his club before one. It's yet to be confirmed, but it's looking promising.'

Priestley glared at him. 'You could have told me,' he said reproachfully. 'I feel soiled by what I did. You could have spared me that.'

'I would have done had I known what you planned to do, but I didn't want to raise your hopes, so I thought it better to wait until we were certain. But let's talk about Mackay. He's the only one on our original list of four who can't prove that the murder weapon didn't belong to him.'

'He didn't recognise it when you showed it to him at the Expedition Office,' said Priestley, fighting down his irritation with an effort. 'In fact, he gashed himself trying to pick it up – he didn't know how sharp it was. If it had been his, he would have been more careful.'

'He may have allowed himself to be cut on purpose, to mislead us. He's intelligent enough to have thought it through. And there's the fact that the blow was executed with surgical precision.'

'That may have been chance. Bradwell's report said the killer may have jabbed wildly, and just happened to catch Scudder in the throat.'

'No, it didn't. It said he couldn't tell what had happened – the blow may have hit the larynx by chance, but equally, it may have been deliberately aimed.'

'I take it, then, that you favour Mackay as your next villain?' asked Priestley unhappily. 'Be it on your own head, Will.'

Taylor shook his head. 'Our feisty Scot is no higher on my list than Marshall or Yaxley. Marshall is certainly ruthless enough to kill, and his religious convictions worry me – they seem at odds with the rest of his character.

'And Yaxley?'

Taylor shrugged. 'I have yet to gain his measure. He's made virtually no impression on me at all, except for having powerful views about biology and evolution.'

Footsteps outside the cabin made them both glance up, and Adams entered. The expression on his face was one of cautious relief, and he looked both ways along the passageway before closing the door behind him.

'I understand Helen came to see you,' he said in a low voice. 'It was against my advice, because you can't begin to imagine the family difficulties she will experience if it becomes known that we…I'd have given *anything* for her not to have gone through what must have been a bloody embarrassing and awkward interview.'

'She was a good deal less awkward and embarrassed than you are,' said Taylor. He smiled. 'I wish you luck and happiness, and I hope you can be together openly when you return.'

Adams did not return the smile. 'Thank you. But this isn't the end of the matter. You accused me of murder, and I want an official apology from you and your chief bloody superintendent.'

'Think before you demand that,' warned Priestley. 'It might lead to questions about how Taylor came to realise you were innocent. No one knew about the accusation outside the expedition, and I suggest you let sleeping dogs lie.'

'Damn you, Priestley,' snapped Adams. 'Are you threatening me?'

'No one's threatening anyone,' said Taylor soothingly. 'And you shall have your apology. You can have mine in person, right now. I'll write officially when—'

'No,' said Adams tiredly. 'Priestley's right, damn him. I'm just angry that Helen had to come here and talk to you. Here, shake hands with me, Taylor, and let's say no more about it.' He grasped the inspector's hand but only looked with disdain at Priestley's when the geologist extended his as well.

'It was my fault, not his,' said Taylor. 'If you're going to blame anyone, it should be me.'

'I can accept gross stupidity from *you*,' replied Adams. 'You're a dim-witted policeman. But this bloody whipper-snapper…he should have known better.'

'Priestley didn't—' began Taylor.

But Adams turned on his heel and walked out.

As it was nearing six o'clock, and there were sounds that said the dock was coming to life, Taylor and Priestley went to see whether either of the surgeons had arrived. They had, although they had come to the ship with very different intentions. Marshall was there in his Sunday best, wearing a neatly pressed suit and a clean collar. Mackay was dressed in rough clothes, clearly intent on using a day when the docks were closed to go about his own work. Yaxley was also there, sleeves rolled up and an expectant expression on his face.

'I thought you were jesting when you said you intended to pack the medical supplies today,' Marshall was saying to the Scot. 'It's Sunday, man. You should be in church.'

'I'll have plenty of time for religious reflection when we're south,' retorted Mackay irritably. 'Until then, God can wait, because I've got a lot more pressing business. Oh! Good morning, vicar. You're up early.'

'I thought I'd drop by before morning service at St James's,' said Reverend Vallen. If he had heard Mackay's remarks, he gave no sign of being offended. 'I wondered whether you and any other expedition members who are free tonight might care to join me for supper. Nothing fancy, you understand. Just cold meat and boiled potatoes.'

'Thank you, vicar,' said Marshall politely. 'I shall be delighted.'

'Good, good.' Vallen smiled happily. 'You must come, too, inspector. You won't be the first policeman to enjoy a cup of tea in my drawing room, and I'm sure you won't be the last.'

Taylor did not think he would be particularly welcome, especially if Adams were there. 'I have a cricket match today,' he hedged. 'Perhaps another time.'

'There will be thunderstorms this afternoon, and your game will be rained off,' predicted Vallen. 'So I shall look forward to seeing you at the vicarage. We dine at seven.'

'Cricket?' asked Marshall disparagingly. 'On a Sunday? Who are you playing? The patrons of a tavern?' The contempt in his voice was brazen.

'The Ecclesiastical Commission,' replied Taylor evenly. 'A team comprising deacons, vicars and even a bishop.'

While Taylor asked his remaining suspects more questions, then returned to the station, Priestley walked with Vallen as far as his church, and then took a cab to his lodgings. He wrote several letters to friends and a telegram to his father, describing in detail the distinctive design of the cap, although the post office was closed, so they could not be sent until the following day. Then he went to chapel, and showed it to the more educated members of the congregation, pulling it from his pocket so many times that the brown paper soon became tatty.

He met with little success, however, and returned to his rooms frustrated. He tried to take his mind off it by reading *Antarctica* by the Swedish explorer Otto Nordenskjöld, but soon fell asleep over it. When he awoke, the sun was shining brightly, so he ate some sandwiches left for him by his landlady, and went to see if Taylor's match was in play.

It was being held in a pleasant park, with a row of ancient elms on one side and gracious buildings on the other. By the time he arrived, the opposition were all out for two hundred and fifty-seven, and Taylor's team was currently forty-three for two. The day was warm, the surroundings peaceful and Priestley would have been content were his mind not so full of dark thoughts. He became gloomy and unsettled, a mood that was reflected in the sky, which had started to cloud over.

He flopped on the grass next to Taylor, who sat apart from his fellow players. Priestley was not sure whether it was a ploy on the inspector's part to be left alone, or whether the other cricketers had deliberately shunned him.

'Batsman's wicket, is it?' he asked, nodding to where a board showed the high score of the Ecclesiastical Commission.

Taylor grimaced. 'Not a bowler's certainly. I performed abysmally, and the captain asked whether the Headless Bishop was affecting my concentration. I came here to escape the damned Headless Bishop.'

'Don't swear,' said Priestley mildly. 'It makes you sound like Adams.'

Taylor groaned as the batsman took an ill-advised sweep that knocked the ball directly into the hands of the cleric at long leg.

'I've started my enquiries about the cap,' said Priestley conversationally, propping himself up on his elbows and tipping his head back to stare up at the massing clouds. 'No luck so far. Do you have anything to report?'

'A lively interview with Mackay, during which he became incandescent with rage and challenged me to a boxing match – if I win, he will confess to murder; if he wins, I will concentrate my enquiries on thieving dockhands.'

Priestley stared at him, troubled. 'He offered to confess?'

'Only because he thinks he wouldn't lose. Then I cornered Marshall emerging from church, and he managed to steer me into a debate about the legalisation of prostitution. I've no idea how. I suppose I was just too tired to stop him.'

'He has opinions about such a matter?' asked

271

Priestley doubtfully.

'Very strong ones, and it's clearly a subject that interests him. I suspect you'll hear all about it when you're in the Antarctic. Then I tried to talk to Yaxley, but he refused to speak to me, claiming that O'Brien had advised him against it. But then things took a turn for the better…Oh! There goes Hyde, caught behind. I'm up next. Don't leave.'

He walked to the wicket, and Priestley lay back down again, but did not remain prostrate for long. Within minutes, the first drops of rain began to fall. He sat up, and watched the umpires discuss whether to continue.

'Excuse me, young man,' came a voice at his side. It was an elderly clergyman with a cane. Priestley scrambled to his feet and removed his hat. 'Forgive the intrusion, but I never forget a face and I believe I've seen yours recently – at a reception given by Lady Wallaston. Your name is Priestley – a memorable one for a man in my vocation – and you're part of the expedition that's about to sail south for the glory of King and Country.'

'Yes, I was there,' said Priestley, flattered to learn that he should be recognised by strangers.

'Hah!' said the old man, pleased. 'I knew I couldn't have been mistaken. I hope you don't mind me charging up to you.'

'Not at all. I'm only here to watch a friend.'

'It looks as though play will be suspended.' The clergyman waved his cane at the sky, obliging Priestley to duck or risk being hit. 'The clouds are very black. Come and sit with me in the pavilion before we get wet. We can't have you catching a cold before you go to the Antarctic.'

'Yes, sir,' said Priestley, smiling as he followed him across the grass to where tea and sandwiches were being served. The clergyman eventually introduced himself as Cecil Franks, a retired canon from St Paul's Cathedral.

'I saw you talking to young Taylor just now,' said Franks, cheeks bulging with cucumber sandwich. 'Is he the friend you came to watch? He's usually a respectable off-spinner, but he gave us a miserable performance today.'

'I didn't see it,' said Priestley. 'I came too late.'

'His wife makes fairy cakes for us most Sundays,' the clergyman went on. 'Well, that's what she calls them, although it would be a very formidable sprite that laid claim to one. And her sausage rolls…well…' He shook his head and adjusted his false teeth, as if they had endured some uncomfortable experiences with Ruby's culinary offerings in the past.

Priestley pulled out the cap, feeling he was being disloyal to Taylor by listening to disparaging remarks about his wife, and keen to change the subject. 'I don't suppose you recognise this, do you, sir?'

Franks stared at it for some time. 'No,' he said eventually. 'It looks a little like my old diocese colours, but the shield is different. I can't help you, I'm afraid. Has someone lost it?'

Priestley nodded, but did not elaborate.

'How is Taylor bearing up under all this nastiness surrounding the Headless Bishop? He's a good chap, and it has grieved me to see all those tales about him in the papers.'

'I think he's wearing down,' said Priestley unhappily.

'He's strong, but there's only so much a man can take.'

They sat in silence for a while, then Franks began to ask about the expedition. Priestley was relieved to discuss something more cheerful, and it transpired that Franks knew Reverend Vallen and expressed his hope that Nigel would find a place on *Nimrod*.

'He attended our Cathedral school,' he said. 'Lovely treble until his voice broke. So, he's a zoologist now? How time flies! It seems only yesterday that he was heading up to Oxford. Charles Vallen must be very proud. Give him my regards when you see him.'

'I'm dining with him tonight, sir,' said Priestley.

'He performs copious amounts of charity work, and has been a key figure on the Police Benevolent Committee. In fact, it was Vallen who raised much of the money for the convalescent home built for officers injured in the line of duty. You should get him to find funds for Shackleton. Gathering cash isn't easy, but he has a rare talent for persuading wealthy people to part with their lucre to advance worthy causes.'

'He's already been very good to us,' said Priestley. 'He's been holding regular events in his parish to generate funds, and he persuaded Lady Wallaston to have that reception.'

It occurred to Priestley that the canon might have noticed something at the party that he had not. Priestley had been preoccupied with making a good impression on potential benefactors – and with extricating himself from the raspberry tart incident – but Franks' attention had been on the expedition members. He began a detailed interrogation that had the elderly clergyman's eyebrows rising in surprise, but felt vindicated when he learned answers to several questions.

When Priestley had finished, Franks stood to leave. 'Good luck on your expedition, Priestley, although I'm sorry you'll be leaving London so soon. Poor Taylor needs a friend like you.'

Taylor, back in his Sunday clothes, did not relish the prospect of an evening in company. He wanted to review statements and reports at the station, although he suspected it would be a waste of time. Unfortunately, rain was now falling steadily, and the game had been abandoned: Vallen would know he was lying if he claimed the cricket had run late. He was trapped.

He watched Priestley talk to Canon Franks, and felt his eyes begin to close. He took a deep breath and stood upright, fighting off the exhaustion that threatened to overwhelm him, a deep, utter weariness that not even cricket had been able to relieve. Perhaps he should have gone home instead, but he knew he would not have been able to sleep in his silent, empty house. He sighed, wondering how much longer his life was going to be dominated by murder – and whether Ruby would ever forgive his chronic neglect and return to him.

He looked again at Priestley and Franks, supposing their conversation was about Lady Wallaston's party – he knew from his enquiries that Franks had been among the guests. He could not imagine the canon in evening attire, as would have been necessary at such a formal occasion, because the man was so unashamedly slovenly. The thought made him stand up straighter, as the germ of an idea began to form in his mind.

Scudder had been killed late at night on a dark quay,

275

when he had been wearing formal clothing identical to that donned by every other member of the scientific staff. What if Scudder had not been the intended victim? What if he had been mistaken for someone else? The killer had certainly been harried, because he had neglected to retrieve the murder weapon. And, despite the late hour, there had been people wandering around – England, Marshall, Murray, Adams, Helen Underhill, Mackay, the officers and men on watch, to say nothing of the docks' night-watchmen. Perhaps the killer had panicked, and had targeted the wrong man.

But if Scudder was not the intended victim, then who was? Adams, for breaking social convention and courting an attractive widow in mourning? One of the hopefuls, to eliminate a competitor? Murray, because his poor health might be a liability to the expedition? The fiery Mackay or the biting, disdainful Marshall?

Taylor frowned. Marshall. The surgeon was desperate to be second-in-command, even claiming he had been promised the position, but it looked as though that honour would go to Adams. Moreover, Marshall had tried very hard to have Adams blamed for Scudder's murder, and had been delighted when Taylor had made his accusation. Was Marshall the culprit, and it had not been Scudder he had intended to kill, but his rival for the post?

'I have some information for you,' said Priestley, making him jump by speaking behind him. 'Shall we walk across the park and take a cab to Rotherhithe? I had the foresight to bring an umbrella, but it's a bit late for you – you're already soaked. I shall tell you what I've learned as we go.'

Taylor indicated that he was to begin, suspecting that the geologist would not like knowing the line his thoughts had just taken.

'It's about Mackay. Canon Franks says that according to Professor Rice – whom Mackay was drinking with before he left Lady Wallaston's house – Mackay was drunk to the point of virtual insensibility *before* he went to the Queen's Head.'

Taylor nodded slowly. 'It would explain why he wasn't attacked. The Queen's Head patrons are rough, but they don't stoop to trouncing helpless drunks.'

'This professor – a medical man – believes Mackay would have been capable of very little that required any coordination. Do you think that's enough to eliminate him as a suspect? He was physically incapable of stabbing a man in the neck?'

'If he was able to go from Lady Wallaston's house to the Queen's Head, drink more beer, and reel to the ship, he could also thrust a knife into Scudder. However—'

'He was too intoxicated for anything as precise as avoiding major blood vessels but severing a windpipe, though,' interrupted Priestley. 'If he struck the fatal blow, then it was not surgical neatness, but chance.'

'Granted, but most murders involve alcohol in one form or another. In Mackay's case—'

'But Davis had to help him into bed,' persisted Priestley. 'He was hopelessly inebriated, and inebriated men make stupid mistakes – he would have muttered something about the murder, or he would have had blood on his hands or his clothes. Davis would have noticed.'

In all Taylor's years as a detective, he had never

known a drunk to cover his tracks successfully. Despite the fact that Scudder had not shed much blood, a fellow barely able to stand would almost certainly have trodden in it. Taylor had inspected the clothes of all the expedition members personally – he had not trusted Grant's reports about them, thankfully – and there had been no stains on Mackay. Even the soles of his shoes had been free of it, although deeply ingrained with the oily soot and coal dust that coated the quay.

'I had eliminated Mackay today anyway,' he said. He shrugged at Priestley's surprise. 'I tried to tell you, but you kept interrupting. There was a message for me at the station this morning, about the letter opener.'

'From the "expert" you sent it to?'

Taylor nodded. 'Wild was right to say that buying RNR paraphernalia is difficult. It is, and Mackay, as a Royal Navy surgeon, would not have been eligible to purchase any.' He saw Priestley's disappointment that his own efforts to exonerate the Scot had been superfluous, and hastened to reassure him. 'That, along with your findings about his physical state, is sufficient to eliminate him from our list.'

Priestley looked pleased. 'Good. That means all our suspects from the shore party are in the clear except Marshall and Yaxley – and I'm sure we shall find something to exonerate them, too.'

Taylor hoped not, because otherwise the case would remain unsolved. 'There's one thing we should consider though. We have been working on the supposition that someone had taken against Scudder. What if we're wrong? What if Adams was the intended victim?'

Priestley gazed at him, rain hammering around them,

immediately understanding the route the inspector's thoughts had taken. 'You think Marshall wanted to dispatch Adams, because he thinks he should be the expedition's second-in-command? It was dark, and he made a mistake? I suppose it explains why he told you to investigate Adams virtually the moment you arrived.'

Cabs were in high demand because of the rain, and Priestley and Taylor were obliged to walk the entire way to Rotherhithe, black muck from the pavements splattering up their legs, and water forming a gritty paste with the soot and grime under their feet. Even so, they were an hour too early to call on the Reverend Vallen, so they visited *Nimrod* first, where Priestley wanted to check that a box of books he had taken to the ship had been stowed below decks and not left out in the wet.

When they arrived, Shackleton was there, in company with a tall, strapping young man attired in a very expensive suit. The fellow's hands were in his pockets, and he moved with an easy confidence that suggested he was used to things going his way. When Shackleton beckoned Priestley over, the stranger's face broke into a grin of excited delight.

'Priestley?' he asked, gripping the geologist's hand with warm enthusiasm. 'I *am* pleased to meet you. We're going to be working together – I'm your new assistant.'

'Sir Philip Brocklehurst,' said Shackleton, making the introductions. 'The latest member of the expedition. I'm sure the two of you will get along famously.'

Priestley returned the handshake with genuine friendliness. He had taken an instant liking to the newcomer's affable manners and debonair charm. 'I wasn't expecting another geologist, but your arrival means we can spend more time on granitic intrusions.'

'Granitic what?' drawled Brocklehurst. 'You're going to have to explain a lot to me, I'm afraid, old boy. Just because I'm to be assistant geologist doesn't mean I know anything about rocks.'

While Priestley launched into an eager explanation, all else forgotten now an opportunity to discuss his real work had arisen, Taylor turned to Shackleton.

'How can you afford an assistant geologist, Mick?' he asked in a low voice. 'I thought funds were tight.'

'They are,' replied Shackleton with a grimace. 'And Brocklehurst's appointment will cause bitter disappointment in some quarters.'

Taylor stared at him. 'Are you saying you have appointed *this* fellow to the last post? But I thought that was to go to a biologist – to one of the hopefuls.'

'It was. But as I've come to know him better, I've realised that Murray is such a fine scientist – despite his physical limitations – that he'll be able to manage the biological programme alone, or perhaps with a bit of help from the surgeons.'

'You're right: this *will* cause bitter disappointment in some quarters. Yaxley and Nigel Vallen have been giving everything they have for the chance to join you. And now you give the place away to someone else? Jesus, Mick!'

'I know, I know. I feel terrible about it, believe me.'

'And from Brocklehurst's remarks, it seems he's not even properly qualified,' Taylor went on. 'Even I know what granitic intrusions are!'

Shackleton rubbed his hand across his face. 'He can't

paint or draw, either, and I really did want an artist to join us. My friend Edward Wilson did wonders for Scott's expedition. His illustrations were highly praised by natural historians, and his paintings have been shown at exhibitions.'

'So why appoint Brocklehurst?' asked Taylor in incomprehension.

Shackleton's smile was rueful. 'Because he donated two thousand pounds to the expedition. You don't need me to tell you what a bonus such a sum will be.'

'He's *paying* to go?' asked Taylor incredulously.

'He's offering a donation,' corrected Shackleton primly. 'It is hardly the same. And two thousand pounds will solve a lot of problems.'

'Money seems to be the root of everything,' said Taylor glumly, thinking about Chief Superintendent Hamilton playing poker with the press to increase his budget.

Shackleton nodded. 'I informed Yaxley and Nigel about the situation this afternoon – O'Brien withdrew yesterday – and they took the news like gentlemen, which is what I'd expect. They're both good fellows, and if a windfall comes our way, I'll gladly sign them both up.'

Taylor smiled, but the whole affair had a distasteful feel, and he wondered what Priestley would think when he learned what had happened.

Chapter 12

Not surprisingly, Priestley was uncomfortable with the notion of imposing on the Vallens after Nigel had received such a blow to his hopes, but his concerns were groundless. Nigel had accepted with dignity Shackleton's argument that an assistant geologist would be of more use than another biologist in a continent comprising mostly rocks and ice. Yaxley was less sanguine, and pointed out that if that were true, why had they been labouring – literally – under the premise that a biologist was to be appointed?

Needless to say, it was the main subject for discussion over the dinner table, present at which were all three thwarted hopefuls – now dubbed the 'hopelesses' by a callously witty Marshall. The surgeon was slightly subdued, though, and Taylor wondered whether he was simply on his best behaviour because a vicar was present, or if there was a more sinister reason for his restraint.

'Shackleton told us that Sir Philip's application arrived only lately,' said Reverend Vallen soothingly. 'But that if it had been received earlier, he would have been appointed at once.'

'I believe him,' said O'Brien, who had been enjoying the Vallens' hospitality since Murray's lecture, and was evidently too comfortable to leave. 'Brocklehurst is fit and eager, and has many well-placed friends.'

'Money,' said Yaxley bitterly. 'Sir Philip is the heir to Swythamley Park, a large estate in north Staffordshire, so lord knows what financial considerations he offered Shackleton.'

'There's still time for more funds to come in,' said Priestley encouragingly, while Taylor stared at the opposite wall and said nothing, although it occurred to him that the two thousand pounds was unlikely to remain secret for long. 'I was told only today that Lady Wallaston is going to have a word with the Bishop of London about a charity concert on our behalf.'

'Dear Lady Wallaston,' said Reverend Vallen fondly. 'She organised a similar event when I was raising funds for the Police Convalescent Home – founded with the aim of nursing injured officers. I expect you've heard of it, inspector?'

Taylor nodded. 'I was a patient there last year. It's a fine place.'

Vallen beamed. 'I know a man shouldn't take pride in his own good works, but it's always uplifting to hear one's labours are appreciated. Lady Wallaston raised three hundred pounds with her concert, and I have every faith that she'll do the same for the expedition. Don't despair, boys. I'm sure the money will arrive one way or another. God works in mysterious ways.'

'I'm going to sell my grandfather's collection of Dickens first editions,' said Yaxley to Nigel. 'They're worth a small fortune, and the money will allow me to buy my own equipment and make a donation towards my keep in the south. I wish there were more, so I could fund you, too.'

'You should save your money,' said O'Brien gloomily. 'Antarctica is a vile place. To quote Captain Cook, it is "doomed by nature to perpetual frigidness; never to feel the warmth of the sun's rays; whose horrible and savage aspects I have not words to describe".'

'That's how I imagine it,' said Taylor, thinking Cook's stark analysis was probably far more accurate than Priestley's fanciful descriptions. He shifted uncomfortably in his rain-soaked clothes. 'Worse even than London on a wet afternoon.'

'I have a few bits and pieces from *my* grandfather, now you mention it,' said Nigel eagerly, ignoring them both and speaking to Yaxley. 'He was a post-captain in the Royal Navy, and brought trinkets from all over the world, which he told me are priceless. We shall *both* go south, Yaxley! Raise a glass with me!'

In his delight, Nigel knocked over his wine, and during the cleaning up there was a knock on the door and the last guest arrived. Mackay had been drinking, and sailed into the parlour on a waft of whiskey fumes.

'It would be a great kindness if you could wet the whistle of a thirsty man, vicar,' he slurred, as Marshall scowled disapprovingly. 'Anything will do – you know what they say about us Scots – but a wee dram would slide down a treat.'

'We don't serve spirits on Sunday,' replied Reverend Vallen politely. 'But you may have a little port mixed with water. Nigel will set it up for you.'

Taylor watched Nigel pour a miniscule amount of the

fortified wine into a cut-glass tumbler, then fill it to the brim with water. The youngster studied the pale pink mixture for a moment, obviously deciding it would not do. To rectify the matter, a generous dose of cochineal was added, which gave the beverage the appearance of thin blood. Mackay sipped it with considerable wariness, trying without success to identify the flavour. His lips were soon stained so scarlet that he looked like a Bermondsey prostitute.

'This is going to be a long evening,' Taylor whispered to Priestley. 'Nigel and Yaxley are valiantly trying to look on the bright side of a black situation, and Mackay is drunk so it won't be long before Marshall yields to the temptation to make tart rejoinders – a clerical presence notwithstanding.'

'Marshall's angry with you,' Priestley muttered back. 'He keeps scowling in your direction, and I can't help thinking that it's because you eliminated Adams from your inquiries.'

'We should engage him in conversation, and see if he lets something slip.'

Priestley sighed. 'I suppose you can't afford to take a rest from your duties, even on a Sunday. And I suppose *I* shall have to do the same. However, I cannot afford to spend too much more time on Scudder.'

'Because of your new assistant?'

Priestley nodded. 'I've thought from the start that there should be more than one geologist – the amount of research to be done is astronomical. But Philip will need guidance, so I must think very carefully about my work from now on.'

'Philip?' drawled Marshall. Priestley started guiltily,

not realising the surgeon had been listening. 'You're on a first-name basis already?' His expression was malicious as he raised his voice, as if mentioning the fellow who had destroyed the aspirations of Nigel and Yaxley amused him. 'But he's an excellent choice. I've always said geology was under-represented.'

'Yes, but so is biology now,' said Reverend Vallen, passing around a tureen of potatoes that had been boiled grey. 'And that's a terrible pity.'

'Why?' slurred Mackay. 'Rocks remain in the Antarctic all year, but animals and birds go north for the winter. Priestley will have subject matter to pore over long after the last wee penguin has flown away.'

'I thought penguins were flightless,' said Taylor.

Marshall smirked, then addressed Vallen. 'Mackay believes geological research will yield more important results than biology, although I disagree. I think the study of these unique adaptations will allow us to understand evolution and natural selection in a way not possible since Darwin visited the Galapagos.'

'My dear sir!' cried Vallen, handing him a plate of thinly sliced meat, some of it hard at the edges and smelling as if it should have gone to the cat several days before. 'Surely you don't *really* believe that? You're a God-fearing man! You *must* see that these unique creatures are exactly the way God created them?'

'Well, yes,' said Marshall, a little uncertainly. Then his tone became patronising. 'But science teaches us other things as well. For example, it seems to me that penguins have a common ancestor with tropical birds. They must have migrated to the Antarctic millions of years ago, to take advantage of the plentiful food supplies in the southern oceans. Then, because all their food was taken from water and there was no need for long migrations, they lost the ability to fly. It's a perfect example of natural selection.'

'Millions of years?' echoed Vallen, appalled. 'But God created the world on the twenty-third of October in four thousand and four BC. How can this process have taken millions of years?'

'Geology teaches us otherwise, vicar,' said Marshall politely. Taylor watched in fascination, sure that anyone other than a priest would have been treated to a sharp put-down. 'We have solid proof in rocks that the Earth is considerably older than five thousand, nine hundred and eleven years, and that it was once very different from how we know it today. Look at the dinosaurs. Their bones have been found with fossil faunas that indicate they inhabited a world—'

'No,' interrupted Vallen firmly. 'That is simply not true. God created fossils when He created everything else. It says so in the Bible, and I'm sure you know Genesis and Proverbs Eight, to say nothing of the beginning of the Gospel According to John. Geology is a wicked subject that will take us from God, and we mustn't allow it to drag us down such an iniquitous path.'

'I beg to differ,' objected Priestley, as Marshall was uncharacteristically at a loss for words. 'Geology pertains to the study of the Earth and what it can tell us. It isn't wicked. I don't have any difficulty in equating science with my religious beliefs.'

Vallen was becoming animated. 'Charles Darwin, in *On the Origin of Species*, said that geology…inspector! Are you all right?'

Taylor jumped in alarm, then gazed in dismay at the mess of gravy that filled his plate and had flowed onto the once-pristine tablecloth. Some of it had left the table altogether, and was dripping on the floor, while the jug was almost empty. Marshall laughed.

'You like a little sauce with your meat, do you, inspector? So much so, that the beef is an inch under the surface and you have left none for anyone else!'

'That is the kind of thing Nigel does,' said Vallen, jumping up to stem the brown tide with his napkin. 'So we're well equipped to deal with it. It's one reason why I have plain floorboards in the dining room, when the late Mrs Vallen always wanted a rug.'

'He was asleep,' slurred Mackay gleefully. 'I thought *I* might be the one to be overcome with a great feeling of lassitude, but it was Taylor.'

'Actually, he was so interested in our debate that he didn't watch what he was doing,' said Priestley, leaping to Taylor's defence. 'It's a tribute to the quality of the conversation at Reverend Vallen's dinner table.'

'Thank you,' said Taylor in an undertone, during the interlude afforded by the arrival of more gravy and the changing of the tablecloth. 'But I *was* asleep. I was dreaming that Marshall had confessed to killing the Headless Bishop.'

'Wishful thinking,' said Priestley. 'I hope dessert is better than the main course – and not just in terms of the conversation, either. I'm not in the Antarctic yet, and I object to starvation rations.'

The following day was overcast, so dawn came later than usual. Taylor rose in the dark and went to work before it was fully light, arriving just as the cleaners were leaving. One of them, a tiny, wizened man who had once been a chimney sweep, shyly confided that *he* didn't believe Taylor was as inept as the newspapers had reported. Taylor nodded his thanks for support of sorts, and went to his desk.

There was a note from Hamilton saying that there had been another death over the weekend – two drunks had fallen fighting in the river and one had not survived – and so the next case would be Taylor's. He frowned in puzzlement: even with the Mayfair strangling, the next incident should not have been his. He spoke to the duty sergeant, and learned that Andrews' leave had been extended, leaving a rotation of three detectives rather than four.

'And Hamilton agreed to it?'

The sergeant shrugged. 'Andrews is our best detective; he told me so himself. Hamilton would not dare deny him.'

Taylor returned to his office, and regarded the towering mass of paperwork with a sense of despair. He was rapidly becoming overwhelmed, and wondered again whether it was what Hamilton intended. If so, the strategy was working.

Grant arrived two hours later, sullen and resentful, to report that he had been unable to match any missing tramp to the description of the Headless Bishop. Taking pity on him, Taylor told him to abandon that line of enquiry and prepare the final file for the Poplar Workhouse case instead. Grant snatched the papers angrily.

'Arresting Vine was good, but you shouldn't have nabbed Hopkins first,' he said sulkily. 'You nearly caused a grave miscarriage of justice, and it hasn't gone unnoticed. All I hope is that *your* mistake doesn't reflect badly on *me*.'

It was hardly a fair or an accurate summary of what had happened, and Taylor did not grace it with a reply. It was already nine o'clock, and he could not justify wasting time debating the matter with the likes of Grant. He left the building, intending to ask Adams if he thought Marshall wanted to be second-in-command badly enough to kill for it. He knew he had latched on to the notion like a drowning man, but it was the only way forward that he could see. He had not gone far when he spied a familiar figure.

'I've just been to the Post Office,' said Priestley cheerfully. 'And sent a dozen letters to friends, and a telegram to my father about that cap.'

'I'm going to speak to Adams,' said Taylor, uncomfortably aware of how much hope he was pinning on the young man's efforts. 'About Marshall. And while I'm there, I shall tell him again that you argued his corner when he was a suspect.'

'Thank you,' said Priestley, although he had a bad feeling that it was already too late, and that irrevocable damage had been done. 'Incidentally, there's something you should see.'

With resignation, Taylor saw he held a copy of *The Star*. 'No. There comes a point where it's simply better not to read that stuff.'

'You'll want to see this,' said Priestley. 'Faris has reported a new lead in the Headless Bishop case: he says the victim might not be a clergyman after all, but a silversmith.'

Taylor stared at him. 'A silversmith?'

Priestley nodded. 'An expert was shown a photograph of the Bishop's body – taken before you were careless enough to lose the corpse – and was able to identify forearm burns consistent with marks earned in the business of silversmithery. You have been informed of this lead, but the public should be aware that you haven't seen fit to follow up on it yet.'

'Hamilton,' said Taylor in a low voice. 'I told Hamilton the lie about the silver burns.'

'So, now you know who's been telling tales,' said Priestley. 'The man trying to destroy you is your boss – whom you've suspected of manipulating the press to secure better funding.'

'Not the press,' corrected Taylor tightly. '*The Star.* More specifically, Faris.'

He turned and strode away abruptly, leaving Priestley to run after him. He jumped into the road in what the geologist thought was a wildly reckless manner in order to flag down a cab, and told the driver to take him to Fleet Street. Alarmed, Priestley scrambled into the vehicle after him.

'You're not going to confront Faris, are you?' he asked uneasily. 'Is that wise? He may use what you say to do you even greater harm.'

'*Greater* harm?' asked Taylor in a soft voice that was distinctly unnerving.

Priestley said nothing more, sensing a deep rage he dared not agitate further. When they alighted at the newspaper's premises, Taylor stalked towards the entrance, then immediately changed course when he saw Faris walking up the road towards them, his nose buried in a copy of one of his own papers.

'Ah, inspector,' said Faris with a sly smile. 'I was hoping I might have a word with you, and here you are. Tell me about this silversmith business.'

'Where did your information come from?'

Faris tutted. 'A man in my profession gets good at hearing things, just like in yours.'

'I made it up,' said Taylor. Faris gaped. 'I wanted to see who was revealing details about the case, so I fabricated a series of lies and spun them to different people, to trap the informer.'

'If you did that, then you already know who told me,' said Faris, although he looked uneasy. 'You just need to equate the right lie with the right person.'

Taylor took a step closer. Although there was nothing overtly threatening in the move, he still towered over the reporter in a way Faris clearly found unsettling, because he blanched. Priestley braced himself to intervene.

'It was Hamilton.'

A flash of surprise crossed Faris' face. 'Hamilton? *He* wouldn't tell me anything.'

Taylor's eyes narrowed. 'You're lying.'

'I'm not! It wasn't Hamilton.'

'Then who was it.'

Faris edged away. 'I'm not saying. *I* don't want to end up headless, like your Bishop.'

'Why should you be afraid of that?' asked Priestley, puzzled. 'We're talking about a corrupt police officer here, not a killer.'

'I don't know what you're talking about,' and Faris shiftily.

'I think you do,' said Taylor. 'To fund an effective police

292

force requires a great deal of money, which we don't have. What better way to rectify that than to terrify the public into thinking that its safety is compromised by incompetent officers?'

'Your words, not mine,' said Faris. 'But that's not the whole story, of course.'

Disliking the grubby reporter and his sly replies, Priestley stood on Faris' other side, knowing it would unnerve him. 'Then what *is* the whole story?'

'I can't say,' snapped Faris, trying to push him away. 'Who are *you*, anyway?' His eyes widened. 'I know! You're one of the men from the Antarctic expedition. You must have something to do with the murder of that scientist, Brice Scudder.'

Priestley was about to inform him that he had no idea what he was talking about, when Faris shoved him away again.

'Oh, no!' he cried, suddenly alarmed. 'I don't want anything to do with *that* business. Leave me alone.'

'What business?' asked Taylor, moving to block his escape.

'That affair at the docks,' cried Faris, becoming more frightened by the moment. 'I don't want…I can't risk…' He looked around him with wild eyes, seeking a way out.

'Someone told you there had been a murder at the East India Docks,' said Taylor, regarding him thoughtfully. 'But, after one unsuccessful attempt at trying to pump me for information, you abandoned the matter. That's unlike you. Did someone order you to—'

'I don't want anything to do with it,' repeated Faris, white-faced and visibly shaking now. 'Leave me alone. I don't know anything about it.'

Taylor and Priestley watched in confusion as the reporter put his head down and battered his way past them, breaking into a run the moment he was free.

'Someone has threatened him,' said Priestley, as he and Taylor walked towards the docks. 'He was terrified once he realised who I was. And do you think he was lying when he denied that Hamilton leaked the information? He must have been! No one but Hamilton should know about the silversmith burns.' Priestley snapped his fingers. 'Grant! You sent him for a pencil, but he may have heard anyway. And then there's the pathologist – Bradwell.'

'Robert is one of my closest friends,' said Taylor shortly. 'He'd never talk to Faris.'

Priestley looked across the grey smear of the river, and did not reply. On reflection, he was inclined to dismiss Grant, because the sergeant was not clever enough to play such a complex game. That left Hamilton and Bradwell, and both were strong contenders as far as Priestley was concerned.

They said no more until they reached *Nimrod*, where Adams was grudgingly helpful, knowing that Shackleton could not have an unsolved murder hanging over his head when they sailed. Unfortunately, he was unable to say whether Marshall was the kind of man to kill.

Meanwhile, Marshall claimed he was far too busy to answer questions, acidly pointing out that he alone had kept the Sabbath, and so was behind with his work. Then Shackleton arrived amid a flurry of activity, and the surgeon seemed to realise that it would not look good to refuse his co-operation in front of the Boss.

'Harangue me *here* if you must, Taylor,' he said, not bothering to look up from the papers he was studying. 'I'm too busy to go up to the officers' cabin. Be careful, boy!'

Taylor turned to see Nigel next to the gun cupboard. The lad was still hard at work, despite his disappointed ambitions, and had been set to packing cartridges in watertight containers. While Taylor knew there was not too much that could go wrong with such an operation, it was still not a task that he would have allocated to the clumsiest person he had ever met. As it was, Nigel had dropped a box, and cartridges were rolling across the deck. The young man began to collect them, fumbling horribly under Marshall's critical stare, and letting one slide out of his awkward fingers for every two he grabbed.

'Please come upstairs,' said Taylor, partly because he didn't think Marshall would be happy once he heard the nature of the questions, but also because he disliked the surgeon's bullying.

'I need some tea,' said Marshall, determined to oblige on his own terms. 'I'll drink it up there, and you can interrogate me for as long as it takes me to drain a pot.'

Priestley followed him up the ladder to the deck, with Taylor bringing up the rear, but the inspector had not gone far up when he realised he had left his hat behind. He climbed back down the steps to collect it, then stopped.

Nigel, still kneeling, was no longer collecting the spilled ammunition. He had one of the rifles out of its fastenings, and was holding it across his knees. He leaned down and slowly picked up a cartridge.

'What are you doing?' asked Taylor sharply, making him jump. 'Don't load that.'

Nigel grinned sheepishly, and the rifle slipped from his hand to the floor, making Taylor leap to one side, concerned the weapon might discharge. Nothing happened.

'I've never seen this model up close,' said Nigel, retrieving it. 'I wanted one as a boy, but my father said it was too dangerous. I joined a gun club once, and won a competition, but he still wouldn't let me have one.'

'He was right,' said Taylor, taking it from him to ensure he had not slipped a cartridge home, then stowing it in the cupboard. 'You don't want anything to do with firearms. They have a nasty habit of going off.'

'I had hoped to bag a seal, and bring its skeleton back for the Natural History Museum,' said Nigel wistfully. 'But that's unlikely now. Still, my father says he'll do all he can to raise the funds for the last position, and he's quite good with money.'

'I hope he succeeds,' said Taylor, closing the cupboard door.

'Well?' snapped Marshall, pouring himself some tea, but not offering any to Taylor or Priestley. 'Make it quick. The morphine tablets are due to arrive this morning, and I don't trust anyone else to check the order. I don't want to be in the Antarctic before realising that we only have half of what we asked for, or that the dosage is too low or too high. You'll agree, Priestley, I'm sure.'

'It *is* important,' said Priestley. 'But so is solving the murder. Besides, I thought Mackay counted in the medical supplies last week.'

'Some of them, but not the morphine. You won't be so smug when you fall on an ice axe and spill your guts into the snow. Or when you slide down a glacier and your tibia is poking out of your thigh. Compound fractures are terrible injuries under those conditions.'

Taylor regarded him uneasily, wondering if there was a threat in the doctor's vivid descriptions. It made him uncomfortable, knowing that in such a distant place anything could happen, and there would be no police officers to prevent mischief.

'You tried to have Adams blamed for killing Scudder,' he said bluntly in the hope that Marshall would blame him, not Priestley, for any unpleasantness. 'Why?'

'Because I thought he was guilty,' replied Marshall, eyeing him malignantly. 'And so did you, for exactly the same reasons. You haven't deigned to tell me why you suddenly deemed him innocent, so *my* analysis still stands, as far as I'm concerned. I remain convinced that he's the culprit, and if you had any sense, you would, too.'

'There's a possibility that the killer might not have intended to kill Scudder at all,' said Taylor. 'He might have been aiming at Adams, but in the dark and with everyone in evening dress, he made a mistake.'

Marshall stared at him. 'Oh, I see. You've allowed Adams to wriggle out of trouble, so now you need a replacement suspect. You've selected me. Well, it won't work. I *don't* approve of Adams, and I'll be livid if he's appointed second-in-command over my head – in fact, I'll probably throw in the whole thing – but I certainly don't go around killing folk I dislike.'

'I'm glad to hear it,' said Taylor dryly. 'Or there wouldn't be many people left.'

Marshall went to stand by the porthole. 'I find human beings a wicked, selfish, querulous race, and few individuals command my respect. I should never have become a surgeon, dedicating my life to healing their diseases and sewing them up after their foolish mishaps.'

'You have a compassionate bedside manner, I see,' said Taylor. 'I only hope your colleagues don't require your services too often in the Antarctic.'

'I couldn't agree more,' said Marshall, turning back to face him. 'It would be a waste of my valuable time. However, I also hope no one *here* needs a murder solved, because you clearly aren't up it, Taylor.'

'No?' asked Taylor tiredly. 'And why is that?'

'Because there's a flaw in your logic. It *was* dark that night, and we were all dressed alike. But even so, no one could have confused Scudder for Adams, especially at close range. So where does *that* leave your theory?'

A constable was waiting for Taylor when he finished talking to Marshall. There had been a fatal road accident involving a hansom at Piccadilly Circus, and foul play was suspected. It was Taylor's next case, and it was with a feeling of frustration that he took a cab from the docks.

As he went, he was acutely aware that he had failed to solve a second case within weeks. Worse, he had let down Shackleton, Priestley and everyone else who had put their faith in him. He would still try, of course, but with only three detectives available, it would not be long before yet another case intervened, and then another, and even if he gave up sleeping and eating altogether

– and he had already pared them back far more than was healthy – there would still not be enough hours in the day.

However, when he arrived at Piccadilly Circus, he discovered the incident was not suspicious at all. A motor-car had made a loud, mechanical pop near a horse, causing it to bolt into oncoming traffic. It had collided with another carriage, the unfortunate passenger of which had been killed.

However, although there was no foul play and therefore no need for a detective, Taylor was obliged to remain, because the constables in charge were inexperienced and had scant idea how to proceed. It would have been irresponsible to leave them, so he spent the rest of the morning and part of the afternoon teaching them what to do.

Meanwhile, Priestley, uncomfortable with Marshall muttering vicious comments about snivelling police informers, visited the British Library, where he spent several unsatisfactory hours trying to find references to college colours. He had arranged to meet Brocklehurst at two, and they went to the Lyons Café on The Strand, where he found himself increasingly delighted with the prospect of working with the baronet.

Sir Philip was eight months younger than Priestley, and they had a good deal in common. They walked back to the ship together, where Priestley gave his new colleague a detailed tour, during which Marshall's unpleasantness seemed far less of a trial. Brocklehurst had an easy, carefree manner that appealed to the other members of the expedition too, and it was not long before there was an atmosphere of cheerful gaiety aboard *Nimrod*. Marshall found himself shunned for his ill temper.

Eventually Priestley left Brocklehurst with Adams and Murray, and went in search of Taylor, finding him at his station.

'Is this it, then?' he asked, easing inside the small office and keeping his voice low, acutely aware that unfriendly ears might be listening. 'You have your next case and ours is relegated?'

Taylor smiled tiredly. 'Not yet, although it won't be long – when the weather is this hot, it always brings out the worst in people. But I can't talk now. I must go to the mortuary, and make sure those constables did what I told them. If I don't, and they do something wrong, the mess will take even longer to sort out.'

'I'll come along.' Priestley tried to sound nonchalant, but inwardly braced himself for another distressing experience.

Taylor looked at him in surprise. 'I thought you didn't like the place.'

Priestley smiled ruefully. 'To be honest, I'm so pleased to be given a colleague like Brocklehurst that I wanted to share my enthusiasm with a friend. I want to tell you what it means for our scientific programme.'

Taylor led the way out. He was bemused but flattered that Priestley had chosen him as the recipient of his confidences, and the comment about friendship was strangely touching.

Priestley talked non-stop all the way to the mortuary, which transpired to be a lengthy journey, because traffic was almost at a standstill. Taylor was one of those rare people who could listen without interruption, although his few remarks indicated that he was paying careful attention; he was not like Priestley's mother, who nodded and smiled at her son's eager monologues, but whose mind was on something entirely different.

When they arrived at the grim building, Priestley saw that daylight did nothing to improve its appearance, which was dirtier and shabbier, although perhaps now more functional than sinister.

Bradwell had taken Taylor's warning to heart, because the gates were firmly shut and the visitors' door was locked. They were obliged to resort to furious hammering before someone came to let them in, exhorting them to be patient while he wrestled with the locks. It was Peter Marshall, the doctor-in-training and cousin to the expedition's surgeon. He grinned cheerfully and ushered them in with a courtly bow that would have put Sir Walter Raleigh to shame.

'Enter,' he said in a sepulchral boom. 'But abandon all hope.'

'Don't,' chided Priestley uncomfortably. 'Not in this place. It's not decent.'

Marshall raised his eyebrows. 'You've got to joke – you'd end up crazed if you didn't. It's horrible here – all blood, guts and one-way journeys to the cemetery.'

'I know,' said Priestley. 'But jesting…well, it's not right.'

Bradwell emerged from his chamber of horrors, wiping his hands on a towel. 'You need to learn there's a time and a place for everything, Marshall,' he said, although without rancour. 'It was inappropriate behaviour that brought you here in the first place, if you recall.'

'What did he do?' asked Priestley before he could stop

himself. He did not really want to know, and Marshall's sudden scowl – one that made him look uncannily like his sullen cousin – indicated that he still thought the punishment unjustified.

'I've no idea,' replied Bradwell. 'Bart's Hospital was impressively discreet, saying only that he and his friends needed to learn some respect for the dead.'

'Bradwell isn't a bad sort,' said Marshall, when the pathologist had taken Taylor to his office, where they began to sift through paperwork. Priestley could tell from Taylor's resigned expression that the constables had bungled whatever they were supposed to do, and that he was obliged to rectify the matter. 'He could have made life miserable for us, being sent here in disgrace, but he's a good chap.'

'Yes,' said Priestley noncommittally. He was still not sure what to think about Bradwell, and only wished Taylor had not claimed him as a friend, far from certain that his role in the leaked information was innocent.

Marshall laughed. 'Of course, it's probably because he was in trouble a lot when he was a student. I've heard he was a bit wild.' He sobered suddenly. 'But we probably shouldn't have done it, and we're lucky Bart's didn't throw us out.'

Priestley had the feeling that he was about to be confided in, and tried to forestall the confession. 'I should be getting back to—'

'We stole a corpse,' blurted Marshall. 'We visit mortuaries as part of our anatomy course, along with the men from Guy's, and Bradwell showed us four bodies that were destined to be used for the advancement of science. The one that had been allocated to us was ancient, whereas Guy's was getting three really fresh ones. So we decided to put matters right. We took one of the ones that was supposed to go to Guy's.'

Priestley regarded him in distaste. 'That was disgusting.'

'Yes and no,' said Marshall defensively. 'Why should Guy's get the best cadavers? It's hardly fair! Besides, our plan backfired, because when we got it home, there weren't any organs in it. They'd all been removed.'

'Did you take it from here?' asked Priestley, suddenly wondering whether he was about to uncover the mystery of the Headless Bishop's disappearing body.

Marshall seemed to know what Priestley was thinking. 'No – we took it from the van that was loaded in the yard, ready to go to Guy's, so don't think we swiped the Headless Bishop. Our corpse had its head, hands *and* feet. And there was no mitre carved into it, or a smashed kneecap. When we showed up at anatomy with an extra cadaver, our professors immediately assumed the same as you – that it was the Bishop – and were in a right royal panic. But they piped down when they saw our corpse was different.'

'Where's it now?' asked Priestley.

'Buried in Highgate Cemetery. The professors wanted it shoved in the ground as soon as possible, before Guy's found out.' Marshall blanched suddenly. 'You won't tell anyone, will you?'

'What did it look like?' asked Priestley.

His heart was beginning to thud. Of course the authorities at Bart's would not have associated Marshall's theft with that of the Bishop, because of Faris' inaccurate reports. They would not know that the Bishop was complete in all respects, and they obviously had not clarified the situation with Bradwell, either – that would have begged the question as to why they were asking, and the hospital obviously wanted the matter hushed up. They had not even told Bradwell why the students were being punished, and he, tolerant old rebel that he was, had not asked.

Marshall shrugged. 'About fifty years of age, grey hair. Green eyes, I think.'

Priestley felt his ebullience begin to fade. Taylor's description had the Bishop as a much younger man. But perhaps the inspector had made a mistake: he was not a pathologist and so not qualified to estimate the ages of corpses. 'Was there a stab wound in the chest?

'No, of course not! We took an unwanted cadaver, not a murder victim. We're not *that* callous, or that stupid.

Priestley's disappointment was complete. 'When did you do it?' he asked, persisting anyway.

'It *was* the same night that the Bishop went missing, as it happens, but that was just a coincidence.'

Feeling Bradwell should be aware of what was happening in his domain, Priestley marched into his office and repeated the tale. Marshall was irked, but then somewhat vindicated, when the description of the corpse failed to match that of the Bishop in terms of age, build, hair colour, and other physical characteristics. He shot Priestley a smug, arrogant sneer that was redolent of his cousin.

Priestley turned to Taylor, who had listened to the exchange with some bemusement. 'I thought I'd discovered something that might help you. It didn't occur to me that two bodies would go missing on the same day.

'They didn't,' said Bradwell a little indignantly. 'I lost one: the Headless Bishop. The others, all present and correct, were shipped off as planned the next morning.'

Priestley was confused. 'But that can't be true. Marshall admits to taking a fifty-year-old man with grey hair, and you lost a thirty-year-old man with dark hair. Something is awry.'

Bradwell waved an airy hand, and spoke more casually than Priestley felt was warranted. 'Leave this with me. I shall make one or two enquiries, and contact you if I learn anything pertinent.'

Priestley watched him complete his paperwork with Taylor, a feeling of unease uncoiling in the pit of his stomach.

Chapter 13

Because Priestley had been so eager to talk on the way to the mortuary, Taylor was surprised to find him silent and withdrawn on the return. The inspector supposed he was disappointed that Peter Marshall's confession had led nowhere, other than to suggest that Bradwell had lost more bodies than he had realised. But such a revelation was not a bad thing – it might make the pathologist more careful in future: Taylor had long been concerned that his friend might fall foul of burglars.

Meanwhile, Priestley's exuberance had vanished. He had not liked Bradwell's casual reaction to the news that more than one body was missing, and it again made him wonder if the man might have stirred up the press to shift the focus from his own ineptitude. But there was nothing he could do about it, so he decided to visit the Expedition Office, to check on some specimen labels. It was already eight o'clock and he felt as though he should at least do *something* useful that day He alighted in Regent Street, leaving Taylor to travel to his station for more paperwork.

When he arrived, the office was deserted except for Shackleton and Nigel. Adams was speaking at the Army

& Navy Club, and the others had gone to support him. Shackleton had been unable to join them, because of a function later that evening, while Nigel had remained to monitor any visitors who might want to see the exhibition. When Priestley arrived, Nigel was just ushering out two retired seamen, listening politely to their inaccurate reminiscences of when Captain Nares led the British Arctic Expedition of 1875.

'Deaths,' one of them said. 'Galore.'

'And scurvy,' added the other salaciously. 'Dangerous place, the Antarctic. You should watch yourself, lad. Polar bears and great vicious walruses, too.'

'Captain Nares explored the Arctic, sir,' explained Nigel patiently. The two men looked blankly at him. 'We're going to the *Antarctic*. The opposite end of the Earth,' he added a little desperately when no gleam of comprehension was forthcoming.

'It's all the same,' said the first knowledgeably. 'You mark my words. Far too much ice, man-eating bears, cannibals, walruses and those wicked black and white birds…'

'Penguins?' asked Nigel, startled.

The old man nodded sagely. 'That's the ones. Evil brutes. Turn your back on 'em for a second, and they'll have you. You watch yourself.'

Priestley found himself smiling, but Shackleton was exasperated. 'No wonder we're not raising money,' he said in an undertone. 'People don't even know where we're going, and have the most extraordinary notions of what we'll find when we're there. One woman asked me today which "part of the South Pole" I planned to visit.'

Priestley listened patiently.

307

'I've been hearing this sort of nonsense all day,' Shackleton went on irritably. 'Nigel is a saint, the way he deals so politely with such inanities. It's a wretched shame we can't afford another scientist. Still, I stand by Brocklehurst. And this is for you, by the way.'

Shackleton handed him a telegram. It was from Priestley's father, and as the geologist opened the envelope, he was aware of the Boss trying not to look interested, while Nigel's face was transparently hopeful. Inside, the message was brief, but it told him all he needed to know. It read: CAP McGILL UNIVERSITY CANADA STOP FATHER STOP.

'Is it about funding?' asked Shackleton, trying to sound casual, while Nigel seemed to be holding his breath.

'McGill University,' said Priestley in immense satisfaction, barely hearing him. 'I've done it! I've found out in a day what Greasy Grant failed to do in weeks. The man is an incompetent!'

'Are you referring to *Sergeant* Grant?' asked Shackleton, puzzled. 'Is it something to do with Scudder?'

'No, I'm sorry. It's something else entirely. Will Taylor was having trouble identifying a body, and I've been able to trace part of the corpse's clothing to this McGill University. I've never heard of it, though.'

'It's in Montreal,' said Shackleton. He looked bemused. 'Your telegram isn't from that fellow John Gray, is it? The one who applied to join us, but never came back for his second interview?'

Priestley was startled by the question. 'No. Why?'

'McGill,' explained Shackleton. 'Gray is the only person I've ever met from there. They say it's a very good university, but I don't know anything about education overseas – and not much about it in England, to be honest. It just crossed my mind that he might have written to you with an explanation of why he failed to come back.'

Priestley rubbed his chin. 'Do you remember when that was, exactly?'

Shackleton watched Nigel take a brush and began to sweep the floor around a case that held a small model of *Nimrod*. 'Lord! I hope he doesn't knock that over. It belongs to Joyce.'

'Gray,' prompted Priestley. 'When was his second interview?'

Shackleton didn't take his eyes off Nigel. 'It was the sixteenth of June. I remember it well, because it was the same day as my sister Kathleen's birthday.'

'The Headless Bishop was found on the fifteenth of June,' said Priestley.

Shackleton gaped at him, Joyce's imperilled model forgotten. 'What are you suggesting? That John Gray is the Headless Bishop? What in God's name led you to that preposterous conclusion? Besides, wasn't the Headless Bishop a clergyman?'

'No one knows what he was – *The Star* gave him that name.'

'But this is a big leap of faith, Raymond – to claim that Gray and the Bishop are one and the same, based on identifying a cap.'

Priestley nodded. 'Yes, it is a big leap, and we can't even be certain that the cap belonged to the dead man. However, we have a chap from McGill – a university in Canada that can't have too many of its graduates in London – who disappears on or around the fifteenth of

June. And we have a body discovered at the same time in the presence of a McGill cap.'

Shackleton continued to stare. 'I don't like the sound of this. Gray might not be the victim at all – he might be the killer. And we have Scudder dead. Do you think he somehow learned that Scudder was the one who argued against him after his interview and did away with him?'

'It's possible – but how would he have found out? Presumably, such things are confidential?'

'Scudder had a loose and spiteful tongue,' said Shackleton. 'You'd better tell Taylor all this – tonight, if you can. I hope to God it provides the break he needs to lay this nasty business to rest.'

Priestley nodded. 'But there's one more thing I need to know. Gray must have mentioned a family – a next of kin – on his application form. If there's anyone in this country, the police will have to go and speak to them.'

Shackleton went to a cupboard and unlocked it, rummaging until he found what he wanted. Inside a manila folder was Gray's application, which included personal details, qualifications, experience and a photograph. It showed a strong, handsome face with a slight smile playing around the lips. Priestley wrote down the address of a cousin in Bromley.

'I suppose you intend to go, too,' surmised Shackleton disapprovingly. 'To speak to this cousin about Gray's whereabouts – or even hope he might be there, and confesses to killing Scudder?'

Priestley smiled. 'There's a train to Bromley every morning at ten past eight.'

Shackleton was not happy, but noticed the determined jut of Priestley's chin and knew he would not be denied.

'Very well, but be careful. Brocklehurst is a fine fellow, but he can't manage the geology alone.'

Priestley set off for Taylor's station, but when he arrived, it was to be informed that the inspector had been summoned to an incident in Battersea. Grant was in the office, labouring sullenly over a pile of papers, but neither he nor anyone else was willing to supply Priestley with an address, so that he might speak to the detective in person.

Disappointed, Priestley wrote Taylor a brief message, stating that the cap belonged to a McGill University graduate, possibly one named John Gray. He included the Bromley address and the recommendation that they go together the following morning to visit Gray's cousin. The train left Battersea Park station at ten minutes past eight, and he would meet Taylor on the platform.

High wispy clouds streaked across the sky the next day, and the stunted trees outside Priestley's lodgings swayed and quivered in the wind. During the night, the breeze had veered away from the southwest, and was coming from the north, with cooler, drier weather. It was a relief, and Priestley was in fine humour as he waited at the station.

Recalling how Taylor had almost missed the train the last time, he was not overly concerned until it was actually puffing out of the station – with neither of them aboard – at which point he became irritated. The cap represented a major breakthrough in both cases, and he felt Taylor should have made the rendezvous – or at least sent a constable with an explanation if other work had intervened. He waited another forty minutes, until the next train was due to leave, then boarded it alone.

His annoyance did not last long. He hardly needed a police inspector with him when he spoke to Gray's cousin. Moreover, he had a perfectly valid excuse for visiting: Gray had been on the brink of being accepted on the expedition, and Priestley was only ensuring that the application had been officially withdrawn. It occurred to him that he might find Gray there – that he could come face to face with the killer of the Bishop and perhaps even Scudder, too – but he pushed that thought from his mind. It was broad daylight, and he was going to a respectable village in Kent. Nothing bad could happen to him there.

The London Chatham and Dover Railway train chugged through the clutter of identical houses and the puffing factories of south London. Then chimneys and buildings gave way to allotments and trees, and eventually to open fields, villages and farmland. Bromley was a large settlement in a low valley, and its houses were well-spaced and varied in design. It was the kind of place where wealthier clerks lived, who could afford more pleasant surroundings and did not mind the daily commute to the City. Priestley alighted amid a furious hiss of steam, and asked a platform guard where he might find Holmesdale Road.

It did not take him long to locate George Gray's cottage, although it was a stiff walk. It was located on a track that led off the lane to Camden Park, standing alone on a rise that overlooked a brick-works and the railway line. Priestley marched up the garden path, and knocked on the door. For the first time, he felt uneasy: Taylor was used to dealing with such situations, but

Priestley was not and should have waited for him. But it was too late now, and he squared his shoulders as a shadow appeared on the other side of the stained-glass door. An elderly woman with white hair smiled expectantly at him. Behind her was a man of the same age, bent almost double; he held a toy soldier in one hand, and a tiny paintbrush in the other.

'Who is it, Maude?' he asked softly.

Priestley flashed his most winning smile, wondering whether Gray was lurking upstairs, preparing to hurtle down with a specially sharpened paper knife. 'My name is Raymond Priestley, and I'm with Mr Shackleton's expedition…'

Maude's face broke into a wide smile. 'You've come about our John! Is he to go with Mr Shackleton? We expected him to tell us all about it, but he never did. Come in, come in. The kettle has just boiled, and I'm sure you'd like a cup of tea. George? Fetch out the china, will you? We have a visitor, sent by Mr Shackleton himself.'

In a small but comfortable room that overlooked vegetable plots – regimented rows of carrots, onions and potatoes, as neat as the model battlefield in the front room – Priestley was treated like a lord. He was given the best chair, poured tea in a delicate service that was apparently only used for very special guests, and provided with more cakes and biscuits than even he could manage. Then they began to talk about John.

'He's not a cousin really,' explained Maude. 'He's our nephew's son, but we've always been close. We didn't have any children and our nephew died young, so John lived with us for a number of years. Then he went to Canada.'

313

George took up the tale. 'After university in Montreal, he went to sea with the sealing ships in Spitsbergen – that's in the far north. After a couple of years he returned to Canada to work for the Hudson's Bay Company.'

'Then, when he came back on his holidays to visit us,' continued Maude, 'he saw an article in the paper about Mr Shackleton. The next day he went to volunteer.'

'When was this?' asked Priestley.

'About a month ago. He said he'd be staying with a friend in London, but that he'd let us know how he did.'

'Has he?'

Maude shook her head. 'But that's not unusual. Our John's always been a bit of a wanderer, and we never know where he is during his vacations.'

George smiled affectionately. 'Usually, we find out when his postcards came.'

Maude nodded at her husband. 'Remember when he told us he was going walking in the Lake District, but then a card came, and he'd gone to Egypt instead? Egypt! Our John loves to travel.'

'And you haven't seen him since the day he went to volunteer?' asked Priestley.

George shook his head. 'The next time we get a postcard, it'll probably be from Antarctica. I expect he'll find a letter-box somewhere, because he knows how much we like his cards.'

'We've kept every one he's ever sent,' said Maude with pride. 'Would you like to see them?'

Priestley started to demur, but George was already heaving himself out of his chair, returning a few minutes later with four large books, all filled with cards and the dates they were received. The last one had been in

314

March of that year, when Gray had been working in the Hudson's Bay Company offices in Ottawa.

'Did he play cricket for McGill?' asked Priestley, thinking about the hat.

'Rugby,' replied George.

'Does he have a college cap?'

'Bless you, Mr Priestley, what funny things you ask,' said Maude, passing him another slice of fruitcake. 'He does have a college cap – a terrible shabby thing he bought in Montreal years ago. He won't throw it away, because he says the new ones are either too big or too small. He'll wear that cap until it falls off his head.'

'This friend he's staying with,' said Priestley. 'Do you know his name?'

'No,' replied Maude, exchanging a questioning glance with her husband. 'He never said, and I don't like to pry. He's not a boy any more, and it's not our place to poke into his business. But he has friends all over the place – from McGill, his school in Chichester and his clubs.'

'Clubs?'

'Activity clubs. George has been a member of the Dragonfly Society for years, and he used to take John with him. I think that's why John joined others when he got a bit older. At one time, he was a member of five, with gatherings each day of the week – there was natural history, bellringing, shooting, botany and butterflies.'

'Is there any way to find out the name of this friend?' asked Priestley.

'Why?' asked Maude, suddenly nervous. 'Is there something wrong?'

Priestley saw he was on the brink of upsetting them, and hastened to put their minds at ease. 'Not at all, but

Mr Shackleton is keen to speak to John, and this is the only address we have.'

'We don't know it,' said George. 'But his best friend should. He's a chap called Harry Fletcher, who lives in Cambridge, next to Hughes Hall. If anyone knows where our John is, it's Harry.'

Priestley left Maude and George with the sense that he had managed the situation rather well. He had the name and address of a man who might be able to provide Gray's current location, and he had asked his questions in a way that had left the elderly couple with no idea that he suspected their kinsman of murder. The more Priestley thought about the facts, the more convinced he was that he had solved both Scudder's murder and some of the mystery surrounding the Headless Bishop. He walked jauntily, heading down the hill towards Bromley Station.

He had not gone far when he became aware that someone was walking behind him. The track was a lonely one, shielded from the main road by hedges. It was rutted and overgrown, and deep pools of muddy water had gathered from the recent rains. It was not the sort of lane where many people would be walking.

He started to turn, but before he could, he was hurled to the ground. Then the breath went out of him as his assailant dropped onto his back. Hands took a grip around his neck, pushing his face into a puddle, so he could not breathe. He struggled hard, but his assailant had the advantage, and it was not long before Priestley felt himself grow weak from lack of air.

Although the Battersea incident – a brawl in which

316

knives were drawn – kept Taylor busy until well after two in the morning, he was still at his desk by six o'clock, knowing he needed the quiet time before his colleagues arrived if he was not to drown in the teetering files and reports that needed his urgent attention. He was also keen to avoid Hamilton, not yet sure how to address the silversmith leak.

He began by looking at what Grant had accomplished the night before, pleased to note that the sergeant had done as he had been told with a modicum of efficiency. He felt that the case against Vine was fairly watertight now. There was only one thing left to do before he passed the paperwork to the Crown Office and its prosecutors.

'We're going to the gaol,' he said to Grant, when the sergeant arrived a couple of hours later. 'To interview Billy Hopkins. I want to ask him again about this man he claims offered him fifty pounds for his false confession.'

Grant was sulky, his whole demeanour suggesting he did not want to go. 'That's a waste of time. He's already told you he doesn't know, and I'm sure he's telling the truth. He was scared to death when he thought his so-called benefactor might leave him to hang, and he would have told us anything he knew.'

'Probably, but we need to be certain. Vine's defence council may try to shift the blame to Hopkins at the trial, and we should trace this fellow if we can.'

Grant grumbled all the way to the prison, some of his comments verging on the insubordinate. Taylor tuned them out, and thought wistfully of Priestley's intelligent, mannerly company. He wondered whether the geologist had had any luck with the cap.

They entered the grim confines of the gaol, hearing

317

the echoing voices from the cells, the clatter of metal plates and cups, and the distant booms of slamming doors. They spoke to Hopkins in a filthy room that bore the wholly inappropriate title of Police Interview Suite. Taylor had been in it dozens of times, but never failed to be affected by its air of dismal hopelessness. Hopkins seemed to sense it, too, because he was frightened.

'Tell us about the man who offered you fifty pounds,' said Taylor. 'Let's start with where you met him. Was it before the explosion or after?'

'And if you lie, I'll break your fingers,' added Grant, shoving past Taylor and making the prisoner cower away in terror.

'Leave,' Taylor ordered his sergeant abruptly. 'Wait outside.'

'But—'

'Go,' said Taylor, fixing Grant with an intimidating stare of his own. Grant backed out, shooting first the inspector and then the prisoner a glare of pure malice. Hopkins started to cry.

'Please,' he wept. 'I can't tell you nothing.'

'This is your chance to co-operate and redeem yourself in the eyes of the law. If you help us, I'll ask the prosecutor for a lighter sentence. We're going to find out anyway, so you may as well reap the reward.'

'You'll find out anyway?' asked Hopkins, staring at him with sudden hope. 'How?'

'From witnesses, who saw you talking to him,' lied Taylor.

'Then it was *after* the explosion,' said Hopkins, relieved. 'I was asleep before. I went down to look at the laundry with everyone else after the bang, and he got me then.'

'Did he talk to you before or after the police arrived?'

Hopkins hesitated. 'After.'

Taylor regarded him soberly. 'And which of the police officers was it?'

Hopkins looked down at the table. 'Him what was just in here. Grant.'

Taylor asked a few more questions, saw Hopkins returned to his cell and summoned Grant. The sergeant's eyes were watchful, and he knew immediately that Hopkins had confessed. He sagged, leaning against the wall and closing his eyes, pinching the bridge of his nose between a thick thumb and forefinger. Looking at him in distaste, Taylor supposed it was the man's slippery ways that had earned him his nickname.

'Why?' asked Taylor simply.

Grant shrugged. 'He had a record for setting explosions, and there he was, watching this one with shining eyes. It was obvious he was the culprit, but he denied it. I offered him fifty pounds for a "false" confession, to get him down to the station without any trouble.'

Taylor spoke in a low, controlled voice that made the hair stand up on the back of Grant's neck. 'And then what?'

Grant swallowed. 'You already know – I got the wrong man. But we needed an arrest! We had the Headless Bishop and Scudder unsolved, and another lost case would have seen me out of the running for inspector for sure. Hamilton said so.'

Taylor raised his eyebrows. 'He did?'

'He's taken an interest in me.' Grant was sullenly

defiant. 'He said I have the makings of an inspector, but only if I play my cards right. He told me to watch what you do, and make adjustments if necessary.'

'Make adjustments?'

'That's what he said. He told me the Bishop was going to be mentioned in the House of Commons, and that heads would roll. He said one might be mine if I didn't make adjustments.'

'Hamilton lied to you,' said Taylor in disgust. 'Heads probably will roll, but yours wouldn't have been among them, not as long as you are a sergeant. He's using the Bishop to prove to the public that we're under-funded, under-manned and obliged to recruit second-rate detectives. And you have played right into his hands.'

'I don't see how—'

'Your aggression with suspects and witnesses impedes early solutions. You try to follow leads, but lack the imagination to do so successfully. You don't do as you're asked. You're corrupt. Your assistance on a case is more hindrance than help, which is why Hamilton insists we work together. He has used you to achieve his own ends.'

'No!' cried Grant, stung. 'I don't believe...' He trailed off, and Taylor saw him reconsider. It was some time before he spoke again. 'Why would he do such a thing?'

Taylor thought the answer was obvious, as there were not many officers with Grant's uniquely unpleasant combination of talents, but he felt the sergeant had heard enough unhappy truths for one day. He said nothing. Grant was also silent, and did not speak again until they were outside the prison.

'Will I lose my job?'

'Yes.'

Grant's face was savage and vengeful. 'Then Hamilton will lose his, too! I think it was him who talked to Faris about the Headless Bishop, and *him* who started the tales about your competence. And last night, I saw him steal a letter addressed to you. That boy Priestley left it.'

Taylor shrugged. 'I doubt it was important.'

'Then you'd be wrong.' Grant raised his hands when Taylor regarded him questioningly. 'He scribbled it on a bit of paper, so I read it. It wasn't like it was in a sealed envelope or anything.'

'What did it say?'

Grant seethed with resentment, and it was several moments before he could bring himself to speak. 'Priestley said he'd traced the cap.'

'No wonder you didn't tell me sooner.'

Grant glowered, but continued. 'He got the address of the Headless Bishop – or the Bishop's killer – and he wanted you to catch the ten-past-eight to Bromley, so you could tackle him together. I imagine he's there right now, confronting the fellow.'

Taylor gazed at him in horror, then broke into a run.

There was not a vast distance in terms of miles between the gaol and Bromley, but it seemed one of the longest journeys Taylor had ever taken. He commandeered a motor van from the prison, with a driver, and urged the man to tear along the streets at a pace that was far from safe, using all his knowledge to direct them along little-known shortcuts to avoid being caught in the capital's notorious jams. The driver caught his sense of urgency, and drove with all the skill and determination he could

321

muster, hand constantly on the horn.

Eventually, the crowded streets gave way to suburbs, and then they were dashing through the countryside itself, scattering startled pedestrians and once swerving dangerously to avoid another vehicle chugging along in the opposite direction. The resulting lurch almost sent Taylor tumbling through the door, while the driver swore and gripped the steering wheel with knuckles that were white.

'These things will never catch on,' shouted Taylor, above the howl of the engine. 'They may be faster than a horse and cart, but they're too damned dangerous.'

'Especially you're forced to drive like a lunatic,' muttered the driver. 'Here's Bromley. Where did you want to go?'

'Holmesdale Road,' he said, repeating the name Grant had given him and hoping the sergeant had not misremembered. 'Do you know it?'

The driver shook his head, then jammed on the brakes. 'There's a policeman. He will.'

The constable was a large, ponderous fellow with a highly coloured face and a handlebar moustache. 'Now, sir, the best way is if you—'

'Get in,' ordered Taylor, flashing his official identification and moving over to make room for him. 'Direct us as we go.'

Obediently, the policeman crammed himself inside the van and the driver resumed his breakneck journey, hurtling along the High Street, and following the main road up a hill, to where houses gave way to farmland.

'There is Holmesdale Road,' shouted the constable, his shaking finger showing his terror at the ride. 'But you

322

won't get this here vehicle up the track. Not with all the recent rain, and…what's happening up there?'

The driver had pulled up at the entrance of the lane, affording a clear view to where two figures wrestled in the distance. One was on top of the other, hands around his throat. Taylor shoved past the constable and began to run. He shouted, and the uppermost man started in alarm, scrambled to his feet and darted away, thrusting through the hedge and leaving his opponent sprawled on the ground. Taylor recognised Priestley's jacket, and raced towards him, heart thudding in his ears. He reached the geologist and hauled him out of the puddle.

Priestley's eyes fluttered open. He gazed blankly for a moment, then struggled to sit.

'Someone tackled me,' he choked. 'From behind.'

'He fled when he saw us coming.' Relief flooded through Taylor. He had been sure he was too late, and that Priestley was dead.

'Don't let him escape! It's the Headless Bishop's killer!' Priestley shoved Taylor hard. 'Go after him, Will. I'll catch up.'

Taylor was reluctant to leave Priestley, but the constable was lumbering towards them and the terrible fear Taylor had experienced when he thought Priestley had been murdered was suddenly replaced by a cold, hard rage. When Priestley pushed him a second time, he leapt to his feet and raced to the gap in the hedge.

He shot through it, a distant part of his mind noting that, by the way armfuls of hay from the adjoining field had been laid out, someone had been waiting on the other side for some time. Had he seen Priestley visiting the Gray's cottage, and lain in ambush?

Meanwhile, Priestley's would-be killer had made good time across the field and was scaling a stile at the far end. Taylor's hard sprint up the lane had left him winded, and he was unable to go as fast as he would have liked, although he was certainly gaining on his quarry. He reached the end of the field, vaulted over the stile, and found himself on land belonging to the brick-works.

Pallets stood everywhere, and there was a jumble of sheds and outbuildings, any one of which might provide refuge for a fugitive. He looked around desperately, not sure where to start. He picked a couple of shacks at random, ignoring the questioning yells of workmen who wanted to know what he was doing.

'There!' yelled Priestley, catching up, and pointing to where a dark-coated figure was aiming for the railway line. He coughed, spitting mud. 'He's going to cut back into Bromley.'

They set off in pursuit. The fleeing figure glanced behind him, then increased his speed, although his movements were becoming slower and more laboured. He reached the railway track and clambered up its low embankment. A train was coming in a fury of smoke and steam. Its driver saw the figure on the track and blew the whistle, just a toot at first, and then more urgent when the figure remained where it was.

Taylor powered towards it. He could not see the killer's face, because the sun was in his eyes and the fellow wore a hat that shaded his features, but he sensed the challenge nonetheless. The man was standing still, daring Taylor to catch him.

The train was closer now, whistle screaming so hard that it hurt Taylor's ears. Then the man turned away with a jaunty wave and dropped down the embankment on the other side. Taylor ran harder, thinking only of the taunting gesture. He reached the bank and started up it, but someone grabbed him from behind and brought him down in a bed of nettles.

Then the train was there, wheels thundering and screeching on the rails, and Taylor's body shook as it sped past. It seemed to go on forever, forcing him to put his hands over his ears. Finally, it was past, and he stood on unsteady legs.

There, in the distance, was a single vehicle moving slowly along the road that lay on the other side. Two people were in it – one the man he had chased, and the other some passing local resident, who had responded with innocent kindness to the fugitive's plea for a lift.

It was over. They could never catch a moving motor-car. Taylor felt like screaming at the top of his lungs, to give voice to the anger and frustration that turned his legs to jelly and his stomach to acid. But he didn't, and only stared silently at the vehicle until it disappeared behind a row of houses.

'He was daring you,' said Priestley unsteadily. 'He wanted you to chase him across the track, because he knew you wouldn't make it. He tried to kill you, too.'

'Damn him!' snarled Taylor. 'Bastard!'

'Don't swear,' said Priestley. 'It makes you sound like Adams.'

'The young man is right, sir,' said the constable, as he, Priestley and Taylor walked slowly back to the lane. 'You wouldn't have made it across the track. That fellow knew exactly what he was doing, and you're lucky your friend stopped you.'

'Did you see his face?' asked Taylor hopefully. 'Either of you?'

Both shook their heads. Then they were silent again until they were in the van, when Priestley gave a detailed account of his near drowning.

'So we saved each other today,' he concluded soberly. 'You drove him away when I was on the verge of expiring, and I know you'd be dead if you had tried to cross the tracks, as Gray wanted you to do.'

'Gray?' asked Taylor.

'John Gray – the owner of the McGill University cap, and the man who murdered your Bishop and probably Scudder, too. He applied to join our expedition just over a month ago, and he failed to appear for his second interview the day after you found your Bishop.'

'Why would Gray kill Scudder?'

'Probably because Scudder was less impressed with him than Shackleton or Adams, and may have said so – Scudder had a blunt tongue. Or because he's a deranged killer. We can't give this monster normal motives, Will. He isn't like us.'

Taylor smothered a smile that the young man should think he needed such a lecture. 'Go on with your story.'

'His family haven't seen him for a month.'

'Then perhaps Gray *is* the Bishop,' suggested Taylor, 'given that the cap was near the body.'

'That's what I thought initially, but if that's the case, then who killed Scudder? No, I think my theory makes the best sense. You can ask Gray about the Bishop when you catch him, which should only be a matter of time now you have his identity. I can even give you a

326

photograph, because there's one with his file.'

'But you didn't actually *see* him just now, did you?' asked Taylor.

Priestley shook his head. 'No, I told you: he attacked me from behind. But you were closer than me, and he looked right at you when he taunted you.'

'But the sun was in my eyes and his hat concealed his face, as I'm sure he knew. He's too clever to be identified so easily.'

'It *must* be Gray,' said Priestley with complete conviction. 'Why else would he be all the way out here? He was going to visit his relatives. No other explanation makes sense.'

Taylor supposed he could be right, but events had moved so quickly that he needed to think before he committed himself. When they reached Bromley, he dropped the constable at the village Post Office, and ordered him to send a telegram to the police in Cambridge, asking them to send an officer to speak to Harry Fletcher as a matter of urgency. Then, the constable was to keep a discreet watch on Primrose Cottage, in case Gray returned.

The driver brought them back to the city at a considerably more sedate pace than they had left it. Taylor listened again to Priestley's account of his visit to Maude and George, and was inclined to concur that they knew nothing about John's whereabouts or activities. The constable had described them as honest chapel folk, respected in the community and unquestionably decent.

Loath to leave Priestley alone, lest he become a target a second time, Taylor accompanied him to the ship, intending to ask one of the expedition members to keep an eye on him until Gray was caught. He was sure Wild or Joyce would oblige. Or perhaps Nigel Vallen would offer him a room at the vicarage, where he could take refuge with O'Brien for the night. He felt an acute sense of guilt about what had happened, knowing he had dragged Priestley into a danger that was part of a day's work for policemen but was wholly unacceptable for scientists.

When they walked into the officers' cabin, Marshall glanced up irritably, making it clear they were interrupting. Reverend Vallen was with him, writing at Marshall's dictation.

'I found myself with a spare hour, and Dr Marshall is using me as scribe,' the vicar explained. 'Anything to help.'

'Anything to make up for the fact that the expedition is now without one of its rifles,' countered Marshall acidly. 'Young Nigel has broken one. I thought a gun was a pretty tough piece of equipment, but he seems to have done something to the firing mechanism, so we're obliged to replace it.'

'It was an accident,' said Vallen defensively. 'These things happen.'

'Especially to Nigel,' said Marshall, turning back to his work. The fact that his behaviour towards the clergyman was brusque was indicative of the depth of his frustration.

'You were left a message a few moments ago,' said Vallen, ignoring him. He handed Taylor an envelope. 'It is urgent, apparently, but we didn't know where to find you.'

Taylor opened it, and his face broke into a smile. 'It's

from Bradwell. The Headless Bishop has been found.'

'Oh,' said Vallen in distaste. 'I assumed it was something more...prosaic.'

'It's all very simple and rather stupid,' said Taylor. 'Apparently, the medical students at Guy's got wind of what those at Bart's were planning, and decided to one-up them. They exchanged one of their "fresh" corpses for one that Bradwell had done an autopsy on – which is why Marshall and his friends found it sans organs when they got it to their own hospital.'

Marshall looked up from his work. 'You mean Peter, my cousin? That young tyke! I thought he must have done something very bizarre to make Bart's give him mortuary duties during his vacation. Brazen young fool!'

Priestley saw he was amused, however, as if such a prank was something he might have done himself. He was also aware of Vallen's horror, and although he sensed such a discussion would be distasteful to a cleric, it could not be helped. Priestley wanted answers.

'That explains how Peter Marshall and the others ended up with the fifty-year-old man, but not what happened to the Bishop.'

'Early the next morning, before Bradwell was there, a couple of Guy's students arrived to put *their* corpse back into the van,' Taylor continued. 'But they weren't the same students who had visited the night before...'

'And so the Bishop was put into the van rather than the one they should have had,' surmised Priestley in understanding. 'I see! And like Peter Marshall, the Guy's students didn't connect the Bishop with the body they took, because it didn't match *The Star*'s misleading descriptions. Hamilton must have been delighted – the theft of the corpse fitted his plan rather nicely.'

Taylor agreed. 'But even though we have the Bishop back, Bradwell says he can't tell us much. He remains an unidentified male with a single stab wound to the heart. Unfortunately, his head has been anatomised, so any identification from the face is now out of the question.'

Vallen gazed from one to the other with an expression of utter distaste. 'I'm not sure I understand. And you are talking about the poor unfortunate who was decapitated at Fountain Dock? And that his head is on him? But how can that be?'

Priestley took pity on him. 'He was never headless, handless or footless, sir. That was rubbish invented by the press.'

Vallen shook his head, and his expression was pained and rather sad. 'What a wicked world we live in. Such a wicked world.'

'Thank heavens for the Antarctic,' said Marshall piously. 'God's last remaining Eden.'

Chapter 14

Priestley would not hear of being allocated a bodyguard, asserting that he was quite capable of looking after himself. Taylor pointed out that he had almost been drowned, but Priestley replied tartly that Taylor was just as likely to fall prey to the killer's antics, given what had happened at the railway line.

In the end, they compromised, with Priestley agreeing to remain aboard *Nimrod* that night, where Cheetham and then Davis would be on watch with their men. Brocklehurst would also be there, because he had promised to complete an inventory of the equipment for the ponies by one in the morning; Cheetham would drop the finished list at the Expedition Office on his way to his lodgings, so it would be on Shackleton's desk when the Boss arrived in the morning.

Taylor returned to his station to organise the hunt for Gray. He remained uncertain whether it was Gray who had killed Scudder and the Bishop, but obviously the man needed to be caught and questioned. He was confused by the whole business: it was true that both victims had died within three miles of each other, but he found it difficult to connect a stabbing at a disused wharf with the execution of a scientist at the East India Docks.

By evening, twenty-nine police officers had been given a description of Gray and ordered to arrest him on sight, with the warning that he was extremely dangerous. Hamilton listened carefully to the briefings, leaving Taylor to wonder how much of the information would be fed to Faris. He again considered tackling his chief, but Hamilton's antics seemed to pale into insignificance when compared to the increased pace of his investigations, and he decided he did not have time for a confrontation, especially one that might result in his dismissal unless very carefully handled.

He went looking for Gray himself, disguised in a shabby raincoat he kept for wandering the less salubrious districts of the city after dark, but he did not expect success, and he was not surprised when his ambling resulted in nothing more than three solicitations from prostitutes.

He caught a cab home, hoping Ruby would be reading in her favourite chair, but the house was deserted. There was an unpleasant smell in the kitchen, and he was repelled to discover her meat pie alive with maggots. He threw it away, located the last of her scones and choked it down with an oily rind of cheese, trying to recall when he last had a proper meal. Then he went to the parlour with a glass of beer, intending to devise a plan of action for the following day.

A sharp rap on the front door woke him, and the sodden rug by his feet indicated that the glass had slipped from his hand as he had fallen asleep. He glanced at the clock. It was half past two, and he had been dozing for almost an hour.

A constable stood there, hunched under his cape in the darkness. Rain was falling steadily, and the cobbles glistened wetly in the light from the recently installed street lamps.

'You've caught Gray?' asked Taylor eagerly.

The officer shook his head. 'There's been a murder, sir.'

Taylor, to whom these words whispered in the dead of night were wholly familiar, reached for his coat. 'Where?'

'East India Docks, sir,' replied the constable, easing into the porch to escape the damp. 'Body found about an hour ago. I've got a cab waiting for you.'

Taylor's blood ran cold. 'Do you know the name of the victim?'

'No, sir,' said the constable. 'Only that it's a young man.'

Taylor urged the cab to drive so hard and fast through the deserted streets that it broke an axle, and he was obliged to run the last half-mile. Rain drove into his face and soaked through his clothes as he tore along, trying to keep his mind concentrated. There were several young men on the expedition, and there was no reason to assume it was Priestley who had been killed.

But, of course there was a reason: the killer had tried once already, and might be afraid the geologist would identify him. Taylor ran harder, breath coming in short gasps and blood pounding in his ears, although he knew that a minute or two would make no difference to the outcome.

He arrived sodden and breathless, to find Ives waiting, a miserable expression etched on his face.

'Another death on my dock will finish me,' he wailed. 'I don't suppose you could put in a word—'

But Taylor was gone, racing up the South Quay to where the now-familiar masts stretched skeletally into the night sky. He could see people gathered around someone on the ground, men who turned at the sound of his rattling footsteps. Marshall was there, standing slightly apart and identifiable by his stocky shape, and First Officer Davis, taller than the others. The newcomer – Brocklehurst – was there, too, and so were others Taylor did not take the time to identify.

'It's Yaxley,' said Priestley, stepping out from behind a pile of crates, where he had been sheltering from the driving rain. 'Poor Peter Yaxley.'

'What happened?' gasped Taylor, taking a lamp and crouching next to the body, trying not to show unprofessional relief.

'I found the body,' said Davis, who huddled unhappily inside his sopping watch coat. 'It was just like before: I relieved Cheetham at one, did a check of the ship, and when I came out with Berry, there was Yaxley.'

'It's the same as what happened with Scudder, sir,' said Berry. 'The killer waited until Mr Davis and me were checking the holds, and made his move when we were below.'

'What about Riches?' asked Taylor, looking around uneasily. 'Where's he?'

'Here, sir,' said Riches, stepping forward. He held a cloth to the back of his head, and Marshall hovered solicitously at his elbow. 'We changed our tactics a bit after Scudder, so that one of us stayed on the quay while the other two checked the ship. But some bugger knocked me on the head.'

'A stunning blow,' elaborated Marshall. 'There won't be any lasting damage, although he'll have a headache tomorrow. So, inspector, it seems our killer was so delighted with his success the first time that he simply repeated the operation.'

'Not quite,' said Taylor, lifting the tarpaulin with which Davis had covered the body. It was an ugly sight, and he was aware that only Marshall did not look away. 'Yaxley has been shot; Scudder was killed with a blade.'

'I heard gunfire,' volunteered Brocklehurst. 'At least, I *think* I did, although with the docks so close to the iron works and a cement factory, I can't be certain.'

'Neither can I,' added Priestley. 'Although I certainly heard a loud crack.'

'*I* didn't,' said Marshall. 'The first I knew about it was Davis yelling at about half past one.' He crouched next to Taylor, peering at the body in the unsteady light of the lamp. 'This looks to have been fired at very close range, wouldn't you agree, inspector? You must have seen your share of these things.'

'Enough,' said Taylor soberly. 'The bullet entered Yaxley's head just above his left ear, and exited taking the right side of his skull with it.'

'Sweet Jesus!' whispered Brocklehurst, turning away.

'You'll be doing this to seals in a couple of months, so don't be too prissy,' said Marshall sharply. He looked the baronet up and down, adding acidly, 'and I'm sure you must have bagged a pheasant or two on your family estate.'

'It's not the same,' said Priestley, leaping to his new friend's defence. 'This was Yaxley, and we knew him.'

He turned to Taylor, who was tucking the tarpaulin around the body, gesturing for the waiting constables to remove it. 'Yaxley, Brocklehurst and I were working in the captain's quarters – England said we could use them, so Davis could sleep in the officers' cabin – until one o'clock.'

'I finished my inventory, and gave it to Cheetham, as we'd agreed.' Brocklehurst took up the tale. 'I'd planned to return to my hotel at that point, but it was pouring with rain, so I decided to spend the night aboard, instead. Yaxley elected to go home, though. He left at ten-past-one, and that was the last we saw of him.'

'How long after he left did you hear what you thought was gunfire?' asked Taylor.

'Four or five minutes, no more.' Brocklehurst looked at Priestley for confirmation.

Priestley nodded. 'But we didn't think anything of it – we'd no reason to believe it was gunfire, and it was just a loud bang that could have been anything. Then, about fifteen minutes later, Davis started yelling...' He trailed off.

'Has anyone left since this happened?' asked Taylor.

'Cheetham and his men left before Yaxley did,' replied Priestley. 'Everyone else is here.'

'Good,' said Taylor. 'I want everyone to go on board and wait for me. Marshall, tend to Riches. Davis, you needn't worry about the quayside tonight – no thief is going to make off with your materiel when the docks are swarming with policemen.'

Taylor began to organise his officers, looking around for Grant before remembering that the sergeant would not be there. A grubby and distinctly sullen letter of resignation had been on his desk earlier that evening; Grant was taking his leave before he was dismissed.

Ives confirmed that Cheetham and his two sailors had left the docks soon after one o'clock, shortly before a sharp report that he had assumed was a motor-car. He also reported that a search of the quay had revealed no hiding killers, but it was such a vast area, it was impossible to be sure. Taylor ordered a second, more comprehensive search using his own men, although he doubted it would yield fruit. The killer would be long gone, escaped during the thirty minutes or so between the shooting and Davis' grim discovery. Eventually, he was able to start speaking to witnesses.

'Do you think Gray did it?' asked Priestley, when he was summoned to the officers' cabin with Brocklehurst, to give their account in more detail.

'Possibly,' replied Taylor cautiously. 'However, I think we can safely assume that Scudder and Yaxley were killed by the same culprit. I don't see two murderers with designs on your expedition, despite the fact that the methods of execution are different. Will you show me the gun cupboard?'

Priestley led the way to the locker, leaving Brocklehurst to dictate his statement to a constable, then gasped in horror when he saw that the lock securing it had been broken. He wrenched open the door. 'One rifle is missing! So, now we know where the weapon came from.'

'We know more than that,' said Taylor. 'We know the killer is definitely a member of the expedition: no one else would have been on board.'

'No!' objected Priestley. 'Gray is the killer. We've all

but proved it.'

'We haven't though, Raymond. How could Gray have come for the gun with Cheetham and Davis on watch, and you and various other expedition members wandering all over the place? He'd have been seen. And you all know what he looks like, because you've either met him or seen his photograph.'

'This gun could have been stolen at any time during the day,' argued Priestley. 'Just because it's loss is discovered now, doesn't mean that the killer is one of us. We keep the cupboard locked, but we don't inspect it every five minutes, and all sorts of people could have got at it – including dockhands pretending to help with the stowing.'

Taylor nodded slowly as incidents and discussions snapped together in his mind, and with it came understanding. 'You're right – at least in part. The gun was taken earlier in the day. However, I stand by my conviction that it was stolen by someone connected to the expedition, not by a random thief.'

'Someone connected…what do you mean?'

'Nigel Vallen. I saw him playing with a rifle myself, and he told me he has an interest in firearms. Marshall also accused him of damaging a weapon, which means he was in the locker more than once. He was a member of a gun club once, and wanted a rifle of his own, but his father refused him permission to buy one.'

Priestley gazed at him. 'Maude Gray told me that John was in a gun club too.'

Taylor rubbed his chin. 'Is it too tenuous a connection? Is it possible that Gray's friend in London is a fellow shooting enthusiast? Such as Nigel Vallen?'

'But Nigel can't be the killer!' objected Priestley, appalled. 'Because…well, because he's Nigel?'

'Let's think it through. Scudder wanted O'Brien as the expedition's third biologist – he didn't want Nigel. Yet Nigel was desperate to go south, so he killed the man who was pressing for another candidate.'

'But Nigel has an alibi for Scudder's murder,' protested Priestley.

'His alibi is O'Brien,' Taylor pointed out. 'Who isn't exactly stable. He's also currently staying in Nigel's house – under Nigel's sway. Now, let's say it was Nigel who tried to drown you—'

'But it wasn't,' protested Priestley. 'It was Gray.'

'You can't be sure, because you didn't see his face. The man I chased could have been Nigel, although I confess he seemed less limber than I imagine Nigel would be. But let's leave speculation aside for a moment and concentrate on facts. Who did you tell about visiting Gray's family? And don't say Grant knew, because he was with me when you were in Bromley.'

'Hamilton,' flashed Priestley. 'You told me yourself that he stole the letter I wrote, asking you to come to Bromley.'

'Grant lied about that,' said Taylor tiredly. 'I found the letter in a jacket he left behind – he told the tale out of spite, to force me into a confrontation with a man who can demand my resignation. And to avenge himself on you for being a better detective than him.'

'I am?' asked Priestley with a sudden grin.

Taylor gestured irritably. 'Think, Raymond. Who else knew you planned to visit Gray's family?'

'Shackleton,' said Priestley. 'But it certainly wasn't

him who attacked me!'

'Who else was there when you talked to Shackleton?' Taylor was becoming impatient.

Priestley stared at him. 'Nigel,' he admitted eventually. 'Nigel was sweeping up. He wasn't part of the conversation, but he probably heard it.'

'Did you tell Shackleton which train you intended to catch?'

'I told him the eight-ten, but you didn't turn up, so I got the next one.'

'Whoever attacked you was probably hiding behind the hedge when you arrived, intending to kill you *before* you could speak to the Grays. However, you were late, and he might have assumed you'd had second thoughts. He fell asleep, exhausted by his early start to arrive ahead of you. You walked past him, perhaps waking him, so he waited, ready to strike when you left.'

'But why?' cried Priestley. 'What can Nigel have against me?'

'Other than going on the expedition of his dreams, while he stays at home? Nothing, probably. What else did you discuss with Shackleton? That you'd identified the cap as being from McGill?'

Priestley nodded slowly. 'Yes. He probably heard me make the association between McGill and Gray, too.'

'And he knew it was only a matter of time before you guessed that Gray was his gun-club friend, *and* that he'd murdered him in order to get on the expedition himself.'

'Oh, come, Will!' cried Priestley aghast. 'Now you're letting your imagination run wild! You think Gray is the Headless Bishop?'

'You thought so yourself initially,' said Taylor. 'The

340

Bishop was a man of about thirty with dark hair; so was Gray. And think about the location of the murder: the rectory, where Nigel lives, is within spitting distance of Fountain Dock. It wouldn't have been difficult to kill Gray and take his body to the nearest accessible part of the Thames, intending for the tide to carry it away. It was stripped naked, so the police would never be able to identify it—'

'Except for the cap.'

'Except for the cap, which was lost in the darkness. You saw what it was like there, and you heard what Long Ron said about the killer muttering as he left, carrying his victim's clothes, expressing remorse. Nigel is the kind of fellow to feel sorry for killing a friend.'

'Will!' cried Priestley, appalled. 'I can't believe I'm hearing this! Nigel isn't the killer. Not clumsy, amiable Nigel!'

'We know he was in the gun cupboard today.'

Priestley was silent for a moment. 'Then why would he want Yaxley dead?'

'It was a mistake. Yaxley was not his intended victim, Brocklehurst was.'

Priestley gaped at him. 'Philip? But that makes no sense!'

'It makes perfect sense. Brocklehurst had been working on an inventory, which he had promised to complete by one o'clock, so Cheetham could drop it at the Expedition Office. He decided at the last minute to stay on board, but Yaxley went home. Yaxley was killed at about ten past one – at exactly the time Brocklehurst should have been leaving.'

'But why would Philip be a candidate for execution?'

'The answer to that is obvious,' said Taylor impatiently. 'Because he was appointed to the post that had been promised to the hopefuls. Everyone has been saying that Nigel had the best chance, and then all of a sudden here is Brocklehurst, stepping in with no experience and a privileged background. Of course Nigel is resentful.'

'Sir!' called a constable, opening the door tentatively.

Marshall was with him. 'He has a telegram for you. Urgent. Did I just hear you tell Priestley that you might have a suspect at long last? Who?'

'Nigel,' said Priestley unhappily. 'Will thinks he killed Scudder, Yaxley and Gray.'

'*Nigel*?' repeated Marshall incredulously. He started to laugh, but stopped when he saw Priestley's bleak expression. 'You're serious!'

'Yes,' said Priestley wretchedly. 'I still can't believe it.'

'Neither can I,' said Marshall. 'Especially Gray. I thought he and Nigel were friends. They certainly acted companionably when Gray came for his interview, and I assumed it was Gray who had encouraged Nigel to apply – or vice-versa.'

Taylor nodded his satisfaction at the information, while Priestley gaped. 'Why didn't you mention this before?'

Marshall was startled by his vehemence. 'Why would I? I didn't think it was relevant to anything, and I thought you saw them together, anyway. It wasn't a secret.'

'Telegram from the Cambridge Police,' said the constable, breaking into their discussion with a voice that indicated he thought what he had to say was more important. 'Their machine has been broken, hence the delay. There's a letter for you, too, sir, but it's been hanging around a while.'

Taylor opened the telegram, and pushed the letter in his pocket. It bore Grant's untidy scrawl, and he did not want to plough through a justification of the sergeant's unsavoury actions while he was on the trail of a killer. He scanned the telegram, then handed it to Priestley.

'There's your evidence,' he said. 'Harry Fletcher says the friend Gray has been staying with in London is Nigel Vallen, an old acquaintance from his gun club. Fletcher adds that Nigel's address is a vicarage in Rotherhithe.'

It was dawn when Taylor, a revolver in his pocket, and five armed constables arrived at the vicarage. Priestley had insisted on accompanying them, and Taylor had refused. However, when it became clear that the geologist was going to make his own way to Nigel's home, and that it would be safer for all concerned to have him where they could see him, Taylor relented, but ordered that he was to remain in the cab until he was given permission to leave it.

The building was in darkness. Taylor ordered three constables to the back of the house, sent another to guard an alley that ran along its side, then knocked on the door. His hand was in his pocket, fingers gripping the gun, and he was unsettled to find they were unsteady. He disliked firearms, especially having been shot once in the line of duty. There was no reply, so he rapped harder. A light went on in an upper window, and he stepped away from the door, so he could see the constable in the alley. The man shook his head: no one had made a bid for escape.

Steps sounded in the passageway, and another light went on.

'Who is it?' called a voice. Reverend Vallen.

Taylor stepped closer to the door, the gun heavy in his hand. 'Police,' he called back. 'Taylor.'

'Taylor?' echoed Vallen, and there came the sounds of bolts being drawn. 'I'm afraid you're rather early for refreshments. When I said you were always welcome for a cup of tea, I wasn't anticipating you'd take up the offer at such a peculiar hour.'

Taylor did not reply. He waited until the vicar had opened the door, then pushed past him into the hallway, ignoring the man's protestations. He checked quickly that the front parlour was empty, and bundled the priest inside it, the last constable at his heels.

'Nigel,' he said, quelling the priest's increasingly agitated complaints. 'Where is he?'

'In bed. But I—'

'Where?'

'The first bedroom on the right, upstairs. But what's this about? I object in the strongest—'

Taylor cut him off, ordering him to stay in the parlour, then ran up the stairs to the room Vallen had indicated. It was in darkness, but the light from the hall illuminated someone lying in bed, and he could hear soft breathing. Gesturing for the constable to draw the curtains to let in the grey light of dawn, Taylor pulled the revolver from his pocket and advanced across the room. Gripping the weapon in his right hand, he hauled away the covers with his left.

Nigel came awake with a start. 'What—?' he began. He saw the barrel of the gun and his jaw dropped in terror. 'Father! Help!'

'Stand up,' ordered Taylor. 'Put your hands on your

344

head. Now!'

Frightened by the cold authority in the inspector's voice, Nigel did as he was told, standing rigidly still while the constable patted him down, then pushed him against the wall. Taylor searched the room quickly, looking under the bed, then moving to the desk. It was an old one, and delivered his hip a painful knock as he tried to move around it. He winced.

'I'm always doing that,' said Nigel, giving him a wan smile and trying to conceal his horror with normal conversation. 'You'll have a nasty bruise tomorrow.'

Taylor made no reply, but bent to where a suitcase had been pushed underneath it. He tugged it out, noting the initials 'JG' engraved in its ancient surface.

'It's locked,' said Nigel, stating the obvious.

'Where's the key?'

'I don't know. It belongs to a friend. You mustn't tamper with it. It isn't yours—'

He stopped speaking when Taylor took a pocketknife and broke the lock with a snap. The inspector opened the lid, and rifled through the contents.

'These belong to John Gray,' he said. 'Where is he?'

Nigel was uneasy. 'I don't know. He left, but didn't tell me where he was going. He just wrote me a note saying he'd be back, and would I mind keeping his things. He's always doing that sort of thing. He just gets the urge to wander, and off he goes.'

There was something oddly convincing about Nigel's tale, and Taylor began to wonder whether Priestley might be right after all: that Gray, not Nigel, was the culprit. But there were too many questions with such a solution, and he pushed the doubts from his mind. He resumed his search, but there was no rifle.

'What did you do with the gun?'

'What gun?' Suddenly, Nigel looked decidedly furtive. 'I don't own a gun. My father doesn't approve of them. I told you that the other day.'

'The gun you took from *Nimrod*.'

Nigel swallowed hard, and his eyes darted from constable to inspector. 'I didn't take anything.'

'You'd better get dressed,' said Taylor. 'You'll be coming to the station with us.'

While Nigel pulled on his clothes, Taylor inspected them for blood, but there was nothing. Eventually, Nigel was ready and Taylor indicated the younger man was to precede him down the stairs. Nigel baulked.

'There's been a mistake,' he said unsteadily. 'I don't know what you think I've done, but—'

'Tell us at the station,' said Taylor shortly. He was suddenly very tired, and wondered whether he would have the energy to listen to the lies and excuses that always fell from the mouths of killers once they had been caught. And Nigel had been more ruthless and cunning than most.

'The vicar has gone to use a neighbour's telephone,' said one of the constables as they arrived downstairs. 'I couldn't stop him.'

Taylor pushed Nigel into the parlour and closed the door, shutting him inside. He knew from his previous visit that the windows had been painted shut, so escape was impossible, and he did not want to detail two of his constables to escort Nigel to the station when he needed them to search the house – the vicarage was large and

346

rambling, and it would take too long with a smaller team.

'A police officer with a gun couldn't stop an unarmed priest from leaving?' Taylor asked shortly.

'He was angry, sir,' objected the constable. 'He said he was going to telephone Chief Superintendent Hamilton and register a complaint, and I thought that if I tried to prevent him, he might tell Mr Hamilton we were heavy-handed. Besides, laying hands on a holy man don't come natural.'

'All right, Matthews,' said Taylor wearily. 'It's not him we want anyway, although I'd just as soon he was here when we search his house.'

'Search a vicarage?' asked Matthews uneasily.

'We need to find the weapon that killed Yaxley. Start in the attics and work down. And don't forget to check for loose floorboards.'

'Very well, sir. Shall I let the scientist in? He's outside.'

Taylor supposed there was no danger now that Nigel had been apprehended. He nodded, and Priestley came bounding into the hall, full of questions.

'Did you find the gun? Is there *evidence* that Nigel killed Yaxley?'

'Not as such,' replied Taylor, trying to keep the exhaustion from his voice. 'But I can prove Gray was here. There's a suitcase of his clothes upstairs, and Nigel freely admits that he visited.'

'You're limping,' said Priestley, watching him move towards the parlour. 'Did Nigel put up a struggle?'

'Just banged my—' Taylor stopped speaking abruptly, and a smile spread across his face, although it was humourless, and Priestley thought it rather nasty. 'I bashed my hip on Nigel's desk, and he said he does it all the time. There was a bruise on the Bishop's hip, just like there will be on mine tomorrow. Gray is the Bishop, and Nigel *did* kill him.'

'Perhaps.' Priestley supposed the evidence was mounting up. 'But what about Yaxley and Scudder? Nigel has an alibi for Scudder.'

'No, he doesn't. He was with O'Brien for a while that night, then he came home, where his father was waiting. Both went to bed. But look at the size of this place. Vallen wouldn't know whether Nigel was here or not. Nigel must have slipped out again.'

The door flew open, and Reverend Vallen stood there. He wore a coat over his pyjamas, and his chest was heaving from a brisk run. His hair was awry, and he was furious.

'I've just telephoned Chief Superintendent Hamilton. He orders you to desist whatever you're doing and leave. I sit on the Police Benevolent Committee, and I have many friends. Your behaviour is unacceptable, inspector. I shall not allow this matter to pass unremarked.'

'I apologise for the inconvenience, sir,' said Taylor. 'But we have reason to believe your son has murdered three people. I suggest you—'

'You can suggest whatever you like, but you will leave my house immediately,' ordered Vallen coldly.

'I'm afraid we can't, sir,' said Taylor gently.

'Then you can wait in my parlour until Hamilton arrives and orders you himself,' snapped Vallen. 'He won't be long. Nigel can keep an eye on you, and if you've harmed a hair on his head, I shan't be pleased. I am going to dress.'

He turned and walked up the stairs, bristling. Taylor

gestured that Matthews was to go with him, and told two other constables to resume their hunt for the gun – the remaining pair were scouring the garden. Perhaps Hamilton *would* arrive and tell him to desist – it would not surprise him – but he would not stop until directly ordered. Reluctantly, the constables obliged, clearly unhappy with aggravating a clergyman.

'I've just thought of something,' said Priestley, catching Taylor's sleeve as he started to open the parlour door. 'If Nigel did kill Gray, and Reverend Vallen knows, then it might be Vallen who's been telling Hamilton to spread lies about the Headless Bishop. Vallen seems to think he can order Hamilton around…'

'Hamilton might lie and scheme to improve his department's budget, but I don't think he'd lie and scheme to conceal a murder.'

Priestley increased his grip. 'I'm serious, Will. Vallen has just ordered a senior police officer to come to his house at dawn, and Hamilton is complying. You've suspected for a while that Hamilton is corrupt, so don't expect him to be on your side when he arrives.'

'Sir,' said one of the constables unsteadily, emerging from a door that led to the cellar. 'You should see this.'

'What?' snapped Taylor. 'Just tell me.'

'It's O'Brien from *Nimrod*. He's been stabbed.'

'Oh, no!' cried Priestley, gazing at the crumpled form in the cellar's farthest corner. 'You were right, Will! Nigel *is* the killer! But why murder O'Brien?'

'Because he's been staying here, and he discovered those,' said Taylor, nodding to where cufflinks lay on the floor beside O'Brien's outstretched hand. They bore the

McGill shield. 'He must have worked out that Gray had been murdered, and confronted Nigel with the evidence – a fatal mistake. He should have come to the police.'

'And there,' said Priestley, pointing with an unsteady finger. 'A coat, trousers with braces, a white shirt and socks stuffed into shoes. The items Long Ron saw the killer carrying away. It was Nigel. He stripped his friend's body and brought the clothes here, not imagining that anyone would ever find them.'

'Finish the search,' Taylor instructed the constable. 'Get Jackson to help. And then parcel up these items. If we can prove they belong to Gray, we'll have enough to hang Nigel.'

'And Yaxley's murder?' asked Priestley softly.

'We need to find the gun for that. Come on. I don't want him alone longer than necessary.'

Priestley followed him into the parlour, where Nigel was sitting on the sofa, knees pressed together and hands clasped in his lap, looking for all the world like an elderly spinster. His face was shiny with sweat.

'We found O'Brien,' said Taylor, sitting on a chair opposite him. 'He's been stabbed, just like Gray and Scudder. And we found Gray's clothes in the cellar, too. We know what happened. Gray came to stay with you while he met Shackleton. Initially you were pleased, but he had excellent qualifications, and you saw you were a very poor second. You murdered him, leaving his body for the Thames to carry away.'

'I don't know what you're talking about,' said Nigel hoarsely. 'I told you: John has a habit of wandering off, and he left me a note. You can see it, if you like.'

'You took care to ensure the body wouldn't be

identified by its clothing,' Taylor went on. 'But you reckoned without a witness who saw you, and who pulled the corpse above the water line.'

'There was the blanket you wrapped him in, too,' added Priestley. 'The good quality blanket that no pauper would have wasted, but that wouldn't be missed from the house of a vicar with a good living.'

'But your plan worked anyway,' continued Taylor, 'because there were false reports that impeded my investigation, and no good leads. Then you learned that Scudder favoured O'Brien, so Scudder had to die, too – you knew O'Brien wouldn't persist once his lover was dead. Moreover, Scudder's death meant another position open on the expedition.'

'This is all wrong,' said Nigel weakly.

'But then the unthinkable happened,' said Taylor, watching him intently. 'First, one position was cut because there isn't enough money, and second, Brocklehurst was appointed. So, Brocklehurst had to go. You waited until he finished his inventory – at one o'clock, just as promised – then you shot him with the gun you stole from *Nimrod*. However, it wasn't Brocklehurst you killed, it was Yaxley.'

'Yaxley?' asked Nigel unsteadily. 'Peter is dead, too?'

'And now we find O'Brien murdered in your cellar,' finished Taylor. 'Your ruthless ambition has claimed four promising lives.'

'No!' cried Nigel, jumping to his feet. Taylor stood, too, hand gripping the revolver in his pocket. 'I admit I stole the rifle. It was wrong, but I wanted something of *Nimrod*'s before she set sail and I've always yearned to own a gun. But the rest is completely untrue.'

351

Priestley stood near Taylor, trying to keep the distaste from his expression. He had liked Nigel, and saw his actions as a betrayal of both the expedition and Shackleton.

'Your conclusions could not be more wrong,' said Vallen, walking into the parlour, now fully clad in clerical dress. He strode towards the grandfather clock that showed the hour was a little past seven, and opened its door, as if to wind it. 'Leave him alone.'

'How do you explain the body in your cellar?' asked Priestley. He swallowed. 'O'Brien's.'

Vallen moved suddenly, and had whipped a rifle from inside the clock-case before anyone realised what he was doing. Taylor started to tug the revolver from his pocket, but Vallen's reactions were frighteningly fast, and he used the rifle's long barrel to dash the weapon from the inspector's hand. The handgun skittered across the floor, while Taylor clutched a numb wrist: the vicar had packed a powerful swipe.

'This is loaded, inspector, so I recommend you do as I say, unless you want to spend another spell in the Convalescent Home. Nigel, pick up the revolver.'

Nigel gazed uncomprehendingly at his father, but did as he was told. 'I…I don't understand…'

'Come and stand by me, son. Don't worry. Everything is under control.'

'My constables are all over the house,' warned Taylor. 'You won't escape.'

'Actually, two are shut in the cellar, two are locked in the garden shed and Matthews is dead. I'm afraid I was obliged to stab him.'

352

'Stab him?' cried Nigel. Taylor closed his eyes sick with horror: Matthews was a married man with small children. Nigel dropped the revolver in his agitation, but Taylor was too stunned to capitalise on his clumsiness. 'You killed a policeman?'

'It was unavoidable – he found my muddy clothes and guessed it was I who tried to drown Priestley in Bromley yesterday. But he is of no consequence. Hamilton will be here soon, and he'll know how to resolve the matter so that Taylor is blamed.'

'But why?' asked Priestley hoarsely. 'What will you gain from that?'

'Exoneration – I'll be a victim, not a suspect. Hamilton will convince everyone that a deranged inspector, driven to despair by his failures, went on a rampage during which police officers and two members of Shackleton's expedition lost their lives: you and O'Brien. Nigel will certainly be appointed if *you're* dead.'

'Hamilton won't condone murder,' said Taylor with more conviction that he felt, watching Nigel fumble with the pistol. The lad was moving as though in a daze. 'So put down the rifle—'

'Yes, he will,' said Vallen firmly. 'He appreciates my fund-raising abilities too much to refuse my requests.'

'His tales to Faris,' said Priestley in disgust. 'They were your idea?'

'Actually, they were *my* tales,' boasted Vallen smugly. '*I* told Faris what he might or might not write, coloured with details Hamilton had confided to me – I'm a priest, so he never suspected me of leaking information. I encouraged Faris to speculate about the Headless Bishop, as he so prosaically refers to Gray, but I forbade him to pen a word about Scudder. I don't want adverse publicity to deter prospective sponsors for the expedition.'

'It was you who threatened Faris?' Taylor was amazed that a clergyman could control so wilful a character. 'He was afraid even to mention Scudder's name when I met him in Fleet Street.'

'Good,' said Vallen with satisfaction. 'Obedience is a virtue I greatly admire.'

'And all so Nigel can go south?' asked Priestley. He gripped Taylor's shoulder, warning him against futile heroics. He recognised the expression that lit Vallen's face: it was the glow of the fanatic, and he knew Vallen would shoot Taylor without a moment's hesitation. 'Why is it so important?'

'Because he wants me to disprove the link between geology and biology, which has been used to add credence to Darwin's theories,' explained Nigel miserably.

Taylor stared at him in confusion. 'I have no idea what you are talking about.'

'Enlighten him, Nigel,' ordered Vallen archly.

Nigel swallowed hard. 'Because it's covered with ice, Antarctica has remained just how God created it, with no weathering or erosion. I'm to prove that the world isn't millions of years old, but that the first day of creation began at nightfall preceding the twenty-third of October four thousand and four BC – less than six thousand years ago.'

'Exactly,' said Vallen with profound satisfaction. 'Evolution will be proved a malicious, blasphemous heresy, and people will revert to their former beliefs – the ones they held before geology polluted and corrupted

354

men's minds.'

Taylor continued to gaze at him. 'You did all this to disprove evolution? You killed Gray, Scudder, Yaxley, O'Brien and now Matthews for a *theory*?'

'Ours is a noble goal,' said Vallen loftily. 'And God obviously wants our success, because everything is working out perfectly. As soon as Hamilton arrives, you'll be off my list of concerns, inspector, and Nigel will take Priestley's place on the expedition. Just as God intended.'

The only sound in the parlour after Vallen made his crazed declaration was the rhythmic ticking of the grandfather clock. Taylor had encountered lunatics and fanatics many times during his years on the Force, but there was something about Vallen that told him the priest would be far more formidable than all the others combined.

'I need to sit down,' he said, indicating his damaged arm. He forced himself not to flinch when Vallen brought the rifle to bear on him sharply, and took a tentative step towards a chair by the fireplace, where there was a set of brass pokers that might be used as weapons. 'I think I might faint.'

Vallen grimaced. 'Very well. Look out of the window, Nigel, and see if Hamilton is coming. I don't want to waste all morning on this disagreeable business.'

'Hamilton does everything you ask, does he?' asked Taylor, making a show of flexing his wrist, then casually dropping it towards the handle of the largest poker. 'Because it was he who encouraged Grant to pervert evidence and take the law into his own hands. Was that on your orders?'

'I suggested Hamilton should tell Grant that he might be in line for promotion,' replied Vallen. 'I know Grant, because he comes for tea. All Hamilton had to do was plant the seed of hope, and ambition drove Grant to hamper your work, as I knew it would. Hamilton did not need to issue specific instructions to Grant, because Grant's reactions were so predictable. He didn't earn his nickname for nothing, inspector.'

'Will thought Hamilton's mission was to secure better funding for his station.' Priestley saw what the inspector intended to do and took a small step in the opposite direction – Vallen could not cover them both if they were separated, and perhaps one might prevail. 'And he was right up to a point...'

'But I didn't know that Hamilton was dancing to another tune, too,' said Taylor. 'You fed Faris lies about the Headless Bishop, not only to highlight police incompetence, but to draw the investigation away from Gray by causing confusion and muddying the situation with lies and misinformation.'

'You probably told Hamilton to overload Will with work, too,' added Priestley. 'So he wouldn't be able to solve the murders you committed.'

Vallen inclined his head. 'You're a clever boy. It's a pity we have to kill you. I shall ask Hamilton if there's an alternative, because, unlike most of your colleagues, you appreciate the importance of serving the Almighty.'

'Yes, he does,' said Taylor quickly. 'Persuade him to join your cause. Killing him would be a waste of a brilliant mind created by God.'

'Our reasoning was correct when we analysed these

murders,' said Priestley, ignoring Taylor's transparent attempt to save him, sure Vallen was not so stupid as to fall for it. 'Except that the killer was not Nigel, it was you. And no wonder you haven't raised much money for the expedition. You've been so busy buying Hamilton that you've none left for Shackleton.'

Nigel turned from the window, his face wet with tears. 'I don't believe any of this. You're playing some sort of parlour game, like we have at Christmas. My father would never do any of these things. He's a *vicar*!'

'A vicar who wears a cross that imprinted itself on Gray's corpse,' said Taylor, shifting on the chair so Vallen would not see when he grabbed the poker. 'Now we have Gray's body, we can match the two. Your cross cut into his chest when you killed him.'

'No!' shouted Nigel, tears springing in earnest. 'You're making it up. Stop it!'

'And finally, there's this,' said Taylor, reaching with his left hand inside his pocket to withdraw the message Grant had sent him earlier. 'Nigel mentioned at dinner on Sunday that his grandfather was in the Royal Navy. He was not – he was in the Royal Naval Reserve. Grant checked it for me. The letter opener that killed Scudder belonged to Vallen – a family heirloom.'

'No!' cried Nigel desperately. 'Ours is far sharper than everyone else's, because I use it for preparing zoological specimens. Our knife isn't the one that killed Scudder. What you showed me in the Expedition Office wasn't ours!'

'You didn't see it,' Taylor pointed out. 'Wild kept you away from it, lest you hurt yourself.'

Vallen was wholly unconcerned by the allegations.

'You'll never prove anything. And here is Hamilton at last – come to clear up the mess you've made with your meddling. Sit still, inspector: I *will* shoot you if you try to escape. The work of God is at stake here, and I can't allow anyone to stand in its way.'

Chief Superintendent Hamilton had raced out of his house the moment he had received Reverend Vallen's furious and confusing telephone call. He was unshaven, his collar was askew and he had not taken the time to comb his few remaining hairs across his balding pate. He had come alone, not taking the time to summon reinforcements.

He heard the vicar calling him from the parlour and entered, gaping in alarm at the scene in front of him. Nigel was in tears by the window, playing with a revolver in a way that made Hamilton want to leave; Vallen was standing by the grandfather clock with a rifle; Taylor was slumped by the fireplace, his arm dangling in an awkward, painful way that suggested it was broken; and the young scientist named Priestley was regarding Vallen with a rank disdain that Hamilton was certain the vicar would not like.

'We've been hearing how you have helped Vallen pervert the course of justice,' said Taylor. His voice was cold, and the chief superintendent wondered exactly what the priest had been saying about him.

'Five men are dead by his hand,' added Priestley, equally icy. 'Gray, Scudder, O'Brien and Yaxley, killed to ensure Nigel travels south with Shackleton. And Matthews, one of your own men, stabbed to keep him quiet. He intends to kill Taylor and me, too. And you

358

have aided and abetted him every inch of the way.'

'How do you think we should proceed?' asked Vallen, addressing Hamilton as he might arrange a tea party. 'I was tempted to spare Priestley, who could have been an asset to our sacred cause of disproving the theory of evolution, but I don't think we can trust him not to betray us. Thus, you must arrange his death so Taylor is blamed for it. I shall ensure the press thinks so, too – Faris will oblige me.'

Hamilton gazed at him aghast. 'What are you talking about? We have no common cause, unless it's to improve my station's budget. And I don't even understand the theory of evolution, let alone have a stance on it. *Please* don't tell me these accusations against you are true?'

Vallen regarded him with pursed lips. 'I thought we understood each other. Are you telling me you didn't look more deeply into my reasons for asking you for various favours?'

'I did not!' cried Hamilton shocked. 'Why should I expect ulterior motives? You're a vicar!'

While Vallen's attention was on the chief superintendent, Taylor made his move. He seized the poker and leapt to his feet, holding it like a cricket bat to strike the rifle from Vallen's hands, although he did not manage to do it before the furious priest had pulled the trigger and fired off a round. The shot was deafeningly loud in the confines of the room. Simultaneously, Hamilton leapt to his inspector's assistance. Meanwhile, Nigel, his natural clumsiness exacerbated by distress, sent three shots into the general mêlée before Priestley was able to wrest it away from him.

The skirmish was over as quickly as it started, leaving

two men with gun-shot injuries. One was a flesh wound and the other was mortal.

'No!' cried Priestley, gaping at the carnage. 'Sweet God, no!'

'Don't swear,' gasped Taylor, almost inaudibly. 'It makes you sound like Adams.'

Cape Royds, September 1908

Philip and I saw the sun today – not just a sliver, but for the first time in months, the whole sun, free of the horizon and free of clouds. It was indescribably beautiful, and it marks a new beginning, the challenge for which we've all been waiting since we were in London.

And it comes not a moment too soon. When fifteen men of action are crammed together in one small hut for months of endless darkness, someone is bound to unravel. Not surprisingly, the first to do so was Mackay. Two weeks ago he leapt on Roberts and started choking him, because the cook put his foot on Mackay's locker to lace up his boots. 'Bobs' would have had serious problems if Mawson hadn't gripped Mackay by the throat with an even firmer grasp, and turned him back to his bed.

The agonising, dragging monotony of winter has brought out the best and worst of our party. On the one hand, the Boss kept almost everyone content and focused on our goals with his exceptional ability to treat each member as though he were part of a team and yet, at the same time, the most important person there. On the other hand, even some of the good times brought tension. In May most of us were greatly amused when the artist whom the Boss hired before we left England dressed up like a woman and behaved very affectionately to everyone. But he was so pressing in his attentions to Mackay that the quick-tempered surgeon told him he would spit at him unless he backed off.

If there was one specific occasion that gave proof of how close – and how distant – we'd all become, it was our party to commemorate mid-winter. In the midst of a somewhat rowdy celebration, Roberts led a reprise of the raspberry tart incident, putting a specially made pastry on Shackleton's seat. It was only in the laughter and cat-calls that followed that I finally felt able to admit to everyone that, in fact, I had been responsible for the original event. At Lady Wallaston's party, I'd just started eating a large tart stuffed with cream and raspberry jam when I set it down for a moment on my chair while I fetched a glass of lemonade. As I moved away, I saw a stout lady in what I think was later referred to as 'her best black bombazine' sit on that chair. She gave a small screech, which was the beginning of quite a scene. I never went back into that room; I never even looked back, as I made my way to the garden. An amusing incident, but one that prevented me from seeing Scudder leave that fateful night. I wonder whether I might have been able to stop him if I had – not to avert a murder, but because the Boss had asked us all to stay in the hope of earning donations.

As if in honour of my confession, the Boss made one himself. He had been given, immediately before his departure from home, a present for me from Ruby Taylor. He had forgotten to pass it on, but he did so now. It was heavy enough that I thought it was a large book, but it turned out to be a packet of her shortbread, harder than the ice outside and twice as durable. We laughed – both certain that the many months had not changed the consistency or impermeability of it one bit.

But even that party couldn't bring good nature out in everyone. Marshall, for one, remained as venomous as ever. Late that night, he confided to Mackay that he didn't approve of Wild's boisterously friendly talk and loud singing. He was, he said, 'seriously thinking of getting Wild outside to give me a hand with the ponies and then giving him a damn good hammering.' Even Mackay found that too miserable for words.

And so it went on throughout the long winter, not long after the beginning of which, Murray's health required him to be confined indoors. I was placed in charge of his dredging – so that he at last got the assistant biologist he'd once expected, while the geology was continued by the Prof and Mawson. I'd go out with a packed lunch and stay at the dredging site all day, only coming home for dinner. It was colder than I can say, but at least it wasn't dull. Philip was recovering slowly from the frostbite he'd suffered on Mount Erebus. It was pretty lonely, except that the Boss would come along sometimes to dig and yarn and sing. After a few hours he'd leave, but at least he came regularly, the only chap who did.

Then after a month of me being out there every day, Adams appeared. At first, I assumed he'd come to check on me because he was, after all, second-in-command. His visit started tentatively, but after a while we shook hands – as well as one can through two pairs of gloves and heavy wolfskin mittens. He came back a few days later and we had a nice natter, and then he reappeared the next day. We never talked about Helen, Will Taylor, the murders or our respective roles in them, but I was pleased to see that he'd finally forgiven me, and that we could develop a friendship.

Not that it changed certain aspects of him, which still are hard to take. Shortly after the sun started flashing its face for a brief while each day, but before it had truly risen, the Boss began sending out different groups to man-haul supplies south, towards where the journey for the Pole will start. It's brutal work, putting five hundred pounds on a sledge, tying three men to it, and heaving it twenty miles across uneven, sticky ice. The first time out I went with Adams and Mackay, and for three days we marched to a monotonous repetition of blasphemy every few steps from Adams. It was so incessant, it disturbed even Mackay.

My duties away from the hut meant it took me most of the winter to finish the report that Shackleton wanted. It was difficult to write when the others were around, since the Boss didn't want any of those involved to know what I was doing. Certainly Marshall and Mackay won't feel flattered by the way I remember things!

Now I've finished it, and I think I've received the best reward of all. The Boss recently announced the make-up of the three sledging parties, and since our group grew to fifteen after we left England, there will be some men obliged to stay at the base and help Murray carry out his biological studies. The Prof, Mawson, and Mackay are going to leave first, trying to reach the South Magnetic Pole, while carrying out scientific studies all along the way. The main thrust of the expedition, of course, will be led by the Boss himself, heading towards the geographical Pole with Adams, Wild, Marshall, and the surviving four ponies. What will they find as they pass over the Great Ice Barrier? Is there solid land there, or will everything be covered by ice? Will there be mountains, glaciers, frozen lakes? And will they bag the Pole? I wouldn't know why not – if confidence and ability count for anything, then the Boss will be the one to get it.

But surely the best journey has been given to me, along with Philip and our Australian colleague Armytage. We'll start shortly after the Boss leaves, with a trip to the lower slopes of Mount Erebus, where we're going to look at some unusual parasitic cones – oh, and just for Philip, some granitic intrusions. Then we're going into the mountains west of McMurdo Sound to – as the Boss put it the other day – 'look at rocks.' What could possibly be better? Since signing on, I've been dockhand, lecturer, administrative assistant, sleuth, common labourer, seal and penguin skinner, pony-carer, assistant biologist and sledge-hauler. And, of course, report-writer. But now – now I'm going to be what I want: a geologist.

Meanwhile, my thoughts often stray back to that last, terrible scene in the vicarage at Rotherhithe. Nigel shot his own father dead, which was perhaps the best outcome for all concerned, even for Nigel himself. I had a letter from him the day before the expedition left: he intends to go back to Oxford and train for the priesthood. I hope he'll make a better one than his father, and religion will be safer for such an embarrassingly clumsy fellow than biology in distant regions.

Hamilton survived the mêlée, of course, and is still in charge of the station. Like the political man he is, he weathered all the charges against him, and even managed to win more funding, thanks in part to a gloomy piece by Faris in The Star. It included an apology to Will, which I hope will mend London's opinion of him, just as I hope he mends from the bullet in his arm, which I also hope hasn't affected his bowling, his chief concern in the fuss that followed the confrontation with Vallen.

If only he could only see us now! His old friend Shackleton soon to be world famous by bagging the Pole. And me solving a lesser-known but even harder to resolve riddle: the discovery of what on Earth could possibly be harder than one of Ruby's biscuits.

Historical Note

The British Antarctic Expedition (BAE) led by Ernest Shackleton in 1907–09 was one of the most successful in the history of polar exploration. It sailed on the former sealing ship *Nimrod*, which had been refitted at the East India Docks in the Blackwall section of London between June and August 1907. Shortly after Shackleton set up his base at Cape Royds on Ross Island in February 1908, he sent out a party to conquer Mount Erebus, the great active volcano named for the part of the underworld in Greek mythology through which the dead passed before reaching Hades. Five of the six men who attempted it – his second-in-command Jameson Adams, Eric Marshall, Alistair Mackay, Douglas Mawson and T.W. Edgeworth David – became the first ever to gain the summit, only Sir Philip Brocklehurst not reaching it due to severely frostbitten feet.

The next spring, after the long, dark Antarctic winter, three major exploring parties were sent out. One, consisting of Raymond Priestley, Brocklehurst and the Australian Bertram Armytage, made a geological investigation of the unique area today known as the Dry Valleys. Another, led by David, who was known as 'the

Prof,' and also including Mawson and Mackay, made the longest unsupported sledging trip in Antarctic history. The three men reached the region of the South Magnetic Pole, which they claimed for Britain, before racing back to the coast just in time to be picked up by *Nimrod*, the captain of which was on the verge of abandoning them to their fate. They were rescued primarily due to the efforts of John King Davis, still the first mate despite Captain Rupert England having been replaced due to Shackleton's dissatisfaction with him.

The third party – Shackleton, Adams, Marshall and Frank Wild – crossed the Great Ice Barrier (now known as the Ross Ice Shelf) and ascended the previously unknown Beardmore Glacier to the Antarctic Plateau. They then struggled on to 88°23'S, only 97 geographical miles from the South Pole, before, running out of food, they turned back. Their nip-and-tuck return journey was one of the great sagas of Antarctic exploration, particularly coming on the heels of a magnificent outward journey that reached a place 366 geographical miles farther south than any other man had ever been.

Upon the expedition's return to civilization, Shackleton became an international hero and was knighted. He later led two more expeditions, on the first of which – the Imperial Trans-Antarctic Expedition (1914–17) – his ship *Endurance* was crushed in the ice of the Weddell Sea. Shackleton held his men together for months on the sea ice, then led them in small boats to Elephant Island. There, he left most of the party under the command of Wild, while himself making a remarkable open boat journey to South Georgia, after which he organised the rescue of his men. In 1922, at the beginning of his next expedition, he died of a heart attack at South Georgia.

Wild served under 'the Boss' on all his expeditions, and after Shackleton's death, took command of that final venture. He also served as base leader during Mawson's Australasian Antarctic Expedition (1911–14), which was the greatest scientific expedition ever launched in the far south. Neither of the other two members of the farthest south party – Adams and Marshall – ever returned to the Antarctic, although Marshall did later explore an unknown region of New Guinea.

Davis captained *Nimrod* on her way back to England from New Zealand and went on to become the most experienced sea captain of the 'Heroic Age' of Antarctic exploration, including serving as master of the ship *Aurora* on three Antarctic voyages during Mawson's expedition.

Several years after the end of the BAE, Mackay and biologist James Murray joined Vilhjalmur Stefansson's Canadian Arctic Expedition (1913–18). After their ship was crushed in the ice, Murray, Mackay and two others left the main group to try to reach mainland Siberia. They vanished without a trace.

Priestley became one of only a few men to serve under both Shackleton and Robert Falcon Scott, when he joined the latter's last expedition (1910–13) as a geologist. He eventually turned to academic administration, and in due course became the Vice-Chancellor of, first, the University of Melbourne and, then, the University of Birmingham. He later was knighted, served as acting director of what became the British Antarctic Survey, and was president of the Royal Geographical Society. He died in 1974, seven months before his friend Philip Brocklehurst, who was the last surviving member of Nimrod.